Dale Cottell

Scent of Lilacs

A love story

Dale Cathell

authorHOUSE™

1663 LIBERTY DRIVE, SUITE 200
BLOOMINGTON, INDIANA 47403
(800) 839-8640
WWW.AUTHORHOUSE.COM

First published by AuthorHouse 07/20/05

ISBN: 1-4208-5786-X (sc)
ISBN: 1-4208-5787-8 (dj)

Library of Congress Control Number: 2005904634

Printed in the United States of America
Bloomington, Indiana

This book is printed on acid-free paper.

Acknowledgments

I want to expressly thank my 'readers', Janet Cherrix (who a long time ago I nicknamed One High Hip and who was one hell of a body-surfer), Gail Whaley (who gives me some class and an insight to another world), Phyllis Mitchell (who tried to get me to keep the f- words out, for the most part successfully, I think), Nancy Howard (an editing guru, among many other things, who is still trying to get my lays, lies, and laids straight), and my younger sister, Joanne (the ultimate English teacher).

Readers perform the functions in independent publishing that assistant editors do in commercial houses. Their suggestions were invaluable and most appreciated. Many of their suggestions are in the final product.

I have attempted to accurately portray the sword fishing industry off Block Island in the 1950s before the advent of long lining. However, the literature on the subject is sparse, as is my experience with that very special form of 'darting' swordfish. Any errors in my portrayal of the industry is inadvertent. Likewise my descriptions of Block Island are based primarily on my observations during a visit to that very special island. I did however have the benefit of an out of print book by a Mr. Downie that I attempted to use to infuse myself with the history of the island. If I got it wrong, I misread my (Mr. Downie's) history. My admiration for the food at the Hotel Manisis is based upon personal experience.

The sections dealing with the asbestos and liquor industry mass tort cases are completely fabricated, but are based, roughly, on the knowledge I've gleaned over the years from the briefs of innumerable attorneys litigating mass tort cases. I don't know that it has happened as I portray it - but it could.

The love parts of the book are imaginary - of course.

Prologue
JULY, 2003

I am an old man now. Seventy-three. Feel it, too. I've come to this beach in the lee of a large rock framed by the dunes and bayberry bushes of Block Island, the Ocean View bluff, the *Hotel Eva* behind us, to be with you again.

I know I must look strange. Sitting in a straight-back white metal chair by a table in the middle of an isolated beach, finishing the writing of this journal as we watch the scarlet splash of the sun rise in the east, rising from the sea as it did so many years ago.

I'm white haired and wrinkled now. I'm wearing a black dinner jacket, a pleated shirt, a black bow tie and matching cummerbund, black patent leather shoes, my finest evening wear. At least, I think I look my best in it and now I want to look my best.

Not for the great billfish that brought me here that earlier time and that may even still swim in the now, to me, almost mythical seas of long ago, maybe down at South Channel, No Man's Land, off Montauk Point or the dumping grounds. Maybe their offspring wait for me. Wait to get even. If they do, I'll be dressed for it. But, I'm not dressed for a trip to the fishing grounds. Nor am I dressed to ride in the horse carts - they're long gone as well-at least the way they used to be. Nor for the vixen standing now in the dunes behind us, wondering what we're doing sitting here listening to the music. Not for those that find me, those who will be looking for me, but for you. I'm dressed for you.

I'm finishing this journal here on the beach with you, writing of all the memories. The good ones of our time. A bottle of champagne on the small round-topped table beside us, chilled from the morning dew, and two long stemmed glasses beside it glinting pink from the rising sun, love songs playing on the radio, happy songs as they always were. The songs that played on the night we danced. Danced with the scent of lilacs.

Now, the *Hotel Eva* hovers above us; the Great Salt Pond and its inlet to the northwest are as they were in that other time. And the harbors of all the other islands to the south - down to Key

West even, are in my memory still. As I look back I'm thinking of all the lives I've met as I've traveled through my own. Mostly, I'm lost in my memories of you.

The gun in my pocket reminds me, now satisfyingly, of promises kept. My promises to you. To the Captain. The same gun I used at the Jackspot. Just hours ago.

I talked with you again as I arrived this morning, was taking a bath the morning after an old man's trip to the Jackspot of his youth. I've talked with you many nights. Most nights, really. One way or the other. For more than fifty years. Some would say, if they knew of it, that I was crazy, am crazy. I know, though, that my talks with you kept me sane.

I've never stopped the dreaming, never stopped the memories, never wanted to, never wanted to stop loving you. And the dream talks were what I had. Mostly all I've had of you for fifty years. My talks with you led me to the successes that I've had in my life. Business, professional successes, not personal ones. At least most people who knew me, know me, don't consider my personal life to be a success. When you are single and powerful, an advisor to Presidents and you're forty-three, you're Washington's most eligible bachelor. When you are powerful, a billionaire, an advisor to Presidents and still single thirty years later, you're eccentric, or worse. They didn't know, couldn't know, that I had been married all the time in my dreams, was married in my mind. You never let me come to you, yet you took the best part of me.

You knew, somehow, what I had not the slightest idea of, that power and wealth was to come to me. And that I would use it wisely. You promised though, that I could come to you sometime and until then we were to be together across the divide of our physical beings, together in our dreams.

We became lovers, almost, on this beach - the beach where we're sitting now. At this very spot; at least I tried to have Julian place the chairs and table so. Here beside the rock we sheltered behind that far ago night when you brought me here to lie in the snow, to let me know that you were woman-built.

I have not forgotten you. Can't forget you. Never wanted to.

I was twenty then, hiding from the poverty of my life and other things, another thing really.

Came for the swordfish. Found them. Found you. The story of the journal I leave is the story of the scent of lilacs, the story of loving you.

BOOK ONE

Chapter One

JULY 4ᵀᴴ, 1952

INSHORE

They were headed for a first landfall at Block Island. The run from Annapolis down the bay to Cape Charles had been easy. The remnants of the northeaster had backed to the northwest blowing about ten to fifteen. They'd been able to fly a spinnaker most of the time. Letting the big balloon pull them down the bay. Even with a bone in her teeth it had been almost leisurely, with a following wind and sea on her stern they'd been able to lie back in the cockpit relaxing, except when one of them had to go below to stir up another batch of martinis. Then they'd reached the ocean. It changed, the leisure part of it. The wind was off the port bow. They'd pulled the spinnaker in before they'd made the turn north.

From then on they'd driven her hard all the way up the coast from the mouth of the Chesapeake, beating her into the wind as much as possible, falling off some when they had to. Working the sails constantly. Tacking to seaward to catch the Gulf Stream. They'd stopped drinking martinis when they'd made the turn north, too hard to mix and drink when the boat started rising to her bow with every wave, some of them large, left over from the northeaster. But they hadn't stopped drinking, just switched to beer. They had gotten half-drunk and intended to stay that way, or more so. To them the party was the important part of the trip. The contest was the excuse.

The four of them had known each other since their college days at Harvard. Two of them had gone on to become lawyers, one was a medical intern at a prestigious hospital in Washington and the other an administrative assistant to a congressional committee. His brother was the committee chairman and had gotten him the job, was grooming him for a congressional seat, the very one the brother held. The brother was running for senate in the next election, intended to become the junior senator from Massachusetts.

1

The family wanted the younger brother to take over the congressional seat from the second district - wanted to keep it in the family. Belonged to them, didn't it?

The lawyers worked for a major Washington firm, but, more importantly they were tied to the family, to the fortunes of soon to be Senator O'Brien and his brother, Cliff. They expected to coattail themselves into prominence, become people on the 'national scene'. Become lobbyists, pundits, political operatives, whatever scraps came their way. Lucrative scraps. All of them were linked by ambition and past, following the same star, with a vested interest in the star.

The head partners at the law firm had encouraged the two lawyers to take the trip, to always be available when Cliff O'Brien called. The partners were playing the come, betting that sometime in the future the relationships could be parlayed into a win-win situation, a series of win-win situations. All they needed were door openers, and the two junior associates could already crack open doors in town, later if they got the right ride they could open them all the way. They didn't have to know much law, the firm had real lawyers, good lawyers that could take care of the legal things. The youngsters just had to know people, have access to the political swingers.

The Congressman, and his younger brother had showed up on the radar screens of the partners two years earlier as comers. Then had come the applications from the two associates a year later. Manna from Heaven. Bread on the doorstep.

They'd been hired, no one checked their transcripts, didn't check their references once they realized there was a letter of recommendation from the potential senator for each of them. Didn't really read the letter either once the signature was recognized. Influence was the commodity the firm offered and the two were hired. In short order they had become the younger O'Brien's baby sitters. They had been made to understand that was their function in the firm. They knew it was all they had to offer the firm, but it was what they wanted anyway. They'd protect Cliff, stroke him, whip him when they had to, anything to get him moving up the ladder once his brother made way for him. Dragging them behind up the same ladder, just a rung or two below. They were inextricably bound to the younger O'Brien, sycophants. They had already started the process of getting him elected to his brother's seat.

It was a given that the brother would move over to the Senate, it was to be the 'O'Brien seat, wasn't it; they had to insure that Cliff would replace him in the House of Representatives.

When Cliff had called, told them he was entering the *Party Time* in the July 4th weekend race to Newport, that they'd be partying all the way up and back, would go over to Block Island and run the summertime girls, all they had to do was tell the partners of the invitation; they were virtually ordered to go.

They'd gone way out to sea once they had left the Chesapeake, wanting to stay way off, riding the edges of the Gulfstream north, avoiding as much as they could the Labrador Current's wind driven southern push. Early on the morning of the fourth they passed thirty miles off Montauk Point, turned inshore, heading for Block Island, intending to round the north side, cross the sound and run on up to Narragansett Bay and Newport on a port tack. There were several sails they could see inshore of them and as they made their turn inshore they could see in the distance off their starboard side a swordfishing boat.

As they switched to a port tack, a stay turnbuckle high on the main mast gave way. It had been unchanged, uninspected for years, had developed a spot of rust, then began to rust through and through. When it separated the stay failed as well, putting extra strain on the other stays. At the moment the turnbuckle gave way the boom was traversing from starboard to port as they switched to the port tack; a second stay parted, then another and suddenly the mainsail split from the twisting tension. It popped. It had all happened in seconds. They rushed to lower the sail to take the pressure off the mast, made it in time, but they'd lost the mainsail. The mast was sprung as well, unseated. They were effectively out of the race. They took the reefs out of the jib and five hours later were sitting in the boat yard on the mainland while the mast was being reseated, the stays repaired. They never bothered to check in with the race organizers. Wasn't any need to check in a no finish, or at best, a last place. No glory in it.

They spent Saturday night in Newport. Drinking, partying, being obnoxious generally. Had they not been with O'Brien they would have been kicked out of the club and every place they went during their pub crawl. As it was, they were thrown out of one bar; they'd made a mistake in entering a fisherman's bar. When they'd gotten obnoxious, the fishermen had beaten the hell out of them and literally kicked them out into the street.

They were still hung-over, half-sick, bruised even, when they returned to the yard at midday on Sunday. O'Brien charged the repairs, they loaded up, used the auxiliary motor to get out in the bay, raised sail gingerly and sailed into the sound intending to head back to the Chesapeake. Within the first half hour all four were taking turns vomiting over the side. So they took some hair of the dog that had bitten them the day before. Didn't help, they were still sick, drunk again too. As they approached Block Island a decision was made to head for the calm water of New Harbor, to have another night ashore, to recover maybe. Good intentions.

They tied up to an un-designated mooring buoy at four in the afternoon. Soon they were all asleep, two below, two in the cockpit. At eight O'Brien awakened, still half drunk. Woke up the others. They piled into the dingy, almost sinking it. As it was, once they were all in it only had inches of freeboard. They got the kicker, the small outboard motor started, carefully made their way over to the shore a hundred yards or so from the harbor master's office. Found an old stub piling to tie off the dingy. At the car stand on Ocean Road they rented an old Buick sedan, drove down the coast a mile or so to Calamity - a seafood restaurant and bar.

They filled up on lobsters, two each, baked potatoes and salads. All the time throwing zombies down on dares. By ten they were all drunk again, obnoxious. Throwing money around, too. Made no difference, they were asked to leave anyway. They drove up on Water Street, went to Maggie's, the swinging bar, the place where the summertime girls congregated to dance, to see and be seen and to have a good time.

By midnight they were too drunk to care what happened, care what they did. O'Brien had twice fondled a waitress. The last one had hit him with a tray. He'd started to hit her then but one of the lawyers had stopped him. A little later he had approached another girl at the bar. When she turned away from him in disgust, he'd called her a whore. She'd turned, threw her drink in his face. Walked off. When he tried to follow a bouncer intervened. He swung at the bouncer. The bouncer hit him, putting him on the floor. Then grabbed him by his belt and began dragging him to the door. When one of the lawyers tried to intervene the bouncer had dropped O'Brien, cold-cocked the lawyer, picked O'Brien back up and threw him out on the street. The other three were following through the door, two of them holding up the semi-conscious lawyer. Soon they revived O'Brien and the dazed lawyer. They went looking for where they had left the old Buick. It was twelve-thirty. They found the Buick and designated the intern to drive, he'd drunk less than the others. He got it started, they climbed in still complaining about the "Block Island whores", "damned sluts," and reverting back to their Harvard days, "townie sluts,' 'worthless poor ass cunts." They kept up the drunken insulting complaints as the car began to move, swaying, but at least in motion, O'Brien in the front passenger seat. They went north on Water Street until it turned into Dodge Street. Soon they came to a four way intersection. O'Brien yelled, "Turn here."

The intern turned left on Old Town Road when he should have turned right. They rounded a curve and almost hit a woman walking on the shoulder. The intern had to swerve the car sharply. O'Brien yelled, "Stop the car!" The intern pulled to the side of the road. O'Brien got out. The woman was standing several car lengths behind their car. O'Brien approached her, staggering a little, smelling of alcohol.

"We're sorry about that, miss. Didn't see you until it was almost too late. You okay?"

Eva answered, "I am now. You should be careful how you drive on our roads. A lot of people walk from place to place at night."

"I said we were sorry."

"Okay.."

"Do you know who I am?"

"No."

"I'm Cliff O'Brien."

Eva stood there silent, worried. There was no other traffic on the road and there were thickets on both sides, no nearby houses.

"I know you've heard about the O'Briens even on this pissanty island."

She moved, turned to the side so as to walk around O'Brien. He moved in front of her, stopping her advance, leaned over her, casting

5

his alcohol breath all over her. He looked at her closer, beginning to notice her beauty even in his drunken state.

"My brother's going to be the Senator, I'll be taking his place as the Congressman from Boston."

"Let me by please. I don't know you, " she answered.

"No reason to be uppity. You ain't nothing but an island slut. I told you who I am."

"You're drunk." She said, trying again to walk around him, noticing as she did another man get out of the car. O'Brien stepped in front of her again. She had to stop or bump into him. "Get out of my way."

"I ain't too drunk to give you what you need."

"Get out of my way."

He reached for her then, for her dress, grabbed it and ripped it down the front, pulling her bra down as well, exposing her breasts. He leered at them, said "God damn!" She turned to run and he grabbed her hair, pulled her back. She slapped him then. Clawed for his eyes. Instinctively he hit her, hit her hard. She fell from his grasp onto the ground. Unconscious.

The other lawyer got out of the car then, staggering some also. Approached them. The three of them looked at each other. The other lawyer said, "We've got to go. Come-on, a car will be coming and it will be too late to get away from here."

"We've got more of a problem than that," the first lawyer said, the one who had gotten out of the car and had heard and seen what had happened, "he told her his name. She knows who he is. When she comes to, the first thing she'll do is turn him in, tell what Cliff did."

"We're still better away from here," the second lawyer said, "we can get on the boat and down the coast. When they try to say we did it we can say we weren't here, couldn't of been Cliff."

"Won't work. Cliff got in that ruckus at Maggie's with the bouncer. If she identifies us, the bouncer may remember us. The 'weren't there story' won't work. Too many people know we were here."

"Even if they figure it was Cliff, with his family he'll just get a slap on the wrist, like when we were college."

"This isn't Massachusetts. The O'Brien name isn't going to carry the day out here."

"Most that will probably happen," the other lawyer said, "is a fine, maybe we can get it settled, pay her some money to forget the whole thing."

"Can't very well do that out here on the road, with her lying there unconscious. By the time we got that arranged, if we could, it would be too late to do anything else if she didn't agree."

"It was just a drunken slap."

"It was more than that, he ripped her dress almost off her. And it wasn't a little slap. He punched her. She'll be bruised tomorrow. She's going to wake up with her tits out; she's not likely to forget any of it."

"What do you suggest?"

O'Brien spoke then for the first time, the situation itself having sobered him, partially, "There's another thing. This gets out, there's no House of Representative's seat for me. My brother will probably lose the Senate race. Everything we've been planning on is at risk. It's too important, too much at stake for a snap decision on the shoulder of a road on this goddamn island. Grab her feet," he said to the lawyers, as he grabbed her under the shoulders. They lifted her into the back seat of the car. O'Brien got in back with her, the two lawyers got in the front seat. "Get us back to the dingy. We'll take her with us until she wakes up and we can make a deal with her, do something, think on it more ."

They made their way to where the dingy was tied off; O'Brien said to the intern, "Drive the car back to the rental place. If there's no-one there leave the keys under the door. Then come back here, wait, and we'll have the dingy back for you as soon as we can."

The night was dark, no cars on the road, little light. They carried her to the dingy, put her in the bottom, climbed around her getting in themselves. They were afraid the noise of the motor would attract attention so one of the lawyers rowed toward the *Party Time* while the intern drove back up the road toward the car rental place. The sailboat was a long way out in the harbor and they were worried about being seen, but they had the girl in the bottom; she couldn't be easily seen anyway. It took them twenty minutes or more to get to the *Party Time*. When they got close, O'Brien, riding on the stern thwart said, "Row her around to the offshore side."

With the two lawyers holding the dingy steady, O'Brien lifted the woman over the *Party Time's* gunwale into the cockpit. She began to stir. As he picked her up to carry her below, he said to the others, "Go back, pick Mike up, I'll get the boat ready."

They pushed off as O'Brien took her below. He'd already figured out what needed to be done, ultimately. Knew, too, what he wanted now. He took her up forward, laid her on the bunk. Turned the light on. Looked at her breasts for a moment, felt himself getting hard.

She began to moan as he ripped the rest of the clothes from her. Right as he thrust himself in her, squeezing her breasts as he did, she opened her eyes, realized what was happening and screamed. He drew back, hit her, said "Scream, I'll kill you." She had started fighting then, scratching him, hitting him as he entered her the second time. She fought him, bleeding heavily now from her vagina. She began to moan, over and over again,

During one point in the rape she reached up to scratch his neck and her hand become entangled in a necklace, the chain on which his cross and his crew award hung. He grabbed her hand and threw it away from him. The chain broke and she grasped it. He was intent then, he was about to finish, wasn't paying attention to other things. Didn't give a damn what she broke.

He thrust more rapidly now. She had stopped fighting, stopped scratching, became stoic, he had already taken what meant the most to her in the world. Another stroke, a hundred more, made no difference. Now she thought of surviving. But she knew that survival was probably not going to happen once she had come to, realized he was raping her; it was no longer a drunken accosting on a country road, it was a kidnaping and a rape. His family was a prominent, wealthy, Massachusetts family. Members of what the rest of New England called the Boston Gang. They'd do anything to get what they wanted. That meant that she was going to die as well; be murdered. He had too much to lose if she lived. She closed her eyes, began to pray, aloud.

"Dear God, look after Mama and Daddy when they find out what's happened to me." He was thrusting more rapidly now, listening to her words as he grunted on her.

"Dear God, look after Hank. Thank you for giving him to me even if it was only for a little while. Look after him." O'Brien grunted rapidly as she finished her prayer. He climaxed, began thrusting slower. She stopped praying, opened her eyes as he lowered his upper body on her, her face above his shoulder. She looked at the bulkhead behind her rapist. Focused just for a moment on one thing hanging there, it was an award of some kind, crossed oars on a plaque. She realized then that the chain she had in her hand also had crossed oars hanging from it. As he laid on her, as he began to slip from her, she scrunched the chain in her fist, making it as invisible as possible. Soon he got off her, stood with his penis hanging out of the fly of his trousers; he hadn't even bothered to undress. He looked at her, "Damn if you're not a good piece of ass. Tightest cunt I've ever fucked." She didn't respond. Just glared at him, then looked around, saw a corner of her dress on the edge of the bunk, grabbed it and pulled her dress over her, covering her private parts, her breasts.

"Ain't no use to try and get away. Only one way out of the cabin, that's aft at the cockpit. I'll be there." He left the cabin.

Soon she felt the dingy strike the side of the boat. The sailboat rocked a little as she felt the others climb aboard. She could hear them murmuring for a while, then could hear them unmooring from the buoy. She heard a small engine start up, then the wash of the water as the boat began to move. After a half-hour the noise of the motor stopped, she heard sails being raised and the boat took a steady list to starboard as she felt it go on a wind driven starboard tack.

After the sails were set, the boat on a course which would carry it around the north end of Block Island, the four men gathered in the cockpit. The intern, Mike, who had returned the car asked then,

"She's below?"

O'Brien answered him, "Yes."

"She okay?" John asked, as the two lawyers sat on either side of O'Brien.

"Depends."

"What's that mean?" Earl, the other lawyer asked.

"Well, she's been fucked. So I guess it depends on whether she liked it or not. I liked it. She was my first virgin."

"Jesus!" Mike exclaimed.

"She's lying up in the forward cabin. She's as beautiful a woman as any of us are ever liable to see again. You ought to get some of it. I got a feeling it ain't going to be around long."

Eva heard the companionway hatch open, felt him come in, looked up. It was one of the others. She pulled her dress up, wasn't enough of it to cover her. She knew it was too late to plead with any of them. She wouldn't give them the satisfaction of begging for what she knew was beyond their intention to give. If they let her go, one of the so-called great families of Massachusetts would be involved in another scandal, one they might not be able to control, the scions of the family would be brought down, one in prison. She knew instinctively that there would be no bargaining. She wouldn't bargain anyway. She knew that they would kill her. Why beg? She just looked at the man standing in the companionway. Then he closed the hatch and she saw him undoing his belt. He pulled the remnants of her dress away from her naked body. She lie there unmoving, her hands clinched into fists.

Soon he was on her. In her. She waited for the right moment, right when he was climaxing and suddenly pushed her left index finger and nail all the way in his eyeball, hooked it, and in a split second his eyeball was lying on his cheek. She didn't know how she knew to do it. She just did it. He fell off her, screamed, and she heard the others coming. The hatch was opened and the other three stood there looking at their friend, at Earl. She didn't bother covering herself. They weren't worth wasting modesty on. They were scum.

"Oh, God dammit", one of them said, she thought it was the one who had been driving when the car had passed her on Old Town Road. Two of them then helped the one she had injured and they took him out, the other one grabbed a medical kit and went out closing the hatch behind him, turning the light off as he left. She lie there in the darkness, hearing the water rushing by, hearing faintly the wind in the sails. Wondering how they would kill her, where they would put her body over, would it be found.

Out in the cockpit the men looked at each other. Earl was moaning loudly, holding his head as the intern pushed his eye back in its socket, taping a bandage to it tightly and giving Earl a pain killer from the medical kit, but he kept moaning as O'Brien spoke:

"You know we've got to do it."

"Do what now?" John replied, as Earl lay moaning.

"If we let her go, we're all finished." O'Brien responded, "No Congress, no Senate for my brother, no big time jobs down the road for two of you, more than that even, no high-paying jobs doing nothing at your big law firms. It's all finished if she ever gets ashore alive."

"You're talking about killing her?" Mike, the intern, said, "Killing her?"

"Either she's finished or we're finished. That means all of us, even you Mike. No big time medical practice, you'll be dispensing pills in a dispensary in the wrong side of a prison."

"I haven't done anything. All I did was drive the car."

"That's all it takes," John, the lawyer, said, "makes you a principal in the first degree, principal to a kidnaping. You might not get as much time, but you'll still be an old man before you get out, even if you can survive in prison, stay sane after you've been gang raped, buggered, a dozen times."

"I don't care, I'm not murdering anybody." Mike said. "She's just a country girl. She doesn't know anything. Probably won't even tell."

"You might be willing to take that chance, but I'm willing to bet that the rest of us aren't," O'Brien said, "anyway who is she, a nobody, just island snatch. There's not anyone that counts that'll care what happens to her. Just a nobody on a nowhere island."

The three of them stared at each other for minutes as Earl lay on the deck, moaning louder now. Then O'Brien said, "I'll do it." He took a club out of the compartment under the wheel. Went below.

She heard the hatch open. Looked in his eyes. There was nothing there. She knew this was it. She steeled herself, clenched her fists tighter. She was praying when he hit her the first time. Five, six, seven times, then she was unconscious. Felt nothing else. He continued to beat her around the head mostly. Then he saw she was still, hands tightly clenched. He went back up to the cockpit, leaving the hatch open.

"It's done. Now let's think about where we're going to put her over. Don't want her to wash up down home, her body get caught in commercial gear there. Besides I'm not wanting to sail two days with a dead girl aboard. Need to get rid of her somewhere up here, then get on home before she floats up and they find her."

As Earl began to moan even louder, the other lawyer, John, spoke up. "We might be able to make it look like an accident. We can come about, get over to the west, off Mohegan Bluffs. The coast is rocky there. Tide's coming in, be high tide in two hours. Tide will wash almost up to the base of the cliffs. If she washes up there they might think she killed herself falling down the bluff, falling on the rocks. If they don't find her, she doesn't wash up for a couple of days her body might be so decomposed that they won't be able to figure anything about it."

An hour later they were sailing a half-mile off the rocks at Mohegan Bluffs, the Southeast light blinking off their stern, off the starboard quarter. O'Brien said "I'll need some help getting her up. Come-on, John." He and John went below to the forward cabin. She was bloody, no movement at all, in the dimness from the cabin light it appeared she wasn't breathing. She was dead. They thought she was dead.

In another moment they had her naked body in the cockpit. "Wait a minute," John said, "we need to dress her as best we can, if she washes up it'll look better if she has some clothes on her." He went below, got her undergarments, what was left of her dress, came back up. He slipped her panties on, then her bra, and fastened it. Looked at the dress, said "There's no way it'll ever stay on her. We'll just put it over with her, hope it washes up near anywhere she washes up.

"Lets ease her over the port side, the offshore side. Don't think anybody can see out here, its so dark. No need to take chances though. Need to wait until the Southeast Light comes around, then ease her over right after it passes."

They rolled her body over into the sea.

Chapter Two

SPRING, 1951

LEAVING

I had started my journey on an island far to the south. I had been raised 'on the boats', as they called it then. Kids like me, raised by families that made their living on the water. I grew up, as did most of us, spending my after school hours first on the back bays behind North Beach, they call it Ocean City now, running trot lines when I was ten, supplying the restaurants on the island, the tourist island - Ocean City. Usually, as it was with me, we'd graduate to working on the 'sport' boats in the summer time, the 'head boats' first, and then on to the sport fishermen, the trolling boats. There would be blue fishing in late May until mid-June when school tuna would arrive and we'd 'pull' tuna until the marlin showed up toward the end of June or the beginning of July. They'd hold us until September and the beginning of school.

Later, as we got older, in the winter and early spring, we would go commercial fishing on the weekends, on the draggers at first, usually trawling for flounders on the bottom. Later, we'd go potting offshore on the sea bass boats in the spring.

When I got older, and bigger, especially bigger, I'd spend weekends during the winter and spring on the sea clam boats. Converted trawlers usually, that would force the clams from beds eight to ten miles offshore with hydraulic water pressure, to be scraped up by the dredges, the scrapes dragged on the bottom beneath the boat.

It was heavy work, especially the clamming. All of us could barely wait for the bluefish to arrive. We could get off the commercial boats then. Go to trolling on the weekends when we weren't in school. Hard work still, but not so hard.

We were a tough bunch. Thought we were, and we were. Boys still, really; but boys of the sea.

I was as tough as it got. From somewhere, my anger I guess, I got the thirst for it. For the fighting. It didn't make me particularly loved in some quarters. The 'right' quarters. High society. At least what passed for it in Ocean City. The rich folks. Their daughters were off limits to such as me. So they thought. Their daughters thought differently. That's what counted. I didn't give a damn for the parents, anyway. Really, I didn't care much for the girls, either, except for one thing, the one thing. The 'poking' part. The local girls were only wintertime things. Usually.

In the summer, every week at eleven on Saturday morning all the tourist girls would leave. Their week's vacation was over. At three in the afternoon another batch would show up to begin a week. The same lies would last a guy all summer. If you couldn't make out in Ocean City in the summer you had big problems; you'd better find a fat girl, a skinny one, ugly or something, maybe a preacher's daughter. Come to think of it, not a preacher's daughter; they were high up the scale; wild ones, the daughters of the cloth.

By the time I was twenty I was wild as hell. Ran with a wild bunch. Mostly fishermen who were the sons of fishermen. We fished, fought, and fornicated. All we could.

The controls were not like they are now. No one asked how old you were. They just looked. If you were big enough, you were old enough. Big enough to get your elbows on the bar. Big enough, and bad enough, to stare the bartender down. But nobody cared much in those days. No one who counted.

My journey began in one of the boardwalk bars. "Crab Junction." It was only early April - a cold April. We'd just come in from clamming with the wind blowing out of the northwest - blowing cold, blowing hard until we'd gotten under the beach, then it was just cold. Like the beer we were drinking now.

They were big mouths from the University of Maryland. They'd been on the national championship football team in the late forties, forty-eight I think. They'd begun to 'pot' already, big guts on them from the beer they'd been swilling and they still thought of themselves as both big and bad. Big they were, the three of them. But bad was mostly a memory, though they didn't know it - yet. A memory compared to me and Jimbo.

Our muscles didn't come from trainers, two hour workouts, where the most that could happen might be a strained or pulled muscle.

Ours came from twelve to fifteen hours straight of lifting forty pound shovels of clams above our heads, seven feet, into the cages that held the clams on the heaving decks of the clamming boats. All day long. They came from hour after hour of pulling nets as hard as one could pull. And in the summer they came from 'wiring' tuna, forty, fifty, hundred pound tuna, bigger even, truly wild creatures, not make-believe like football players. And the marlin, too. Hundreds of pounds of wildness, sometimes, with the big blues - dynamite in their fluorescent suits.

Our life wasn't about who won or lost a game. Our lives were made up, in large part, of contests on the decks and in the cockpits of boats, over living and dying. Far at sea, sometimes twenty, even sixty miles at sea, with waves as high as the flying bridges on the sportfishing boats, waves that sometimes swept the decks of the trawlers clean, taking everything over. Us, too, more often then we wanted to remember. Sometimes so wild out there that to make a mistake was to invite disaster, dying even. And we did. The fishermen of the coast. Even as young as us. The wild ones. We used up our quota of fear at sea. Wondering sometimes, too often, really, whether we'd make it home. Home to the beach. Two or three paunchy ex football players didn't compare with a four or five hundred pound mako shark, or even a hammerhead, or a marlin, a blue marlin green to the boat, or a sea, a twenty-five-foot sea coming up out of nowhere, or a line squall coming off the beach with winds of a hundred miles an hour in the gusts of the leading edge. Or coming home over the bar in a southwest wind blowing a gale, the tide ebbing, the boat overloaded with full cages of clams, only two feet of freeboard left, in the winter when death comes in fifteen minutes in the water. In the days before survival suits.

So when the big one pushed me aside at the bar, I didn't say anything. I smashed my beer mug in his face. Right out. No talking. We didn't waste words. Words never stopped a fight, at least none of ours. I thought nothing. I just hit him. And it started. Before it was over we wrecked the bar. And it was owned by a friend of ours. He used to be a friend.

But that's not why I left, the trashing of 'Crab Junction'. It was the big one, the one I hit first. I'd broken up his face. His jaw, both sides. His nose. And I fractured his skull. I only hit him once. With the mug. They made them thick in those days. Solid. It fared better than he did.

The following evening when the clam boat came in, the Chief was there on the dock, the Chief of Police, waiting. He'd been a wild one in his time, a fisherman. He'd gone the route a score of years before us.

"Hank," he said. "You've got a problem, a big problem."

"What's that, Chief?" I asked.

"The fight last night. There's trouble."

"What do you mean? He's the one that started it. He shoved me. Then I hit 'im. That's what happens you shove somebody you shouldn't."

"He's still in the hospital, Hank. He may not make it. He's not come to, yet. You've broken his face up; fractured his skull. His jaw, too."

"What would you have done, Chief? If he'd shoved you? Moved out of his way? You never moved out of the way in your time."

"That's the problem, Hank. It's a different time. It don't work no more the way it used to. You know who his uncle is?"

"No. But I get the feelin' he's somebody. And I got the feelin' you're goin' to tell me."

"His uncle's a big time banker. A rich banker from Pennsylvania. And there's goin' to be a lot of pressure to do somethin'. To do somethin' to you."

"I didn't start it."

"I don't think that's goin' to make no never mind, now."

"I don't think you came here just to bring me a situation report, Chief. You tryin' to suggest somethin'?"

"Hank, if I were you, I'd get gone. I wouldn't leave any word behind, either. They don't know for sure who you are; what your name is, or really what you look like. But when the guy gets out of the hospital, if he gets out, they'll be down here tryin' to find you, tryin' to identify the guy that did the damage. You need to go away, and stay away, 'til this blows over."

Chapter Three
ASSATEAGUE

When the chief left, I went to Mr. Bob's house. Mr. Bob was an icon from the gambling days, ran a casino on the boardwalk before they were closed down. He'd kept the money though. There had been plenty to keep.

Over the years I'd taken him a lobster now and then when the scrapes of the clam boats brought one up, or one wandered into a bass pot. Taken him bluefish cheeks, too. He loved those cheeks. I wasn't there now with lobsters, fish or anything else. I needed help, a place to stay while I thought things out.

I knew I could go to Hatteras, Florida, the islands, find work on the boats. For Ocean City boys that was never any problem. But everybody knew I had started going south in the winter to fish. That's where they'd look for me even in the spring - if they identified me, if somebody talked.

Mr. Bob let me in. Charles, his brother, and both their wives were there. I knew them all. He asked me to take a seat, got me a beer. Then asked:

"What's on your mind, Hank? Got a problem?"

I answered him. "I need some place to stay for a couple of weeks. I need to get out of town; there's been a fight and I didn't lose it. I was wonderin' ifin I could go down to Green Run for a while until I figure it out?"

Green Run was a hunting camp down below Fox Hill Levels on Assateague Island to the south of Ocean City. No bridges to it. No roads. Isolated then, much more than it is now with the bridge they finished in the early 70's.

"Sure," Bob answered. "No problem. I'll get the keys to the club."

I left and called Jimbo. Asked him for a ride down to South Point on the mainland - about eight or nine miles south down Synepuxent Neck. We went by Law's Market where I left a part of my clam share money with old man Laws. Paying for provisions. If he found out about the fight, he'd keep his mouth shut. We were locals. Not 'come heres.'

17

That's what really mattered back then. Less now. It was the same at the liquor store.

Jimbo took me down to the ferry dock at South Point. Left me there so he could get back without anyone knowing he'd taken me to the ferry.

The ferry was on the way in, about halfway on its return trip. Hot Pot Pie, the operator, had probably been fishing on the beach. Early in the season for it, but not too early. If you wanted to make sure he'd be there when you wanted to go over, you had to make arrangements ahead of time - or take your chances. He fished a lot.

After a while - it was a slow ferry, he was approaching the slip. He saw me and waved. He'd been friends with my dad. That was before my dad shipped out on the *Marcella* and she capsized trying to get in the inlet in a southwest gale. They never found my dad. He was just gone. I was five years old when it happened. But Hot Pot Pie had remembered all the days he'd spent with my father drum fishing down the beach. He'd looked after me some.

He backed the small ferry into the slip. Threw a line on an offset pile just to hold her off the dock. The wind was blowing in. He walked to the rear of the ferry, said:

"Hey Bub, what's up?"

He had always called me Bub. Don't know why. Just did.

"I need to get on over to the beach as soon's you can go back. I've had some problem above. Need to be gone 'til it sorts out."

"Hop on," he said, "might's well get "er done now."

I jumped over what passed for the transom. The ferry was a monitor barge with no discernable difference at either end. Just an old barge that had been outfitted with a side mounted gas engine that had just enough power to let the barge put, put, put, across the bay and up the gut to the ferry dock on Assateague.

About a half-hour later we were pulling in the gut. Pretty soon I was ashore, waving as Hot Pot Pie headed back across the bay. It was almost dark now and I could barely make him out, highlighted by the last rays of a falling sun shining in the west behind the mainland.

I hoisted my duffle bag on my shoulder and began to walk south down the beach across the darkening levels to the west of the dunes. I stayed west because I didn't want to come across anyone who might have come over earlier for night fishing on the surf bank. Besides, it was easier to walk on the packed clay and sand of the levels than on the open beach to the east. It took me a half-hour, little more probably, to walk the mile or two down the levels amongst the bushes and stunted pines of the barrier island. For a while I was walking amongst ponies, stunted descendants of horses that swam ashore after the wreck of a Spanish galleon centuries before, or so it was said. Didn't bother them, they didn't bother me. I jumped a fox as I came up to the shanties that made up the camp. Shanties didn't do them justice. They were more than shanties. Actually, very nice considering where they were. But shanties are what everybody called them. And shanties, then, they were

I let myself in and grabbed the hurricane lantern that always hung by the door. The last person leaving always had the job of filling the tank at the bottom with kerosene from the drum in the kink bushes - squirrely bushes that never knew where they wanted to grow next. Grew 'ever-which-away'.

I lit the lamp. Put the provisions that needed to be kept cool in the metal lined chest Bob and Charlie let hang down into the water of the gut near where the shanty was built. Then took the other two lanterns outside and filled their tanks. Soon I had light - that warm peachy light a lantern gives off. I set about squaring things away, getting a fire started and such.

Then I got drunk.

Then I went to bed.

Same things, mostly, every night for a month.

Sometimes though, especially when the moon was from three quarters up, through full to a quarter down, I'd take a bottle and go over to the east side of the dunes after dark. Make sure no-one was fishing nearby and I'd lie there sipping easy whiskey on the east slope of the dunes looking out over the moonlit dappled sea, drawing sustenance for my soul from those resting in her depths. My dad was there, a dad I hardly remembered. I wondered, lying there on the cool sands of spring, what advice he'd give a son in the position I was in? What would he tell me? Even though the answers didn't come directly, I knew the answer. To be a man. Always. But, the question for me was how to be a man in my present circumstance? To allow myself to be drawn into the grinders of the powerful? No, I didn't think so.

One windless night in late May I went all the way down to the high tide mark where the waves of the tide before had undercut the beach, leaving a cut-out bank. I lie there with the sand bank as a back rest, looking at the beauty of the twinkling sea and sky. After a while, I became aware of a pod of porpoises hunting just beyond the shore break, almost on the beach. Not twenty yards from where I was. It was as if they were speaking to me. Inviting me to join them in their migration north. Giving me a sign. Making me think that maybe the answer was to head north, or at least somewhere farther away until everything blew over. If it did.

It was a month after I arrived at Green Run, when I came back to the shanty after an afternoon of wading the eel grass for soft crabs. They had their first shed a month early over here on the sea side, the coastal bays - probably the salinity caused it. In any event, I'd stopped when I'd gotten a dozen. Didn't take long. I had three doublers. They add up a lot faster when you're soft crab wading. So I'd sat out on the marsh in the lee of a marsh clump basking in the sun and thinking about what to do next. I was getting a little tired of soft crabs. But they were there if you knew how to find them, and I did. And oysters, too. There were two natural oyster bars nearby in the bay, thigh deep at low tide, shallow enough that you could pick them up by hand. Big old oysters that had never been commercially 'scraped' or 'tonged', the tastiest in the world. 'Salts', we called them for their high salt taste. Same as Chincoteagues, or Blue Points from up in Long Island Sound. Oysters that were saltier than their Chesapeake Bay cousins because they lived in salt water fresh in from the ocean. 'Salts' marked also by the sharpness and points of the shell that were missing in their kin from the inland bay. I'd brought some Oneida crackers down with me, some other crackers in tins, and ketchup, too. Wasn't much finer eating than a fresh caught 'salt', laid out on a cracker, with a drop or two of ketchup on him. At least for the first couple of weeks.

But, now I knew I'd have to go somewhere for some supplies soon even if I was to stay on into the summer - but that was unlikely, too many people over on the beach when it warmed up. I was still thinking on it as I walked up to the shanty. By then it was almost dark. Jimbo was sitting on the porch waiting for me. He made my mind up.

"Jimbo. Whatcha doin' down here?" I asked. "Its not that you ain't welcome, it's been a bit lonely the last couple of days."

"Hits about to get a lot noisier." Jimbo answered. "Somebody down here fishin' seen the smoke comin' from the potbelly. Went back and told ever'body and now they's thinkin' maybe the man done the damage in the fight is hidin' down here. They still ain't sure who it be. But they's acomin' in the mornin'. I got Hot Pot Pie to bring me over. He's waitin' at the gut. Get your things. You got to get."

In an hour we were on the ferry heading to the mainland. It was pitch black now. Overcast, no moon. A slight wind causing a little sea. A little spray slurping over the gunwales. We were all standing in the wheelhouse. Jimbo, Hot Pot Pie and me, talking. Mostly about what I was going to do.

Hot Pot Pie said, "Look they's was atalkin' for awhile about whoever done it must of headed down south - Hatteras, maybe even Florida. They 'spect' you cause you're gone - but they don't know for sure 'cause nobody done any talkin' on it. But they's known you go south sometimes. You need to find some other direction."

Jimbo, interrupted: "Hey, you know where you ought to go? North, up to New England. To the swordfishin' grounds. None of us ever done it. Be differ'nt. We ain't got much chance down here to get in that stuff. Too hard to bait 'em. Now looks to me to be the time for you. They do a lot of it off a islands up there. Islands way out - not like here a half-mile or so. Up there the islands, some of 'em anyway is ten, twelve miles out. Nobody 'ill know you and they ain't easy to get to. You can hire out on a swordfishin' boat. You might even like it."

By the next morning Jimbo had taken me to a truck stop just outside Wilmington, Delaware, where, with a promise to help unload the truck, I got a ride on a sixteen-wheeler hauling a load of rock (striped bass) up to the Fulton Fish Market in New York. It was June 12th, 1951.

When we had the truck unloaded, the driver helped me get a ride on a truck heading back north after delivering a load of codfish to the market. Late that afternoon we arrived at Point Judith, Rhode Island. I couldn't see it for the fog, but I knew that one of the islands I was heading for, a swordfishing island, Block Island, was just offshore. Twelve miles, maybe.

I could see a boat, a green hulled working boat coming out of the fog through an opening in a breakwater about a half-mile to the left up the waterway from the dock. Ivory white topsides. It wasn't overly big. Maybe 35-40 feet. But it had a red mast with an open platform at the top and an upturned pulpit at the bow, with yellow kegs showing midships. A small red dory was being towed behind the bigger boat. It was a swordfishing boat.

Chapter Four

THE EVA

She was called the *Eva* and appeared to me to be what we called down home a flounder dragger size. But, she wasn't rigged for trawling, for dragging nets. Had no nets on her either. She'd been either built or modified for swordfishing.

At the top of her mast was an open platform with metal spikes set in the mast from the deck to the platform to act as a ladder. Up forward, the pulpit extended upwards some from her bow, maybe out about seven or eight feet, with cables extending from the deck of the pulpit to the sides of the bow and to the mast as well and with a cable rail attached to stanchions affixed to the edges of the pulpit. Although the commercial boats in Ocean City did not have pulpits, I'd seen them on some of the sport fishing boats, in fact had worked on boats with them, but they were mostly for show and much smaller than the one I was seeing now. It was rare for a swordfish to be found basking on the surface as far south as the mid-Atlantic and even when one was seen most boats didn't have harpoons and would try to 'bait' them instead - drag trolling baits as close to the fish as possible. It was rare when a basking swordfish would take a trolled bait.

Just forward of the mast on the *Eva* was a small wheel house, not much bigger than the man that was standing at the wheel as she approached the dock. Not enough room in the wheelhouse for bunks, galley and the like. I presumed she was primarily a 'day' boat, a 'short tripper' - a boat that returned to port on most nights. The boom attached to the base of the mast extended almost to the stern and was canted at about a 45-degree angle off the deck. There were several kegs on the deck and tubs of line attached to the kegs. To the side, lying against the port gunwale were harpoons with the darts reattached. All the gear was neatly stowed. The vessel appeared in great shape for a boat involved in a commercial fishery where boats usually looked like hell.

I could only see two men aboard her. I'd been told that usually swordfishing boats, even the smaller ones, had crews of three or more.

Usually, the harpooner (what they called the 'sticker'), the operator, (usually the captain), sometimes an observer in the crow's nest and the keg man, the person who threw the keg over after a fish was darted, or 'ironed'. On the bigger boats there might be additional dory men who would chase down the darted fish while the mother boat went after other fish. The dory men would subdue the 'ironed' fish by lancing, then making it fast to the dory and wait to be picked up by the mother boat. *Eva* was a small boat, though, had only the small dory, so I wasn't sure whether she used the dory system, or subdued fish one at a time by having the mother ship chase down the kegs, one after the other if more than one fish was struck before the first fish was brought to the boat.

As she approached the Port Judith commercial dock, I could see six or seven swordfish on her deck, already dressed out. I asked a dockworker who the captain was and the boat's home port.

"She be a Block Islander, "he responded. "Her captain is one of the Stinsins. He's an islander."

Soon the *Eva* was in the unloading slip, dock lines were thrown to her and she was made fast to the landing dock. The two men aboard her began to attach lines to the tail of one of the larger swordfish, probably around five hundred pounds when she'd been whole, fastened it to a block on the end of the boom, pulled it up, and swung the boom over to the dock where dockhands unfastened the fish, and dragged it inside the fish house, while the boom was used to land another of the big fish. The smaller fish were manhandled directly to the dock. Then the dock hands swung a wide hose over the boat, up near the wheelhouse where a large compartment was attached. One of the men on the boat opened a hatch to the compartment and crushed ice flowed from the hose, until it overflowed to the deck. The hose was swung back over the dock and the hatch to the boat's compartment was closed.

After the fish were landed, the man that had been giving the orders climbed up on the dock and went inside. He was a big man, as big as me, six foot, maybe two or three inches above it. Probably weighed two hundred and forty or so. And it wasn't fat.

I waited for him. After about twenty minutes he came outside, counting money, and proceeded to give some of it to the other man who had been on the boat. That man then walked off the dock and up the street. I approached the man who had disbursed the money; he appeared to be the captain.

"Captain," I said, "I'm Hank Gaskins. I'm from down south a ways, been workin' on draggers, clam boats, doin' some sport fishin', matin', as well. I've come up 'ere to see if I can get some work on a swordfishin' boat. I'm looking for a ride over to Block Island to see if anybody over there needs a hand. Any chance I can get a ride across with you, instead of waitin' for tomorrow's ferry?"

He looked me up and down for a minute. Guess he liked what he saw, or at least I didn't turn him off. Then there was the general helpfulness of one seaman to another. And, although I didn't know it then, his crew had just quit and he was really shorthanded. Not many fishermen were still wanting to go 'sticking' swordfish. It was hard work, and dangerous, too. He'd already been operating a man short in this early part of the season, now he was two down. So he was in a bind of his own. Made me look all the better, I guess.

"Get, aboard," was all he said. I'd learn that he didn't talk much, only when it was needed. That way he was listened to whenever he had something to say.

We got on the boat, me with my duffle bag, and went toward the wheelhouse. He went in, turned the engine over, told me "Make her loose." I put the duffle bag alongside the wheel house.

With his eyes on me, I went forward and unfastened the bow dock line, threw it up on the dock, then did the same with the stern dock line and we slowly made our way out of the unloading slip. When we cleared the slip, he turned her to port, went slowly down the channel so as not to create much wake and in five or ten minutes he turned her to starboard and we went through the opening in the breakwater, proceeded generally eastward toward the island. By that time I was standing next to him in the wheelhouse.

"What'd you do?" He asked. I had expected the question. Fishermen don't just up and leave their home port. Usually, they have to leave. Like me.

"Got in a fight with a rich kid. He got hurt and his family wants some flesh."

"Fair fight?"

"Sorta. He was a football player, outweighed me by 50 pounds are more."

"What happened?"

"We'd just come in from sea clammin'. Were havin' a beer at the bar on the dock, when he came in and shoved me aside. I hit him. Problem was, I had a mug of beer in my hand when he shoved me, so I hit him with it. It broke up his face some, had to go in the hospital. The chief of police asked me to be scarce. I always wanted to try what I heard about this fishin' up 'ere. Got my share money, headed north. Ended up in Point Judith. I come from an island, always lived on one, know what it's like. The energy of it. There's Block Island where we're headin'. Seemed natural to go to 'er.

"Captain, I don't start 'em, but I got to own up, I usually finish 'em."

"You didn't start it, then?"

"No sir. I didn't. But I didn't run from it. Ain't got much run in me."

"Ain't got much run in me neither," Captain Stinsin said then, "can't have much run in you out 'ere when things get tough, and sooner or later they's gonna' get tough. That's what happened to the man just left the boat. That big fish came to the boat, appeared almost dead so we just tail roped 'er, didn't bother to lance 'er, hauled 'er on board with the boom. She come aboard too green, revived and knocked him plum overboard. He got mad when I didn't stop right then and get 'im back. Hell, I knew he could swim. I had to kill the fish afore she tore hell out of the boat. Only took me a minute or so to lance 'er. I was back to 'im in five minutes. Hell, this early in the season ain't much out there to get you. But he got pissed off. You can swim, I hope, better be able to if you're a gettin' in this business."

"Yeah, I can swim, but, I ain't lookin' to. I was raised to know about 'a hand for the boat and a hand for yourself'. I always aim to stay on the boat."

"So you ain't never done no swordfishin' afore? Whosoever takes you on got to hope they can teach you 'fore you get yourself hurt or kilt?"

"Well, like I said I ain't aimin' to get hurt. Damn sure ain't gonna get kilt. And, I'm a fast learner. Where I come from you got to be careful no matter which fishin' you be doin'. If you're trawlin', ever'thing got strain on her; if a cable snaps it can kill you, if you get caught up in it it'll drag you over and down and there ain't no way to get the gear back aboard afore you're drowned. When you're pullin' strings of bass pots they's always a load of weight on it and anything can happen. I don't think I'm gonna forget how to protect myself up 'ere. It's all the same in one way, the sea can kill you - don't give 'er no chances, got to make 'er work to kill you."

"When you ready to start workin'?" Captain Stinsin asked.

"Soon's I can find a boat that'll take me on." I answered.

"I'll take a chance on you," he said, "but, you got to know this is the very beginnin' of the season. It's early. We won't get too many for a while yet - till mid-summer. "Em fish we just sold at the dock were three days worth - three short trips. We're into short trippin', boats that do 'er day at a time. 'Cept for the sellin'. Sometimes we ice 'em a day or two, then over to Point Judith. But the fishin' is out in the mornin', back in the evenin'. Mostly. Early to late."

"It's probably better that way, for me," I responded, "give me more chance to work into learnin' 'bout it, with the fish bein' sparse, and the 'short trippin'. Mostly, that's what I done down home. Day at a time. "

"Well, afore you agree to sign on, you got to know 'bout the money. Usually, we need to carry two men, 'sides myself. I've done 'er by myself when I had to, but not liken it much. She's really a three-man operation. The bigger boats uses more men, even. We really need three, but we make do with two when we have to. We work shares. Cause you just learnin', for the first two weeks you'll have to work on a half share. After that, if you still want to be 'ere, and I want you 'ere, you go to a full share. The boat always gets a full share and I always get a full share. We'll be tryin' to get another hand, and, ifin we do, he'll get a full share, but with another man, if we do 'er right we'll get more fish and the shares will be bigger anyway. That sound ok to you?"

"Yeah, that'll do. Sounds fair. I've always worked on shares when fishin' commercial."

"When we're working her two handed," he continued, "I'll run her to the grounds where the fish be, or I think they be and you be up on the mast lookin' for 'em. Usually, up north here, they's finned out. The dorsal and tail fin 'ill be out. Ain't like 'em marlin down south;

swordfish dorsals is fixed, they can't put 'em down. The fins'r up all the time. So ifin you see one tailin', 'specially if the tail is out pretty good, the dorsal'ill be showin', too. If the sea is really calm, they's easy to see. If it's rough, you have to look harder cause they's in and out more, 'dippin' I call it. You can still see 'em some though, even when they's down, maybe down in the water two, three feet. We 'stick' 'em too, when they's down, though usually they's up. It be better when they's up, the water don't throw off the lookin' and stickin' too much, refraction, I think they call it, when the water, she throws off your aim.

"When you see one, you yell down to me, I'll look up and you point whereaway she be. Soon's I see 'er, you get on down and take the wheel, throttle 'er right down 'til we're barely makin' way to the fish. While you're comin' up on 'er, I'll get in the pulpit with the 'stick'. When I strike the fish, I'll yell 'she's 'ironed'.' When I yell that, you leave the wheel and run to the gunwale and get ready to throw the keg over when the line is finished runnin' out the tubs. There's 'bout four, five hundred feet of line, still you don't want to be dallyin'' any. I'll be bringin' the stick back aboard dropping it up in the bow, then takin' the wheel. You point 'er out to me and we'll chase the keg down as she's tirin'. If there's more around, we might leave the first fish on the keg while we try to 'iron' anothern. Sometimes we get two or three on the kegs at a time when the fishin' is hot. Ifin we get another deck-hand, we might use the dory to chase the first one down no matter how big she is, while the other two of us 'iron' some more. But, once you get 'em darted and kegged, you got to be careful the dart don't pull out. That's why with a big fish, 'specially ifin we think it ain't darted real good, we try to land 'em with the dory, more give to it and it don't yank the dart out so much as the big boat does. Sometimes though, we ain't got a lot of choice, have to leave the dory with the first fish 'stuck' ifin the next fish gets to hell and gone. Then we have to chase the second fish with the *Eva* no matter how big the fish is, leave the dory with the first fish. It can get confusin' sometimes when you ain't got but the one dory. And it can be dangerous. These fish ain't like them marlin. They's sometimes come after the dory. They'll try to stick 'er or break 'er up. They's brave fish. They's used to fighin' off sharks up 'ere, 'specially the big makos. They take care of 'emselves right good."

28

"I'll handle it," I said, "take a bit to get used to it, but not long. It's a fish and it's the ocean. That's what I come from." I responded.

We rode on to the east-northeast for a while and soon the island began to come through the haze, rising out of the sea. We were heading for the northernmost end of the island. I would learn that there was a harbor on the near side of the island - the southwest side as we came up on the island. It was called New Harbor because it had not been dredged out until the late 1800s. Gave me some idea of how old the island settlement was. In Ocean City we didn't have a real ocean harbor until the thirty-three hurricane cut the inlet through, and to me that was a long time ago. We weren't heading for New Harbor though, but for what they called Old Harbor around on the east side. They didn't make things anymore complicated then they had to on the island. Guess it comes from having to be self-reliant so far off the mainland. At home I'd swum the half-mile to the mainland just to show I could. But, ten or twelve miles is a mite too far. Way out here they had to take care of most everything by themselves.

As we got closer, heading around the north end, I could see that the island stretched down pretty far to the south. On the northerly end, the end we were rounding, there was a fairly high bluff, with a lighthouse that looked to be on the westerly side of it, on a sand spit. I would come to know it as "North Light." It took us a half an hour or so to come up on it, then round the north end, Sandy Point they called it. We continued around what they called "Clayhead," and then to the south I could see the lights of a harbor, with the lights of a large hotel hovering above. Another fifteen minutes and we were coming up to a large breakwater extending easterly from the island. There was a smaller right angled breakwater to the north of it, with an opening between the two which was the entrance to the harbor. We entered and went to starboard, to the north part of the little harbor, close up to the inside of the smaller breakwater. Captain Stinsin told me:

"That third buoy from the end's ouren. Take that boat hook up forward and when we get up on the buoy, you'll see a stringer from it, snag it with the hook, pull it aboard and then make the bow line fast to it with the clasp. Then let 'er go over. We'll take the dory to the breakwater and make the stern fast to the cleat up on the jetty."

Soon the *Eva* was secure in the harbor, with the dory fastened to the stern line. Captain Stinsin said then,

"Hank' we got to take 'em kegs, sticks and darts, get 'em ashore and in the truck. Can't be leavin' 'em in the boat once the tourists start usin' 'ere in June, 'specially 'em college boys, that fraternity stuff. They'll steal 'em, they tell me they hang on the wall in these houses they live at, and the littler 'uns is the boys whats got to steal 'em. I just take 'em to the house, lock 'em up in the shed, bring it all back the next sailin' mornin'."

After three short trips with the dory, we had all the gear ashore, including Captain Stinsin's ditty bag and my duffle bag. It took two trips for us to carry it all up to the parking lot. On the last trip as we were walking, he turned to me, said,

"Don't s'pose you got anywheres to stay?

"Nope, not yet, was fixin' to find me a roomin' house." I answered.

"Well, you might's well stay at the house tonight. Can look for a permanent place to stay tomorrow. We won't be going out for a day or two. Stay with us this evenin'."

Chapter Five

EVA

We walked off the breakwater carrying the last load, then got in a pickup and proceeded up a street called Water Street, then up Dodge Street to where the street sign said Old Town Road. There we took a right and rode up a winding road, a house here and there, separated by several thickets and wood-lots. Half-way up that road was his house. It was an old house, built by his grandfather in the late 1800s he would later tell me. It was a story and a half, typical, I would learn, of many houses built on the island in that period. He drove the pickup into the back yard and I helped him put the gear in the shed. He locked it and we both walked around to the front of the house, up the steps of the porch. It extended the width of the front of the house, had several chairs and a chaise lounge with cushions, all centered around a small table. I would learn that this was where he had his morning coffee when he wasn't sailing. Especially in the summer. He walked to the door, opened it.

I followed him in the door of the house. It opened into a small parlor, or living room. I could see through part of it to a kitchen beyond a dining room. There were two women there. The older one was in front of a stove, the other was just bringing china and silverware into the dining room to set the table. While I had been mooring the boat, Captain Stinsin had radioed his wife that he was bringing a guest for the evening. Like many island couples where the husband swordfished, they had set up radios so that they could talk while the husband was at sea.

The older woman, Captain Stinsin 's wife, was about fifty I guessed, several years younger than he. She was a beautiful woman still, a mature woman. Her stance bespoke a woman sure of herself. And, in time it would be clear to me that they were sure of each other - in love with each other.

The other woman, the one just coming into the dining room was very young, not much more than a girl, really. Younger than me, I guessed. I didn't have to guess about anything else. She was simply beautiful. She had styled her honey-blond hair upswept in some fashion, held together with a bow at the back that together framed perfect facial features. There was no single element of her face that made it beautiful. It wasn't the kind of face where I could look at her eyes and say they were perfect and that's what made her so beautiful, though they were perfect deep blue eyes, or say her beauty rose from the classic nose, the cheekbones raised just right, the ears peeking out of the finely textured hair, the creamy smooth complexion. It was impossible to focus on her separate features at that first meeting because I was overwhelmed with the whole of her. She wore a high-necked silk blouse, with full sleeves down to tight cuffs at her wrists, with a ribbon belted around her waist and a long skirt. I didn't have to look to see if she had a good figure, it was just there. Had I seen her, a stranger, walking down a street anywhere, I would have simply stopped and looked. Stared at her, I guess. She was just that kind of a beautiful woman. The type of woman you look at, and then, when she's passed, look skyward and say: "God, you got it right that time!"

Captain Stinsin, motioning me forward, introduced me.

"Rebecca, I want you to meet Hank Gaskins. He's signed on with me for the season. He's from down south, from an island in Maryland."

Rebecca, his wife, had started toward us when we first came in the door, wiping her hands on a towel. She came up to me then, held her hand out, said: "It's nice to meet you, Mr. Gaskins." She spoke with almost perfect diction, no accent, no rough grammar like the Captain and me. I would learn that she was a school teacher. College educated. Her daughter, Eva, had just gotten home on summer break from the University of Rhode Island. The daughter had a summer job at the best hotel in town. A management job of some kind.

"Just call me Hank, ma'am," I responded to Mrs. Stinsin, as I took her hand in mine, bowing my head slightly as I did. "Hit's a pleasure to meet you."

"This is our daughter, Eva," Captain Stinsin said then and I knew why his boat was called the *Eva*.

She came toward me and when she got close, went as if to shake my hands, but remembered that she was holding china and silver wear. She adjusted and with her left hand, held the items to her chest while she held her right hand out to me.

"Mr. Gaskins," she said then, "it's nice to meet someone from away from here for a change - especially in the early-season. Especially a fisherman from somewhere else. You'll be the one that'll be taking care of Daddy when he's out fishing."

"Hello, Miss Eva," I responded as I looked down to take her hand, "I'll be a fishin' on your boat with Captain Stinsin, 'cept that I imagine he'll be takin' care of me, for the most part, at least for a while."

I realized, after a moment, that I was lingering with the handshake, holding her hand a little long, looking at the delicate fingers in my rough paws, before elevating my head to look into her eyes. When I did, deep blue, almost purple eyes, looked into my soul. I had to look away. Couldn't bear the scrutiny of her gaze. I was frightened, even. My heart had stopped, I think. I know I wasn't breathing. In that instant I knew that she knew all my innermost secrets, things even I didn't know were in me. Inner levels unknown so far to me. In that first glance, she captured my spirit and made it hers. It was like we were alone. Even then, I couldn't go on. Couldn't think of a thing to say. And she saw it. She rescued me. She broke the spell with a giggle - not a girlish giggle, but a happy laugh of discovery, for her as well as me. I even smelled her then, caught the scent of lilacs.

Her mother interrupted:

"Will, take Hank upstairs to the rear room. He's a tall one and there is more head room there. Open the window on the rear and he'll get all the air he'll need. Hank, there's a bathroom halfway down the hall. I put a towel and washcloth in there earlier on the edge of the tub. When you get yourself settled, come on back down. We're just about ready to eat."

We went up stairs, then down a hall that led from the front to the back of the house. The hall stopped at a door that was open and I could see a bed through the opening as I approached.

"This is where you'll be for the evenin'," Captain Stinsin said, "tomorrow we'll get you set up in a roomin' house, probably up by the Hill Top Hotel, they take roomers in several of the homes up there and I think the Hill Top has special rates for single fishermen."

He left me then and I looked around. It wasn't really a full two-storey house. The upstairs side walls were really knee-walls, with the ceiling angling up from about knee-high to the peak in the middle of the room. There was only headroom for me in the middle third of the room, to the sides I had to bend over. The bed was in the exact middle of the room, but with the headboard up against a window at the rear of the house. Out the rear window, through the blue and yellow flowered curtains, I could see across a field to another house and a road, a road I would learn was named Ocean Avenue. Beyond it I could see a pond of some kind, shining through the fog in the quarter-moonlight. After a moment, I turned, put my duffle at the end of the bed, went back down the hall to where Captain Stinsin had pointed out the bathroom. I threw some water on my face, washed my hands and tried to calm down the mess my hair had become in the wind out on the Sound. Then I went back downstairs.

By then the table was set and Captain Stinsin was sitting at the end of the table nearest the parlor, with a steaming tureen of soup in front of him.

"Sit down, Hank," he said motioning to the seat to his left, "Rebecca usually has a hot pot of corn chowder for me when I come in from fishin'. Today, she's put just about everythin' else in it, as well. Oysters, clams, some kind of fish, looks like little ling cod. Vegetables, too. If you don't like this, you've done come to the wrong island."

I walked around him, took the seat to his left where he had directed me. Eva then walked into the dining room with a bowl of mashed potatoes, followed by her mother with the main dish, a baked rockfish it looked like to me, though they called them stripers. Eva sat down on the side of the table to her father's right, across from me, where every time I looked up I'd be looking at her. Her mother took a seat at the end of the table nearest the kitchen. When we were all seated, Captain Stinsin said:

"We'll have the blessin' now. 'Dear God, bless the people of this house, bless all the people of Your house 'ere on earth. Bless the food we are about to eat out of the bounty You provide us. Keep these women safe from harm. Keep this young man who has joined us for this meal safe at sea as he goes upon 'er again. It's his first time up 'ere with our way of things and he'll need Your protection 'til he gets the right sea legs for what we be a doin'. Keep me safe, too. Bring me home to Rebecca, to Your daughter who you lent to us to love for our time 'ere. Look after Eva, your precious jewel, our's too. In your son's name. Amen.'"

We all joined in with our own amens. For them, because it was their way, me because it felt right to join in. When I unbowed my head my eyes automatically rose to meet Eva's, precisely as hers were rising to meet mine. I had to look away. I knew my face was red in that instant. She was really having an effect on me.

Captain Stinsin ladled a large portion of the chowder into a bowl and asked me to pass it down to his wife, then he gave a portion to Eva, then to me, and finally to himself. For a while we ate, mostly quietly, except for the occasional "Please pass me." After the fish and vegetables were finished, Mrs. Stinsin said:

"Eva, why don't you go in and cut everybody a piece of the apple pie you baked this afternoon?"

In a couple of minutes Eva was back with portions of pie for everyone, serving her father and mother first, then coming around behind me, and reaching over my shoulder, placing the slice of pie in front of me. So close I could feel her presence, an aura of her.

I said, "Thank you," and she returned to her seat across the table from me. I couldn't just keep looking at my plate, but every time I looked up, across the table at her, I was consuming her with my eyes. Couldn't help it. To stop I just started looking first to my left at Mrs. Stinsin, then to my right at Captain Stinsin. Left to right and back as we began to talk, but I could see my attempts to avoid looking Eva's way tickled her. She could barely keep from laughing. She knew full well the effect she had. She was so beautiful, I don't imagine it was the first time she had seen such a reaction.

Eventually, we finished dinner and after the table was cleared, moved into the parlor. Soon we began to talk.

"I met up with Hank at the dock in Point Judith; he was waitin' for a way to the island, said he wanted to try swordfishin'," Captain Stinsin said, starting the conversation. "He's been doin' lots of commercial fishing, sport fishin', too, down south in Maryland. They catch a lot of marlin down there, but not many swordfish. Ain't the same down there with 'em. Don't stay on top, much, like 'ere."

"What made you want to come up here, Mr. Gaskins?" Eva asked. "Your season's got to be coming on down there."

"Lots of reasons," I answered, knowing that Captain Stinsin was listening closely, because he knew the real reason. I wanted to be careful, not lie, but not tell the truth either. I continued, "I've always wanted to try the harpooning of 'em; they's really hard to bait when we see 'em on top down home, so we don't get much chance at 'em. Knew this place was a pretty good hot-spot, a friend of mine suggested I should come and the time seemed right." I'd managed an answer without lying. I looked over at Captain Stinsin who had a slight smile on his face. I had walked around the complete truth - but I hadn't lied.

"Clem got knocked off the boat by a big-sized fish today." Captain Stinsin said. "I didn't stop to pick 'im up right away cause I needed to lance the fish. Only took me five minutes to get back to 'im, never got more then a couple hundred yards from 'im. Had 'im in sight the whole time. He's a heck of a swimmer, besides. But, he got way mad anyway, wouldn't hardly talk to me, 'ceptin' cussin' me real good. Thought we'd get to fightin' afore he calmed down some. Anyways, soon's I paid 'im off at the Point Judith dock he told me off and left. There I was, already short a hand and the only hand I had done walked off. Then Hank 'ere, he walks up wantin' a ride to the island lookin' for work on a swordfishin' boat. Don't know whether he's any good or not, but I do know - there he was. We'll find out about the good part soon enough."

"Isn't that going to be dangerous," Mrs. Stinsin said, "breaking in a new hand when you're shorthanded?"

"He says he can handle 'er; says he's a hand for the boat one for hisself trained down south. He's done a might of sea clammin' down there in the winter and it don't get much more dangerous than that; also says he ain't got any run in 'im. We'll see 'bout that, too."

"Mrs. Stinsin, I think I'll be okay," I said. "it's a boat, it's a fish, and it's the sea. That's all I've known since 'afore I was eleven. Been on the water one way or the other all my life. Been at it so long, don't 'member what it feels like to take a level walk even when I'm on the beach. Long as Captain Stinsin stops harpoonin' them fish that likes to knock crewmen over, ever' thing be fine." "Hank," Captain Stinsin said, "up 'ere we 'stick' fish, or we 'iron' 'em. Harpoonin' is what 'em fancy sport fishermen do - or try to do. You don't want to be talkin' too much 'bout harpoonin' 'hereabouts - might cause you to be a 'laugher'. You start out that-away, and you'll be fightin' afore you know it."

36

Eva, spoke up then. "Mr. Gaskins" she started. But, I interrupted her for a moment.

"Miss Stinsin," I said, "ifin its right with your parents, I'd just soon you call me by my given name, Hank. Just feels funny bein' called Mr. when I'm not but one or two years older than you."

"Daddy?" She asked her father.

"Hit's okay," her father responded, "but, Hank you might's well call 'er by 'er's, too. No need to be too formal, things ain't formal most of the time 'round the island 'ere. "Cept for church."

"Hank, I think you'll find most of the people on the island to be friendly," Eva continued, "its not the full season yet, most of the tourists don't come over until well into the summer. Right now there are mostly locals and like most people anyplace they're going to be curious as to who you are. There won't be much jealousy about you taking a job on the *Eva*. Everybody up here is generally shorthanded. The Captains have to check around all the time for hands.

"Most of the young people can't wait to grow up and get off the island. I don't know why. I love it here. The boys that do want to stay in the area generally move over to Point Judith where they can get on bigger boats that go out to the banks for days before they come to port. Over there, too, it's a lot easier to get anywhere else - Providence, Boston, anywhere. When it storms, especially in the winter, we can go weeks without being able to get a boat from the island to the mainland. But, that just makes it special to me. Living here is like an adventure. Right now, of course, except for summer and holidays, I'm off-island at school. But, I'll be back permanently as soon as I can. I've been promised a manager's job at the Ocean View once I graduate. So I've planned it to come home."

"Yeah, island livin' is differ'nt," I responded, "more so I 'spect, up here where you're lots further out than down home. They's energy in island people; more dependence on each other."

"You might get a little grief from some of the guys when they find out you're staying' here," she said, "but don't worry about it, they'll get over it."

I answered just as her father was about to speak: "I'm just staying for tonight. Captain Stinsin is goin' to help me get set up, get a room or somethin' at a place, or near a place, called the Hill Top. So they won't have to worry none on me stayin' 'ere. But the truth is, I can understand 'em not wantin' a stranger around."

Captain Stinsin interrupted then and I feared I'd gone to far, gotten to familiar. If I had, he knew how to handle it it.

"Hank, we've had a long day, both of us. It's time we went to bed. We'll get on over to the Hill Top first thing in the mornin'."

With that, we broke up and I went on up to bed.

Chapter Six

THE HILL TOP

The next morning, after a big breakfast of eggs and fresh 'tinker' mackerel, they called them Boston mackerel, that had just been caught the day before, Captain Stinsin and I walked up hill farther inland. At first we didn't say much. Then he spoke.

"We be goin' tomorrow, 'bout first light. When they's 'ere at the island this time of year tain't no need to get out there too early, 'cause the fish don't rise until the sun's up good. They go down, too, when the sun gets a goin' down fast. But, they ain't 'ere much yet, so your first trip I think we'll be goin' down 'tween Montauk Point and South Channel - be a might further trip down there."

"Why is it that they only come up mostly midday?" I asked.

"Don't really know for sure," he answered. "my daddy always thought that they feed mostly down deep, probably why they's so hard to bait on top down south, and that they do most of it at night. Most these fish we catch in close 'ere are females, big fish, breedin' size. We think, maybe, that down deep where they do their nighttime feedin' the water's real cold - at least lots colder than it is on top. We think that what may happen is that they feed heavy down deep at night and eat so much that they's come on up in the daytime when the sun's up, lookin' for warmer water to help 'gest what's in 'em, and then just lie there, almost 'sleep, lettin' what they's just et settle good, afore the next night's feedin'. Don't know whether it's right or not, but it's good as any other reason."

"You know, I've only seen a couple down home in my time." I said. "Seen on top, I mean. And mostly it's a far piece out, but ever' now and then, somebody 'ill spot one in close just lyin' there. Most boats down there don't have nothin' to stick 'em with, so they have to try and bait 'em."

"You got 'er right now, we call 'em 'sticks' up 'ere," Captain Stinsin interrupted, "and the points we be callin' 'darts' or 'irons'. We dart 'em or 'iron' em, we don't harpoon 'em up 'ere. You need to 'member that, or you might be a butt."

"What you mean 'a butt'," I asked?

"They'll laugh at you. You say you ain't got no run in you. You'll be showin' it ifin you ain't careful, you start gettin' yourself laughed at."

"Anyway," I continued, "what you say 'bout the reasons for 'em lyin' on top sounds 'bout right, 'cause they's sure don't look like they's a feedin' when we see 'em down south; we troll baits right over the swords down home and most they usually do is just sink, go down."

"'Nother funny thing 'bout 'em, up 'ere," Captain Stinsin said, "is that afore they's stuck, they's a lot more likely to shy away from a dory than they are from a big boat. You can get up on 'em, sneak up on 'em lots easier from the *Eva* than the dory. Most of us think's it's because they relate the dories to sharks, 'specially makos. Makos eat up on 'em a lot, other sharks, too. But the makos is the bad 'un far as they're concerned. Swordfish 'll turn on the dories, too. Most of us think they do 'cause they think the dory is a mako and that they need to get free by killin' it. You got to be careful when you in a dory. 'Til you got 'er lanced, till you kill it, especially when she's got a considerable bit of line out, you best off standing on the gunwales and transom, cross the corner we calls it, in case the fish rams the bottom. That way it won't pierce your feet. Just put you in the water. Funny, they attack the dories, but not much done about attackin' the men ifn' the men get in the water."

By this time we were walking up another street to the left that took us to a small rise and there on the right was the Hill Top Inn. It was a large white building with a porch in front, columns and such, with steps going up to a lobby off the porch. There was a separate bar at ground level to the left of the porch and in the rear I could see what looked like small cottages for the help. We went on up the steps into the lobby of the hotel. Nice enough, I guess, but not five star. But, I wasn't looking for five star. Right then I just needed a place.

Captain Stinsin knew the man behind the desk and before long had it arranged that I could have one of the rooms in a cottage out back. I would learn that several of the crewmen on swordfish boats stayed at the Hill Top.

I thanked Captain Stinsin for his help. Right before he left he told me, "Be on the breakwater where the boat be, 'morrow mornin' daybreak. Five o'clock. We be gettin' out the harbor soon's there's enough light to see by. Got a far piece to go where we be goin'. "

"I'll be there." I said.

I got my clothing gear out of the duffle bag, put it in a small dresser along the wall of the room I had just rented. I decided to take a walk around the island. We'd gotten in virtually after dark the night before and I'd really only seen a small part of it on the way to the Hill Top with the Captain.

Chapter Seven

BLOCK ISLAND

I walked back down toward Old Harbor, took fifteen minutes. Wanted to make sure how much time it would take for me to get to the boat in the morning. Near the harbor, Old Town Road bore to the left and became Corn Neck Road, which ran along a beach I would learn later was called Crescent Beach. I walked north on that road, alongside the beach for the first part. I could see that this part of the island looked to be the lowest part, but even then it was higher then where I came from. Lots higher than Assateague, too. Ahead the land rose, and behind me, too, there behind Old Harbor and inland, it appeared to be higher still. It wasn't like the sand-piles I had called home. Where I was now, Crescent Beach, looked to be on a lower saddle of the island that stretched east to west. North and south was higher. All over the island as far as I could see the fields and marshes were sprinkled with wild-flowers, golds, blues, whites with a small clump of red flowers here and there. And everywhere you looked there were lilac bushes with their light purple flowers casting their scent downwind. In the setting of the green fields, with the brown marshes and the blue green sea as a backdrop the vista across the island became a painting, a landscape.

The ocean to the east was to my right as I walked. Blue green like it was down home close to shore. To my immediate left there was a series of little blue ponds glistening in the morning sunlight, or maybe it was one pond with lots of coves, guts and things. They kept on until considerably after I walked on by the intersection of Beach Avenue. I would learn that Beach Avenue ran on over toward the New Harbor and the Great Salt Pond. Beyond New Harbor and the Great Salt Pond was the sea to the west that they called Block Island Sound. I was curious about the west side but for now kept on going north, walking up Corn Neck Road. After a bit, probably a half-mile, Corn Neck Road moved inland, moving away from Crescent Beach. I walked on up the road which was gradually rising toward the bluff and a lighthouse I could see in the distance across another rather large pond or series of ponds. The area was overgrown with underbrush and warped and withered trees, reminded me of the trees on Assateague. Twisted by the wind and salt spray. In an hour or so I was at the north end of the island. I'd passed a few houses on the way up and there were driveways to the side of Corn Neck Road, leading, I presumed, to houses or small farms and the like.

Pretty soon I came to a dirt drive to the east off of Corn Neck Road. It was the first drive that didn't have a mailbox at the end, so I decided to see where it went. In another ten minutes I was standing at the edge of a huge dune, looking back to where I had started my walk. I could see the Old Harbor, its breakwaters and above them on another high bluff, a large hotel. An unusual hotel. It looked to the east out over Old Harbor to the edge of the sea.

Even from the distance, I could see an elongated front facade, with a cupola atop a center section that was a story higher than the three or four stories of the remainder of the building. It was clearly the largest structure I had seen in my walk. I'd missed it, except for the lights in the darkness last night and so far today when I went on Corn Neck Road it had been at my back and I had been too busy looking ahead. But, from where I was I could see that it would clearly be the epicenter of the summer season.

I looked to the north and could see that I was almost at the end of the island; it just stopped, maybe a half-mile from where I was standing, bending a little to the left, toward the northwest as it did. I climbed down the almost vertical face of the dune or bluff, carefully, to the beach, walked on around the north end, realizing as I did that I was walking around the end of the island we'd sailed past the night before as the *Eva* rounded the island heading for Old Harbor. Like her, I rounded the headland, but in the other direction. Another ten minutes and I was at the absolute northernmost part of the island, a slightly northwest spur, a sand spit actually, the one they called Sandy Point; a little to its south, between it and a pond called Sachem Pond, was the lighthouse I had seen earlier in my walk. There were ponds stretching below Sachem Pond back in the direction of the center of the island. It didn't look like it was very walkable and I had no desire to get bogged down in the mud on my first full day, so I began to retrace my steps back down Corn Neck Road. I guessed I'd gone a total of two or three miles by that time.

In a bit I arrived back at the intersection of Beach Avenue and decided to take it. It ran almost at a right angle to Corn Neck Road. Soon, maybe a quarter-mile farther, I ran into Ocean Avenue, which I would learn was the road between Old Harbor which I had already seen, and New Harbor to the west. I went on down to New Harbor, passing the Narragansett Hotel on the left as I got down near the docks.

New Harbor appeared to be a little upscale as far as the boats were concerned. Mostly, over at Old Harbor were working boats. New Harbor looked like a 'swells' harbor, sailboats, cruisers, and such. Play boats. There were a few work boats here and there, but many more yachts and sailboats. Some of them very big. One or two sport fishermen, but none I recognized. They were primarily home ported in New England ports.

I didn't stay long, wanted to see as much of the island as I could in the day I had.

I'd already walked a good piece. Was hungry. As I walked back up Ocean Avenue in the direction of Old Harbor, I came to a small food store with a lunch counter. Went in, had a sandwich and a soda, and headed on out. Soon I was back down in the Old Harbor area past where I had turned to go north on Corn Neck Road. There was a small turnaround, or traffic circle, with a statue in the middle of it. There didn't appear to be much vehicular traffic. There were fish houses, some stores, and restaurants between the street I was on and the harbor. A ferry had just docked and quite a few people were beginning to circulate in the area. They were going in the restaurants, the stores, and some of them were carrying bags into some of the small hotels along Water Street, that was aptly named because it was the last street before the beach and the water of the harbor. I noticed a jitney with the words Ocean View Hotel loading up passengers, then heading up to the large hotel I had seen from the dunes at the north end of the island.

I walked on up the road to the hotel grounds. It was even more impressive from close up. It was an expensive hotel, unlike my digs at the Hill Top. The people sitting in the chairs on the veranda, playing croquet on the lawn and milling around, were dressed up, the men in jackets and ties. I would learn that the Ocean View was the queen of the

Block Island hotel industry. Built years before by Nicholas Ball, it had been Block Island hotel royalty for eighty years or more, built in 1873 after Ball convinced the federal government to begin construction of the Old Harbor breakwaters. It was here, at the Ocean View Hotel that Eva worked and where she anticipated being made a manager when she graduated. She was already a concierge. She had worked at the hotel in the summers in various capacities since she was 14 years old, had quickly worked her way up the ladder. She was smart. Her looks didn't hurt either, I thought.

Soon, I walked on past the Ocean View, first on Spring Street, going south or southeast, down the easterly edge of the island. It was generally higher here, the elevation of the road generally considerably farther above the level of the sea than had been Corn Neck Road. Shortly, I could see another lighthouse ahead on the left. Before long I was at the road that led to the lighthouse. It had a sign that said "South East Light." I walked on by, not knowing whether the lighthouse was open to the public. The road kept going up until I realized I was considerably above the level of the ocean. Higher here than when I had been on the north end of the island. I then came to a little fork in the road and, wanting to stay as near the sea as I could, I bore left. The road here changed its name to the Mohegan Trail. Soon, there was a sign indicating a path to "Mohegan Bluffs." I took it and within a hundred yards I was standing atop a high bluff, two or three hundred feet above the sea. There were steps and a path leading down and soon I was on a sandy beach, with rocks and such strewn about, some of them big, with a considerable sea with a right break coming in from the southeast . I could see, to the west now, down the beach, scattered surf fishermen, beach-goers, shellers, whatever, here and there.

I stayed awhile, down near the water, comfortable as I always am near the sea. Leaned my back up against a big rock at the foot of the bluff, just looking out to sea, thinking as I had done on Assateague just days before. Wondering, what tomorrow, and its tomorrow, would bring. I was looking forward to it. Already, I liked the Captain. He was plain speaking, and was putting lots of trust in me to be the person I said I was - a person with no run in him. Mrs. Stinsin had treated me like there wasn't anything strange about a kid from Maryland showing up on a dock in Point Judith looking for a job on a swordfishing boat and appearing at her home for dinner, out of almost nowhere. I was already taken with Eva. Found it hard to look at her she was so beautiful. And she was nice. Treated me nice; teased me a little with her knowing smiles and laughter, but even that was done right. Made me embarrassed; not angry.

Eventually, I climbed back up the bluff, hit the trail again and soon reached the intersection of Lakeside Drive. The trail didn't appear to go much further, so I headed back north on Lakeside Drive, going, it looked like, up the center, or almost the center of the island. Before long I was walking by a small airfield I guessed (wrongly) was private and then walked on until I was in the vicinity of the Hill Top. I went to my room, laid down and fell asleep.

I awoke around five o'clock, went down town, I guess it was downtown, found a small restaurant and had dinner. I had them make several sandwiches for the next day, stopped by a store on the way back and got some drinks, went in my room, set the alarm clock and sacked out. The alarm went off at 4:30 in the morning and soon I was sitting at the Old Harbor breakwater aft of the *Eva*. No-one was aboard her and I wasn't sure of Captain Stinsin's likes and dislikes so I didn't go aboard, stayed on the breakwater until, about fifteen minutes later, he pulled up in the parking lot and I went to meet him to help with the gear.

"You could'ave got on 'er," he said, as I came up to him on the parking lot.

"Didn't know for sure," I responded, "didn't want to start out on the wrong foot. She's your boat and I didn't know how you want to be runnin' this 'ere deal."

"You're the crew." He said, "that means she's your boat 'til I tell you she ain't. You don't have to be waitin' on me to board 'er. There's always things need stowin' away, things to be made shipshape, lines to be checked and such. You just figure she's yourin, treat her like she's much yourin as mine. That'll get things done right. Straight up. We got to trust each other where we goin' and what we be doin' out there, got to trust each other ashore as well. Want you to be 'memberin' that. 'Member it 'bout ever'thing. Lets get on 'er, get to goin'."

46

Chapter Eight

SOUTH CHANNEL

It only took us minutes to get out of the harbor and another five minutes or so to round the south breakwater, put her a little south of east and head on out towards South Channel, but running a little off the direct course to the channel so that we would be down a little toward Montauk Point, the very tip of Long Island. We'd be fishing on the inshore side of the channel, where the bottom comes up some and where the water gets a little warmer.

In a couple or three hours we were coming to where Captain Stinsin wanted to concentrate, a point near the channel that put the *Eva* at the off-shore point of a triangle, with Montauk as another point, Block Island the other. Captain Stinsin slowed the boat up some, not too much though. He wanted to be able to cover as much water as possible, but not so fast we would risk missing what we should be seeing.

He turned to me, said, "You might's well get on up 'er. The platform on the mast. You got to be lookin' all the time. There's a little too much chop right now for the best seein', but she'll probably smooth out some 'round ten. Ifin you see any fins, tail or dorsal, anything, even ifin you can't see 'er real good, give a holler, point to it, and keep a pointin' until I'm a comin' up on 'er."

I went on up the mast, climbing the spikes set alternately on either side, until I climbed up on the platform. It had a small pipe rail, about waist high to keep the lookout from falling and to give him a steadying handhold when the seas would get up a little. The boat began to run a pattern, about a mile to the south, one to the east, than back north - but not so far to the north, then west but not so far to the west as we'd gone to the east, then south again, further south than before. I figured it out after the first circuit. He was running a pattern to cover most of the water, but moving the pattern itself to the south and east as he made each circuit. That way he'd cover more ocean, but not miss much that was in each piece of it.

For a while, considerable while, I didn't see much. Birds. At one point a bunch of porpoises, maybe as many as fifty or so went on by the boat, going south to north. I'd first seen them way to the south and almost called out, but caught myself in time. We cruised around for another hour or so. Then I noticed something off to the southeast a little, the boat quartering toward it already, maybe a hundred and fifty yards, that hadn't been in that piece of water the last time I'd looked in it. I waited for a couple of seconds to make sure. Then I yelled,

"There she is."

Immediately, Captain Stinsin came out of the wheelhouse and looked up at me. "Whereaway?" he yelled.

I pointed to the tailing and breaching fish, "About a hundred and fifty yards, thataway", I answered. I could see the fish a little better now. We'd come up on her a little because we were already heading in her general direction. I could see she was a good size fish. Certainly, 'sticking' size. Maybe in the three hundred pound class. Anyway, a big fish to me. Captain Stinsin cut back on the throttles, put the bow right on the fish, and started easing up toward where I had been pointing.

"Get on down, I see 'er," he yelled up to me. "I need you to get on the wheel while I get ready to "stick" her."

I climbed down fast as I could, rushed into the wheelhouse to take over conning her. Captain Stinsin went on up on the pulpit, picking up one of the harpoons, a 'stick' he called it, that had been made ready on the ride to the grounds. He had attached one end of a line to the eye of the 'dart', the other end ran toward midship where the tubs of line and the kegs were.

I could see the fish up ahead, maybe forty, fifty yards now. I cut back on the throttle, getting her to settle in more, still making way though toward the fish, but slowly now, easing up on the fish..

Captain Stinsin was getting on out on the end of the pulpit, the 'stick' in his right hand, the line from the dart running along the 'stick' clasped beneath his hand firmed up on the 'stick', with the line running from under his hand into the water back to where it rose, went over the gunwale into one of the line tubs and then to the keg. Another line led from the end of the 'stick' to a forward cleat where Captain Stinsin had made it fast when he went up on the pulpit. When the fish was 'ironed', the dart would break loose from the 'stick' and the line would run free back to the line tub and the keg and Captain Stinsin would pull the 'stick' back aboard as he came back into the boat.

As we came up on the fish, Captain Stinsin yelled back to me, "Slowly now. Try to put me right over 'er right shoulder. Slowly. Slow now. You're gettin' it. There!" And with that he had thrown the harpoon, the 'stick' and 'dart'. I could see it strike high up on the fish's right shoulder, just underneath the dorsal.

I put the engine in neutral and began to run to the line tub on the starboard side of the boat, the side Captain Stinsin had thrown the 'stick' from. At the same time all hell broke loose up forward. Upon being struck the swordfish had immediately gone airborne. It was a big fish - to me. I figured three, four hundred pounds now she was out of the water and I had a good look at her. She crashed back into the sea, then charged off to starboard on top of the water, crushing water, then exploding it skyward. In a second the fish jumped again, leaving the white water it had created for another trip skyward, by now dragging the line from the tub so fast that it was almost smoking as it rubbed across the gunwale going out. By then I was at the tub, getting there just in time to pick up the keg attached to the line as the last of it left the tub. I threw the keg over and our fish, my first fish, was 'ironed' and 'kegged'. By now Captain Stinsin was back in the well of the boat. Just going into the wheelhouse.

"Keep your eye on the keg." He yelled. "If I lose sight of 'er, it'll be up to you to get me back on it." He finished.

The keg was rushing in a fairly straight line, generally southward from the *Eva*, occasionally disappearing under the water for short periods. Every so often the fish would breach, sometimes jump, usually a good distance from where the keg was, but mostly she stayed down, fighting the keg.

After a while, maybe five minutes, Captain Stinsin leaned out of the wheelhouse, turned to me, by now I was standing to the right and a little forward along the starboard gunwale. "Get up on to the platform," he said, "look out for more of 'em. They's solitary fish, but sometimes when the water, she's right for one of 'em, they's be more up on top. Keep a lookin', ifin you see anothern, give me a yell and we'll make up our mind ifin its right to 'iron' 'er while we the got the first 'un on a keg."

"Gotcha, Captain," I responded as I turned to the mast and climbed up to the platform. From there I could see the 'ironed' fish, about

49

a hundred yards out, maybe a little more now, directly off the bow. The Captain had gotten the boat in gear and advanced the throttle, heading generally south after the fish. We were gaining some on the keg. In another ten minutes we were within maybe forty yards of it, when out of the corner of my left eye, to the east, maybe a couple of hundred yards, I saw something. I turned and focused on it, and there was another tail and dorsal fin, another swordfish basking on the surface.

"Captain!" I yelled down to the wheelhouse, "there's anothern off to port, 'bout a couple hundred yards. Looks 'bout the same size as the one we got stuck." It couldn't be made out from the deck level and he left the wheelhouse unattended, climbed halfway up the mast, looked up to me and said:

"Whereaway?"

"There!" I pointed off to port, actually off the port bow, almost level with the stuck fish. "To the southard!" I yelled, "Seaward." I finished.

"I got 'er." Captain Stinsin said, "keep a pointin' at 'er, and we'll get on up to it in a short piece.

"You got to keep a lookout for the keg all and the same time," he yelled up as he turned to the wheelhouse, "keep me aknowin' where each of 'em be." He concluded.

The next fifteen minutes were hectic. Captain Stinstin would yell up, "where be the fish?" I'd point toward her and he'd con the *Eva* in that direction. No sooner than he'd got that direction and responded, he'd yell up again, "Whereaway's the keg? Keep your eye on that keg; she be a bird in hand. We got 'er, don't know ifin we'll get the othern." I'd point to the keg, saying, "It's there, Captain." He'd look that way, but all the time keeping the *Eva* quartering away from the keg, going after the other fish.

"Soon now," he yelled up, "get ready to get down 'ere."

After another minute he yelled up, "now." I climbed off the platform as fast as I could, Captain Stinsin was running to the gunwale, the port side this time; that's the side we were coming up on with this second fish. He was grabbing another "stick', pre-rigged as before and heading up to the platform. The keg from the first fish was clearly visible to starboard, about a hundred fifty yards off, slightly south of the line with the new fish and the *Eva*. As we came up on the new fish, I throttled back slowly, keeping an eye on the new fish, while at the same time trying to frame the piece of water where the keg from the first fish was.

I gradually reduced the speed until we were just crawling up on the second fish. She was hardly moving, just a small wake around her dorsal and a slight movement of her tail, just now and then, not much. I could see the Captain getting positioned on the pulpit, keeping the stick and dart lines apart, and getting ready to sling it at the fish. I looked at her again and realized for the first time now that we were close that she was a really big fish, considerably larger than the fish we already had 'ironed'. A real "hoss," we would of said down home if she'd been a blue marlin.

Captain Stinsin yelled, "Watch it close on this one." as he threw the 'stick' at the fish, again impaling the 'dart' just behind the dorsal to the right. There was an instant explosion, Captain Stinsin barely had time to let go of the dart line, the stick popped back at him as if it was on elastic, almost hitting him on the head. As I started for the line tub I slipped and fell. Upon feeling the 'dart', the fish immediately began a high speed dive, taking out line faster even than the first fish, in fact so fast that by the time I recovered my footing and got near the line tub I saw all the line go over the side, dragging the keg along before I could get to it and throw it over. As the keg passed over the gunwale, it hit it sharply, breaking off a foot-long section of the wooden gunwale cover. As soon as the keg hit the water, the big fish dragged it under and it was gone from sight. Now we had two fish stuck, one to the west, hopefully worn out considerably and one just stuck that had sounded almost straight down and might come up almost anywhere.

"Keep a look out." Captain Stinsin said as he arrived back at the wheelhouse, "we're just goin' to lie 'ere a bit, 'till I get afeelin' 'bout, whichaway this un be goin'. Keep a eye on the first un, on the keg over to the westward."

I looked at it again. It was moving slower now. The first fish tiring more. The *Eva* lie there almost motionless, only enough way on for steerage, for another five minutes or so; me constantly looking at the keg to the west, now almost motionless itself, with the first fish up on top now, seeming to be wallowing some.

51

Just then, maybe a quarter mile away, the keg from the second fish popped up, clear of the water even, as if it had come to the surface from a great depth, which I presumed it had. I thought the second fish was gone for a moment, pulled loose from the dart and gone. But just about the time the keg was falling back to the surface the huge fish lunged straight up from the water eight feet or more, almost landing on the keg when it fell back into the water. The fish then took off straight east, dragging the keg behind so fast that it was making a clearly visible wake of its own, even from a quarter-mile away.

Captain Stinsin came from the wheelhouse then, gesturing for me to come with him as he went toward the stern, toward the dory. "Both these fish be big on's, we goin' be losin' one or the other of 'em ifin we don't use the dory. Hate to put it on you the first day, but you'll need to go in the dory and get the first fish while I chase this big 'un'," he said. With that he grabbed the line, pulled the dory up alongside. Shortly the dory was being dragged alongside the *Eva* as the larger boat kept moving slowly to the east in the direction of the big fish.

Captain Stinsin, "Put the oars in 'er, Hank. Then get in 'er," he said. I did, and shortly he was handing me two lances, long poles with comma-shaped lances on the end, lances with the point forward, and a cutting edge on the outside of the blade. "When you get up on the keg, 'member, you grab it, get it in the boat and pull the fish to you, slow like. Keep clear of the line you get in the boat, ifin the fish has another run in 'er, you ain't wantin' to be a steppin' in the line when she's a runnin', he said. "Now, when you get 'er to the boat, you want to tie 'er loose to the side, maybe just hold 'er loose to it, take the lance and drive it deep's you can, right 'longside the dorsal. But as far forward as you can, almost above the gill covers; do it too far aft and you'll be damagin' the meat and that'll keep the price low. Do 'er right, and you'll kill 'er - still. Won't move atall. If that happens, put 'er in the dory. Ifin you can't get 'er in the dory by yourself, make 'er fast 'longside', then wait and I'll be back to get you after I get this othern. You gotta be careful now, you recollect what I done told you 'bout 'em sometime attackin' the dories. Keep your eye on 'er. See you in a bit," he finished, as he cast off the line from the dory and headed to the wheel house.

As he left, I yelled at him, "Hey! How you gonna boat that big fish ifin you get up to 'er?"

He pointed at the boom, the block and tackle, said "I'll lance 'er, tailrope 'er, and sling her in with the boom. Don't you go aworryin' 'bout it; look to yourself."

Soon the *Eva* was heading to the east in the general direction of George's Bank, a far piece from where we were. I got the oarlocks in the gunwale holes just forward of midships, got the oars through them, put some gloves on and stood up to get my bearings, realizing as I did that I was fast becoming alone on the ocean as the *Eva* was receding to the east. Funny, the ocean was a lot bigger now, giving a lot of truth to the old saying that "the ocean she is so big, and my boat, she is so small." That was my exact circumstance. I'd been a lifetime, short as it had so far been, at sea, almost every day, but since I had graduated from crabbing and clamming in the coastal bays down home to the offshore fishery, commercial or sport, I hadn't been quite as alone as Captain Stinsin had just put me. I wondered now, about the 'long trippers' that went to sea for several days, out on the offshore banks, or farther even, that used dories extensively, would have several out from the mother-ship at a time. Too far for them to even try to make land. Where I was, if Captain Stinsin didn't return for me, I still had a chance to make Montauk, or depending on the direction of the current and the winds, the islands to the north, maybe even back to Block Island, though it'd take a full day, maybe more to row to shore, that's if the current and wind would allow it.

I looked around, then, to the west mostly, a little south of it. At first, with the swells, swells that were a little higher now that I was in a small boat, my eyes barely above surface level, I couldn't see the keg. But in a minute or so, I picked it up on the top of a swell, not much more than three or four hundred yards away. I took my bearings on the sun and a cloud that appeared to be holding fairly steady in the sky, didn't bother to get the compass out of the forward compartment, didn't need it to run down a keg so close. Could adjust a couple of times on nature's landmarks, the cast of the seas and the clouds, and be up on the fish in ten, fifteen minutes at the most. That's what happened. I was at the keg in short order. It was moving off, but only a little.

I shipped the oars, laid them in the scuppers, reached over the side grabbed the keg and slowly and carefully pulled it into the dory, laid it in the scuppers atop the oars. I then began to pull in the rest of the line slowly, until only about fifty yards was left between me and the fish.

I could feel intermittent surges, pulls really, coming from slow sweeps of the fish's tail, but they didn't feel especially strong or brisk. The fish was down now, but I was able to gain line consistently, until down in the deep I could see the glow of the fish as I pulled it up. Soon I could see its tail sweeping, slowly though. In another five minutes it was almost awash alongside the dory. But, I should have known it wasn't over. While almost awash, it still remained dorsal high, not on its side like a truly beaten fish, like marlin coming to the boat down home after an hour on 80 pound, when they had no fight left, just lying there on their sides. I should have known. Right as I reached with one hand for a lance, the fish jumped, thrashed off about twenty, thirty yards, line burning my hand even through the glove as it ran out before I could let go. Just as I was bracing myself for the take-up when I'd have to let go and throw the keg back over, the line stopped going out. I looked out, and here she came for the boat.

Before I could get braced, she hit the boat head on, piercing the side of the dory, driving the near gunwale almost under the water and catapulting me overboard on top of the fish. Before I knew what had happened, I was astride her, the tail in front of me with nothing beyond it but the open sea, my rear to the boat. But, I was almost as quick as she'd been charging the boat. In an instant I had reversed position and headed the seven or eight feet back to the dory, literally climbing up the fish. I grabbed the gunwale with one hand, thrust off the fish with my left foot, and was over the side back in the dory. Couldn't have been more than three or four seconds. Don't think I was even a hundred percent wet; hundred percent scared I was, though. I paused for a moment, the fish's sword was through the side of the dory and she was thrashing side to side trying to pull it out. I looked around, found a lance and in another instant had killed the fish.

I sat down on the thwart, the seat I had rowed from as I made my way to the keg. I just thought of a lot of supposes. Suppose I hadn't landed on the fish, but had gone to the side and under, fully clothed, boots and all. Could I have got them off, the jacket, the boots, in time to keep from drowning. Suppose the fish hadn't got stuck in the dory, would she have turned on me. I know Captain Stinsin said they didn't attack people; but that fish had been plenty mad to charge the boat and marlin had killed people before, maybe not intentionally, but they'd killed before, one way or the other. Suppose the fish had sunk the dory. There I would have been, miles and miles at sea, no boat, trying to swim as long as I could, or trying to climb on a keg tied to a big swordfish, but, in any event, knowing I wasn't going to make it. Suppose, with the dory sunk, Captain Stinsin couldn't find me when he came back.

After a minute of rest, I calmed down. Took my boots off and drained them of sea water. Got myself in order. The dory wasn't sunk, I wasn't on the keg, I was in the dory, relatively safe, the fish was dead. Everything was ok.

Damn sure was different, though, than the marlin fishing I'd done down home. Every bit as exciting - more so for sure. Now I had to figure out what to do next as I waited for the *Eva* to return.

That reminded me, where was she? Where was Captain Stinsin? I stood up, the dory listing a little to the side the fish was stuck in, but steadier from its weight. I looked around, figuring out general east from the sun and the set of the sea and the same clouds I'd been watching while I was rowing, though they'd changed their shape some. Looked there to the east first, then all around. Not a boat in sight, not from where I was. I was still alone, me and the fish.

Figured I might as well get her loose and in the boat if I could. She hadn't been able to get herself unstuck before I'd killed her. Fish, especially bill fish, don't swim backwards much, least I hadn't seen any in reverse. From the compartment under the thwart, I got the marlinspike that Captain Stinsin used for a bat to stun the smaller fish that he didn't want to lance. I grabbed it by the small end, got myself steady up against the gunwale, leaned over and struck the end of the fish's bill (or sword) and in four or five hits the fish floated free of the boat. I dropped the marlinspike, stuffed a rag into the hole - with the fish free it was above the water line, anyway. I grasped the line to the fish and held it steady, pulled the fish back to the boat, guided the tail within reach, grabbed it with one hand, then both hands. In another minute I had wrestled her into the boat. She was probably three hundred pounds hanging weight, but when you pull a fish into a boat with the low freeboard of a dory, a lot of the weight of the fish stays in the water when you first get the tail part in, then as you drag it on over the gunwale, the weight you've already pulled in, even though its dead weight, helps you pull more in, until the fish is balanced on the gunwale, or transom if you're pulling over the stern. You're never pulling much more than half the weight. Once she's balanced, it only takes a little pull and the rest flops in with what you already pulled in. That's what happened.

Soon as she was in, I went about getting the dory shipshape, getting the dart out of the fish, coiling the line, taking all the gear, including the keg and stowing it in the stern. The fish lay midships, just about in the middle all the way around, its tail stuck under the rowing thwart where I would be sitting if I rowed. The killing lance I put with the others in the scuppers.

When I had it all done, I stood up, looked around again. It was about one o'clock now. I'd been messing with this fish for forty-five minutes or so; figured the *Eva* would be coming back for me by now. I didn't see her anywhere. Didn't see any boats. Saw nothing but the sea and the sky and the dory I was in. I'd been at sea a lot. Spent most of my life on it. Doesn't always work out just the way you want it, but some how or another things work out some way, usually, so I didn't panic. I was hungry, though. Everything had been going on so fast, getting the fish 'ironed', both of them, and launching the dory that I'd forgotten my sandwiches. I expected there was water up forward in the dory, well found vessels always carry 'just in case' water. Man can last a long time without food, but, water, that's different. I checked the forward compartment and there was a gallon of water sitting on life preservers.

As for food, if it was a real long time, if the *Eva* couldn't find me, I could eat the fish if I had to. So there wasn't any emergency yet. Just a reason to be uneasy. Down home, not counting wind, the drift inshore would be south, off-shore, north. Up here though I didn't know the drift. But, even then, if it didn't get real rough, I figured I'd be okay. Montauk, Long Island was down to the south some, Nantucket, Martha's Vineyard, Cape Cod, up to the north, Block Island to the northwest . I had oars and a strong back; if it came to it I figured I could make it somewhere. Might take a day or two. Might have to row at night. I could do that off the lights, the lighthouses. Block Island had two, one on its southeast side, one on the north, I'd be able to see them if it was clear. Montauk Light was down to the southwest some. Long as I could see, fog didn't roll in, I'd get to one place or the other. Besides, I felt that Captain Stinsin would be back. The fish he'd stuck and chased had just taken him further than we'd figured it would.

I still couldn't see him, couldn't find the *Eva* on the horizon two hours later. Still wasn't fretting too much, but I wasn't the happiest camper on the sea. Then about 3:30, off in the southeast, I found a little bump on the far edge of the sea. In another thirty minutes I could make out a boat, and in another thirty Captain Stinsin was throttling down, pulling the *Eva* alongside the dory. He came to the *Eva's* gunwale and threw over a line. I made it fast.

"See you got that fish in the dory by yourself. She's right smart size," he said, 'bout three hundred pounds looks like. She'll dress out 'bout two forty, two fifty." With that he threw a tailrope down, "Wrap it 'round 'er tail, then get on up 'ere," he said "and we'll yank 'er on in." Don't need to use the block and tackle, we can get it done just as good without usin' it".

I climbed over the *Eva's* gunwale to help him pull the fish on in the boat. The dory drifted on back astern as we got the fish situated. When I first rolled off the gunwale on the *Eva's* deck, I saw a giant fish, twice the size of the one in the dory, or maybe even bigger.

"Damn," I said, seeing the fish, "that's a lot of fish for one man to be a gettin' into a boat." I knew then what I'd just thought before, Captain Stinsin was a real man. He could do it as well as talking about doing it. I could see gear strewn around, not where it belonged. Line, kegs, lances and the like. Not shipshape like he kept her. A little bit of a mess really.

Like I said, he didn't talk much. "Weren't easy. Needed doin'. Got done," he said, as we pulled the other fish on in the boat.

"I'll get the gear stored," I said then, as I moved towards some of the mess.

"It took a bit longer to get 'er kilt than I figured on," he said, "it were so late when I got 'er aboard and I knew I'd gone a far piece. I was worried I was a gettin' short on time to get back to you afore darkness come down. Didn't want to be leaving a new man out at night on his first trip. Don't want to leave any dory-man out after dark atall.

So I didn't want to take the time to clean up afore I started for you; when I was runnin', I was lookin', didn't figure it to be too smart to leave off the lookin' whiles runnin', just to get 'er cleaned up. Figured we'd get 'er squared away when I found you, ifin I found you."

"What to you mean, 'ifin'?" I reponded.

"Kiddin' son, just kiddin'. Ain't never left no man out 'ere permanent, don't aim to start now. I'll always come. You can count on 'er. Let's get goin', we can start our run in now, gonna be too late already to get over to Point Judith, so we'll be takin' the fish over there early in the morning, leave for fishing from there. It'll be a long day."

"What 'bout the fish?" I asked.

"We dress 'em out anyways," he answered, "they don't take 'em whole over at Point Judith. Only pay on dressed fish and dressed weight. Don't blame 'em none. I wouldn't take whole fish either. Been times when fish'll show up that gets jellied. Nobody knows for sure what causes it, but some thinks it's 'cause some fish ain't dressed soon enough or good enough, 'specially when they's off 'long-tripper' boats. They make a rule though, applies to ever'body, can't blame 'em, once the fish gets on the dock you can't tell what kinda boat she come off of if the tags get lost."

Captain Stinsin put the *Eva* in gear, advanced the throttle, and we started the long ride back to Block Island. I cleaned up the mess, got the gear stowed and when I was done, Captain Stinsin came aft, left the boat running for home; he had lashed the wheel to keep her roughly on course for Old Harbor.

"Hank," Captain Stinsin said, "come on back and watch me dress 'em fish. From now on you'll be doin' most of it. Once we get 'em dressed, we'll put 'em in that little fish hold, fish box really, right behind the wheelhouse, then ice 'em down. Ifin we was agoin' on over to Point Judith right smart, wouldn't have to ice 'em too much. But it'll be mornin', need to keep 'em cooled down good. "

"Captain," I responded, "'spect it's the same as dressin' out marlin, makos even, big tuna. I've done some of that back home, 'specially when they come dead to the boat. Why don't you stand by, watch me dress 'em, see I do it right, ifin I don't, you can stop me and I'll get 'er right."

I didn't need any help and that was settled on that first day on the water with Captain Stinsin. But he had a piece of curiosity that had been biting on him ever since he returned to pick me up. "Hank," he asked, after a while, "how come you was so wet when I got back to you?"

"Captain," I said, "that was a wild fish. She come on to the dory, charged it she did, when she got to the boat there was a lot of thrashin' goin' on, splashin' and such. Afore it was over, I got wet from it."

"I saw she put a hole in the dory," he said.

"Yeah," I said, "had to use the marlin spike to knock 'er bill back out, I'll plug her permanent tomorrow."

"Well, yeah, ok, but how'd you get so wet, your socks is soaked, ever'thing you got was soaked when I got to you?"

"Don't you worry on it none." I answered. "Just got wet, that's all you need to know."

He laughed then, said, "Ain't often I get a hand in the water two days runnin'. Least you got back in 'er," he finished, and headed back to the wheel house. He knew. I just left it be. Wasn't any use trying to talk it away.

I joined him in a few minutes and we continued westward. The sun was setting; moon rising. There was still a little time of the month moon left, about a quarter-moon, and some light glowed from it as it came up to replace the sun. The night was clear. One of those nights at sea where the moonlight bounces from the water's wrinkles and the stars twinkle so clearly it's like they join to become one beautiful thing, and it feels like you're sailing right in the middle of it all; that it spreads out from you, all around.

After an hour we could begin to see yellower lights, not clear white like the stars or the moon's reflections, but yellow-blurred land lights. In another hour we could make out the darkness of the land, sprinkled with the yellow light dots. Thirty minutes later we were pulling into Old Harbor, tying up at our mooring. After putting more ice on the fish it was done with. The first day of fishing was over. Around seven hundred pounds of swordfish I figured. Dressed weight. Only two fish. Not bad.

"In the mornin', early, three-thirty," Captain Stinsin said, "we got to get over to Point Judith to sell 'em fish so's you can see what's it's like.

Hereafter, we'll only go over ever' two, three days. By goin' over early, we'll still get a full day in on the water after we sell the fish."

"I'll be here." It was already ten o'clock. Only five and a half hours until we set out again.

Chapter Nine

THE GRIND

By quarter to four the next morning we turned to port as we came out of Old Harbor and began our run to Point Judith to sell the fish. In an hour or so we were pulling up at the unloading dock. It opened generally around four, five in the morning and there were already people moving about. We used the boom to swing both fish up on the dock and they were taken inside the weighing shed. Captain Stinsin climbed on the dock, the tide was lower than it had been two days ago when I was first here and it was necessary for him to crawl up a short dock ladder.

Soon he was back aboard, started the engine. I loosed the dock line, threw it on the dock; he put the *Eva* in gear and we were heading out again. This time it took us an hour and a half longer to get to the edges of South Channel where he wanted to go because we were coming from farther away. We took her south, past the south end of Block Island, and ended up a little farther south than we had the day before, nearer Montauk Point. Around ten thirty I spotted the first fish. It was swimming slowly south, its dorsal and tail fin full out of the water, even a part of its shoulder humped up some. I yelled down and we went through the same drill as the first fish the day before. Had her 'darted' in no time.

It was a smaller fish, around two hundred pounds. While Captain Stinsin was maneuvering the *Eva* to the keg, I didn't see any other finning fish. Soon, the Captain yelled up to me on the platform.

"Get on down 'ere, Hank. She ain't big. We'll just tailrope 'er and manhandle "er onboard."

I climbed down as fast as I could, went to stand by the Captain.

"When we get up on the keg, you take that ol' boat-hook in the scuppers, there on the port side. Use it to grab onto the line and then pull the keg inboard. When you get it in the boat, give me a holler and I'll be to helpin' right smart at it. If afore I get to you that fish tries to make another run, just let the line go and throw the keg back over. Ifin she's too green and you hold 'er too tight, might pull the dart on 'er.

Ifin you have to let 'er go, we'll just take after 'er again. Ifin you can hold 'er 'til I get there, we'll be able to gentle 'er a little bit, then get that tailrope 'round 'er. Once we get that on 'er, she's ouren, don't make no difference then if the dart does pull out."

Soon she was aboard and I was back up the mast. Twice more that day we went through the drill. Only got one of the fish though, the dart pulled on the other while she was still on the keg. The other fish we landed was about three hundred pounds. On the way in, we dressed the fish, put them in the fish hold and iced them down. We got in late again, and the Captain said, "We'll just leave 'em 'iced down 'til after tomorrow, maybe next day. Don't want to make a habit of runnin' on over to Point Judith ever' day, lessen I got a real load on 'er, or they's fixin' to spoil. Ain't warm up 'ere yet, they'll hold up good for a couple of days."

On the next day we had four fish aboard the *Eva* by twelve thirty when it clouded up and began to rain. When it did, Captain Stinsin said, "We might's well call it a day, the sun leaves this time of year, the fish leaves, too, mostly. We'll motor on over to Point Judith and off-load these fish, with the two days we got right smart of 'em. That way we won't be a wastin' a day 'cause of rain."

We offloaded at Point Judith, were back in Old Harbor before nightfall.

We lay in the next day, fixed things on the boat. Something was always breaking. If there's any constant about a boat it's that something always needs fixing. Maybe that's why we talk about them in the feminine case.

The next day, the one after, and the one after that, we were back out catching fish, generally catching more fish as the season progressed. We didn't fish on Sundays, though. That was the Lord's day, Captain Stinsin said, "And I'm gonna give it to Him." I was thankful that he did. Sundays and rain, hurt your pocketbook, but helped your soul, body too. Especially when Mrs. Stinsin always invited me over for Sunday dinner. The dinner was always fine. Eva was finer.

After awhile on some Sundays after dinner, Eva and I would take a walk. It was her idea. I was just too much off my feed when I was around her to suggest doing things. I didn't know how to act with a nice girl. I'd known some, but mostly they'd been kept away from me.

Eva was unique. Her parents treated her different. It was almost as if she was the parent and all of us the children. I came to understand that she controlled everything around her. There was never any question about taking advantage of her. I didn't even think about it. I just did what I was told. I saw enough though to know that she didn't have any steady boyfriends, a beau, a man, whatever. Sometimes I'd spend a whole afternoon walking and listening to her talk about the country, about the world sometimes. But mostly she talked about Block Island, how she loved it, about its history. About her family. About what was important to her. She'd say how important it was for people to be true, to be loyal, to always tell the truth.

It was rare when I could look at her eyes for long. Beautiful deep blue eyes, like the color of the off-shore water back home in mid-summer. We called it 'deep blue', almost indigo. That's what she had, 'deep blues', eyes the color of the deep sea. Couldn't look at them at all when she was looking at me. When she'd catch me looking at her eyes, I'd have to look away, though as I did I'd see her smile sometimes. I'd never had a shy moment before in my life that I could remember, but on those Sunday afternoon walks I wasn't what I used to be. I was becoming someone else. Part of it, maybe, was that she was Captain Stinsin's daughter and he and I were friends already, becoming better friends every day on the water. But that was only a small part of it. She captured my heart on those Sunday afternoons, but I didn't know how to let her know. I just went where she went.

Chapter Ten
THE SUNSET

Late one Sunday afternoon as we were finishing dinner, Captain Stinsin reached in his pocket and handed me the keys to the pickup, saying, "Ain't no need to get wet walkin', never know when she'll come to rainin'." There wasn't a cloud in the western sky. The Captain continued, "Don't figure you'll steal the truck. Can't get anywhere anyways, being she's an island we be on. Be careful, now, be gettin' dark afore too long."

"Come on Hank," Eva said, getting up from the table and turning to her mother, "we won't be long mama; we'll help you clean up when we get back. We'll just ride down to Conneymus Road, out near Southwest Point. It's been a little far for walking. With the pickup it's a lot nearer. And that's the best place to see the sunset."

With her directing me, we drove down the middle of the island on what she called Center Road. We took a right off it onto Conneymus Road which soon became a dirt road. It ended on a bluff facing almost due south-west. The windows were down and a nice breeze was blowing in from the south, enough breeze that it ruffled her hair. I just sat there didn't know what to say. Really couldn't think. Didn't know what to do. If she wanted me to do anything? I started to put my arm around her shoulders, when she said,

"Let's just talk some." I put my arm back on the steering wheel. "Sure.' I responded.

"Tell me more about yourself?" She asked.

"What do you want to know? You already know where I come from, things like that."

"Your family, tell me about Ocean City. Why'd you leave? How bad was the trouble? Had to be something that made you come up here. What about school?'

"There's not much telling, nothing interesting. I'm more interested in you."

"We'll do it my way," she said, "there's lots of people on the island that can tell you about me. You're the only one that can tell me about

64

you. And I need to know so start talking. Unless you're afraid. Unless you have something to hide like being married or something."

"I ain't married. Never even thought much on it. You want to know 'bout things, I'll do my best. I've told you 'bout Ocean City some. She's on an island, not much like this 'un or nothin', not round, not much width to 'er. She's long, 'bout eight or nine miles long now, not much more than a mile wide and that only up in the north end, way up near Delaware, beyond the city limits. The city starts at the inlet to the south, goes up 'bout twenty blocks. Got carnival rides and things like that at the south end, cottages and such spread north up the boardwalk, several, I guess ten or twelve hotels up on the beach front with a boardwalk in front of 'em. Boardwalk stops 'bout fifteenth, sixteenth street. Nothing much 'bove it 'cept sand dunes and beaches on the ocean side, marsh and such on the bay side. Really ain't much of nothin' on the bay side, it's all over toward the sea-side of the strip. Ever'thing's centered to the ocean. I thought there was some big dunes down home, up north 'bove where the hotels is. We used to go up and party some where they was, but since I come 'ere I know 'em dunes just babies up next to your bluffs.

"Ain't nothin' much to 'er, just the hotels, tourists and things go with 'em. Outside that onlyest thing is mostly the fishin'. Back afore the thirty-three hurricane all the fishin' was done off the surf bank. Big fishin' camps got set up. Operators owned 'em and the gear, and the locals worked out of 'em. Kept the boats up on the beach most of the time, boats two, three times bigger than you all's dories up 'ere. Lots heavier too. They'd get 'em down to the water with horse carts, launch 'em through the surf and then oar out to the traps, we called 'em pounds. Later on some, most of 'em, got engines in 'em, but they still had to oar 'em through the surf out beyond the break. Then cut the engine on and motor on out. Just 'versed 'er on the way in. Most ever' body's daddy when I was born had worked in the pound fishin', one time or the other. It was dangerous work. Get caught in a storm, onlyest thing you could do was run for the beach and try to get the boat on the beach through the surf without capsizing. Lots of 'em used ter get kilt doin' it.

"In thirty-three a big storm come up. 'Til then Ocean City weren't on no island of its own. It was just the north end of Assateague Island that run on down to Virginia. All of it had a bunch of bays behind 'er, stretched all the way from Delaware Bay to the Chesapeake.

"When that storm was over an inlet had cut clean through the island, washed most of the fish camps to sea. They kept 'er open, got the gov'ment to build jetties, most like similar to what you all got at Old Harbor. Ain't quite so big. North from it is Ocean City, south of it is Assateague. Anyways, once the inlet got cut through didn't have to launch 'em pound boats through the surf no more 'cause a commercial harbor sprung up on the mainland, 'cross from the island - 'bout half-mile or so."

"Did you work on the pound boats?" Eva asked.

"Weren't born early 'nough. Time I was born it was mostly over, " I replied, then continued, "they went out through the inlet and fished the pounds outta there for awhile, then the operators started bringin' trawlers and such in 'cause they could operate outta there once the inlet was made. Most I remember 'bout it when I was a kid was 'em blowin' up the pound pilings. They weren't usin' 'em none and the Coast Guard, or some such, said they was a hazard to navigation.

"You'd be on the boardwalk, maybe the beach and you'd hear this big boom, look out and there'd be splashin' and things goin' on out there. Last man killed in the pound fishin' industry blowed hisself up. Old man Simpson it were. Know his kin."

"What about yourself?" She asked. "Tell me about you."

"Well my dad was a local, family been 'round since afore the Revolution. One time they were farmin' on the mainland, but 'em days weren't much money in it. Anyways, once the men started comin' up from Ocracoke lookin' for work and the only work they had experience with was fishin', some money men from Baltimore financed and set up the fishin' companies, the camps for the men, the processin' and such. By the time my daddy was born it was mostly fishin' or nothin'. He worked some in the camps, then when the companies went to trawlin', draggin' nets, he went to work on 'em boats. He was workin' on the Marcella one day, out draggin' when they should a been layin' at the dock. Had to work though. You ain't out there catchin' 'em, you ain't puttin' no money, no food on the table.

"They's out over night and there was a storm down below Hatteras they didn't know nothin' 'bout. Whiles they was out, the storm got over the Cape and went back out to sea some and started throwin' big seas up the coast. Out where they was it was mostly big long swells, not peakin' up or nothin'. It weren't 'til they got close to the inlet the next afternoon that they realized how big they really was. The swells were peakin' up big when they got in the inshore shallows, were breakin' all out in the inlet. Had the inlet closed out. They didn't have no choice but to try her anyway, didn't have 'nough fuel to get anywhere else, chances were the sea was breakin' the same ever'where anyway, didn't have enough fuel to lie hove too back offshore, they'd need to keep power on her to keep her head into the sea, so they tried to run the inlet between the breakers. Didn't make it. She capsized. Broke up. Nobody's seen my dad since. The rest of 'em washed up, crab eaten' and ever'thing. He didn't.

"My mom went to work, doin' whatever she could in the hotels. I went on the water when I was eight, workin' for a cousin of my father's. Workin' the pealer floats, dippin' the softs out right after they shed to keep the other crabs from eatin' 'em and to keep their new shells from hardin' up. Got a little older, one of my dad's friends, Hot Pot Pie, took me with him when he worked the pots and trot lines. Mostly used me at first for cullin', later went to dippin' on the trot lines, then as I got older started handlin' the pots. 'Bout time I was twelve Hot Pot Pie got out of it, went and got a job runnin' the ferry to Assateague.

"I started goin' to sea then, workin' the head boats that went bottom fishin', fishin' mostly for porgys, sea bass and 'taugs. Fished mostly the wrecks, sometimes a place called the 'Bass Grounds', 'bout ten, twelve, maybe fifteen miles off, 'pending what kind of fishin' we was doin'. In the fall we did a lot of sea trout fishin' on weekends, driftin' inshore twenty, forty foot of water. By the time I got two summers under me haulin' back on the anchor four, five times a day, mostly in deep water, I'd picked up my shoulders, filled out big most ever'where for a boy my age. My dad had been big, I was followin' 'im. By fifteen I was six foot, weighted a hundred eighty pounds, solid. Grown another three, four inches since then, another fifty pounds too, I guess. Once I hit fifteen I started workin' on the marlin boats, we'd blue fish in the early summer, then tuna, then 'bout the end of June start workin' hard on the marlin. Sometimes we'd get ten, fifteen a trip. Course you ain't always gettin' em, sometimes you get nothin'.

"I'd save up some money each summer, but I spent a lot of it on runnin' round and things."

"What things?" She asked, interrupting me.

"You ain't got to know ever'thing." I responded. "Least not right now. Ain't the time." She was smiling and as I looked at her, said

"Go on, then. Now that I have you stopped I want you to get going again - but sooner or later you'll be telling me everything I want to know."

"You're goin' to need to be careful 'bout what you think you want to know. I weren't no angel."

"I gathered that," she said, "but keep on going, give me everything that you will tell me now."

"Anyways, then, most time come fall there weren't much money for school clothes and things. My mother didn't make much. She couldn't help much. And she'd begun to drink heavy after my dad got killed. The winter when I was fifteen, mostly takin' care of myself, bringin' as much money in as she was, right after Christmas she stepped in front of a truck. Ain't never wanted to know whether it were an accident or not. They said it was. The cops. I just 'cepted it. Still choose to 'cept it. Don't want to know no different.

"I let the apartment we'd had go, got me a room over at Mable Pierce's roomin' house, near the docks. Had no money, so I had to work on weekends, other times, find ways to make do. The big money in the wintertime when the marlin fishin' was over, was in the sea clammin'. Hard work, hardest I ever done. They converted old trawlers to doin' it there's so much money involved. They pull a scrape across the bottom with a water jet just in front of the mouth of it that excavates the clams out of the bottom on top of it, then the scrapes gets 'em. "Bout ever' half-hour or so they pull back on the scrape, bring 'er up and empty it on the deck. Ever' thing comes up with it, anything layin' on the bottom, but if you're in the right place they's plenty of clams. Then the deckhands, that's me and 'em like me, take big shovels and shovel 'em up 'bout seven or eight feet over the sides of big metal cages into the openin' at the top. All day long you do it until all the cages the boat 'ill carry is full. Then head 'er on in, cleanin' up much as you can on the way. Eighteen hours sometimes. Then you do 'er the next day. Ever'body works on shares. So they just keep 'er goin'.

"Usually, I'd make 'rangements for the weekends on a particular boat for the whole school year. One of the regular deck hands would get a day off when I worked. But, there was plenty of work and not many strong backs that could stand up to it for long. They's always on the lookout for strong backs. I always had all the work I wanted. Kept myself in livin' money. Doin' 'er since I was fifteen. Summertimes it was back on the marlin fishin' boats; on a good boat with the weather for you, you could make as much as clammin' and the work weren't so hard, hard but not so hard, and lots more fun than shovelin' clams.

"I just kept that up, even after they graduated me from the high school just to get rid of me. Kept right on goin' with it, the fishin', didn't know nothin' else. Then I started goin' down to Florida, over to the islands in the winter. Did that the two winters 'til the last 'un. Anything beat clammin' once I didn't have to go on to school. Don't know why I come up early from Florida this past spring. Just did. Had to work for a while. Then I left to come up 'ere."

She interrupted me, "What about school?" she asked. "When I'm around you I see how smart you are, Daddy tells me you're the quickest learner he's ever had on the *Eva*, but sometimes you don't talk like you've been to school at all. You're real corn pone sometimes. Daddy talks funny, too. Both of you speak a different English than I've learned in school."

"I know I ain't sophisticated in my way of speakin'. It ain't that I don't know better. If I take my time and think on it, I can mostly get 'er right. I speak this way for maybe a couple of reasons. Mostly, its that when you're at sea you ain't got much time, no inclination either, to take time with the way of speakin'. Something gotta be done now, it's got to be done now, can't be worryin' 'bout how you speak on it. Way it goes on the water. Maybe it's the same with both of us - your dad and me. 'Nother thing, most tourists that come down home think we speak with a southern accent. Ifin we do, maybe it's 'cause most of us come from them that come outa Ocracoke, fifty, sixty years or so ago. It's almost a heritage. I'll be workin' on it some now that I'm up here. On my language. It'll be hard, though.

"Far as school's concerned, I figured I was better off out of it, guess they agreed 'cause they graduated me out."

69

"You and daddy sound almost alike," she responded, "I've been trying to teach him to clear up his manner of speaking. Get him to talking right, but I haven't gotten far with him yet. Now there's two of you. I've more on my plate than I anticipated. But, that's something I can keep on with as long as you're here. How long are you planning to stay?"

"When I came up 'ere, I was only plannin' to stay for the one swordfishin' season. Wanted to see what it was like. Been real lucky signing on with your daddy. He's ateachin' me all of it. Ain't 'ever learned so much so fast as I'm a learnin' now. Its the right kind of fishin' for me. Know I'll stay the season. 'Riginally planned to head down south this comin' winter, don't know now. I'm likin' most ever'thing up 'ere I do, what it is I see." I said finishing, looking at her until my eyes were cowed by hers.

"What 'bout you? Tell me about you."

"Don't think so."

"What do you mean you don't think so? I've told you a lot 'bout me. It's not fair for you not to do the same."

"Hank," she said, "I'm not going to tell you about myself."

"That's not fair."

"That's the way it is. You see there's a difference between us, between men and women."

"I know that."

"Not that, silly. I'm not talking about looking different. Women need to know different things than men. Women need to actually know about men. But men need to wonder about women. It's not a matter of being fair or not fair. Women need the security of knowing what is, men need to wonder what will be. That's why we interest each other. We're just different in what we need to know. You wonder about me, I want you to keep on wondering. Why would I do anything to take that away? It's what you need, the wondering."

And that was it that sunset.

For the next month or so, other than the Sundays, it was just the fishing, day in, day out, sometimes into the night working on the boat, the trips to Point Judith. Wasn't much else to do. No time to do it anyway. Hard work. Partying, I guess, was there. I could hear the noise up at the Hill Top bar some nights after I got home, but I didn't join in much. They were locals, hard for a new guy off the boats to get accepted. Sometimes I'd stop in for a beer on the way out back to my room, but wouldn't stay long. But, really, I was working too hard to get it started - partying and such. Trying to get my feet on the ground. Usually tired. Not wanting to embarrass Captain Stinsin, his family either. Eva, especially. I was only around her on Sundays, usually. Occasionally I'd have to drop by to pick up something for the boat from the shed at back of the house, but normally I was real early or she was working late. But, for some reason, a reason I didn't fully understand, I cared what she thought, or would think, of me, based upon what I was and did. Because of her my social life was limited to Sunday afternoon walks on the island.

Chapter Eleven
AUGUST

By August the fish were really there. We'd usually have a load by three o'clock. Had to take extra ice with us when we planned to go over a day's fishing to the next, before we took the time to go over to Point Judith. It was a hard grind. Four or five o'clock in the morning, depending on whether we had to go over to Point Judith before the day's fishing. Until dark most nights. Fishing hard all day long. Six days at sea, one on the beach, the next six at sea, and again and again. On the way in after a mid-August trip, Captain Stinsin said,

"Eva 'ill be comin' tomorrow. We'll be 'short trippin'. She asked it. I said it'd be okay. It's her day off at the Ocean View. She usually comes out two, three times a summer. Put her up on the platform. She's got seein' eyes, like youren. Any problems with it? 'Er comin'. "

She hadn't told me that she went swordfishing with her father. All I could think of at first was how I didn't want her out there because it was dangerous. I knew she wasn't really fragile, but she looked it. Mostly, she'd just been so feminine, so woman-like that it was hard to picture her on a working boat. Yachts and sailboats, but not commercial swordfishing boats. This was thirty years before women got involved in commercial fishing, even swordfishing. I didn't think it was done. I didn't want her out there because I was afraid she'd be hurt. To me she was breakable.

I didn't want her there at first, then I realized I also did want her there. Wanted to spend more time with her. Not to talk. Not much time for talking when you're swordfishing. Just wanted to be around her. Wanted to see how she handled herself on a boat. Wanted her to see how I did.

While I was thinking on it, Captain Stinsin spoke again, "She asked me to see if it were okay with you. Said if it weren't, she wouldn't come. She ain't really no problem, Hank. Done it before. Mostly she looks for 'em, don't generally get involved with the rest of it, lessun we get more than two fish ironed. Even then she knows what to do. I taught her just like I'm teachin' you."

I thought for another moment, then asked, "What 'bout there bein' no head on this 'ere boat. You and me just whip it out, piss over the side, sit on the gunwale for the other if we have to. We ain't gonna be able to do it with her aboard."

"You just sing out, 'Eyes forward.' She'll look off the bow 'til we's finished and tell 'er its clear."

"What 'bout her? She can't be gettin' it done over the side. Women ain't built for it."

"Who says? She can get 'er done over the side quick as you, almost. Ifin it gets rough, she uses a bucket. She just yells out 'Eyes forward' just like us and we pay attention to what's ahead 'til she clears it for us. Told you she's been out 'ere before, knows the drill, ain't never been no problem. Won't be tomorrow."

"Well, guess it's alright. Won't be first time I've been 'barrassed. 'Sides seems I'm 'barrassed most times I been 'round 'er. She's got my number. Knows it, too."

"Been a noticin' it, some," the Captain said, "seems you pink up when she's 'round. You ain't the first to pink up, you're only the first she's let hang 'round for long. I'll tell her its ok with you. See you at the boat in the mornin'."

We met at the parking lot the next morning. I noticed right away that she wasn't just along for the ride. She grabbed a keg as we loaded up to take the gear to the boat. Made the second trip, also. Carrying her load. Stayed out on the deck with me arranging the gear as the boat cleared the breakwater and turned south and east toward South Channel. We talked a little, just when we needed to, about what needed doing, what we should be setting up next. After about an hour Captain Stinsin called back from the wheelhouse for her to get up on the platform and commence to looking.

When she climbed up on the platform I went in the wheelhouse, stood next to the Captain.

"Hank," he said, "'bout time you get some time out on the pulpit. Get some 'perience on 'stikin' 'em. First 'un she calls down you get on up to the pulpit. Want that dart right up 'longside the dorsal and you got to be careful right smart."

I thought for a moment about doing the 'stickin', then realized I was thinking about enjoying it. Slinging the stick and dart was really the essence of what it was swordfishermen did that set them apart the most. It was the unique way they had of getting hooked up to a fish. After that it was like most other fishing for big fish even though those methods were different as well. Still after she was 'ironed', a swordfish was hand-lined in just like most fish caught on hand-lines. Just that they were much bigger fish, far more dangerous. The harpooning was the most critical part, rest of it didn't work if the dart wasn't placed right or wasn't deep enough.

It wasn't long after, when we heard Eva yell down from the platform that she had a fish in sight. We looked up and saw where she was pointing. Pretty soon the Captain spotted the fish and headed toward her. "You might's well get on out there, we'll be up on 'er in a short bit." He said. I went on out on the pulpit.

In about a couple of minutes he was easing the boat up on the fish, coming at her over her right shoulder. I got everything ready, had the 'stick' all ready to throw making sure the lines weren't tangled, making sure I weren't stepping in any lines, seeing that the line from the dart went down the side of the boat to the line tubs. The fish was a medium sized fish, two hundred fifty pounds maybe. A good sized fish to be on for a first strike. Not big, not too little.

Just about when the pulpit's shadow was about to go over the aft end of the fish, I heaved the stick as I'd seen the Captain do it scores of times. It was a good throw. The dart went in right alongside the dorsal and went in deep. The fish exploded, busted the hell out of the water it was in and took off, all in an instant. I held on to the line from the stick as it broke loose from the dart and it swung back to the pulpit. By this time I noticed the Captain back at the line tub getting ready to throw over the keg. I started to the wheelhouse, noticing that Eva was already there conning the boat as her father threw the keg overboard. Her father yelled then, "Back up there, Eva, keep an eye out for other fish. Hank keep a lookin' on the keg." He finished as he went back in the wheelhouse. I pointed out the direction of the keg and he turned the *Eva* on the course the fish was taking. It took us only ten minutes to come up on the keg. I used the boat hook to snag the line, pulled the keg inboard and began to play the fish on the other end of the line, letting some line go as the fish ran, pulling some in when the fish calmed down some, always careful not to pull hard enough to yank the dart out. Before long I had the fish close to the boat. Then had it alongside, when I noticed Eva standing to my right with a lance held shoulder high and point down. Before I could say a word, she had lanced the fish, perfectly. Killed it instantly. She pulled the lance back out of the fish as I stood there almost dumfounded at seeing this beautiful creature kill a two hundred fifty pound fish without blinking an eye.

"Here," she said, smiling, "lets get her tail-roped and heave her aboard," handing me the line to wrap around the tail of the fish.

Soon I had the fish tail-roped and the two of us, standing side by side, yanked her into the cockpit of the *Eva,* blood flying as the fish flopped over the gunwale. I looked at Eva then, standing there with her hair frizzled some by the wind and the moisture, with a streak of the fish's blood down her right cheek. She was smiling at me.

"I've been doing this since I was fifteen," she said, "I'm a Stinsin. It's in my blood."

"Speakin' of which," I responded, reaching up with my hand and wiping the fish blood from her cheek. She didn't flinch, or pull away when I did. She just smiled as if to say, "See, I'm the whole package."

Three more times that day she spotted fish; about the same size as the first of them. We got all of them, me doing the 'sticking', the both of us working the fish, with her lancing them, then us tail-roping them just like the first one. The next fish she spotted was a big one, four to five hundred pounds. I stuck her just like the other fish, the Captain threw the keg over and we were hooked up again. Just about that time Eva spotted another fish, yelled down, pointed it out to the Captain. He hollered back up,

"How big she look to be?"

"The same size as the one we have kegged." She answered.

Captain looked at me, said "Better use the dory on the one we got stuck."

I pulled the dory alongside, checked that the right gear was in her and looked to the Captain with a question on my face. I wanted to see if he'd try to put Eva in the dory to go after the first fish. If he did, I wasn't going to be quiet about it. I wouldn't be worth a damn on the *Eva* going after the second fish while Eva was in a dory rowing around the ocean after a four or five hundred pound fish. Not after what had happened to me on my first dory trip. But I didn't have to worry. Captain Stinsin could see my worry. He said, "She ain't goin' in no dory, not's long as I'm livin'."

I climbed on in the dory, unshipped the oars, fixed where the keg was and took off after it as fast as I could row, keeping my eyes on the *Eva* as much as I could while I was tracking the 'stuck' fish. Pretty soon I had the keg, started working the fish to the dory. After a couple of runs she was close enough to lance. I killed her, got a line around her tail a minute later. Stood up to begin to work her into the dory. I noticed then that the *Eva* was off about five hundred yards or a bit more. Eva was throwing the keg over. They'd stuck the second fish. I turned to my situation. In two minutes I had worked my fish into the dory. Made things shipshape. Got the dart out of the fish, coiled the line and wrapped it around the keg, put all of it in the bow. I got the oars out and kept the dory turned so I could keep an eye on the big boat. I noticed that the keg was heading my way, the fish swimming toward where I was.

The next thing I saw was a dorsal going by, the swordfish working hard to get free of the dart, Then the big boat went by not twenty yards away. The Captain tipped his hat, Eva stood at the gunwale smiling at me sitting in the dory. After a bit they were back for me, they'd boated the second fish. I handed the tailrope up to Eva, climbed aboard and we used the boom with the block and tackle to hoist the fish from the dory into the cockpit of the mother boat.

Then it was time to head back to the island. It was late, the sun getting lower, the fish would be going down and the Captain wanted to offload the day's catch and the previous day's over at Point Judith. As we turned for home I got the knives and started to dress the last two fish.

"Hank, give me one of those knives, I'll do one of them." Eva said.

"I can get 'em done, no need for you to get all messed up dressing 'em. Ain't goin' to take me long."

"Hank, I've been doing it since I was fifteen."

I handed her a knife and we dressed the two fish side by side. She grabbed a hatchet and chopped the heads off and then we dragged the guts out of them onto the cockpit deck, picked them up and heaved them overboard. Afterwards, we dragged the fish to the fish hold and flopped them on the fish from the day before, we iced down the whole load, closed the hatch and stood back a little.

There she stood, the most beautiful woman in the world with blood everywhere. Dressing big fish is a bloody mess sometimes. She'd gotten blood everywhere, her hair, her face, down the front of her. She was smiling at me; she knew how it must look, knew what I was thinking. Had to know what a sight it was for a man, a man with the feeling she knew I had, to be looking at beauty encased in drying blood and fish guts.

"You need some cleanin' up," I said, "I'll dip some water so's we can clean up some."

I got one of the buckets with a line attached, not the slop bucket, dipped a bucket of sea water up, placed it on the deck. "We got some clean rags forward, I'll get 'em for you." When I returned with the rags and went to hand them to her, she said, "You do it. I don't have a mirror out here, I can't see myself, my face. You do it." I dipped the rags in the bucket of sea water and gingerly wiped the blood from her face and tried to wipe it out of her hair. Couldn't get all of it out of her hair, that would have to wait for later.

The whole time I was cleaning her face she stood there, two feet away, looking into my eyes, smiling. When I was through, and stepped back to see the job I'd done, she reached for me, leaned up and kissed me on my cheek. My heart stood still. It wasn't anything but a peck. But my heart stopped. She smiled again, walked on past me up to the wheelhouse. Later, after I got my heart restarted and I began to breathe again, I joined her and her father in the wheelhouse.

It was late when we got back to Old Harbor from Point Judith. But she didn't slack off any. Carried a full load to the truck just like the rest of us. Captain Stinsin said, "Get on in Hank, its late, I'll drive you up to the Hill Top." I climbed into the cab of the truck, Eva in the middle. I was conscious on the whole trip of her hip and mine touching, of the sides of our bodies touching - and she wasn't pulling away. She wasn't into making it easier for me. Had a touch of a tease in her. With her, though, the tease was a promise. She did it as a preview, not something put out just to be always drawn back. It was a look at what was worth waiting for. She naturally knew how best to present what she was.

She didn't hide it, but you weren't getting it until the time was right for her and that time carried its price.

When they left me off at the Hill Top the only words she spoke were, "See you at Sunday dinner, Hank." But her smile was playing with me as it always did.

I stayed awake for hours.

It, the fishing, kept on going right through August, then through most of September. Eva went out with us one more time, two days before she left for college. Most of the time we fished generally from the two hundred meter drop-off just south of Nantucket, the 'Dumping Grounds', down South Channel, both sides of it, sometimes within sight of Montauk Point, almost out to George's Bank, wherever the fish were. Long, long days on the water.

Chapter Twelve
THE BAD BOYS

It was about mid-September, after Eva left for college, when I met the 'Bad Boys'.

The swordfish were hot that day, were everywhere. It was if they were stocking up on summer heat while there was some left. We were down off Montauk. Could see Montauk Light in the distance. By noon we had boarded three medium sized fish and were off looking for more. About one o'clock I saw two fish, one about eighty yards from the other. They were almost directly ahead. Maybe a hundred and fifty yards. Even from the distance I could tell they were big fish, could tell it from the distance between their dorsal fins and tails. I looked down at the deck. The Captain had lashed the wheel and was just finishing icing the fish we'd already boated.

We'd learned that it was just as efficient for him to lash the wheel on the general course he wanted to make and for me to go up on the platform to spot fish while he dressed and iced the ones already aboard. He'd grown to trust my eyes. "There's seein' and then there's seein'," he'd said one day. "There's 'ems got strong eyes, can see forever away, can see the horizon better'n 'most anybody, but can't see a darn thing in between; then there's 'em sees things, even if their eyes be weak a bit. Seein' things, things you be wantin' to see is a particular 'bility, a skill. Ain't many got it. You got it. You see things." It was after that when be began the new style, me up on the platform, the crow's-nest, him below dressing the fish, the wheel lashed. Dressing them as we boated them made it easier later when we ran for home if the seas got up in the afternoon. The fish would already be dressed, and I wouldn't have to be stumbling around on a blood-slick deck, with the boat rolling 'ever-which-away', and the fish sliding from one side to the other while I tried to head and gut them and then wrestle them into the fish hold.

I yelled down at him, "Captain, there's two of 'em right off the bow, 'bout a hundred yards and a piece. They look to be big 'uns, both of 'em."

With that he rushed into the wheelhouse, looking where I was pointing as he did. Before long, with me pointing, we had gotten where we needed to be for the closest fish. He yelled up, went for the 'stick' and dart as I rushed down from the platform and into the wheelhouse. In another five minutes we were up on the first fish and he 'ironed' her. She literally exploded right under him, ripped the stick line out of his hand making it swing from its lanyard. The fish almost hit the Captain out on the pulpit and when she landed the splash wet him down good. I heard him yell "Damn," as I went for the line and keg. The fish greyhounding away to starboard looked like a giant white marlin the way it was tearing up the ocean. She had the four hundred feet of line out almost before I could get the keg attached and get it over. Off she went to the south.

"Hot dog," Captain Stinsin said as he was running to the wheelhouse, "she's a big 'un. She might hit six hundred pounds. Biggest one this year. Which way'd you say the 'othern went?"

"She was off to port some, quarterin' away last I eye'd 'er," I answered.

He stepped around the port side of the wheelhouse, looking off the port bow, said, "I got 'er. She's off a far piece, though. Ifin we're gonna have a chance to stick that 'un, you're gonna have to use the dory on the other'n."

I went to the stern, grabbed the dory line and brought her alongside, checked real quick that the oars, including the spare, and the lances were aboard, stepped over the gunwale of the *Eva* into the dory, cast off, waited until I'd cleared the *Eva*, then got set up to row after the darted fish. I wasn't having any trouble seeing her. She was tearing up some ocean, much more than they usually did. Staying on top. I started rowing and within fifteen minutes had come up on the keg. Pulled it aboard and started to close with the fish. She took off as soon as she felt the pressure and I had to let her loose, even had to throw the keg back over. It happen twice more. After maybe another half-hour, I had the keg again and started gingerly pulling on the line, closing with the fish.

She was acting unusual. Not sounding, just running laterally, almost in circles sometimes. Not seeming to pay attention to the dory, me, or even the fact that she'd been 'ironed'. She stayed near the surface, sometimes dorsal out, sometimes not, but always staying up. I hadn't seen one act like this before, but, just figured there was a lot I hadn't seen before about this kind of fishing. I kept on pulling when I could get line easy, letting it go through my hands when she decided to go off a bit, but getting her closer all the time. As she came near the boat she still kept circling; it was like I wasn't there, the dory wasn't, and we were only ten feet from her. It was like she was busy looking for something else.

She was almost jerky, making short movements, head side to side even as I got her almost close enough to reach for the lance. Then it happened. Almost in my face the ocean alongside the dory exploded. Every thing rose up, water, fish, everything. I fell in the dory on my back. Above me the swordfish was pitch-poling four or five feet up or so across the bow of the dory, bleeding. Where her tail had been there was nothing. Just a bloody stump. As I scrambled to sit up, I became aware of a shadow up in the air to my right, the side where I'd been pulling line just a split second ago. There hanging in the air was a huge mako shark - maybe seven or eight hundred pounds.

In the mako's mouth was the rear fourth of the swordfish, it's tail sticking out the right side of the shark's jaws. The mako started to fall back then, scared the heck out of me because it looked like the shark would fall into the boat. Luckily, it didn't; it fell to the side, maybe four or five feet to the side, dousing me with the splash. I sat up as quick as I could, then stood, crouched really, wondering what was going to happen next. I knew of the natural relationship of these two species. The enmity between them, predator and prey. This was the first time I'd seen it.

For a short spell I crouched there as the waves from the entry of the shark back in the water rocked the dory. I looked off to the left and the swordfish was twitching on the surface, trying desperately to swim. What remained of its aft part trying to sweep side to side, but with the great tail gone the fish only twitched. I noticed then, maybe twenty yards to the other side of the swordfish, a dorsal emerge through the surface of the sea and then the tip of a tail. It was the mako. Then I saw another dorsal emerge and it was also a mako, smaller than the first but still a big shark; it had to be or the larger one might have made a meal of it. They began to close with the swordfish, one to either side. I woke up then. Thought, foolishly maybe, that the swordfish was mine, I'd done all the work for it and they were stealing it at the last minute. I grabbed the line that had draped over the bow and hand over hand as fast as I could, I pulled the now almost dead weight of the swordfish toward the dory. The sharks followed and right as the sword bumped into the side of the dory, the big mako attacked the fish in the middle; the smaller shark dashed in and started biting the other side of the fish. I reached over and grabbed the sword, only four feet from where the larger shark had hold of the fish and pulled the sword up on the gunwale. I couldn't get the fish any further. The swordfish still weighed hundreds of pounds and she had a thousand pounds of mako hanging on her. I kept pulling anyway, looking at the sharks eating the fish, trying to rip huge chunks from her. The fish they were tasting was money out of my pocket and the white heat got in me. I held on to the swordfish's bill with one hand, reached down in the scuppers and grasped a lance with my other hand, leaned out over the gunwale still holding onto the swordfish and struck the big mako with the lance. The dory was unsteady, rocking from the actions of the sharks trying to rip chunks from the sword fish and I didn't get it right. In the next second the fire was out of me. Because of the motion of the dory, I had struck the shark a glancing blow down its side, ripping open a long gash, but not a killing blow. The mako exploded and charged the dory and me. Where I had been leaning a second before, the gunwale where my thigh had been, was, almost in an instant in the jaws of the mako and it was thrashing side to side trying to rip a piece off, just as it had been doing to the swordfish. Two words flashed before my eyes as I let go the swordfish's bill and fell into the bottom on the opposite side of the dory. "Augh shit."

The mako held on to the dory for several seconds, sawing from side to side, teeth breaking off and falling into the dory. With a loud rip, a part of the gunwale, the top five or six inches, a bite size part, was bitten off and it and the shark fell back into the water. I stayed still for a minute, until I noticed that line was being drawn from the dory, slowly moving out of it. I got up on my knees and peaked over the side. There, now off fifteen yards or so, the two sharks were still attacking the swordfish, ripping mouthfuls from her, eating her. Gulls, other sea birds, two gannets even, had already gathered, hovering, fluttering above the feast, darting in grabbing the pieces floating away.

I let the line keep going out. I'd had enough. They were the bosses. If they took all the line off, I'd throw them the keg. They could have it all. They stayed there though, not far off, almost alongside the dory, eating on the fish. Me watching. In ten minutes they were through, full I guess, leaving only some of the head and the sword, just a little flesh with it. The big one left the fish, swam slowly over to the dory, turned and swam slowly down the side of the boat, on its side a little, its big black eye looking at me, an eye almost as big as the swordfish's had been. It kept on going aft, then slowly went down, the smaller mako swimming over to it and following it into the depths. I was left there with the mutilated remains of the swordfish awash a few yards away, a raucous chorus emanating from the feeding and fighting sea birds. I noticed now, other dorsal fins, several, but smaller ones, much smaller ones. They were blue sharks come to clean up. There wasn't much left for them. I let them work on her for a while, then pulled the remains to the dory and inboard. In several minutes all the sharks were gone, the ocean clear of dorsal fins.

I just sat there for a bit. I'd seen what I had only heard about. The relationship between the makos and swordfish. This time the makos had won, one had clipped the tail from the swordfish while one of them distracted her. The big one had gone deep while she was protecting herself from the other and had rushed up under her, building speed and taken her tail off, flipping her over from the force of its assault. It had been a classic attack. Without the great tail the fish was helpless. She had no defense and it was only a matter of time. But it was quick. They had killed her fast.

And they didn't always win. Sometimes the swordfish would win, use the great sword to gut the makos, open them up. But, when the tail was gone the rest was a no contest. And I'd seen it up close, too damn close.

I looked off to the southeast and saw the *Eva* coming toward me. In another ten minutes she was longside. I threw the painter, the line, up and soon Captain Stinsin was standing at the *Eva's* gunwale, looking down into the dory where I was sitting on the thwart. He looked at my macabre cargo, the head, sword and gills of a large swordfish, with pieces of intestines floating on the water in the bottom of the dory. I hadn't got around to bailing yet. He took in the missing piece of gunwale, looked at me, and with a weird smile, said:

"I see you've done met the "Bad Boys.""

Chapter Thirteen
LOOKING HOMEWARD

Once in late September, when Captain Stinsin figured the fish had started drifting south, we went down past Montauk on a long day on the ocean. Once past Montauk Point Light, it barely visible inshore, I looked down south. I couldn't see them, but down there I knew were my home places, Ocean City, Assateague, and off their shores, the Jackspot - twenty-three miles out, Poor Man's Canyon farther out, and newer underwater canyons yet to be named.

The summertime girls, too, mostly gone from there by now. They'd had some up in Block Island, but it was a small island with Eva on it. Everybody knows what everybody else does. They didn't interest me like they used to - summertime girls. And Captain Stinsin had kept me so busy and tired, I hadn't had time or the energy to get in trouble with summertime girls, or in bed with them either. And then they were gone.

But, I was homesick some for Ocean City, just a little for a minute there south of Montauk, knowing that if I could have seen so far, I'd be seeing home. Something about home. Only one of them, usually. Bad or good, it's home. And it's a place to be missed if you're gone, no matter how good the place is where you are at any given time. I'd grown to really like Block Island, though. It was a beautiful place. A seafaring place. Surrounded by the sea, immersed in it. The people of the island, many of them, at least the true locals, the generational families, were people of the waters.

During the first week of September Eva had left the island, gone back to school. I'd seen her frequently during the summer when I had to drop by her house to take something to Captain Stinsin, or he'd send me there for something. Then there were the Sunday dinners, the walks. There was the ride to Southwest point to see the sunset. The days on the *Eva*. Everything had been innocent with her, except for the teasing which came as natural for her as breathing.

I'd gone to a party at the Stinsins in mid-August, a cook-out, with lots of people. Lots of young people, young men especially. I didn't know many of them; I'd been too busy working to become a part of a group, was mostly a loner anyway. But the men at the cookout weren't paying much attention to me, either. They swarmed around Eva. No question she was the center of attention for a whole island of males, those under fifty mostly. Just too much for me to put up with. Not like Sunday afternoons when we were by ourselves.

Except for a short greeting to each other when I had first arrived at the party and a couple of words now and then as we passed, there wasn't much opportunity to talk with Eva, be with her. I wasn't much for operating in a crowd, never had been. It wasn't that I was shy. One on one I was as aggressive as the next man. Or at least I had been. For a reason I hadn't fully figured out yet, that had changed. But I'd never been into being a part of a group, all concentrating on one girl, most making fools of themselves. About eleven, I made my goodbys to all the Stinsins, went on home. But, her face had been burned into my mind. Again. I dreamed of her, was dreaming of her when the alarm went off the next morning summoning me to the boat.

Finally, the fishing season 'wound' down. It was the very end of September. Eva had been gone for a month. I figured she had forgotten me. I couldn't forget her. And I really didn't understand. I'd spent the best part of the last five years of my life forgetting things and I'd gotten good at it. But not with her. She had turned the tables on me and I had not the slightest idea how. The fishing had kept me sharp, mentally as well as physically. It was dangerous work that demanded mental concentration. As long as we were fishing my mind was right. On the beach though, ashore, my mind didn't always work right, couldn't figure out things. I couldn't understand what was happening with me because of her. Now that the fishing was over there was no need for concentration. With her gone, there really wasn't anything left to think on. I'd sort of gone brain numb. My brain functioning enough to get me up in the morning, guide me down the street, buy groceries, and get me back to the room.

I had opened a bank account during the summer and had Captain Stinsin deposit all of my share money directly in it when he made the boat money deposits for himself. It was considerable. Captain Stinsin had never taken on another hand, figured that the two of us were good enough for three, I guess. After the first two weeks there had been three full shares, the *Eva's*, the Captain's and mine. We had worked well together, made out fine without another hand. The fishing had been good and we'd 'ironed' our share, more than our share, really. We were probably the high catch 'short tripper'. I'd been able to get by on the remains of my clamming money I'd brought up from home. It was almost gone now, but the swordfishing money would carry me for a considerable period.

I didn't know what I really wanted to do. I was mentally in a funk. I liked it on Block Island. Hadn't met many of the people, I'd been so busy fishing, but the ones I had met, I liked. They minded their business, mostly. I hadn't had a chance to get really involved with the island. I'd been at sea or sleeping almost all of the time. But that had stopped now. I was trying to make up my mind. Winter over here, go home for the winter - sea clamming again, head for the Outer Banks of the Carolinas, or on down to Florida and the islands, sport fishing for the winter.

Going home took care of itself one day the first week of October. I found a pay phone, called home, got hold of Jimbo. He told me real quick not to go home, or to the 'banks' either; there was still a fuss about the fight; they were still looking for the guy who was so good with the mug. He suggested I stay away through another summer. He did tell me, however, that the football player had recovered, no lasting effects, except to his pride, his father's pride as well. Jimbo didn't know about Florida or the islands east of there - the Bahamas. Thought they might be okay, but he couldn't really advise me on that.

I thought for a while about going all the way down to the Keys; maybe over to Bimini, or the out islands to the east of it, but couldn't create any enthusiasm for wintering down there. For some reason I didn't want to leave the island I was on, even with winter coming. There was a hold on me. I thought on it for the next two weeks or so. Then I went to talk to Captain Stinsin, to ask his thoughts on it - what I should do. Wanted to ask him, also, what there was for me to do on the island in the winter if I stayed up here?

Chapter Fourteen
WINTERING

I had called him up on a Saturday in the middle of October, asking when it would suit for me to see him.

"Well, 'morrow's Sunday, church day. We can talk after church. Why don't we meet in church and we can go home afterwards. Rebecca's gonna cook a roast big 'nough for a dozen head. You can have Sunday dinner with us; then we can talk."

"Sounds good to me, Captain," I said, "I'll see you in church."

As soon as I hung up, I rushed on down the street to Captain Stinsin's church to see what time the Sunday services were and then on down town looking for a clothing store or a shop of some kind. I didn't have anything to wear, hadn't even brought a sport coat up north with me. I finally found a consignment shop that was still open and having its second end of the season sale. For almost next to nothing, I was able to buy a used white shirt, tie, and a pair of shoes about two sizes too big, but they were dress shoes. I'd just have to learn how to slop around in them. They only had one sport coat anywhere near my size. It was real tight across my shoulders, but that was partially my shoulders' fault. Most everything I wore, except for bulky sweaters and the like, was tight across my shoulders. Had been since I was fifteen. Found a pair of pants that fit that the lady said matched the coat. The pants and the coat were a little threadbare, lots threadbare really, and smelled musty, maybe they smelled of mothballs a little. But, they were better than fishing clothes.

The next morning when I walked in the church it was already half-full, more maybe. Everyone turned to look at me. I was already self-conscious because of the clothes. But, then the first lady smiled, then another, and more of them. I smiled back, noticed Captain Stinsin standing at the end of an aisle, the second aisle from the front, beckoning me to join him. I walked on down the aisle, shuffled really, wafting mustiness and the scent of moth balls along the aisle, and stepped into the pew where Captain Stinsin indicated, between him and his wife. I wasn't really very familiar with church going. I'd gone some when I was really young, but then slowed down a lot and then quit all together when I turned fifteen and left home and started whoring and fighting and such. So, I was a little uneasy. Not knowing whether I'd remember what to do and when to do it. I made up my mind that I'd follow along. Whatever they did, I'd do. Just hoped there wasn't any 'strike him down' thing going to emanate from on high. I believed in Him and that scared me more than if I didn't.

After church, I stayed with the Captain and Mrs. Stinsin as they moved around outside, saying hello to other church goers, the preacher and anybody around. They appeared to know everyone, of course. Everybody was local there, mostly, anyway, it being October. Most of the summer folks, at least the ones that went to church, were gone now. Be gone until the next season. As we walked around outside the church, they kept introducing me to the people there, introducing me as Captain Stinsin's crew on the *Eva*. After a while most of the people began to leave, most walking, and we joined them, soon reaching Old Town Road and before long we were at the Stinsin house.

The rest of the afternoon was taken up by preparing dinner, Mrs. Stinsin had me peel the potatoes, said "If you can dress swordfish, I imagine potatoes should be easy." She was right of course, but I'd dressed a lot of swordfish since I'd peeled a potato. Twice she had to remind me to peel thin. We had dinner, then Captain Stinsin and I helped clean up the table, washed and dried the dishes and helped her put them away. He brewed a pot of coffee, we filled our cups and all of us went into the parlor. As soon as we were settled, I began the conversation.

"Captain, Mrs. Stinsin, I'm lookin' for some advice on what I should be a doin' now that the fishin' season is over. I'm not much for goin' home, back to Ocean City right yet. I could go on down to Hatteras, they's beginin' to get some big tuna below the Cape in the bight, even fishin' in the winter 'less it gets real cold. I can always go on to Florida, to Pompano, maybe on down the Keys, they know me real well down that way, wouldn't have no trouble hookin' up with a sport fishin' boat, go sail fishin', some marlin out in the stream, smoker kingfish off Boynton Beach. Even over in the islands - Bimini, maybe. I've done 'er two seasons. Made a little bit of a name for it. Trouble is, I don't really feel like leavin' 'ere. Leavin' Block Island. Don't know what it is, just feels like I oughta stay. I probably got 'nough money to make it through the winter, but I don't think much of not workin'. Wouldn't know what to do with myself. I know I could get somthin' on the docks over at Point Judith, but don't feel the same 'bout it over there as I do 'ere. Ifin I was to go there, might's well go on down south 'til spring.

"I guess, what I'm sayin', is I want to winter over 'ere, but, what I'm askin' of you, is ifin I do, what can I get to do. What work is there for an off-islander like me?"

"First of all, Hank," Mrs. Stinsin replied, "you're not an off-islander, really, not if you winter over. You're not a native. But, if you stay most people will appreciate it that you chose to do it. Especially, if you get work. Men that work can be a valuable commodity anywhere," she said, looking at Captain Stinsin as she did, smiling in a private joke way, "especially on an island where some men think it's necessary to drink the winter away. You stay and work it though, you'll find you'll be accepted. Church on Sunday, work Monday through Friday, take off Saturday, you'll fit right in."

"What she's talkin' 'bout," Captain Stinsin said, "is that the people here respect men that work and go to church. She's also diggin' me a little and I might as well tell you 'bout it. When she first growed up, afore she went off to college and such, I was a hell raiser, drinkin', fightin' and such. Livin' in the bars mostly. Workin' on other mens' boats, depositin' my share money on the bars 'bout town, mostly broke by March. It weren't 'til she came back after graduating from college, grownup, filled out and such," With that comment, Mrs. Stinsin picked up a throw pillow from the couch, and did what its name implied, threw it at him.

"You don't have to tell him everything," she said, as he ducked, laughing.

"Guess I'd best throttle back some." Captain Stinsin said. "Anyways, she came back, and I couldn't keep away from 'er, couldn't keep my eyes off 'er. I'd find myself gettin' in the places I knew she'd be, just to be a lookin' at 'er. I was shy for a long piece, mostly couldn't think of how to put the right words in a group for 'er. To speak at 'er. I'd fight any man on the island back then, fight in a minute if they said the wrong thing to me, but couldn't figure on what to say to 'er.

Just a little girl, but she had me goin' all whichaway. Finally, got my nerve up, saw her at the soda fountain at the National one day, sittin' at the counter, went in and sat down next to 'er. Said, 'Miss Pennington, I'm Will Stinsin. Been wantin' to speak with you for a bit, just ain't had the chance yet.'"

"She put 'er hand up, palm first to my face almost, gave a little smile. I thought my heart was goin' to jump right out in my lap. She said then, right out, 'You're a little old to be speaking this way to me, you don't go to church, you drink all the time, party all the time wasting your money, and you run wild women. About the only positive things you have going for you are you work hard, you're good on the sea and you're not bad looking. If you can change the bad things I might enjoy talking with you, but until you do, I won't waste my time on you.' She got up from the counter, walked out and left me there - stunned."

I laughed then, almost couldn't stop. Every time I looked over at Mrs. Stinsin, she had a certain type of smile on her face that got me to laughing again. For several minutes it went on. It was gut laughing for me. I would imagine Captain Stinsin sitting there at the soda counter, big bruiser, barroom brawler, on the receiving end, getting braced by the prettiest girl in town, getting put down. After a while, I got it under control - at least a little bit.

"What'd you do?" I asked.

"I was in church the next Sunday," he said, and that started me off laughing again, until he interrupted me.

"And from that day to this 'un', I ain't done no partyin', I quit drinkin', 'cept for a hot toddy in the winter when she's real cold and I been out in it for a spell and then it's only when Rebecca makes 'em.

"I saw 'er at church every Sunday for two months, never spoke to 'er, but ever' day, ever' Sunday, after the first two or three, if I caught 'er lookin' my way there'd be a smile on 'er face. Come February, think it was February, went to a church supper in the church hall. Got my dinner, sat down, and soon, Mr. and Mrs. Pennington, and Rebecca sat down at the table. Mr. Pennington turned to me, said 'I been seein' you in church regular now for a piece. From what I been hearin' you ain't been carrousin' likens you used to, fact is, you look like you slowed down.'

"Told him then, 'I just got tired a doin' all that stuff'. Fixin' to get to workin' on gettin' ahead. Time, she's a wastin', is what the sayin' is. That's what I've been doin'; don't plan no more on it.' I told 'im. He looked at me, close looked at me, then said, 'Next Sunday afternoon, whyn't you drop by the house for dinner.' I told him 'Don't want to intrude Mr. Pennington, on your family, on Rebecca.' 'Son,' he told me, 'it's 'er I'm doin' the askin' for.' I looked at her. She was blushin' just a little, not too much, she weren't the kind to 'barrass easy even then. She smiled and said, simply, 'It's time, Will, don't you think?' I answered, 'Yesum, I'll be there.' I was. And I still am. The house we're in is the Pennington place. Rebecca 'herited it.

"What I'm tryin' to own up to is that I weren't worth a damn 'til Rebecca got me on the straight. Until I got workin' steady in the wintertime, 'stead of partyin' and bein' drunk all the time, and wild."

He paused for a moment, looked over at Mrs. Stinsin, and I could see the love in their eyes for each other, long-time love, present love. I was envious. Wanted it, too, wanted the chance for it anyway, with someone, sometime. Wanted what they had. Hoped for it. Captain Stinsin looked back at me then, said:

"What most of usens, fishermen, do in the winter is go to paintin', do the outside of the hotels and inns, houses and stuff, 'til it gets real cold, then we does the inside work 'til it warms up again in the spring, 'bout middle of March, then finish up the outside work 'til its time to get the *Eva* ready. Clem was with me last year, but you know 'bout 'im. I'll be starting, shorthanded, on a two-man job at the National come Monday week. Then I got a passel of paintin' at the Ocean View. You want to stay, there'll be work steady-like through most the winter. You can be with me."

"Sounds great." I said. "Let me think on it, I'll know by next Sunday at the latest. Would that be too late for the job with you?"

"No, that'll do," he said, "ain't nobody else 'vailable anyhow. Ifin you 'side to leave, I'll be a workin' one handed. That's what was goin' to be anyways. Next Sunday 'ill do 'er,"

We sat around for another while, talking about the past summer's fishing, some of the fishing in the days when the swordfish were sometimes seen right from the beach and fishermen would row out and 'stick' them. Days gone by now. Even short trippers went a far piece most of the time. We talked then, I guess they talked mostly, me only asking questions, about the history of the island. Mrs. Stinsin was a real historian on it.

Chapter Fifteen

TIMES

"The first person here other than the Indians," Mrs. Stinsin said, "was Giovanni da Verrazano in the early fifteen hundreds."

I interrupted her then. "That's a real coincidence. He was the man that discovered where I'm from. Discovered it, then left it. It was a long time afore it got goin' again."

"It was the same way here. It was almost another hundred years before Europeans came to it again. In the early sixteen hundreds a fur trader, Adrian Block, came here. He's the man that left his name on this island. Then later on in 1636, a man named Oldham managed to get himself killed on his boat in the Sound by Indians from the island. In response men came down from the Massachusetts Colony and burnt the crops and shelters of the Indians who had fled into the swamps. Other expeditions over the next years continued and the Indians were subjected to having their crops taken and their money, too - wampum, that's what it really was called. Later in 1658 the Massachusetts Bay Colony deeded the island to four men. They sold it to another group who wanted to create plantations over here. The land was surveyed and sixteen plantations were laid out with no consideration for the interests of the Indians. Those sixteen surveyed plantations are still the basis of land titles on the island.

"By 1730 or so there were two, three hundred Europeans on the island; the Indians were, for the most part, gone, maybe a dozen or so left. The last Indian known to have lived on the island died in the 1780s. His full name was Isaac Church, but he had come to be called 'Uncle Isaac' by almost everybody before he died. That's where Isaac's Corner got its name. It used to be called Uncle Isaac's Corner, then later on they dropped the 'Uncle' part.

"Mostly from then until the tourist business took off in the last part of the 1800s, the island was mostly farming. Then there always was the fishing. All kinds including the swordfish. There are stories of swordfish being caught as early as 1820 or so. By the Civil War there were whole fleets, sailing schooners, other sailing vessels, going after them in 'no man's land', down in South Channel as well. Most of the fleets came from other ports. Block Island fishermen mostly were loners.

"In both the Revolution and the War of 1812 the British landed on the island. No battles took place here, though. They came, they left, and island life went on. Mostly, the other wars just passed it by. Some of the men fought in the Civil War and the Spanish-American War, and some of them became professional soldiers. Like everywhere we had men fight in both of the World Wars, just recently Korea, too. In the Second World War there were ninety-five Block Islanders that fought out of a population of seven hundred. Two towers were built here, up the north end, to look for submarines. They're still there.

"It was after the War that the tourist business got really big again. Lots of off-islanders began to build houses and such, or buy them. That's pretty much where we are now, the tourist business started up in the 1800s, slowed down during the wars, then started up again. And I imagine it will keep right on growing." She finished. We kept on talking for an hour or so. Talking about general things. After a while I made my goodbys, left, and, thinking all the time, walked on up to my room out back of the Hill Top.

On the Thursday following I was surprised to receive a letter.

Chapter Sixteen
MESSAGE

Dear Mr. Hank Gaskins:

I spoke on the telephone with my parents on Monday. They told me that you're thinking about possibly going south for the winter. What will I do if you're gone when I come home for Thanksgiving and Christmas? Stay!

Fondly

Eva

That settled it. From that moment there wasn't anywhere I wanted to go, but where I was. I started painting with Captain Stinsin on the following Monday, started going to church every Sunday, still stayed away from the partying and the drinking, except that on the way to my room after work, I'd sometimes stop at the Hill Top bar for a beer or two, just for a little while, then I'd go to my room, read until it put me to sleep, dream, then up the next morning and off to work again. I knew what I was really doing. I was waiting. What I was waiting for raised my spirits every day. I tried not to read too much into the letter. Maybe, she just wanted to make sure her father had somebody to help him paint, wanted to make sure that he'd have an experienced hand for the next swordfishing season. Maybe.

When I occasionally stopped for a beer at the Hill Top Bar on the way to my room, I had noticed that someone was painting the walls, painting Block Island landscapes, scenes of the sea and such. One evening, a week or so before Thanksgiving, when I stopped in there for a beer the artist was hard at work. He was working on a swordfishing scene so I was paying particular attention. It was soon clear that he knew what he was doing. The scene he was painting was of a boat, just about like the *Eva*, same size, a pulpit, mast, all of it looked the same. He was finishing painting in a man standing on the pulpit with a 'stick' and dart raised, ready to 'strike' a swordfish basking on the

96

surface. I stayed a beer longer than usual, waiting to see him finish. He was good. In about twenty minutes he stopped working on the picture, cleaned his brushes, leaned a small "Wet Paint" sign on the wall below the scene he'd just created.

He moved over to the bar and took the stool next to me. Without being asked, the bartender put a shot and a beer in front of him. He upended the shot, drank the draft beer in two swallows and the bartender fixed him another combination. That boiler-maker he sipped.

I was naturally curious, the guy was good, his work a little primitive maybe, but, if so, it made it all the better as far as I was concerned, so I turned to him, said:

"Hi. I'm Hank Gaskins. I've been admirin' your work when I've been in here before. 'Night's the first time I've seen you in action. I like it."

"Thanks," he responded, holding out his hand. As we shook, he said "I'm Leatherby."

"Can I buy you a drink when you finish that one?" I asked.

"Time it gets 'ere I'll be finished."

I ordered another round for him and a little later another one as I finished the beer I'd ordered when I first arrived at the bar.

"I've done a mite of fishin' since I growed up," I said, "marlin fishin', tuna, up and down the coast. Been fishin' with Captain Stinsin this summer, paintn' with 'im now, houses and things. Not what like you're doin' in 'ere. You're an artist not a painter. You make it look as good, as real, in a straight way, as anybody I've seen. It's real good."

"I've done some fishin'," he said, "little bit anyway. Mostly from the island. Don't do much anymore; drink's got me and I can't stay sober long 'nough to stay steady on any boat. Ain't goin' on any long trippers, anyways, got too old for it. Still get out now and then on a short tripper when a hand misses the time. Do some other fishin' too, when somebody really needs a mate. Do a lot of odd jobs 'ere and there on the beach, the island. Paint pictures, too, sell a few down by the National, sometimes at the Ocean View when I'm halfway sober. Paintin' this mural's for my bar bill. Long's I keep to paintin' that bartender's been told to keep pourin' 'em shots. That ways I get to do the two things left that's important to me, drinkin' and paintin'."

"Well you're good at it," I said, "I consider it an honor to meet you. The next time you do some pictures of swordfishin', look me up, I'd like to buy one if I can afford it."

"Whether you can afford it 'ill 'pend on how drunk I am when I got one to sell and whether I got any money. Price 'pends on what I need at the time. But, I'll look you up next one I get finished."

I had met one of the island's best known artists. He was almost Grandma Moses in his works' effects. It was really good stuff and I figured his work would stand the test of time.

After that, I'd see him from time to time, just passing usually. We'd speak and then go on our ways. Once or twice that winter I'd see him at the bar, buy him a drink or two, talk a little, then he'd go, or I would.

We were just getting through painting at the Ocean View Hotel, the porch rails, on the Tuesday before Thanksgiving, when Captain Stinsin asked, "Want to go over to Point Judith on the boat tomorrow? Eva's comin' in for Thanksgivin'', she'll be there 'bout eleven. We'd leave 'ere 'round nine. Don't want 'er havin' to wait on no ferry."

"Yes sir," I responded almost before he got his words finished, "I'd like that." I'm lookin' forward to seein' 'er, hope you don't mind me sayin' it."

"It's fine. Figured when I called 'er to tell 'er you might be goin' south that she was goin' to write you. Didn't see nothin' much wrong with it. You learn somethin' 'bout a man when you work with 'im on the sea. You look like you're put together right, almost right. 'Sides, I'd hurt you bad ifin you were to hurt 'er."

"Don't fret none on it," I responded, "don't aim to. But I might's well ask you now ifin its okay if I date 'er, if she'll go with me? Ifin I can determine how to ask 'er."

"Wouldn't asked you to go over there with me tomorrow ifin it weren't right with us. Rebecca and I hold a lot a store in you. We know our daughter, too. That's really 'nough, anyway. But ifin you been worryin' 'bout what Rebecca and I think 'bout you, you can stop your worryin'. See you at the boat 'bout quarter to eight in the mornin'," he finished.

Chapter Seventeen

HOLIDAY

POINT JUDITH

We pulled in the slip at Point Judith just about eleven the next day. She was standing at the end of the dock in a high necked, medium length beige dress, her hands clasped behind her with a matching beige jacket in her hands, her hair up on top of her head and around it, framing the beauty of her face. She had a white ribbon holding her hair up in back. Her waist was tucked in by a brown belt. A bag was at her feet. Wasn't the same Eva, far as looking went, that I'd wiped the fish blood out of her hair, off her face, when she'd gone fishing with us the summer before. Either way, though, she was the most womanly woman I'd ever seen. Didn't really matter much what she wore, what she was doing, she was feminine, always.

As we closed the dock, she just stood there, almost still, standing there beside the bag, just swaying a little, looking at us, looking at the *Eva* as we approached. When we got a little closer, she waved, one hand gracefully waving above her shoulder, a smile, a big smile on her face. As we began to square up alongside the dock, she said, just loud enough for us to hear,

"Hello daddy, Hank. I'm so glad to be home."

"We're glad to have you 'er, sweets. We've missed you hard." Captain Stinsin said as I started to lasso a piling.

Before I could react, Eva had bent, grabbed the bag and threw it into the cockpit of the boat, then had hiked up her skirts thigh high and had leaped down on the gunwale, almost four feet. I started to jump her way, afraid she'd fall. But, she put her hand up softly to me, as if to say, "Thanks, but I'm fine."

She bounded down from the gunwale, rushed over to her father, threw herself, her arms around him and gave him a hug. Really hugged him, kissed him on the cheek. Held him for five or ten seconds, then moved back a step, said

"You smell so good, daddy. Just like you always have. You smell of Old Spice lotion. You must be the only man in the world that still uses it."

That morning after shaving I had also put on Old Spice. Thought about it now, as I stood there with the line still in my hand, the boat still lying there in the slip, in neutral, motor running.

She ran to me then, "Hank, it's good to see you, too, taking care of my daddy." She sort of grabbed my arms up high, leaned forward and sort of touched my cheek with hers, holding her body off a little, but still almost embracing me. She stepped back with a smile, sort of a weird one, then said,

"You too. Both of you wearing Old Spice. I don't believe it. That's funny, after what I said to daddy," she finished and started laughing as she transferred her hands from by biceps to my hands, then just stood there looking at me, laughing, a tittering, lyrical laughter. Got me laughing, too. Then her father. All of us laughing in an unmoored boat in a slip at the dock in Point Judith. She broke the spell, letting my hands go, turning to her father, "Let's head for home, I can't wait to see mama," she said.

With that, Captain Stinsin headed for the wheelhouse, her following and soon we were backing out of the slip then forward, turning up the waterway toward the opening in the breakwater that led out into the sound. I coiled the line, put it up under the bow where it belonged. As I did, I heard her voice, "Hank, come on in the wheelhouse, we'll squeeze you in. It's too cold to stay out there clear across the Sound."

I joined them in the wheelhouse; standing behind them. By the time we had gotten fifty yards up the channel, she had talked her father into letting her run, con, the boat back to the island. She stood directly behind the wheel, with her father quartering her, close in on her right side, me on the left. The wheelhouse was so small that we were all touching. I could feel her excitement as we approached the breakwater opening. She couldn't hold still. Almost taking little hops she was so excited at being home. She turned the boat to starboard and took the *Eva* right down the center of the cut, took a bearing on the island and headed straight for its north end, barely visible in the distance. We hadn't gone a mile when she started singing. Sailor's ditties. But clean ones. She turned to her father,

"Come on daddy, join in with me. I'll sing a verse through first, then you and Hank sing it with me the second time, and the next time. You hear me, Hank?"

"Yes, ma'am," I said, enthralled with her, mystified by her, a little afraid of her.

Her gaiety, her happiness, her shear joy at being home with her family, even with me, was infectious. She reminded me of the brightness of the stars at night, the sparkle of the sun or the moon on the sea. She made me feel good. It was a rapture she was causing by the sheer force of her personality and beauty, not only in me, but in the Captain as well. She was just joy.

We sang ditties for a solid hour, her leading the way, steering the boat at the same time around the north end of Block Island, then heading for Old Harbor. She sang the loudest, made us sing the loudest as we entered the harbor, people on other boats looking at us as if we were crazy. And we were. She made us crazy feeling. Just being in her presence.

Her father told her then, "Let's see if you're as smart bringing the boat to the bow moorin' as you are with the singing."

She put the pulpit right over the float, moved down the side some, I hooked the line, and she put it in reverse, backed her up, not even touching the dory. In five minutes or so, the stern was secured, the dory hooked up to the land line and we were walking up the street. She started singing again. We joined her. Everybody thought we were drunk. I was, and I hadn't had a thing to drink.

God, she was something. One of His special angels, I think. She had to be. There was something extra earthy about her. Almost like she didn't come from where most people do. There must be some unique ingredient that finds its way into the special people. And she was one of them. I was already in love with her and she'd touched me, specially touched me, inside, just the once an hour before. Not like the cheeking, the peck or two. Really touched me, making me feel touched by the way she'd included me in her greeting when she'd hopped on the boat back at Point Judith.

I'd run every woman I could find back home. But, now I was like a little boy. All I could do was stumble along behind her, carrying her bag, as she skipped up the road. The Captain hadn't brought the truck to the dock, we'd both walked down. There she was, an almost twenty year old woman skipping like a kid, followed by a father that loved her the most a father can, loved her to death; followed also by a tamed lion - I might have been a wild lion on the streets in Ocean City, but now the wild was gone. She knew I was hers. I wanted to be hers.

We just followed up the streets to the house. Her duffle bag over my shoulder. Weighed nothing. Guess it did, but I couldn't feel it.

HOME

We went in the house, she rushing to her mother to hug and be hugged, to squeal womanly things to each other. I don't remember exactly what was said. I was in a cocoon, encased in the silk she had been weaving since I first saw her standing on the Point Judith pier. I was inside it looking out at them. After a moment or two, I realized that the women were looking at me, laughing, and Mrs. Stinsin was speaking.

"Hank. Hank!," she interrupted my dream state, "take Eva's bag upstairs, her room is the first one on the right. Hurry now, I'm about to put lunch on the table. Then there's dinner tonight to get ready."

I turned, started up the stairs. I was half-way up when I realized that Eva was following me. When we got to the top, she said "Let me get the door" and brushed past me and went to the first door on the right, opening it and standing to the side of the jamb, gave me just enough room to squeeze past. I touched her lightly as I went in the room. Already today, I'd had more body contact with her than in the six months I had been fishing with her father, on all the Sunday walks of summer, the Southwest Point sunset, when she came along on the fishing trips.

"Put the bag on the floor by the window, please,"she said, "I'll unpack later.".

I walked over to the window and put the bag under the sill, turned to walk to the door. She was sitting in a side chair alongside the bed.

"Talk with me Hank," she said. I stopped and stood there not knowing whether I could even talk I'd been so affected by her presence, and, in any event not knowing what to say. I just stood there.

"Sit down," she said.

There weren't any more chairs, the only other place to sit was the bed, her bed.

"Don't know whether I should," I responded, "your mother, Captain Stinsin, they might not like it."

"Don't be silly. They trust you or you wouldn't be here and they trust me. Sit down. Don't you want to be the first man to sit on my bed?"

I sat down on the bed. Didn't directly answer the question. Couldn't think of a safe answer. No was wrong. Yes was wrong. She knew my dilemma. She'd deliberately put me in the box to see my reaction. And she laughed at it. The quality of her laughing voice was like a musical instrument, a flute, a piccolo, high pitched girly laughter, full out laughter. And then I began to laugh, too. Seeing the humor in it. Here I was a full grown man, tongue-tied, in the presence of a girl I'd known for six months, but a man who now realized that things were being made different. What she had done was to tell me that we didn't have to standoff and play games like other people. We could just be ourselves and in the process turn life into fun.

I tested her then, it would be the only time. "You know" I said to her, "ifin it hadn't been for your letter, I might not be 'ere."

"You would have been here," she responded, "you couldn't leave. I threw my web over you the first time we met. We both knew it. I told mama and daddy in August. That's when daddy let me come fishing with you. I didn't know how long it would take for you to get your nerve up. It's funny with you men that have all the courage in the world when you go to sea and fight with wild creatures, a little bitty girl makes you speechless. I sensed how you felt. You knew it, too. The letter was just a reminder. I meant what I wrote. What would I have done had you gone? You want to know what would have happened? You'd be down south somewhere and you would come in one afternoon from a day's fishing, you'd look up, and you would have seen what you saw at Point Judith a couple of hours ago. I made my mind up this summer. Wanted you to settle some more, season some, before I made your mind up for

103

you. Then daddy called me, told me that you were considering leaving for the winter. So I wrote. Then I knew you'd be here.

"You were so shy when you came to the house those few times this summer that you hardly looked at me. Whenever I knew you were coming, I arranged to be here. Made sure you'd see me. But, I never really caught your eyes the whole summer. Even when we were on the boat together, where you couldn't run off. If you would have looked down deep, if you hadn't been afraid of me, you would have known how I feel when you're around. I couldn't have explained it to you, then. Still can't explain it even to myself. I don't know why.

"I want to spend a lot of time with you. I want to find out why we feel the way we do."

It was probably a minute or more, with her gently smiling at me, before I spoke. It wasn't that I was thinking about what to say. I wasn't thinking at all. Her presence and what she had said enveloped me in a warmth, in a sensory experience I didn't want to interrupt by speaking. I thought my heart had stopped for a minute. Then it was skipping so much I couldn't talk. Maybe I was dying, but it was ok because the all of it felt so good. I was a kid again, there for that minute, with the crush on the girl next door that puts your brain in neutral. But I was a grown man. It wasn't supposed to happen to grown men.

I looked into her eyes. Unabashed for the first time. Really looking. Immersed in the liquid sparkle of her deep blue eyes. I was overboard, swimming in indigo, swimming in the deep sea. Committed. At that instant a casting away of fear. No longer any fear of the unknown depths of the relationship left for both of us to explore together. No more emptiness. It made me smile. Her smile intensified. And I spoke.

"You're right. I couldn't have left. I was shy this summer. You affected me so, I couldn't speak half the time. At the cookout I couldn't stand seein' all the guys hoverin' 'round you. I had to leave. It wasn't my type of thing. All summer I wanted to talk with you like this, but I couldn't get my mouth open when I was 'round you. I was so afraid I'd say the wrong thing, I didn't say anything.

"I've been tryin' to figure out what's been wrong with me ever' since I came to this island. There's been this emptiness I couldn't understand. At the same time there was an energy 'bout me, around me. I think I have it figured out now. Until I saw you, there was nothin' in this world

I had to have. Nothin' important that I was missin'. Then there you were and my heart created an empty space just so you could fill it. But, I couldn't get my nerve up, couldn't figure out how to do it. So I just walked around full of energy but with this empty feelin' inside, this empty space, waitin'. Maybe that's how you tell you feel for somebody. Does the thought of them make you feel empty when they're gone? I guess that's why I was worrin' 'bout leavin' 'ere. Couldn't stand the emptiness, didn't know how to fill it with you gone, when I hadn't been able to fill it even when you were 'ere. Maybe the thought of leavin' was to get away from the emptiness. Then your letter came."

She laughed, not much more than a smile, stood, walked over to the bed, bent down and put her lips on mine, no other touching, just our lips. But it wasn't any peck. Lasted a while. She'd turned something on inside, gave it to me through her lips. I thought I'd stuck my finger in a light socket, hit the funny bone in my elbow. That's how it felt. Thrilled me and scared me.

"Come on," she said after a few seconds, "lets go down, have some lunch and later we'll help mama with dinner. It'll be private tonight, just the four of us. Tomorrow, though, there will be a house full, all the cousins, the preacher, some of the other fishermen, friends. But' it'll be fun. I'll make it fun."

She grabbed me, pulled me up and, hand in hand, led me back downstairs past the dining room table with the lunch settings already on it and into the kitchen where her mother and father were preparing tonight's dinner and tomorrow's turkey. When they saw our clasped hands, they both smiled and I understood. They had known that she had picked me and they knew that Eva got what she wanted. They had already talked about it. There had been a 'what if' family discussion, probably before Eva went off to school. I had already been accepted while I was still trying to figure things out, trying to understand myself.

We moved into the dining room, sat down at the table. Captain Stinsin said grace and we ate. I don't remember what the sandwiches were, what the soup was. My mind was just in an adjusting mode - still assimilating the treasure I was receiving. I looked at her now, almost every second. Couldn't keep my eyes from her's. Making up for all the times of summer when I could've, but didn't, because I hadn't really known how. I hadn't been complete until the few minutes before, when she had made me whole while I was sitting on her bed - the first man ever to be there.

I heard a little giggle from Mrs. Stinsin and looked away from Eva's eyes. Captain and Mrs. Stinsin were both looking at me, and smiling. I realized then that I'd been trying to sip soup from the spoon while looking at Eva. It had dribbled down my chin, some had spilled on my sweater. I could feel my face warming, turning pink I guess, as I put the spoon down, took a napkin and blotted my chin and my sweater. Then Eva went to giggling, not a derisive giggling, but a happy laugh. She knew she was the reason for it, for my inattention to the soup, and it pleased her. It pleased me, too. Not the spilling of the soup, but that everyone knew why.

Soon we were finished.

THE WALK

"Mama," Eva said, "can you spare me for a while? I'd like to take a walk down to the Ocean View beach."

"Certainly, Hank can help."

"Mama! You know what I meant."

"Yes I know, the two of you go on, we'll be fine. But, I'm having dinner early, today, around four, so that we can work on the dinner for tomorrow. Make sure you're back by then."

I'd been thinking (when I hadn't been around Eva) since I had been invited to Thanksgiving dinner, what I could contribute, so I spoke up then, "Mrs. Stinsin, I've decided on what I could do special for tomorrow. Down home we have a thing for what we call 'slicks', they's 'dumplins', made with flour and the essence from a boiled chicken that you don't really have to chew on. Just put them in your mouth, slide 'em around to get the taste off 'em, and they slide down on their own, don't have to work on 'em none. 'Spect they'd work just as well with a turkey ifin there's any drippin's during the roastin' that can be used for flavor. Ifin you have 'nough flour I'd like to try an do some 'slicks' as my part to tomorrow."

106

"I've got plenty of flour, always have plenty of flour, we're biscuit people here on the island, I'll be making a batch. What else do you need for 'slicks' besides the flour and the essence?"

"A rollin' pin and a flat place to roll 'em out thin, place to keep 'em 'til it's time to cook 'em, then a big pot with water and essence to cook 'em up. I can roll 'em up way 'head of time, can cook 'em up a little 'head of time and just let 'em stay in the pot until time for servin'."

"Good," Mrs. Stinsin replied, "then we'll count on them for tomorrow."

Eva said then, "I want you over here early, anyway, so I can be the one to introduce you to my friends and relatives." Then she said, "We'll be back, mama. Come on Hank, let's take a walk." With that she had my hand. We picked up an afghan from the couch as we went through the living room, paused to grab jackets in the foyer and then she led me out of the house and down Old Town Road toward Old Harbor.

Before long, we were walking over the bluff at the Ocean View down a winding pathway through the bushes to the beach. The hotel had been closed since the end of September, so we were alone. The breeze was from out of the southeast, a cool breeze on the right side of our faces as we walked down the bluff, her still leading me by the hand. When we got to the bottom, she pulled me to her, pulling my hand up behind her back and placing it on her left shoulder as she put her right arm around my waist. With a little skip, she synchronized our gaits and walked us down the beach. After a hundred yards or so we came to a place in some of the rocks at the edge of the beach, a place where God had deposited boulders eons ago, just to make a place for us to shelter in, people discovering themselves. People needing a lee shore. She untangled us and said, "Help me spread the afghan, here, next to the rock."

I grabbed one end, her the other, and we spread it where she indicated. She had picked the place, not for concealment, but for protection from the wind. In daytime we could be seen north along the beach all the way to the breakwater at Old Harbor, a couple of hundred yards away. It might have been a nighttime place for privacy; in the daytime it was a shelter from the wind. But, I knew it was a special place for her. A place she came to when she wanted to think, to feel special. I already felt special just by being with her. God! She was something.

107

"Sit!" She commanded. She knew her place. I knew mine. I sat down and she joined me, folding both her legs on the side farthest from me. My legs were bent, extending toward the water. She leaned to her right, resting her head on my shoulder, a small wind swirling around the rock fluffing her hair, strands tiptoing up and down my face, points of fire really where they touched, I was so attuned, so sensitive to her.

"If you haven't guessed," she said, "I'm glad you stayed."

"So am I. I've got to be the luckiest man around. And I've never had any luck before, not this kind. I'm almost afraid of it."

"Don't think about it. Believe me, its real."

"But I didn't know anything."

"I know you didn't. In a way it was fun you not knowing, but then it wasn't, because I could see how it was affecting you. But I didn't know how to get you to see that I felt the way you did."

"But, you can't have known me very well, we hardly even talked."

"Daddy talked. At home, all the time about the kid, the real man he had signed on the boat. All he did last summer was talk about you. When I first told him that I liked you, he went to the Chief of Police and had him call the Chief in Ocean City to find out about your trouble there, to find out all about you. Your problem was what you told daddy it was. We found out that it was your only trouble. He told us, the chief down there, some about your family - not much though, your work and stuff. He also told us that you were a ladies man - that you ran women a lot. Even told us that you were rough on daughters. Are you? Are you rough on daughters?"

How do you answer that question? I answered with a simple question, "Have I acted like it?" She laughed, then said

"I told daddy not to worry about his daughter. That I was more than a match for any good looking woman runner. And he knows that's true. I've been throwing them over the side for years now - not big enough to keep. But I thought you were a keeper; Daddy thinks so, too. Mama took a little longer, but before the summer was over she'd heard daddy talk so much about you, she began to see you, not the barroom brawler you'd been, but the man you had become here since you've been with us, here on the island fishing with daddy. By August I knew about all the things that count the most when a woman is trying to determine whether a person she's interested in is a real man. Firmed it up when we fished together those days on the *Eva*.

"In truth, I could probably have any of the boys around this island, certainly the 'locals'. I know I'm pretty. If I hadn't known it when I was just a little girl, I certainly would have figured it out after the boys seemed to always end up in our yard after school. Some of them lived miles away. I knew, though, even when I was young, that being pretty wasn't something I had done. It was done for me. I didn't claim it, but I accepted it, not as my due, but something that just was. I never let my looks determine who I was. Who I am. I am glad that what wraps around my heart and soul is pleasing to your sight. But, there's more to me then my countenance, my face, my body. I could offer those things to anyone, any boy. He'd be glad. I've been looking for other things.

"I don't know why it's you. You talk of emptiness. I hadn't thought of it that way. But you're right, I think. What I've felt about you when I've been around you, when I've been away, whenever I thought of you, is like a dizziness inside, like it almost draws you in to fill a hollow in the center of your being. Sometimes, just seeing you made me stop breathing. I was like I would forget to breathe."

"I didn't think it would ever happen to me." I said in response, "just wasn't somethin' I was figurin' on. Then I walked in your house that first day and there you were. There's a word I heard the preacher use last Sunday, 'smitten', that was me. I was knocked for a loop from then on. And I don't understand."

"We don't have to understand." she said. "I don't think you have to understand these feelings. It's not like understanding where the fish will be, and when. It's not like making a business decision. It's not something you work up to. Just, all of a sudden it's there. And you're in the middle of the feeling. You can't get out and don't want to."

I put my arm around her then, around her shoulders and her head slipped a little down on my chest. We just sat there, maybe for an hour. Maybe more. Thinking. Our physical contact at most an innocent promise. We talked. Talked a lot about the sea, about the beauty of where we were, about how she loved the island so, would return to it forever. She was excited about the job that had been promised her at the Ocean View after she had her business degree. It would enable her to stay on the island. She wanted to open a book store some day. Maybe a coffee house. And she asked me about myself.

"I don't know. When I first came up here it was just because I had to go somewhere and I wanted to try swordfishing. I wasn't thinkin' beyond it. Then when your door opened and I saw you, I stopped thinkin' altogether. Since then, 'cept when I'm at sea, all I've thought of is you and what was happenin' to me, the empty feelin'. Now, I've got to figure on how to stay 'ere. I've got to find the direction. I'm not the polished kind, I know that. I don't talk right, got the accent and all. No grammar. I never paid much attention in school. Didn't need to speak right to go to sea. Just needed heart and a strong back. I had 'em. Always had 'em. But, I've got to do somethin' now. Can't keep on bein' uncivilized in my talkin'."

"Whatever you do, will be fine. If you want to go on to school, I'll help you apply." She said. "You're smart. You'll do fine in school. It'll be rough at first, but you'll catch on fast."

"The question," I said, "will be whether I can stay away long 'nough to finish college. I may have to go back to Maryland to even get in college. They's a law down there that the University has to take any State high school graduate. So I can get in there.

"You know I could just stay here, save my fish money, paintin' money, put a down payment on a 'short tripper' and keep on fishin'. I'd made a decent livin'. Your daddy does."

"That's for now, she said. "I keep daddy's books for him, make his deposits and everything. In fact I'm the one that made your's this summer so I know how much you made, too. I've been keeping his books for years. I can tell you that the swordfishing is declining bad. Every year it gets worst. Daddy has had his boat paid off since almost before I was born. If he had a heavy boat mortgage right now, he'd be hard pressed to make a go of it. The fish are just going. There are Japanese ships that operate off shore that use a new method, miles and miles of line, and bait the fish down deep at night. They're wiping out the fish. Pretty soon the big American operators will be rigging up for that kind of fishing and the 'short tripping' will become a thing of the past. Won't be enough fish inshore to make it profitable. Daddy and I've talked. Four, five years, is about all that's left of it.

"You're going to have to find something else anyway. You might as well spend the next two winters while I'm at school in a school of your own. Getting set up for something else. There'll be opportunities opening up on the island as the tourist trade builds, real estate, restaurants, contracting, marinas, things to do around the water. All of it is going to come. But you have to get ready for it. I hope you can go next year to college. I'll get all the applications, the one from Maryland, too. We can fill them out over Christmas. You'll get in college, I'm sure of it. You can come home from college, back to the island for the holidays, the summers, when I do. We won't miss much time together," she finished.

We sat there for maybe another five minutes. I was thinking about everything she'd said. About the fishing, about an education, about her and me. Everything I was thinking led to making my home on this island - with her. I guess I made up my mind then, about college. And about her as well. I could see it all, clear. There wasn't going to be much room on this island for an uneducated off-islander, no matter how strong his back. It would be embarrassing for me to be a day laborer somewhere while I was married to the prettiest girl on the island. I could imagine the comments I'd hear, and more important, the ones she'd hear. I knew I had to get myself educated somehow. It wouldn't be fair to her to stay the way I was.

Too soon she said, "The sun's behind the island, that means it's almost four this time of year. We'd better head back." We rose, shook the sand from the afghan, folded it and clasping hands, left the place amongst the rocks. Every now and then as we walked up the beach, she'd lean up, nuzzle my chin and make some remark, sometimes teasing me, sometimes questioning me. Once she nipped my ear. I said then, "You've got to stop that, or we won't make Thanksgivin' dinner tomorrow." She answered, "You've got a lot longer than tomorrow to wait." But she didn't nibble on my ear anymore.

As we started up the bluff, at the first bend in the path a fox was standing. A vixen, beautiful. Big dark eyes looking at us. We froze. The fox stood there looking at us; we looked at her. We must have stood there, the three of us, for a half-minute or so. Then the vixen lowered her head and with a last look at us slowly entered a path in the bushes.

Chapter Eighteen
THANKSGIVING

We had dinner when we got back to the house, a modest dinner. We all pitched in and cleaned up, then went into the parlor with coffee. I mostly sat there at first and watched Eva and her parents joke around. Kid each other. Mrs. Stinsin was like a little girl when she and Eva began exchanging verbal jabs, good humor jabs, woman to woman jabs. Captain Stinsin got a kick out of watching them. So did I. Then they turned on him, kidding him with stories of his past misadventures; the time he'd been so short handed that he was fishing by himself. Sighting fish from the wheelhouse as best he could, then doing the sticking, kegging and everything by running around almost like a madman. While he was standing with the keg in his hands making ready to throw it over, the *Eva* had lurched when a sea caught her broadside and he had slipped into the gunwale, toppled, and gone overboard with the *Eva* in gear. Thankfully he'd gone over with the keg; had to hang onto it with a fish pulling on the other end of the line until a nearby boat got to him and he had let go of the keg and had to swim to the other boat and they fished him out. They turned and had caught up with the *Eva*, still steaming east, but by the time he was put aboard the *Eva* and turned her, the keg was nowhere to be seen. Washed up two days later on the beach below Mohegan Bluffs, line cut near the dart by sharks, the swordfish gone.

I guessed it hadn't been real funny when it happened. Not to any of the fisherman because they knew it could have been any of them, but they must have teased him mercilessly all the same. Probably the talk of the island for the winter, or until the next close-call story. They could laugh about it now, visualize it with humor because it turned out all right. But it hadn't been funny then. I knew the feeling.

Soon they got me laughing at Captain Stinsin, too. That was too much for him. He said to Eva, "Well, our good friend Hank, he knows a little bit more than the two of you 'bout it." They both looked at me. Waiting. I had little choice.

"I went over once this summer," I said, realizing for the first time that Captain Stinsin hadn't told them of my short sojourn in the waters of South Channel on my first day.

"Barely got wet," I said.

"He was soakin' when I got to 'im,"

"I was barely wet."

"Tell us what really happened. You weren't very much to talkin' when I got to you," he said. I decided to tell them.

"The fish rammed the dory, knocked me overboard. She was stuck in the boat. When I went over, I landed on 'er, just turned around and walked right back up 'er to the dory. Now, she weren't happy with it, but I weren't real happy with her neither. And I was almost dry when Captain Stinsin got there. He was gone out of sight when I got knocked over-board. Took him two hours to get back to me. He was just guessin' that I'd gone over."

I had expected them to laugh, but the women hadn't. It was not something in the distant past, it had happened in the season past. Too close for laughter. "Captain Stinsin," that's what Mrs. Stinsin called him when she wasn't pleased, "why didn't you tell me about that?" He'd gotten himself in it, so I wasn't going to be real quick to help him.

"There wasn't anything that had to be told. I didn't think he'd want it told. Knew he wouldn't want it told around town, overboard on your first trip. Didn't want to scare you, either. I 'membered how upset you got the time I went over. All it would have done was worry you, 'bout him, 'bout me. Weren't no reason it had to be told. You all know how dangerous this business is, don't want to be worryin' you more than needs be."

I chimed in, then, finally helping him, "Mrs. Stinsin, I never owned up to it. I never told him for sure that I'd been in the water, told 'im the fish had splashed me wet. I don't think he believed it none, but I never told him different. Far as he knew for sure, weren't nothin' to tell."

"Well if it ever happens again, I want to know," Mrs. Stinsin said.

"Me, too, daddy. You hear it don't you Hank. I want to know," Eva said.

We talked some more, then we all went out in the kitchen to help with the dinner for Thanksgiving day. They had a huge turkey, one

113

raised on the island, ready for baking. What looked like turnip greens to me, lots of them. There were four pies already sitting on the shelf over the stove. There was other stuff too. And there was a big bag of potatoes. I got the short straw again, by acclamation. Also got the instructions about thin pealing. We sat there I imagine for an hour or two. Working on the dinner. Then all of us got our jackets, went out back on the porch and watched the moon play with the stars. Around ten, Mrs. Stinsin said, "It's going to be a busy day tomorrow. Hank why don't you come over around ten or so, you can help. I'll probably need somebody to walk down to the store for the things I've forgotten. Already know that I forgot to get cranberries, I'm sure there's other things. Besides you'll need some time to work on your 'slicks', I'm really looking forward to some Maryland style eating."

"Yes, ma'am ."

Eva said, "I'll walk you to the road."

We stopped in the front yard under a bare oak tree. We just stood there for a minute, face to face, looking at each other. Then she said, "Thank you," stood on her toes and put her lips on mine like she had in her bedroom ten hours before, or was it just a second before, seemed a second. Again, I was shocked, felt an electric shock. She was gone, running in the house. I could hear her laughing.

I walked up the road, then turned left toward the Hill Top. Now I knew what happy was. I'd never been there before. This is what other people had lived for. I had arrived there. I was whistling, singing, I don't know what I wasn't doing as I walked up the road to my room. Got undressed. Never slept a wink.

I went over to the Stinsin house the next day at ten sharp, stopping by on the way at the only store that was open, bought three packages of cranberries. Got to the house, went in the kitchen and began the process of making 'slicks', rolling them out on the kitchen table, making them really thin, almost translucent, ready to drop in the pot later, shortly before dinner. By twelve I was finished with that part. Eva had wanted me around as the people began to arrive, so my being there early had fit into her plans.

The other guests began arriving around two o'clock. As they did, Eva always managed to be at my side introducing me as her friend. I had seen most of them around town during the summer and the fall, many of them at church. Had met some of them. The important thing, though, was that with Eva usually making the introductions an extra message was being conveyed. The rest of the day and evening when I would look around, I'd almost catch them examining me; I could imagine their thoughts, "He's not good enough for Eva. What's she see in him?" What they couldn't know was that I agreed with them. No-one was good enough for her. Not me, not anyone.

She was just different, she saw things inside people that they didn't know were there. Like me seeing things at sea that others looking at the same water didn't see, even though their eyesight might be better than mine. It was in knowing what to look for, the nuances, the little differences that made one piece of water different, and then the ability to read the messages of the difference. I could do it at sea, Eva did it with people. She saw the differences and read the messages. She saw 'things'.

Around two-thirty or so I returned to the kitchen, dumped the 'slicks' into the pot and stood there stirring them while they cooked, every now and then pausing to meet another friend or relative that Eva or Captain Stinsin would bring back in the kitchen for introductions. At times it got crowded with Mrs. Stinsin, usually Eva, a couple of ladies helping them, and me standing at the stove - stirring. At three Mrs. Stinsin started getting people positioned for dinner. She had set up a folding table in the kitchen for the children that were present and a card table in the parlor for some of the adults, the rest of us crowded around the dining room table where we were told to sit, an empty chair to my left and one at the end of the table opposite Captain Stinsin. Altogether, counting the empty chairs where Eva and Mrs. Stinsin would sit, there would be eight people on a table that sat six comfortably. The rest would be at the table in the parlor.

After everyone was relatively quiet, Captain Stinsin gave the blessing. Then Mrs. Stinsin brought the turkey in, a huge turkey, for Captain Stinsin to carve. And the dinner began.

There were probably three or four conversations going on simultaneously at any given time - in the parlor, the dining room, the children in the kitchen. When, however, someone would speak to me, ask a question, or ask others about me, I noticed there was an abrupt silence from the parlor and the dinning room - the kids kept on in the kitchen; they didn't have the curiosity of their parents. Before the dinner was over everyone knew that I was a fisherman from Maryland, had come up to try the swordfishing, had decided to winter over working with Captain Stinsin painting the Ocean View, was going to stay for the next fishing season at least. They also had probably figured out that a special relationship was fast developing between Eva and me.

And I was included in the raves over the food. Everyone loved my 'slicks'. But, I'd made a mistake. Sometimes, later in the year when I would see one of them I hadn't seen for a while, I'd be greeted by a "Hey slick, how you doing." Of course it was for the dumplings. I think. Could have been, now that I think of it, because I'd come up from down south and stolen a treasure.

The dinner broke up late, after ten actually. Clean up had been completed and the last guest left then. Except for me. I walked out back with Eva, stood on the porch looking out over the lights of the island and the lights of the sky - the stars.

"This was as perfect an evenin' as I can ever remember," I said as we stood there, side by side.

She put her arm around my waist, said "I know. It was really fun with everyone wondering about you. All night long, everywhere I looked, they were looking you up and down."

"I know they were. I'd catch 'em lookin' at me. Ever' time I did, they'd look away. Wonder what they're thinkin' now?"

"They're not thinking much, yet. It will take them some time to think about you, before they make up their minds. Here on the island the people withhold judgment until things happen upon which they can truly base a judgment. They're going to be waiting to see how you are, what you do in bad times, in storms and things. That's how a man is measured out here. How is he in the bad times. They'll wait on you. Then, there's me. They might be waiting to see how you treat me. They should be waiting to see how I treat you." She finished.

"Eva! Hank!" her mother spoke from the kitchen, "it's about time for all of us to go to bed, get some rest."

"We'll be right in, mama," Eva said, turning to me and giving me one of what I had started saying to myself was a 'kiss peck', said "What about tomorrow?"

"I'll be paintin' at the Ocean View with your daddy durin' the day. How about checkin' out the movies. They're still open, but this may be the last week. Don't know what's playin', don't know that it makes a difference if I'm with you."

"That's good for me. I don't care what's playing either. Pick me up at six thirty."

We went in the house then, I thanked Captain and Mrs. Stinsin for making me a part of their Thanksgiving, praised the meal and the whole day with them, said my goodbys, left and walked back to my room at the Hill Top.

We went to the movies the next night, played cards afterwards with her parents, then spent Saturday afternoon together just walking up and down the island, talking about everything that young people in love talk about. She told me that she would arrange to get college application forms for me and we'd fill them out together at Christmas. Saturday evening we went to a small party at one of her friend's house. A party I would have called tame in another time, the time before Block Island. A party that the parents joined, stayed home and were a part of. Games and things. Me, generally making a fool of myself, not caring that I was the butt sometimes because it was only when Eva put me there. She would laugh at you, but only after she got you laughing at yourself; then you didn't mind. As I dropped her off at her house around eleven, she said,

"I want you to help daddy take me to Point Judith tomorrow to catch the bus back to school. We have to leave Old Harbor by ten."

"I wouldn't miss it," I said.

She then turned me directly to her, reached up and put her arms around my neck, bent my head down to her and kissed me; it wasn't just a peck. It was the full lipped, full body hugging, melting into one another kiss. A man reacting type kiss and I reacted. After a half minute or so, she pulled back slowly, all of her, from me. She was smiling, said, "You're excited. That's fine, I want you to be, but, remember what I said before 'you've got a lot longer to wait' for that. So do I. We need to know completely what we are together, then there will be a time for it. Lots of times for it." She rose on her toes, kissed my chin, turned and was gone back inside. I floated to my room at the Hill Top.

The next day Captain Stinsin, Mrs. Stinsin and I took her over to Point Judith to catch the bus. It wasn't as happy a time as the outward trip, but it was happy in a different way. We'd, she and I, made our place together. We'd met, so to speak, really met and worked it out. Realized we were in love, beginning a love, that thing that two people reach together if they're lucky.

For the first part of the boat trip she and I were up in the bow together, hand in hand, laughing, talking nonsense sometimes, sometimes not. Talking about the Christmas around the corner. Talking about the next summer. Sometimes talking about how intense our feelings were, how our emotions made us feel weak physically at the same time they seemed to strengthen us mentally. We talked about how different our lives had become in six months, the last three or four days particularly. Too soon we approached the Point Judith breakwater and we walked back to the wheelhouse so she could be with her parents.

We docked and the four of us walked to the head of the pier, to the street where the bus waited. She turned to her parents, thanked them, told them she loved them, and would miss them, kissed the both of them, then turned, I thought to get on the bus. Instead she stepped to me, and there in her parents' presence, embraced me, kissed me, and said "You be here when I get back." Red as a beet, I said "Yes'm." She turned again, stepped on the first step of the bus doorway, turned and blew us all a kiss and was swallowed up for a while as the bus began to move. Before it got to the corner, a window was thrown open and there she was, head out, waving as the bus disappeared from view.

Captain Stinsin had made arrangements to have the *Eva* hauled out on the marine railway at Point Judith. It took us several hours to help get her out, blocked up on the ways so she could get her hull scraped, repainted, get new zincs, have her through hull fittings checked and the like. After she was properly made ready for winter and the next season, she'd be stored, blocked up on the ways until the risk of ice was gone. Then we'd take her home for the next season.

After we had her secured on the ways, the three of us walked to the ferry dock to catch the last ferry for the island. On the trip home we sat together in the ferry's cabin. Captain Stinsin said just one sentence in the ride to the island. "Don't you hurt her." It wasn't a question. It didn't need an answer. Mrs. Stinsin smiled at me. She knew that hurting wasn't what anything was about. She knew I was putty being molded. She had done it to the Captain when they were young; knew Eva was doing it to me. Boy they were special - these Stinsin women. The both of them. From then on she smiled at me every time she saw me. Eva's happiness, my happiness, the Captain's happiness even, was her's as well.

I had never been very partial toward Christmas as a holiday. It had always been, up until now, the period when other people got things, were made happy. For me it had always been the time when contrasts were emphasized, differences reinforced; when you were reminded of your class, your station in life. But now all I could think of was how long it would be until she came back across the Sound, until she returned to our island, until she came back to me, until Christmas.

Chapter Nineteen

THE BOAT

On the first Friday afternoon after Eva went back to college we were quitting for the day, finishing with one of the guest rooms at the Ocean View. Each year some of the guest rooms would be painted, then the next year others, until on a rotating basis all of the rooms would be painted every six years. I asked Captain Stinsin what he was going to do on the weekend.

"Son, I ain't about affordin' all that work on the *Eva* to be done by somebody else. I got a deal with the yard, they just charge me for the haulin' out, and the blockin' 'er up on the stays. They let me do all the other work on 'er. I'll be goin' over there next two, three weekends to get 'er done. Sleep in the cabin, on the floor. It's cold, but I got a small kerosene heater keeps the cabin warm enough to get by."

"Whynt" you tell me you was goin' over to work on 'er." I said. "I can help. I been doin' it seems like all my life. Haul 'em out come fall, get 'em scraped, cleaned up, fixed up, then put 'em back in for the beginnin' of the sea bass in late March, early April, and the run of tinker mackerel in the first ten days of April. Ever' year same thing."

"I ain't said anything, Hank, cause there's no money in it. Ain't got no money for that kind of workin' on the boat. You're paid up when you get your share money. We's square then. The boat scrapin' and paintin' and such comes outta the boat money. That's one reason she gets a share."

"Where I come from," I explained, "ever'body 'spects to get the boat in order. You gonna work on 'er when she's fishin' and makin' money, you're 'posed to work on 'er when she ain't. "

"Well, that ain't how she is up 'ere," Captain Stinsin replied. "We do 'er different. Boat pays it. I save by doin' it myself."

"Look," I said then, "I ain't doin' nothin' on the weekends anyhow. You don't paint on weekends so I don't work then. It wouldn't cost me anything to go over there with you and get 'er fixed up, I ain't makin' anything on the weekends anyways."

"I can't ask you to do 'er."

"You ain't askin', I'm a askin'. You pay my ferry toll over and back, get Mrs. Stinsin to fix the same eats she fixes for you to take over and I'll be there. It's my boat, too. I got an interest in makin' sure she gets done up right. You're gettin' a little old, ain't sure I want to take a chance on you 'memberin' ever'thing needs 'membering."

The next day we rode the first ferry over to Point Judith and went to work scraping off the barnacles and other growth. Got her all scraped down the first day. Early Sunday morning we got the torches and went around and fired the worm holes, killing the sea worms that had gotten in her during the summer. They weren't near as bad up here in the colder water as they were down in Ocean City. Just a few here and there, but we had to crawl under the boat, up and down her to make sure we got all of them. Then we took a hose and washed her down. About one-thirty Captain Stinsin said, "Let's wrap 'er up now, need to catch the two o'clock ferry, so's we can get home and get cleaned up for evening services. We'll start the hull paintin' next weekend. The yard'd put the paint aboard 'er; I already paid it up."

I had wondered about church services. The Stinsins were as regular at church going as I'd ever seen and they'd gotten me started back. It was fitting in well with me, what I'd become now that I realized the opportunity that Eva had made, was making, for me. It was such an important part of her and her family, it had to become an important part of me.

We caught the ferry, got back in Old Harbor around three-thirty. I left Captain Stinsin at the lane to his house, went on up to my digs at the Hill Top. Later, after I had cleaned up, I got dressed in my musty dress clothes and met them at the seven o'clock services.

Chapter Twenty
THE DOLDRUMS

They call them the 'Horse Latitudes', the regions extending between the northern and southern trade winds of the seas of the world, an area of still winds and listless currents, sluggish activity, an area of stagnation. When Eva left for school the 'Horse Latitudes' moved north. At least that's the way I felt. All life had left the island, left my life, when Eva was gone. I became a robot, up in the morning, go to work painting, eat, home, sleep. Up again the next day. Everything important had left. Then I got her first letter asking me to be there for Thanksgiving and the breezes had blown again. When she returned to school, the doldrums returned. Until Monday evening a full week after she had left. The day after our first weekend working on the boat at the yard. That night when I got back to my room after work there was a letter from Eva.

"Dear Hank:
    I'm sitting here at my desk trying to study and all I can do is think of you. I figured that the only way I can clear my mind is to tell you that I love you. I miss you every day. In the morning I'm depressed because I know I won't be seeing you, that you won't be by picking up something for daddy, you won't be with me at Sunday dinner, we won't be walking down the beach, we won't be seeing the sun set at Southwest Point, that I can't kiss you. What makes me keep going is that I know it's just a few weeks and then I'll be able to tease you, hold you, and kiss you again.
    I want to thank you for a wonderful Thanksgiving. Everything was perfect. You fit in as if you'd been part of the family forever. Mama and daddy love you also, I think. Maybe like the son they never had. After me, mama couldn't have any more children so they showered everything on me. It's a wonder that I'm not spoiled. I'm not spoiled am I?

Do you miss me? What a funny question. Of course you do! I miss you, miss you, miss you.

Write and tell me what you're doing. Mama tells me that you're helping daddy with the boat over at the Point Judith yard. That's good. I love it that you get along so well with my parents and that they like you so much. It makes what's happening to us much easier for me, for you too.

I have to get back to my books, try again to study. Please don't think about me between seven and eleven in the evenings. That's when I'm usually studying. If you think of me at that time, I'll sense it and won't be able to study. You can think of me any other time. You know I don't mean that.

I can hardly wait until the holidays. Christmas on Block Island is beautiful. It will probably snow and when it does all the young folks get together, hitch up somebody's horses and go on sleigh rides, make bonfires in the snow, visit each other. I want to do all that with you, show you what it's like. But, I want other time with you. Time just for ourselves, time to wrap up and go on walks along the beach, sit by our special rocks and just talk. Well, not just talk. I want your arms around me; want to smell your Old Spice again. Want to make you blush. Want to be with you now that you're in love with me.

Think of me.

Love

Eva"

It took me three days to reply. To write the letter. The first thing I did was go on Tuesday's lunch break to the only place that sold books on the island that time of year and bought the biggest dictionary they had. Then I bought a book on grammar - the only one they had. It was by Strunk and somebody. When I showed up at the Ocean View after lunch, Captain Stinsin took one look at the books and asked, "Gonna do some writing?" I responded, "Might." That night when we walked home, Mrs. Stinsin was at the end of their path, waiting for the Captain and I imagine waiting to say hello to me. As we got there I said, "Evening Mrs. Stinsin." She said, "Evening Hank." The Captain said to her "Guess, who got a letter yesterday?" He had known when he saw the dictionary.

That night I began to painstakingly reply with the dictionary on my lap, the grammar book on the writing table in my room.

"Dear Eva:

I,too, was depressed until your letter arrived. I knew you'd be busy and wouldn't have much time to write during the first week or so. I knew it, but didn't want to believe it. So I sulked. Kept working, but I'm sure your daddy found me sullen - that's the word for when one sulks isn't it? Anyway, he saw a different me on Tuesday morning. The only thing I remember him saying all morning was that I couldn't sing a lick and he'd appreciate it if I could just hum, or whistle, or anything else.

That evening when we walked home from work, as he pealed off to go up to your house, your mother happened to be standing outside. He said to her, "Guess who just got a letter yesterday?" And boy, did your mother smile as she turned to walk with your father up to the porch.

Yeah, I am helping your father with the *Eva*. I figure it's my boat also. It carries me out and brings me back to you. Besides, I like your father very much and although he still does a man's full day's work and more, he can use the help. It's in the family, anyway, isn't it?

It's a little awkward, me writing. I have enough difficulty putting my thoughts into words when I'm talking, when I'm talking about us with you. I don't know all the flowery words a woman likes to hear and its not like I can ask your mama's advice, so I'll just do the best I can.

I miss you, I need you. The island is only half an island when you're not on it, and I'm only half a man when you're not with me.

I love you.

Hank"

The rest of the week we kept on painting at the Ocean View. Saturday morning we were on the early ferry to Point Judith. As the Captain had said the paint and such was aboard her. We got the first coat, the white primer, on her hull by noon, then worked patching the *Eva's* gunwales and the dory's and patching up other spots where nicks and gouges had marred the surface of the decks and the rails of the boats. Spliced wood into them, sometimes putty was enough. Slapped a prime coat on all the repairs. The next morning we put the second coat, the forest green finish coat, on the hull and I helped Captain Stinsin replace the zincs on the shafts. We made the two o'clock ferry. Then it was church again. And Monday rolled around. There was another letter waiting and this time I answered it by Wednesday.

The next Saturday we put a prime coat on the whole topsides of the *Eva,* then sanded her down Sunday morning. Caught the ferry back to the island, went to church, then home. Spent the next five days painting at the Ocean View, but I also had a letter to answer. Then it was up early Saturday morning for the ferry ride to Point Judith. We put a finish coat on her topsides. I climbed the mast with a bucket of red paint and painted it, and later the boom as well. Took the whole day and a half. The next weekend we painted the trim on her. Traced the name *Eva* in bright red paint on the green of the transom. We then put all the gear in the engine room, locked the hatch and left her there for the winter. We'd get the fishing gear in shape in the spring.

There were letters received and sent each week. I knew she'd be home the next week.

Captain Stinsin and I were finishing painting the kitchen walls at the Ocean View on the 18th of December when he turned to me, "Eva's gonna be home tomorrow." I responded, "I know." He said then, "Like you to go over on the ferry and fetch 'er, first ferry over in the morning. She'll be gettin' in on the bus at eleven-thirty. You can catch the three o'clock back. Hope you can do it, I need to be helpin' 'er mother get ready for 'er comin' home, gettin' Christmas decorations up, getting the tree from down near Satchem's Pond, haulin' it back and puttin' it in the livin' room and such, all 'fore Eva gets home."

"Captain," I said, "you know I'll be happy to go get 'er. Help 'er with 'er things over on the ferry. I was goin' to ask you to let me go with you."

"That's settled then," he said, "let's get cleaned up here; Mrs. Stinsin wants you to stop to the house for dinner. Guess she wants to fatten you up some. There's some kind of sayin' 'bout the 'fatted goose' gettin' kilt', that's you I think. When the women get finished."

At dinner that evening the conversation was all about Eva coming home. What wasn't about her was about me, or about the two of us. Mrs. Stinsin was really working on me and I didn't blame her. I knew where it looked as if Eva and I were heading, where I hoped we were heading, and both of them understood it. They needed reassurance.

"Hank," Mrs. Stinsin said eventually, "you come from down in Ocean City. It's a faster place than the island, especially the way we are in the winter. I don't know whether Eva told you or not, but we've been in contact with some of the people down there. They say you were pretty wild, fighting, womanizing and such."

I interrupted her then, "It's all true, Mrs. Stinsin. I ain't fixin' to lie on it. That's the way it was and that's the way I was. There was a bunch of us that did it, fightin', drinkin', the other stuff. It's all we did. Work, then in the bars partyin' and fightin', pickin' up women, and there was a new batch of women ever' week in the summer. I gotta own up to it. I've known you checked up on me. Eva told it."

"Then you know why I'm bringin' this up."

"Yes'm., I'd bring it up, too, ifin I was you. "

"I'm not worrying about Eva and you doing wrong things. I know her better than that. I know that you respect her for it. She's told me so. But, if the two of you go much further with your relationship you'll be heading toward a permanency. If you're going to change your mind, do it now. If it goes on and then doesn't work out, it may hurt her bad and she's all the Captain and I have, other than each other."

"Mrs. Stinsin, far as I'm concerned it's already headed there. I ain't never seen anything like 'er. Never seen myself this way. Half the time when I'm around 'er I'm like a puppy dog. I ain't gonna hurt 'er, couldn't. I'll tell you right out, I'm lovin' 'er, in love with 'er. She's got me where I'd do anything she wants. She's got me struck right down. She's taken the meanness out of me, she's even got to makin' me sweet, and that's somethin' not many's said 'bout me."

"She's got you right silly, that's for sure," Captain Stinsin interrupted, laughing.

"I think since I've been 'ere," I continued on, trying to ignore him, but noticing that Mrs. Stinsin was smiling, "I've stopped being a boy. Mrs. Stinsin, Captain, she's makin' a man of me. She's finishin' up the job. You all's helpin' with it, too. Didn't have no problem before with the physical part, or the fear part at sea, but, she's givin' me the feelin' part of bein' a man.

"I hope you can understand, I didn't get no raisin' like you've given Eva. Never had no support, don't 'member any of the lovin' like you all give 'er. I was fed and watered some, that's 'bout it. Ever'body just too busy for much more where I come from. We's, boys was anyway, 'spected to make our own way soon's possible. Think you can see that I got big early. I was fifteen, livin' on my own, half the time scared to death but couldn't show it. Weakness ain't what you want to be a showin' in them times, places. I took up with othern like me, I weren't the onlyest one put in that kind of life by circumstances, by where I come out of."

"Well, you haven't been living that kind of life since you've been on the island, even before you and Eva started seriously seeing each other?" she stated, as a question.

"Mrs. Stinsin, when I first came up, when I came over on the *Eva* that first time, I was a new man in a new port. I knew right off that I couldn't start out up 'ere like I left off down there. I probably would have been actin' right for a while anyway. But, I have to admit, heck, ma'am, I'm proud to admit that once I laid eyes on 'er that first night the Captain brought me 'ere, I ain't been the same. I thought somebody had hit me in the head with a hammer. I ain't 'ever been so surprised in my life. I couldn't even talk. I'd never seen anyone so pretty. When she smiled, I'd never seen anything like 'at either. And I never felt 'at way before. It was like she had me 'witched. If I ever go to hurtin' 'er, I'll throw my ownself in with 'em 'Bad Boys'."

Mrs. Stinsin smiled some more. It was clear that the Captain had told her of my run in with the makos. Then she said, simply, "I think we understand each other." "Yes'm, we do." I answered.

127

Chapter Twenty-One

CHRISTMAS

FERRY

I was on the eight o'clock ferry the next morning as she left Old Harbor. I hadn't eaten anything. Too nervous, too excited. It was cold, not bone numbing cold, brisk cold is the best way to describe it. I had a heavy parka on, one that I had also bought at the consignment shop. There weren't any new clothes stores open on the island in December. The consignment shop really hadn't been open either, but the owner was a local and when I explained my problem she had met me at the store and there was a used extra, extra large one that almost fit and was in good shape. I'd bought it.

Mrs. Stinsin had given me a coat for Eva. She had taken warm clothes back with her after Thanksgiving, but her mother wanted her to have something extra for the ferry ride so she had sent over one of the Captain's big heavy coats. It would be large for Eva. The Captain was a big man. Probably bigger than me and I was six feet three, two hundred and twenty pounds by now-give or take. The coat was so big I'd be able to just throw it over her like a tent.

The wind and the sea were calm. Down home we'd call it 'slick'. Mirror like almost. A little fog, just wisps of it, rising here and there where air and water temperature differences came into conflict. But there wasn't much and it just lie there on the water, just a foot or so off it, drifting here and there. Soon we were rounding the bluffs at the north end of the island and heading directly toward Point Judith. I noticed then that off in the distance rising above the mainland was a bank of darkening clouds signifying that a front was moving in.

I stayed outside, up on the bow for awhile, then went inside. I stayed there for the balance of the ride over. Eva wouldn't be there yet, so there was no need to be outside for that first clear glance of her. The bus wouldn't be there until eleven-thirty. I'd have a spell to calm myself. If I could.

Almost from the time we had rounded the north end of Block Island, I had noticed in the far distance that the hills and rises back from the coast of the mainland were snow covered. More than a dusting. We'd only gotten a dusting on the island, but they'd had the full course on the mainland. As we got closer the snow covered hills rising, gradually, to the west, with the framing effect of the darkening clouds behind them, added to the wintery beauty of the Point Judith harbor.

The ferry docked. I had a couple of hours, little more to wait. I left the Captain's coat in the ferry waiting area. Took a walk around the docks for a while, went back inside. I spent the next half hour reading Eva's letters. I'd brought them all - well worn from the reading. I looked outside. The sky had started 'spitting' snow, that's what we called it down home when a snow storm announces it approach by sending outrider flakes, enough to notice, but few enough that each individual flake could be followed to the ground, or past you if the wind was blowing. By now the breeze had picked up. Wasn't complete calm anymore, but still moderate. Didn't look like a lot of wind in the approaching clouds. They just came on, not swirling like high wind clouds. Just darkening as moisture-laden snow clouds do, looking ominous though, playing with us, trying to scare us, before they'd cloak our world in beauty.

About a quarter past eleven, I left the ferry terminal taking the Captain's coat with me, walked outside and down the street to where the bus stopped. I stood there waiting. It was getting colder all the time in the vanguard of the storm.

I heard it first, the bus gearing down as it approached the corner, then I could see it as it turned down the street. My heart was racing. I was short of breath. Almost dizzy in anticipation. The bus went by me by five or ten yards before it stopped. As it did, I saw her. At the front window, puckering her lips at me in a kiss.

I was half-way to the bus's door when it opened and she was on the sidewalk running to me. I barely had time to drop the Captain's coat before she was in my arms.

"Hank. Hank."was all she said at first. Just stood there on her toes, with her arms wrapped around me as far as they could go, the top of her head under my chin. I put my arms under her's, reached around and my hands met behind her back. I lifted her up some - off the ground; she turned her head to me and our lips were together. I almost dropped her. I was being 'shocked' again, my funny bone performing to its name. But then I just pulled her into me more, snuggling within an embrace. We stood there holding each other, kissing, then cheek to cheek. She put her hand up and pushed the hood of my parka off my head, leaned back, took my face in her hands, pulled me down and kissed me again, then stepped back looking into my eyes.

"I needed to do that. I had to make sure it was still there. Couldn't wait until later."

"It's there."

"Yes."

She reached down then, took both my hands, said "Come, the driver's getting my bag out." He was removing her big duffle bag from the underneath cargo compartment, saying as he did, "Here you are Miss Eva; it's been a pleasure having you on the bus, talking with you." It was clear that she'd make a friend of him. "I'll be looking for you after Christmas, have a good holiday," he finished as he turned to get back on the bus. "I'm hoping you'll be the driver then, Bill," she responded. Before she'd gotten on the bus in Kingston she'd never laid eyes on him. But in the hour ride she'd made a friend for life. That was just the way she was.

As the bus pulled away, we turned to each other again, the duffle bag at our feet, the Captain's coat still on the sidewalk several yards back up the road. She grabbed my hands and we just stood there for a moment.

"It's good to be home,"she said, "and it's more so because you're part of it."

"There's no where else I want to be." I responded.

"We've got a little wait, don't we?" she asked, "I guess the afternoon ferry still leaves at two o'clock."

"It's on winter schedule now, three o'clock," I responded, "I thought we'd have some lunch while we waited."

There was a restaurant down the street that had remained open after the end of the summer season. We were soon seated there and eating lobster rolls with fries and cole slaw, good cole slaw. There were other people sitting at the next table so we didn't talk about personal things, about us. She asked about her parents, how the painting jobs were going. Asking whether the Captain and I had finished with the *Eva,* how much snow we'd had on the island, whether there was enough for sledding. We tarried in the restaurant until just before the ferry was due to leave for the trip to the island.

I paid the check. As we left, I picked up her duffle where I had left it in the foyer of the restaurant. I hadn't noticed how heavy it was when I had carried it down the street I was so excited being with her. But it was heavy, made me grunt as I slung it over my shoulder and then held the outer door open for Eva. She laughed at my grunting, said "You've been getting weaker since I left you." As we stepped outside into the gathering snow storm, I answered, "No, I got weaker when you came back." That made her smile, made her radiate that special look into my soul. It said, if smiles could talk, "You please me."

The fire was there. Still. I had known it right away when she ran to me from the bus. As we got ourselves adjusted to how we were going to walk with each other to the ferry with me having the duffle on my shoulder, I thought for a moment that I didn't remember there ever having been a spark between the two of us. Just the fire. We weren't, and then we were. I knew it was something in her. I couldn't describe it, doubted that she could. But we both knew that she had the essence that made us, that changed our separate selves into a single entity. I'd never really known what people meant when they had said that two people were 'a thing'. But that's what we were, I guess. What we really were was a love story. Made one because we loved. Because she knew how to really love. Instinctively. In the best way. And she was teaching me.

As we walked out on the ferry dock, the clouds sent a white blanket of snow softly fluttering down to surround us in its beauty. We boarded, I put the duffle bag down at the front of the cabin and we grabbed a couple of seats where we could see out of the forward cabin's windshield. Within several minutes the deck hands were gathering the dock lines as the ferry eased out of the slip, took a turn to port and slowly made her way down the channel toward the opening in the breakwater. By the time we entered the sound the snow was falling much heavier. Darkening the sky more. Eva, grabbed me by the arm.

"Come on Hank. Let's go up on the bow and see if we can see the island."

"It's gonna be cold out there," I responded."

"I don't care. Are you my man, or not?" She asked, pulling harder on my arm, then releasing it and running to the hatchway and on out to the forward deck.

I rose, put my parka on, grabbed the Captain's coat and hurried after her. Up in the bow was a place, off to the side, where we could sit on a bench in the lee of a compartment, but still have visibility forward. She had stopped and sat down there. I joined her, taking the Captain's coat and wrapping and enclosing her in it. She reached over and grabbed my hand, and we huddled there side by side not speaking at first. Just sitting there in the falling snow. She broke the silence.

"Isn't it great that it's snowing. Now we'll have a Christmas that looks like it's supposed to and we'll have sleigh rides, you can make me a snow man. Have you ever made one?"

"I don't 'member any, but when I was really young maybe I did. I 'member snow ball fights, though, and puttin' snow down the necks of pretty girl's dresses. Sometimes even rubbin' it in their faces, if they were lookin' right."

"I'll tell you right now, Mr. Hank Gaskins, don't think you can get away with putting snow down my dress."

"You don't have a dress on. You're wearin' pants, actually jeans. Got no dress. 'Sides your sweater's so high necked probably couldn't get any snow down it anyhow."

"Been lookin' at my sweater?"

"Only while we were in the restaurant and you had your coat off and then only when you weren't lookin' at me, and that weren't often. 'Cept for that I ain't really seen much sweater, or what's in it either. Don't you worry none. I don't have to see you in a sweater to realize that you're fit for wearin' 'em. You learn a lot from huggin'," I said.

"Be careful, don't go where you don't want to."

"I won't. Question is not about what I want, but about what you want?"

"I want everything you want," she said as she reached over and pulled me to her by the sides of my hood, as close as we could get with my parka and her two coats between us. She kissed me, got me to kissing her, really kissing. She held my head as she pulled back, burnt her deep, deep blue eyes into mine, said "Everything you want in its

132

time." She held me there for several moments, our faces less than a foot apart, just looking at me. She knew that her condition, "in its time," was one I accepted, wanted really, I guess. I didn't want her to be like all the other women or girls I had met, had played with, had slept with even. It was just different with her. It would happen, but when it did it would be right. No sneaking out afterwards. Waking up wishing they were gone, or worse, waking up and wondering who the hell they were. I thought then for a second, held by her just inches away - that she was the light around which my life would revolve. All of the rest of it.

She then drew further away from me, but only to open up her father's coat, say to me,

"Get in here with me, there's room to snuggle. It's a big coat."

"Ask me again."

"Get in here!"

I did. She slipped her arm around my waist, I slipped mine over her's, down across her back. After another couple of minutes, she said, "It's getting warm, we'd better unbutton our coats, just keep daddy's buttoned." Soon we were all snuggled, touching contours, some. Chest to breasts really.

I guess we stayed that way for a half-hour or so, talking about us. She wanted to know how I'd made out waiting for Christmas. Talked about her school, that she was doing well, but that she was bored. That it was my fault. She hadn't been bored until I'd shown up on her island.

By now we were closing on the island. We could see the flash of North Light. We couldn't see the island itself clearly yet because of the snow, it manifested mostly as a darkening of a patch of the eastern sky. As the ferry closed with the island, started around the north end, the snow's effect in the waning sunless light of late afternoon, made it seem as if the bluff on the north end was looming out over the ferry, almost reaching above us as we sat on the bench. Eva reached up above her head as if to touch her island, pretending that it was welcoming her.

In another ten minutes we had rounded the north end and were running down the east side of the island toward Old Harbor. The snow let up some, just for a moment. We rose then, went to the starboard side still encased in the Captain's buttoned coat and leaned on the gunwale,

I did anyway. She leaned on me. She pointed out a place at the very north end of Crescent Beach, back up against Clay Head bluff,

"I went to my first beach party there," she said, pointing. "I was in the ninth grade. I still remember how neat it was to have a fire, roast marshmallows, hot dogs. Make hot chocolate in a pot of water over the fire. Then, later, we sat around on blankets, talked and sang, looked at the sky and moon, tried to find the planets. John Decker tried to kiss me. I didn't like him, but it didn't make any difference. I wasn't into kissing boys. I was waiting, I guess. I've kissed one or two since then," she continued, "but nothing else, no kissing either like we kiss. I've been waiting. How long can you wait?"

"'Til the time is right, whenever it is." I said.

"What about hoping?" she teased.

"Now, tomorrow, next Christmas even. I hope for all of it ever' day. But, hopin' aside, waitin' ain't any problem long's it's you I'm waitin' for. I love you." I finished. She turned into me, laid her head on my shoulder, squeezed me harder. "I know," she said, as she made me look down into her eyes. It was an exquisite time. Snow fluttering into the opening of the Captain's coat, on her shoulders, in her hair, falling between us, and then one big flake fell right on the end of her nose. I licked it. She pushed me away, laughing.

By then we were approaching the entrance to Old Harbor and soon the ferry was being secured in her slip. It was close to being dark out, the days were so short now and the snow was falling even heavier. We went into the cabin where I picked up her duffle bag and with the Captain's coat wrapped around her we walked off the dock toward Water Street. As we got there I started to guide her to Dodge Street, so we could hook up with Old Town Road. She pulled away a little.

"Let's go to my place on the beach, there by the rock under the Ocean View bluff. Just for a little while, a couple of minutes."

"What about your parents, won't they be worried? They probably saw the ferry comin' 'round the north bluffs."

"Not with this snow. It wouldn't make any difference if they had seen the ferry. I'd still be wanting to have a few minutes just with you at our special place. Just the two of us. If they ask anything, I'll tell them. It will be alright. We won't stay long. It's where we had our first real talk, when afterwards I knew that I loved you. It's the first place I want to be."

We walked to the south down Water street. At the circle we went on up the road onto the Ocean View property, then past it to the bluff by the sea. By this time the duffle bag was beginning to put a licking on me. When we got to the top of the bluff, no-one was around and I plopped it down, saying "Don't 'spect anyone be stumblin' on your bag. Ain't no use to carryin' down what's gonna need carryin' right back up." She smiled, said "Don't want you to strain yourself any."

I picked it right back up, put it on my shoulder and began manhandling it down the path to the beach. When I got to the bottom, she said "Why don't you leave it here?"

"I'll carry 'er right on." I responded. She laughed.

Soon we were at the rock where we had sat at Thanksgiving. It was almost full dark now, with a slight breeze blowing snow, lots of snow, in off the ocean. There was only a small shore break coming in off the ocean, maybe a foot, probably less. Some snow had already accumulated at our spot. She told me then "Put the duffle bag down. Spread out daddy's coat so we'll have something to sit on, put the duffle bag at the top of the coat and we can lean against it."

We sat down, arms around each other, getting a little colder in the slight breeze blowing in. She spoke.

"Let's lie down."

We did, and as we settled she unbuttoned my parka, then her coat, then rose and laid on me. I could feel her body from her knees to her lips. She kissed me, pressed into me. Her hips pressing, her breasts pressing, her legs straddling one of mine. We kissed for what seemed like five minutes. As soon as she had laid on me, I had gotten excited like a man gets and was showing it like a man does. So she was learning about my body, too. Not just my shoulders, my arms, but all of it. She pulled back a little, raised up on her arms until the first place where we were touching was at our chest level. She looked into my eyes, said, "Don't tease me about my sweaters anymore. You know what's in them now, you don't have to imagine much. Now, let's get on home."

With that she rolled away and sat up, laughing a little. But the kind of laugh where you know she's laughing for both of you. That was a special secret she had. She could laugh for two people, a group of people even, making it so it wasn't anyone being laughed at. I sat up then. We brushed the snow off each other, stood, she draped the Captain's coat around her and I hoisted the duffle bag on my shoulder. We walked down the beach to the path. She walked, I struggled, up the bluff. In fifteen minutes we had made it back to Old Town Road. Another five and we were at the house.

As we went up the steps the front door opened and Mrs. Stinsin rushed out with her arms open; Captain Stinsin stood in the doorway. Mrs. Stinsin and Eva hugged for what seemed like five minutes. Just stood there arms around each other, squeezing. After a bit, Captain Stinsin cleared his throat, loudly. Eva stood back a little from her mother, laughed at her father's obvious attempt to get her attention, then rushed to his open arms. As she did, Mrs. Stinsin looked at me and smiled. Eva was home and when she was there the whole world changed for everyone around her, for everyone she loved. She brought happiness. It's what she did, maybe her purpose in life, to bring happiness to anyone in her sphere, within reach of her personality. I made up my mind standing there on the porch that I would make her happy. That I'd repay her for all the joy she carried with her to dispense where it was needed, where it was wanted.

Her father took her by the arms, stood her an arm's length away, said, "It's Christmas now you're home. Let's ever'body get on inside, want you to see the tree I fixed up, well your mother and me really."

We walked on in the parlor, Eva saying "It's beautiful," when she saw the tree. I said then, "I'll take 'er bags on upstairs." I went on up and put her bag under the window where I'd put it when she came home at Thanksgiving. As I returned through the doorway she was there. Standing with that smile. We hugged and kissed at the top of the stairs. Getting a start on Christmas.

As soon as we were back downstairs she was on the phone making the arrangements for a sleigh ride on Christmas Eve. Calling around amongst the young people, the friends around her age, getting up a group of four or five couples. She promised that she'd do the fire preparations up the beach by Ball's North Point, up under the bluffs, but where Old Harbor could still be seen in the distance down Crescent Beach. By the time she finished the arrangements, dinner was on the table.

We ate, talking some, mostly about her. How was the school year going? She was getting straight A s, naturally. All of her professors were great, she liked them all, they liked her. How could they not, I thought to myself? She just worked her magic on them like she worked it on me, on everybody. It was impossible to really know her and not like her, love her even. She brightened up everything and everybody.

She and her mother talked a lot about the Christmas preparations, getting ready for Christmas day, finishing up the decorations. They were talking constantly about whatever it is that women love to do at holidays. The Captain and I just sat there listening. He knew when men were surplusage and I was learning fast. There were woman things that were going to be done that didn't need our help and, moreover, stuff we'd better stay out of - just find a corner somewhere, a figurative corner, look into it and keep our mouths shut. That's exactly what we did. Just let them go, half the time I couldn't make much sense of it, but that made no difference. The two of them were almost delirious with happiness that they were together doing what women do at Christmas. It made us, the Captain and me, happy just to see them so happy.

Occasionally, they'd interrupt themselves to fill us in on their plans for the two of us. The first thing they told us was that we were expected to take the pickup down to the area around Fresh Pond, find some dead-fall timber that had been down long enough to get seasoned, cut it up and take it up to Ball's North Point and stack it for the Christmas Eve sleigh ride and bonfire Eva had already planned. Later they paused again to make sure we understood that I was expected to spend Christmas Eve at their house so that I could be there first thing in the morning to see Eva with her presents. Mrs. Stinsin said then, "She's never changed; she comes down those stairs just like she did when she was six. You need to be here to see it. You'll know then what she was like when she was just a little girl."

I didn't have any problem with it. I agreed with everything. Thought then that Eva was turning me into an agreeable person, generally.

A little later Eva and her mother went into the kitchen, cleaning up I guess. Captain Stinsin and I stayed at the table for another moment. He turned to me when they were in the kitchen, said, "Might's well get on up to fresh pond tomorrow mornin', get 'er done. Gonna take the better part of a day." I responded, "Captain, whynt we make it day after, I need to be goin' back to Point Judith tomorrow. Won't be back 'til the last ferry. I need to get to Galilee, got some gifts to be a gettin'. Day after we can get the wood." He responded. "That's good."

It wasn't much later when Eva came out of the kitchen, announcing that she was tired. She'd had a long day with the bus ride, then the ferry ride, the rest of it. She went to her daddy, gave him a kiss on his forehead, said, "Night daddy, I love you." She came past me, paused, gave my forehead the same attention, said. "Night Hank." With that she went on upstairs; the Captain and I went in the kitchen and helped Mrs. Stinsin finish the cleaning up. I was getting good at washing dishes. Peeling potatoes and washing dishes was what my special skill was in the kitchen, that and making 'slicks'.

It was a half-hour or so before we were finished and we all went out in the parlor. As we started to talk, Mrs. Stinsin excused herself, said, "Let me go up and check that Eva closed her door. She's really tired and I want to make sure we don't awaken her." In a minute she was back down, saying "She's sound asleep already. Has a big smile on her face. She'd closed her door, I opened it to make sure she was sleeping and then closed it again. As long as we don't talk to loud we won't awaken her."

We sat around talking, mostly about Eva, them telling me things from her childhood, her early and mid-teen years. Some of them of the insightfulness she'd always had beyond her years. Me telling them of how she appeared to someone from off-island. After a while I began telling them of how I felt about her, how she was affecting me. How she was so extraordinary. How special she was. Eventually, I got up my nerve and came right out and said,

"I'd like your permission to ask her to marry me, not necessarily before she's out of college, but when she graduates and comes home. I mean I'll do the askin' now ifin I have your permission, I want to do it Christmas mornin', just won't plan to get married afore she graduates less she wants it sooner, that's ifin its okay with you for me to ask her and ifin she says yes, and ifin she agrees to wait 'til then.

"I might be goin' off to college, too, she's goin' to help me apply. She's brought the application forms home with her. But, I'd be back each summer for the swordfishin' with you 'til I graduate. I plan to make our home here permanent if she'll have me.

"Captain, that's why I can't go do the firewood tomorrow. Planned to go over to Point Judith on the first ferry in the mornin', catch a cab up to Galilee, they got a jewelry store there. I was a hoping that you could get me one of her rings so I'd know the size. I'll be buyin' an engagement ring so in case she says yes, I can put it on her finger right away."

"Hank," Captain Stinsin said, "what're you gonna do ifin I say, we say, no."

"Captain, I ain't gonna lie. I'll be askin' anyway. I can't help it. I'd do 'er anyways, but, its important to me for you and Mrs. Stinsin to approve of me. Approve of us. I ain't always gonna be poor. I'll be movin' up, gettin' an education, gettin' in business, whatever. I'm smart 'nough, and the onlyest thing I'm afraid of in this whole world is 'er. I love 'er so much it scares me."

"Just wanted to know how much you loved 'er," Captain Stinsin said, "and you've answered it. If you'd challenge me on it, you'd be lovin' 'er all there is. Ain't worryin' 'bout you makin' it, either. I weren't worth nothin' till Rebecca turned me into a man. Eva's already done it with you. Mrs. Stinsin and I have already talked it over, knew it was comin'. Don't worry none, we're glad you're gonna be doin' the askin' and we're hopin' she'll be sayin' yes. She's like her mother, needs a real man." Mrs. Stinsin rose, came toward me. I stood up as she got closer, she hugged me then, said, "Thank you for doing right when you're with her. Treating her like you do. You're already a part of this family."

I thanked both of them, then asked if it was okay if I proposed to her on Christmas morning in their presence. I told them that she was different. That most girls probably wanted to be proposed to in some fancy place, but that I thought it would mean more to her if I shared it with her parents because she loved them so much. They agreed, promised to keep my plans secret until Christmas morning. Even agreed to tell a story for me, a little fib about the next day. Captain Stinsin would tell her that he'd sent me over to pick up a part for the *Eva* that had come in at the marine supply store. That would explain why I wasn't around until dinner time. She might be a little upset when I wasn't there, but if it was for her daddy, or her mommy, I'd be forgiven. I left then, walked up the hill in the heavy snow to my room at the Hill Top.

Chapter Twenty-Two
SHOPPING

I went over to Galilee the next day. Mrs. Stinsin had managed to get one of Eva's rings for me before I left the night before. It was just a matter of finding the ring I thought was right for her, one I could afford. I still hadn't had to touch the swordfishing money; I'd been able to take care of my expenses with the painting money and still had some of it left over.

I spent almost five hundred dollars on the ring. That was a lot of money then. While I was in Galilee I also bought presents for Captain and Mrs. Stinsin, and a bottle of Wild Turkey for Leatherby. I figured he might not have anybody paying attention to him over the holidays and Christmas isn't the time for an drunk to stop drinking. A dangerous time for a man like Leatherby to be sober.

The next day Captain Stinsin and I went down to the area they called "Fresh Pond" and "Peckham Pond," where there were still some fairly overgrown and sort of wild lands. The ponds themselves were freshwater ponds and were in an area where some of the early European settlers had lived for a while in caves. On the west side of the ponds were some wood lots, thickets and such and it was there we went to find dead-falls. We located several downed trees, one would be more than enough to get a bonfire load of wood; besides a pickup only holds so much and the road back into the wood-lot was drifted over in snow banks making it a little difficult to move around. At the same time the ground underneath the snow wasn't frozen hard yet, was a little soft and Captain Stinsin didn't want to overload the truck for fear it would get stuck.

It took us two or three hours to cut the trunk of the tree in fire acceptable sizes. Captain Stinsin scraped the snow off the tree he selected as being properly seasoned, then got atop the tree with a broad-head axe, stood legs apart up the length of the tree and struck the trunk at a point between his outstretched feet. When he was almost through the tree with his cut, he'd climb down and in two or three blows from the ground he'd finish and the piece he'd just cut off would fall on the ground. Then he'd climb back up on the trunk to begin the next cut. In the meantime I split the pieces of wood. We'd brought an iron wedge and a sixteen pound sledge to use in the splitting. With the Captain cutting and me splitting we managed to get the load by around one o'clock. It then took us a half-hour to load the truck; we weren't in any particular hurry. Captain Stinsin had said when we first left the house in the morning,

"Look now, Hank, we don't want to be too 'ficient doin' this firewood business. 'Member, its Christmas time; that's a dang good time not to be around the women no more then necessary, 'til well after dark. When they get the men in sight at Christmas it makes their minds get to racin' 'bout what they can get us to doin' just 'cause we're 'round. Five minutes afore we walk in the house they ain't been thinkin' 'bout one thing needs doin'; soon's we show up 'ere it comes, one thing after 'nother. Ifin we go back too soon we'll be makin' their minds work too hard on it. Gets 'em tired sometimes. We need to take it easy on 'em, stay 'way long's we can."

I didn't reply. I really wouldn't mine it if Eva was telling me what to do; that would mean I'd be around her more. Could see her more. Hear her more, even if Captain Stinsin considered it nagging. But, Captain Stinsin was on my side, on our side really; didn't want to get on his wrong one, so I just nodded that it was okay with me.

Once we got the truck out on the main road where the snow had not drifted as much as it had in some places in the trees, Captain Stinsin drove us on back to the north part of the island. On the way he took a little detour to what we'd call a country store back home. I had seen it passing by but hadn't been in it. We parked the truck outside, its curb side wheels in a snow bank and the road side sticking out. Most everybody parked the same way once the snow came. As we went in, I noticed a potbelly iron stove glowing red in the middle of the store, with several seats, crates, barrels and the like around it. There were three or four men sitting around the fire.

"Hank," Captain Stinsin said loud enough for everyone to hear, "this is where island men come to discuss how to change the world; least we like to think that's why we come 'ere. Truth is, the women don't generally bother us 'ere, leave us alone 'less its an emergency. Its one of 'em un-put down laws and such. Ever' town in the world got a place like this. Where men can hide when the women starts workin' on 'em. 'Bout time you find out where she is on the island.

"Boys," he said then to the men sittin' 'round the stove, "this 'ere's Hank. You seen 'im 'round the island since spring. He's been workin' with me on the boat; turned 'im into a 'sticker' some and he's one of 'em that's got 'bility to see things need seein' when you out there. Ain't brought 'im in before 'cause I didn't know how long he'd be 'round. He's gotten sweet, he has, on Eva. Stayed 'round longer any summer hand I ever had. He's visitin' at the house lots; thought he might need to know 'bout this place."

With that he introduced me to the men around the table, then to the storekeeper and his wife. I'd been seeing them in church every Sunday so I was familiar with them, and vice-versa. The man sort of gave me a wave of acknowledgment, the wife gave me a big smile. It's what you get from church going folks when you join them. We ordered a couple of sandwiches and some hot coffee.

We stayed there for a bit, killing time. Captain Stinsin and the others talked mostly. I mainly listened, only speaking up when their conversation needed me in it. All of the men were swordfishermen and most of the conversation centered around the experiences of the last season and the hopes for the next. Of course, the Captain had to tell them of my first day at it, when I took a wet walk on a swordfish. Later on he added the 'bad boys' episode. But he put in a lot of complimentary stuff also, a lot of it I hadn't heard him speak of before. Then I realized what he was doing. He was, in a way of speaking, paying my initiation fees into an exclusive fraternity. With his stories of me, delivered with the humor of men of the sea, he was letting them know that I was good enough to be one of them. That, like all of them, I didn't have much run in me.

I understood why it was now, why it hadn't happened before, why it might not ever have happened. He knew that my relationship with his daughter was going to keep me around forever. That I wasn't going to be just another itinerant fisherman passing up and down the coast, fishing out of this island one year, someplace else the next. I wasn't the fishing world's version of a traveling salesman. In other words, as far as Captain Stinsin was concerned, I had finally arrived.

Around three or so, we stood to leave. All of the men rose, shook my hand and in one way or another welcomed me to winter on Block Island.

It took us only about fifteen minutes to make our way out Corn Neck Road to where the north end of Crescent Beach met with the bluffs the Captain called 'Clay Head' at Ball's North Point. It was this area that Eva had pointed out two days prior when she and I were standing at the starboard rail looking at the island as the ferry made for Old Harbor.

"This is just 'bout it," Captain Stinsin said as he pulled the truck off the road as far as he could without risking getting stuck. "We got us a right smart carry to get it where Eva wants it. Know right where it is, brought her out to the place one time when she was in high school. Rebecca chaperoned it. They made me go home right after I brought all the food and drinks out 'ere in the truck. Rebecca said weren't nobody goin' to have any fun ifin I stayed. She said she was more understandin' 'bout things like 'at. She's right, too. Later when Rebecca told me that the Decker boy tried to kiss Eva, I almost go out of bed and went over to beat up on his old man. Never liked 'im anyways. Took Rebecca a spell of time to get me calmed down. She said, 'Look at 'er, Will. There hasn't been anything as pretty as 'er on this island in mem'ry. She's 'most a replica of the famous mystery woman, the one in the white dress whose name no-one knows, the one in the picture. Our daughter is so beautiful something would be seriously wrong with the boys on this island if they didn't want to kiss 'er. You're just goin' have to accept it. You know as well as I do that Eva controls things. There's never been anything she hasn't controlled. Usens 'cluded. We've raised her right and that's all we can do.' She was right. She's most always right. One thing 'bout the two of us boy, ifin Eva says yes come Christmas mornin', the both of us is goin' to be hooked up with righteous women. And I ain't talkin' church stuff either, though they be righteous that way, too. You're goin' be findin' that you ain't winnin' any discussions much as you think you should be - just go to waitin'. Waitin' ain't goin' change whose right, waitin' makes it easier 'cause most of the time they's right. 'Em two just knows what no mens ever know. Eva's just like her mother, they seem to know what's goin' on afore it's goin' on."

With that we each grabbed a double armful of wood, headed over the dunes, down on the beach, then up it a couple of hundred yards to a small cut in the bluff right where the dunes and beach met the rise. There were several charred pieces of wood sticking out of the snow in the middle of the area. It was obvious that this was a place where bonfires had been built before. We spent another hour carrying the wood from the truck and on up the beach. We had placed the firewood to the side of the area as we stacked it. I asked him then, "Captain, we ain't goin' be up 'ere with our bunch 'til Christmas Eve, what's gonna keep 'other gang from burnin' up this wood? We worked pretty hard on it today, don't want wrong ones usin' the wood?" "Don't worry none on it." He replied, "This 'ere's Block Island, ain't nobody but locals 'ere this time of the year. Ifin some locals want to build a fire 'ere, they's bring their own wood. Wouldn't use this bunch 'cause it ain't theirs. You can count on 'er. Ain't hardly ever any stealin' on this place. Out 'ere by ourselves in the ocean, sometimes iced in for considerable, can't be havin' any thieves, place ain't big 'nough to tolerate it. That wood she'll be 'ere."

Chapter Twenty-Three
CHRISTMAS EVE

It snowed overnight the night before Christmas Eve. There were maybe eight inches of new snow on top of the ten inches that had fallen during the snowstorm that started when Eva and I had arrived several nights before. Plenty of snow for a sleigh ride. Everything was to start early so all of us could get back at a decent hour. I'd gone over to Eva's at five, the time I was told. I had taken a ditty bag, a bag of gifts, and a change of clothes for the morning.

I had been assigned the job of procuring the hot dogs and fixings, marshmallows and hot chocolate powder. Captain Stinsin had lent us one of his big thermos bottles which we filled with milk to use to make the hot chocolate. Other young people were responsible for the other drinks and the utensils, wire coat hangers for the hot dogs and marshmallows, a pot for the hot drinks.

It was already dark. We were outside waiting and in a little while we could hear the noise of laughing people mixed in with the clip-clop of shod horses' feet on the hard packed snow beneath the fresh snow of the night before. Around the corner came this huge sled pulled by two dray horses. The sleigh was really a modified long bed farm wagon whose wheels had been replaced with runners. There was a two foot high plank rail around the edge of the wagon. The bed was filled with straw, lots of straw, and in it lounged several couples. The driver had a girl snuggled up to him, all of them were wearing heavy coats, scarves and such, wool hats pulled down over their ears. There were openings amongst the outer wear from whence steam from their breaths was rising. Shiny, red cheeked faces peaked out of the clothes, happy faces, Christmas Eve faces.

We loaded our things, including two blankets Mrs. Stinsin had insisted we take, on the wagon bed, as Eva introduced me to ones I hadn't met and soon we were heading off for the north end of Crescent beach. As Old Town Road merged into Corn Neck Road the driver turned the horses to the first opening that allowed the sleigh to go down on the beach itself.

Everybody snuggled to keep warm, most of the couples turned to the ocean as the sleigh made its way north along the beach. Eva had made a place for us in the straw, burrowed down in it until we were buried almost up to our armpits. A bright moon had come up over the ocean; the air was crisp, brisk, a wind blowing down from the north. Wouldn't be long before another storm would move in. We just sat in the wagon listening to everyone talking. Then Eva said, "Let's sing carols." It's what she wanted, it's what we did for the balance of the trip up to Clay Head bluffs to where the firewood was stacked. Captain Stinsin had been correct. It hadn't been bothered.

We got all the stuff unloaded. The other guys and I went to work on trying to get a fire started. We'd had to scrape the snow of the night before off the wood initially, now we were trying to get the fire started with nothing but matches and a little kindling ripped from the pieces of split firewood. The wind was swirling around the headland to the north, sort of being sucked into the little alcove in the side of the bluff where we were. Every time we thought we had it lit, the wind would blow it out. Soon the women were teasing us about our shortcomings in the fire making department. Then Eva was there, "Let me have the matches." She said. Somebody handed her the matches and the wind stopped blowing. The fire caught, she said to us, "Think you great big men can keep it going."

In ten minutes there was a roaring fire there at the base of the bluff. The wagon and the horses were off to the side, still in the glow of the fire-within its realm of warmth. We had put horse blankets on both of them and had put their feed bags on. They stood there as silent observers, just stamping a hoof every now and then. Around the fire were the couples, sitting mostly, wrapped in blankets and quilts, arms around each other, singing. At first we went through their repertoire of Christmas carols.

I was thinking as we sat there for an hour, singing, how different it was here with Eva. I'd never sung a Christmas carol before, except in school. Later as I got older, moved out on my own after my mother was killed, Christmas was just a time for partying, hell raising really, drinking, whatever. But now I was sitting on a blanket on a snow covered beach on an island off the coast of Rhode Island in a group of couples, couples in love, all of whom were compatible with the others, just enjoying each other's company. They had readily accepted me; it

146

was "Hank," this, "Hank," that, "what do you think, Hank?" It was like I'd lived there all my life. It was the way life should be, not the way it had often been for me.

I knew I owed it to her, to Eva. I was with her; that's all the rest needed to know, all they wanted to know. I think maybe that she was their treasure, also, as I knew she was mine. They naturally deferred to her. The girls, too, which was harder to understand. They all loved her. We all did. She was the center of attention, the organizer. She just was it.

After an hour, Eva spoke, "It's time, I think, that we get some hot chocolate in us before we freeze, except that before we do, I want to hear Joey sing "Danny Boy."

With that every body clapped and urged the man that had been introduced to me as Joe Murphy to sing. From the blanket where he and a pretty girl were huddled came this clear melodious voice, a tenor I guess it was, almost at times soprano -like, singing "Danny Boy." When he finished the song the rest urged him on and all of them sang along with him. I mouthed the words as best I could. I caught Eva out of the corner of her eyes looking at me, smiling. After Danny Boy, Joe started right in with another popular song and then another. Often one or more of them would sing along with him.

Soon they stopped singing, pausing, then Eva held her hand up for a moment and they all looked at her. It grew quiet except for the crackling of the fire, the sound of the waves on the beach and the soft whispers of the wind. She started reciting a poem. A poem that probably applied to all of the couples there; I know it did for us.

> "'My true-love hath my heart, and I have his,
> By just exchange one for another given:
> I hold his dear, and mine he cannot miss,
> There never was a better bargain driven:
> > My true-love hath my heart, and I have his
>
> "His heart in me keeps him and me in one,
> My heart in him his thoughts and senses guides:
> He loves my heart, for once it was his own,
> I cherish his because in me it bides:
> > My true love hath my heart, and I have his.'

That's a poem I learned especially for Hank." She said. "It's by a poet named Sidney. I think he knew what love is about. It's a poem I give to Hank, but I give it to all of you, also." She said, and then continued, "Isn't it wonderful that all of us can be together here on Christmas Eve. My toast, our toast, should be, 'to love'."

They all clapped, several came over and just touched her, some not even talking to her, just wanting to be a part of what she was. After a time, she leaned over and up, and kissed me in front of them all, lingered there for a while, then raised her lips to my ears, said, loud enough for them to hear, "My man - get the hot chocolate going before I start to freeze and have to do something silly like hugging you for hours just to keep warm." Everybody laughed, me too. Before long we were drinking hot chocolate, eating hot dogs smeared with mustard, getting the mustard all over everything which, now that I think about it, is one of it's characteristics. Messy stuff, mustard.

A little later we started roasting marshmallows. Before long it turned into a hot marshmallow battle. It started when Eva took a hot marshmallow and pushed it over my nose. Burned me almost, stayed there on the end of my nose with the white liquid dripping into my lap. Soon I had wrestled her down, smearing a marshmallow, just a warm one, all over her face. After a bit, she sat up abruptly, said to me, "Want to lick it off?" I did and I did. She burst out laughing. It was a trap she'd laid for me. She had realized that in the confusion she had pressed her face in the snow and had gotten beneath it into the sand and that the marshmallow mess was loaded with sand that was now firmly mired in and on my tongue. There was no way to win over her, but you always won with her. She was too quick to out wit, but she used her quickness to bind you to her, so you won in the end. And she knew it. It was just the way she'd been made.

By nine-thirty we'd cleaned up at the bonfire and were heading back south along the beach. At Beach Avenue the driver cut across a low spot on the dunes and we rode up the avenue until we got to Center Road. At that point we paused and looked over to the mainland; there miles and miles away we could see the lights rising up the hills back of Point Judith. The moon was higher in the sky now and we could see it, its reflections on the water, and the painting it was doing on the island before us and on the mainland behind. I leaned over to Eva, almost hidden again in the straw, said carefully, I was already trying to improve my way of speaking, "Isn't it beautiful?" She answered, "Yes. And it's special. It's never been this beautiful, the night, the evening, Christmas Eve. You know, I love you." I answered, "To be honest, I know you do, but I don't know why. I don't deserve it. When I truly think on it, I almost can't believe that you love me. I'm just a rough fisherman that got run out of the town he comes from, ends up 'ere, finds you, and you take him. Honest, it doesn't make much sense. And I don't know whether I need to know the whys." She answered, "I give to you the why. Love just is."

Chapter Twenty-Four

THE NIGHT BEFORE CHRISTMAS

We were arm in arm as we walked into the parlor of the Stinsin house. Captain Stinsin and Mrs. Stinsin were still up. As soon as we had taken our coats off in the foyer, leaving the blankets there also as they were damp from the snow, Mrs. Stinsin said, "You've gotten back in time for one of my toddies."

Eva answered, "I was hoping you'd have them. Hank this is one of the few times you'll see my parents drink, when mama makes hot toddies with rum on Christmas Eve. The only other time is on the real, real cold days when daddy's been working outside. Sit down here with daddy while I help Mama."

"Wait a minute," Captain Stinsin said, "what's wrong with your face?" With that he looked at me, "What's wrong with Hank's nose? It's all red on the end."

We hurried to the mirror in the dinning room. The end of my nose was as red as a beet where the hot marshmallow had burned it. Eva's face was a mess; the melted marshmallow was mixed with some mustard she gotten on her face and the mix was stuck everywhere, sand and all. Even in her hair. We were a mess. We looked at each other's reflection in the mirror and started laughing at ourselves, almost hysterical laughing we looked so funny. But, even with the mess she was the most beautiful woman I had ever seen.

"Hank and I had a hot marshmallow fight, daddy," she answered him, "The one I used was a little hot."

By that time her mother was standing in the kitchen door waiting for Eva to come help, standing there smiling at her daughter in wonderment. All her father said was "Ain't I seen ever'thing now. Grown people acting silly."

Eva joined her mother, the both of them laughing. I sat down with Captain Stinsin. "Best get some ice on your snozzle," he said, "don't, she'll be blisterin' right 'ere in the wintertime. Be a might hard to explain. Havin' to tell the men down at the store that some girl, wee girl at that, beat up on it with a marshmallow?"

"I'm not carin' much what most people say 'bout my nose. They ain't got nothin' better to do than speculate on my nose, they ain't doin' much."

"I don't think there's gonna be much speculation after I tell 'em 'bout the marshmallow. Ifin it don't beat all. Her mother never even done it to me. You sure do know how to handle the womenfolk - gettin' beat on with a marshmallow." He finished, having talked himself into another cackling spell.

Eva and her mother came in with steaming cups, gave one to her father, then one to me. They sat down next to us with their own cups. Captain Stinsin made a toast, a blessing really, "To these wonderful women that's with us this evenin'. God, they's been a blessin'. One last thing Lord, make Hank be careful with that nose of hisin, it gets in that hot toddy it'll smart some." He finished, laughing again at his own joke.

We sat around, talking until sometime after midnight. We had another hot toddy before Eva said, "I need to get this stuff washed off me. I'm going up to take a bath, then I'm going on to bed so I can get up early in the morning." She rose from where she had been sitting on the couch with her legs tucked under her, leaning on my shoulder. She kissed her mother, then her father, said good night to them, then came back and leaned over and kissed me, said "Poor thing's got a red nose - just like Rudolph's. See you in the morning." She left then, went up stairs. As the Stinsins and I talked we could hear her running the bath, then singing coming from the bathroom and a little later a "Good Night" drifted down the staircase and we could hear her bedroom door close. Pretty soon I rose to get ready for bed. Said goodnight to the Stinsins, went upstairs and down the hallway, walking lightly as I went by Eva's door so as not to awaken her, to the room at the end, the room I'd slept in on my first night on the island.

I made a quick trip down the hallway, as quiet as I could, to the bathroom, brushed my teeth, took care of what needed taking care of and returned back to the bedroom. I pulled the covers back, got in bed and was sound asleep almost before I finished rolling over.

Sometime later I grew aware of something, there in my sleep. A dream I guess it was. I felt a body, a naked body next to me there in the bed. I started to awaken, but a little finger was placed on my lips there in the dream, telling me to be quiet. Then the naked body slid over on top of mine. I was being kissed as I felt the breasts of a woman, the naked body of a woman on me. Rubbing on my body. I was suddenly aroused, very aroused, and the body slid from mine. The lips that had been on mine, there in my dream, moved to my ear as the body slid to the side. "I love you," was whispered into my ear and the woman in my dream rose from the bed, and, with her naked back and buttocks showing in the moonlight from the window, walked to the door a shift in her hand and through it into the hallway. There in my dream?

Chapter Twenty-Five

THE ASKING

I was aware of a hand shaking my shoulder. It was Mrs. Stinsin standing there in her robe, telling me it was time to get up, Eva was getting ready to go downstairs. As soon as she left I got up, noticed that it was still dark outside, then got dressed and after checking that the bathroom was open made a quick trip there, brushed my teeth, combed my hair some, best I could anyway, and then went back to my room, went in my bag and got the presents I'd brought with me, including the special one, and went on downstairs.

Captain Stinsin was already about, he had a pot of coffee brewing. Pretty soon Mrs. Stinsin joined us. The Captain poured each of us a cup of coffee, poured one for Eva, also, and sat it on the coffee table. The tree was in the corner with all the presents sitting at its foot. I took mine and sat them with the others. The ring I had kept in its ring box, but had wrapped it in a larger package in order to disguise it until the last minute. I'd also bought her a wool sweater without a turtleneck. Had put a note inside the wrapping "To make it easier for the snow." And I'd written home and gotten her a book on my hometown, on Ocean City. Written by the Holland's, two of the town's best historians. I wanted Eva to know more about where I came from; just as I had learned so much about her island from the three Stinsins. I put the ring box behind the others so it would be near the last of the boxes she would open.

In several minutes more she was coming down the stairs in a robe like her mother's. Right away she went to her father, sat in his lap, took his head in her hands, kissed him and hugged him, said "Merry Christmas, Daddy. I love you." After a moment or two, she rose walked to where her mother was standing near the door, took her hands and leaned in and kissed her, then hugged her, said "Mama, I love everything you do for me, I love you. There couldn't be a Christmas without you and Daddy." She turned to me, said "Merry Christmas, Hank" I replied, "Merry Christmas, Eva." She started toward the tree and the gifts beneath it, when she turned, smiling, and said, "You get more than that." She jumped into my arms and there in front of her parents, said to me, "I love the way you treat me, I love the way you feel about me. I love the way you respect me." Then she kissed me, stepped back smiling; the rest of my face now as red as my nose. She had embarrassed me in front of her parents by saying nice things about me, things I knew they loved to hear. She then turned, heading to the tree, saying over her shoulder as she did, "Sleep good last night, Hank?" I didn't answer.

We went about opening presents then, her mother receiving things that women get, her father getting manly things. I was getting things, too; wasn't paying as much attention to what I was getting as I should. But her parents knew why I was mostly silent. Eva didn't, as she sat there almost under the tree facing me, as she handed her parents the gifts she had brought for them, and the gifts Captain and Mrs. Stinsin were giving each other. She was laughing, smiling, she was being Eva. Infecting us with joy. There were the normal expressions of joy and gratitude that I supposed happened all over on Christmas morning. This was my first experience with it. With that kind of joy, that kind of happiness. It was an extra layer on top of the happiness I felt every time I was near Eva.

She then began to open her presents, thanking us, giving me a special smile when she opened the package with the sweater and read the note. Finally, there was the last package and Eva reached for it, turned to look at us, as she had with all the gifts. I'd gotten Mrs. Stinsin to write on the card that it was for Eva, but not had her sign it. When Eva saw her mother's handwriting she presumed it was from her parents. She tore into the package just as she had all the others. I sat there on the edge of my seat, my heart in my throat, butterflies in my stomach, rehearsing in my mind what I was going to say. She got the outer wrapping off, pulled the tissue paper away from the inside. There in the middle of the larger box was a black velvet ring box with a white ribbon tied around it.

Eva stopped laughing, paused, looked at me somewhat quizzically, then looked at her parents also with questions in her eyes, her deep blue eyes. She undid the white ribbon, opened the box and looked at the ring. When she looked back to me a single tear was making its way down her cheek. I was on one knee by then. I said, slowly, being careful

154

with the way I was speaking, "I don't know all the words I should be saying right now, but if I knew them all, I would be saying them and I plan to learn them all. For now I hope these words will do, Will you make me happy forever? Will you let me make you happy forever? Will you let me love you forever? Will you marry me?"

By the end of my proposal she was sitting there with an almost serene look, tears now flowing from both eyes. She said, "Come here." I walked on my knees to her until there was no distance between us. We were touching. She said "Look into my eyes." I looked into the depths of the ocean, I looked into her through the deep blue of her eyes. It was mystical there. It was like being overwhelmed by a storm, but there was no storm there. There was just a deep blue swirling in the eyes I was looking into. It was where heaven was, or what passed for heaven in this life.

"Put the ring on my finger," she said then, pulling back just far enough to present the ring to me and to hold out her ring finger. I put the ring on her finger. She tilted her left hand slightly so that she could see the ring on her hand. Then she looked back into my eyes, said simply, "My man, I'll have you."

We embraced, hugged. I started tearing, tears falling down my cheeks, mixing with the tears on hers as we kissed there on our knees before the Christmas tree on Christmas morning.

I don't know how long it was. My brain had disengaged from me the moment she said she'd have me. I just went into a daze. This wasn't supposed to happen to me. I wasn't supposed to be this lucky. I believed it though. All the evidence was in my arms, or was I in hers? We realized then that there was movement in the room. We weren't the only ones in the room, though a moment ago we'd been the only ones in the special world where our emotions of the moment had taken us. She rose, took my arms and moved me up with her and we both turned.

Her mother was standing in the kitchen doorway, crying. I saw her father disappear around the doorway into the foyer. Eva let me go, said "Mother," as she ran to her mother's embrace. I stood there while they hugged, Mrs. Stinsin smiling at me over Eva's shoulder. She gestured with her head at the foyer door, where Captain Stinsin had gone. I went in that direction, went through the door and there was Captain

Stinsin, tears running down his face. The whole house was crying. If they'd had a dog, the dog would have been crying.

When he saw me standing there he said, simply, "Thank you," put his arm around my shoulder and we turned and walked back into the parlor. The women were still embracing, tearful, so were we. Grown men crying. I didn't even know why I was, I was too happy, but the tears kept flowing. We walked over to the women and as we got close they pulled apart some, Eva reached out to the Captain and myself, "Get in here," she said, and there were four people in one big embrace.

I spent most of the rest of Christmas in a daze, a happy daze. The Captain had decided not to paint any until after New Years so my time was free. Belonged to her, though. We spent hours and hours walking up and down and across the island. Hours walking down the beaches at almost every point of the compass. Hand in hand, arms around each other, going here, there, always together. We spent many hours, mainly evening hours at her special place in the lee of the rocks below the Ocean View, huddled in blankets against the cold. We'd grab our coats, a blanket or two, Mrs. Stinsin would make us a thermos of hot chocolate, sometimes coffee, something to keep us warm as we sat on the beach. As we smooched, I guess that's what decent people call it. Did a little more, but always stopped before going to the place we were saving, saving for when it would mean the most to the both of us. She was a virgin I knew. Couldn't imagine her ever being with a man that way. She told me so and that was it. She simply didn't lie.

We learned a lot about each other, though, that Christmas on the beach beneath the bluff at the Ocean View. I knew there was nothing fake about her. Physically, mentally, emotionally, she was what she appeared to be and better even than I had thought before we got engaged, before we got as close as we became that Christmas.

We talked about family, kids, jobs, homes, pets even. We talked about sex . I told her one night, "I'll never hurt you." She replied, "I know you won't. I'll be in charge, how could you hurt me?" "Sometimes it hurts." I said. "I won't hurt" she responded, "I love you too much. I won't be afraid either. You'd better to be able to take care of what you start, or maybe what I start, when the time comes."

We talked some about the wedding, when, where and how. The where was simple, on the island in the Stinsin's church. There wouldn't be any fancy reception. Why put her parents, or us for that matter to the expense of one at the ballroom at the Ocean View or one of the other hotels? We'd simply have a short social after the wedding at the church hall.

Then, she said, "We'll just get out of there, sneak out the back door as soon as we can, make it to the place we're going and then I'll find out how big you are, how strong. Will you let me hold you?" She asked. "Don't talk like that." I said, as she laughed. She decided that she didn't want to wait until she graduated to get married; we'd get married the next Christmas, six months before she graduated. We would just have to do without for twelve months, save everything for another twelve months.

We filled out applications to several colleges over the holidays, including the University of Maryland. Filled out one for her college, too, although I didn't think I could possibly get in. Didn't hurt to try was her idea. She told me she'd do an extra personal statement for the University of Maryland. When she had it ready, she gave it to me to read. She had told them that they she planned to marry me and she wanted me educated. I bet that's one they hadn't received before. I just shook my head.

Too soon, the holiday came to an end. All of us, the Stinsins and myself, went with her on the Point Judith ferry to meet her bus. We all kissed and hugged, sad to see her go. As we put her on the bus, she turned and said to her parents, "Daddy, Mama, take care of "My Man" until I get back." With that she was gone, and I was alone again. But it was different from any loneliness I had ever experienced. It wasn't frightening anymore, being alone. She was coming back. Coming back to me and I'd be there.

Chapter Twenty-Six
LETTERS

January, 1952

"Dear Hank:

I can't believe how much I love you. I can't believe how much I want you. I can't believe me. For the first time in my life I'm not totally in control. It must be you; that's what I tell myself. And it must be true.

Less than a year ago you were on your island not thinking of me, not thinking of my island, not thinking of loving me. I was on my island, didn't even know about your island, didn't know who it was I would be loving. I knew you were out there somewhere. I knew I'd find you or that you'd find me. But I didn't know when or where. Then Daddy brought you to me.

As soon as you walked through the door, I wanted you. Not just for a toy. A girl like me is surrounded by toys sometimes. They mean nothing. But I could see inside you, could see the goodness there, knew right away that you were no toy. I've never understood how I sense these things. I just do. But that day, that first moment, my senses were overwhelmed. Something inside told me all I needed to know. I knew you felt the same way, but your feelings confused you. You were almost embarrassed at your feelings. The effect I was having on you. I've felt other boys, men, toys, feeling that way before. Standing in front of me, almost speechless. But that was the first time ever that my breath was taken, that my heart forgot to beat, that a weakness was inside of me. Your fate was sealed at that first moment. I knew then what was going to happen. That I was going to have you. I didn't know how long it would take you to understand that we needed to go to the next step. I didn't know how long it would take you to understand what I was going to do to you, I didn't know how long it would take you to understand that we were going to be married and spend all the rest of our lives with each other. But, I knew it was going to happen.

All it took was a little help from me, a peck here, a touch there, a smile for you always. They were all easy to do. I wanted them, as much as you were surprised by them. And we moved forward with a pace that was exactly right for us, I think.

I have to admit that I wasn't positive that you would ask me at Christmas. I knew I'd moved you along, but not too fast. I thought it might take until I returned in the spring, after you had another five months without me, for you to get your nerve up enough to propose. So when you didn't propose Christmas Eve, I wasn't surprised or disappointed. I knew it would happen next summer. I wasn't even thinking about a ring or a proposal as we opened our presents. I was just having a happy time with the people I loved, Mama, Daddy and you on a great Christmas morning. When I opened the package and saw the ring box wrapped in the white bow, I knew I wasn't going to have to wait until summertime to say yes. It was beautiful. Your proposal was beautiful. And it meant so much to me and to my parents that you made them a part of it. That they were there. What more could parents ever ask.

I talked with Daddy and Mama before I left; they told me that they knew ahead of time, that you had told them that you wanted them to be a part of it because you felt that it would mean so much to me. You were right. I love you all the more for including them.

I'm worried a little though, that you may be getting to know too much about me, how I think, how I operate. If you know too much it might be harder for me to surprise you in the moonlight.

I love you My Man.

Eva

February,1952

Dear Eva:

As I sit here with a dictionary and my 'Strunk' book in my lap, I'm wondering if I'm any good at writing letters. Whatever the answer to that is, I do know that I'm very good at loving you. I don't remember having closed my eyes in sleep since you left for school. I go to bed, I close my eyes. There you are on the inside of my eyelids, walking and smiling, teasing, putting marshmallows on my nose. I'm tired every morning from loving you at night - and you're a hundred miles away.

As I'm walking to work, I see your face in all the swirls of the clouds as they float across the winter sky. I never knew before that your features are in every cloud. I never used to see such beauty in them. Clouds used to talk to me about rain and snow, about the winds to come and things like that. They never talked to me of you. That's all they talk of now. I wonder, have I lost my ability to read weather in the clouds? If I have, its because there can be no room to share with other messages in a cloud with you as its passenger.

You make me smile. Here I am, miles from you, writing you a letter and you're making me smile. How do you do it? How do you make me happy when I know you're leading me where you want? I know you're doing it; I couldn't stop it if I wanted to. And I don't want to stop it. How do you know what you know? How do you exert your influence through time and space, over me? I actually smell you now. I feel you sometimes, your arms around me, as much as I did when you were here and we were embracing. I feel your hand on my cheek, your lips on mine. Your hair blowing in my face in the breeze. I walk around hearing things, your whispers in my ears repeating themselves. Saying "My Man"over and over again.

You're a tiring woman, Eva Stinsin. You keep me tired all the time just thinking of you. There's no room left in my brain to assimilate anything else, its already full of you. My heart, the all of me is filled with love for you. Please don't stop loving me, a life without you would be chaos now that you have become everything worth living for.

I walk down to our place on the beach beneath the Ocean View every day. Even when it snows or rains. I don't always sit down, sometimes I just walk through our space to feel the essence of you. I say to myself, "Hank, she did it on purpose.

She left a part of herself here at this place so you can visit with her, feel her, until she comes home." Did you do it on purpose? Leave a part of you behind to comfort me? I think you did. Just another reason to love you.

Summertime seems so far away.

Love,

Hank

March, 1952

Dear Hank:

I read your last letter late at night lying in my bed here in the dormitory. I didn't want to be alone. I wanted to be with you. I wondered as I read your words what it will be like when I use you for that, also. How will it feel? Will it hurt? I don't think so, not for long, anyway. I could feel your hands on my body where they've never really been, but I could feel them, anyway. I felt your weight on me. I felt the all of it. What's going to happen to me up here without you? I had to stop reading the letter. Hold my legs together, tight. I had to think of other things. Of Mama, Daddy, of you on the *Eva* throwing the harpoon, the 'stick'. I had to think about raising our children, not making them. You talk of what I do to you, see what you do to me. Lying there reading your letter, next Christmas seemed as if it were tomorrow.

Did I ever tell you that you're a beautiful man? I don't think so. I was always too busy savoring your presence, to busy being a part of you to stand off and look for beauty. When I speak of beauty, I'm not only talking of you being a 'hunk', that's the word the girls here at school have been using to describe pretty boys. You are one, six feet two or whatever, a couple of hundred pounds plus, long blond hair, hard as a rock, a little boy with his hand in the cookie jar smile, shoulders you can't get in an off the rack jacket. You're a hunk from the outside for sure. I can't wait to see what that hunk can do. Just kidding, I can wait.

My best friend here at school, my roommate, the girl who will be my maid of honor, has been wondering what you're like. Today a group of us were having lunch and there in front of the girls she made me tell her. I said, "He's around six foot five [added a couple of inches], weighs about two hundred fifty pounds [added 30], has long blond hair, reaches his shoulders. Clear green eyes, almost the color of green grapes, eyes that see things, see everything. He has the biggest shoulders you've ever seen, a little bitty waist, not much rear on him, huge arms, working man's arms on him. But gentle hands. Big muscular legs, a huge chest, a hairy chest. His ears are too small for his head," I told them, "but they hear everything I whisper to him, so they're big enough. He's a man full of respect. Too full of respect really, at least he was once. He treats my parents as if he wishes they were his. He looks after my Daddy. He's a man's man, or was until he met me. He has a reputation where he comes from of being able to handle himself. He's not a man for others to trifle with, to laugh at. In short," I told them, "he's a full grown man, keeping size, that loves me." My friend asked me when I finished, "He got any friends?" Another asked, "How many of these guys do you have out there on your island?" Now you know what I tell others, how I tell them how great you are. How easy it is to love you.

I won't be writing for several weeks. I told you before I left that I was taking an extra heavy load this semester and next year too, so I can get out of college earlier to be with my husband. Mid-terms are coming up and I have a lot of studying to do. There won't be time for studying, thinking of you and also writing to you. So I'm going to study and think of you. I know you'll understand. I'll start writing as soon as exams are over, wait until then to tell me again how much you love me.

Each night, though, after studying, when I finally go to bed, I am going to think of you standing before me. Your clothes are off. I'm going to be nude there in my thoughts as I lie in bed. Soon you're with me, your hands on my body where they've never been, my hands on your body where they've never been. I'm going to dream of kissing you when kissing is just a part of what is to come. I'm going to imagine everything. And I'm going to go to sleep with a smile on my face.

Wish me luck on my exams. I love you My Man.

Eva

March, 1952

Dear Eva:

I am alive again. Another wonderful letter. You put sparkle in the lives of everyone that knows you, not just in mine. More in mine, though, I think. I hope. When I think of you nothing is drab, everything sparkles, its like you live in a ethereal world almost, a gossamer place where light plays games, a kaleidoscope where you bring those you love for an extra worldly experience, the experience of loving you. And yes, I do love you. I have been in a different world from the first moment I put my foot upon your island. I felt strange even at that moment and didn't know why; didn't know that an enchantress lived here. A beautiful woman who took my heart as hers, replacing it with her own.

You're much more than the physical parts of you or the combination of those parts. It is what is behind your eyes, the world back there beyond that beauty, the swirling that makes me want to dive into them; it is your laughter, music almost, the way you look at me, the way you have turned me into a musical instrument that you play for your pleasure and for mine, your utter and complete confidence in yourself, and in me too. It's your marvelous, wondrous smile.

No woman was ever intended to be the complete package. I don't think God ever meant to truly make a perfect woman and put her here in this world. It had to be an accident or he'd of kept you for himself. Or maybe you were one of a set of twins and even God couldn't survive two of you; no mortal could. No matter of intent, it was a mistake to send you away. Of such mistakes are miracles made. You are my miracle. I will never know why God gave me such a creature of perfection, but you have made my life.

I think of you in every way there is. When I think of your lips, puckering at first when you teased me with what I told myself were mere peck-kisses, then later when you had all the measurements right, opening them so they melted into mine until we were joined in one point of sensation, I get weak. I'm weak now. If I don't learn how to deal with this sensation we'll need to take our honeymoon next to a hospital so I can be revived after an hour of fully knowing you.

I remember sitting there on the beach on Christmas eve, with marshmallow ringing the end of my nose, liquid dripping from the very end, the burnt end, and you crawling through the snow and sand to get away from me, your derriere (my thesaurus says that's french for rear end), anyway your fanny trying to get away, but not fast enough. Actually, you had so many clothes on it might not have been your rear end. Just a bunch of clothes. It was in there somewhere though, your derriere, and later it wasn't. Later it was in the moonlight. Wasn't it?

Twenty, thirty years from now when our kids are off to college, married maybe, I think we'll look back on this time when I first came to your world of enchantment as a wondrous time, a very special time. I don't think it can happen more than once, not this way, this intensity. I don't think we humans are made to keep love at this level forever; but, I think we're going to find out, going to test it.

It's going to be seven long weeks, or is it eight, until your foot (whatever size it is) steps off Bill's bus over in Point Judith and you step out, run to me, and set me on fire again. I love you every way you are and every way you will ever be.

Hank.

PS. Yes, I bought a thesaurus.

My Man:

Why do you do this to me? Make me think of you every single moment of the day. Sometimes even thinking of being bad again - is it again? Did we both dream it? I'm probably going to flunk out of school I spend so much time thinking of being with you, thinking of being with you in every way, thinking of how far away is Christmas time. Sometimes when I'm alone, I wrap my arms around myself as far as I can, and pretend they're yours. Close my eyes and think of being in your arms. Your big, strong arms. Being protected by My Man.

I want to rub my cheek against yours, feel the bristles singe my skin. I want to feel that tingle that starts in my toes and courses through my body until it feels like my hair is standing on end. I want to feel the magnetism that pulls my body to yours when we are close, face to face. I want to feel the reaction of my breasts to the nearness of you, the reaction of my heart when it feels the beat of yours as we touch. I want those big strong arms to hold me tight and keep me safe. I want you to keep the monsters away. I want you to love me.

Mother and I have been writing each other about the wedding. We know it's not until Christmas, but some things need to get done early. There are no bridal shops on the island, none in Point Judith or Galilee even. Usually the best selection is in the spring. We've decided that she'll come up to school the afternoon of the last day of finals, stay with me that night, and on the next day we'll go to the shops in Kingston and see if we can get a gown. We'll catch the bus to Point Judith the next day and you and Daddy can pick us up there at eleven thirty. Maybe, if the *Eva* is back in the water by then, you can pick us up on her and we won't have to wait for the ferry. That way I can be on our island with you sooner.

Daddy told me that he had a talk with you once, telling you how important it is to stay out of women's ways when they're doing womanly things. He's right. This wedding business is really for women to deal with. So don't be hurt if I don't involve you in a lot of it. I love you, that's why I'll save you a large part of the aggravation of arranging what needs arranging.

You should be hearing from some of the colleges we applied to pretty soon. Let me know as soon as you know whether you've been accepted. We'll need to know where you're going to be next school year, your schedule and everything, so the wedding arrangements can be finalized. You won't have to make them, mother and I will do it and we'll be able to work around both of our school schedules. I hope you've noticed that I have no question but that you'll be admitted, somewhere. Something inside me tells me so and when I feel this way it is so. You can count on being a freshman next September. It's not that I have confidence in you, though I do, or in my own sensory feelings, though I do; it's because God could not have started what he has started with us, unless he was going to give us everything we need. Love like ours begets good things. That's not to say that there won't be hard times. We've been given a great love, we must expect bad things sometimes or why would He have given us the love to surmount the bad times. We'll have them, but because we'll have each other, they will be as nothing.

Sometime between now and next Christmas, you are going to need to go over to the mainland and buy a new suit and sport coat. I don't want to be going to parties and such with a man that smells like a mixture of moth balls and Old Spice. I'm sure the church members will appreciate it also.

I guess that's enough training for now. I'm acting like a wife already.

Of course, wives do other things, too. Things men like. Do you like these other things? Yes, I suppose you do. I know you do. The girl in your dream slid off your body because it was telling her that you like these other things. In a big way, I think she thought; maybe I shouldn't be saying this, maybe I'm being bad again.

Is it okay to talk this way? It must be, we're going to be married. Will you be gentle with me? With you be hard with me? Whichever I ask you to be? Whenever I ask you? Will you teach me all the things I should know? Will you learn all the things about sex I want you to learn, so you can teach me? Are do you already know them all? I think it is the latter. Think of me in your arms. I love you.

Love me, My Man.

Eva

May 10th, 1952

Dear Hank:

Certainly, you will tell your friends of our wedding. They will be able to rent a place for the wedding time. And so what if there is a party? There had better be a party when Eva gets married. They had better invite me to it. You'd better hope they tire me out dancing. You don't want me fresh and full of energy on our wedding night. With all the thinking I've been doing about what will happen then, I'm not sure you could survive if I have all my powers. Invite them. I want to meet them. Who wouldn't want to meet somebody called Hot Pot Pie. My island will survive them. I'll just lay one law down to them when they get here - they can't pass out in church.

So you are afraid, still. You were afraid of me the first time you ever laid eyes on me. And you're nervous. You'd better be. I'm a demanding woman and I will demand that you make me happy, make me happy as a woman. Make me happy in bed. You're going to have to learn how to awaken quicker. A woman can get in your bed and out of it before you wake up. That's what you said. You'd better change that habit. Here you are a great big man, tough, a man that doesn't have any run in him, nervous about the thought of what I'm going to make you do with me. Don't worry, don't be afraid. If you don't know what to do, I'll tell you or I'll show you. I am going to make you pleasure me.

Of course I'm kidding. You're going to have to teach me, but you're going to have a willing pupil.

I'm looking forward to being on the *Eva* out on the grounds this summer. I'm sure I'll be busier than usual with work and the wedding coming up, but I'll make time for a trip or two with Daddy and you. He's been taking me for years now; it's something I wouldn't miss. Besides it's exciting.

This may be my last letter, year-end finals are fast approaching and I need to rachet-up my study efforts. My grades are great and I want to keep them there. I won't have much time to write between now and then and after they're over I'll be home before a letter could reach you. We'll be doing things by then, not just writing about them.

Congratulations on being admitted to the University of Maryland. I knew it would happen. We really won't miss each other too much until after next school year. This next school year we'll be away, except for holiday periods and the summer. But if you weren't going to school we'd still be apart almost as much. And it's worth it, your education. After this year I'll be back on the island full time. Instead of me coming home for holidays, it will be you.

I think how we've handled our parting this school year has pretty much established that we can survive such partings and that we can even thrive, now that you've learned to write love letters. When you and Daddy come to Point Judith for mother and me, you'll need to bring a cart to the bus stop. I'll have all my school stuff, plus the gown if we find one and we'll have mother's bags. Don't even think about carrying all of it at once. I don't want an herniated man in my wedding bed. Speaking of bed, it's eleven o'clock, time for me to get my beauty sleep.

I miss you. And I love you.

Eva

Chapter Twenty-Seven
HOMECOMING

The Captain and I had the boat ready by the twenty seventh of May, were at the Point Judith docks by eleven. I borrowed one of the carts they used to wheel the really big fish into the processing shed. It hadn't been used since the end of the last season, had been left out in the rain and snow. I put a tarp over the bottom where we'd put the women's bags and things. Then the Captain and I went up to the bus stop, me pushing the cart. As we arrived we could hear the bus gearing down just beyond the corner to our left, then it emerged from behind the building on the corner, turned and headed toward us and stopped exactly where we were standing. The third person off was Mrs. Stinsin, the Captain took her hand helping her step down from the bus. As she did, Eva emerged from behind her. When she started to step down I held my arms out to her and she jumped into them, her hands on my shoulders, cheek to cheek, her mouth at my ears. "My Man, I love you." She whispered. As I slowly lowered her to the ground I made the mistake of looking directly into her eyes. For an instant I was lost again in their depths, swirling, my legs weakened, I was momentarily speechless. Eva pushed away then, pushed up on my arms a little so as to say "lower me." As she did she looked away from my eyes and I lowered her. Put her on the ground, leaned over and whispered in her ear, "I love you, too."

She turned to her father, he was standing there with his arms open, she stepped into them and he wrapped her in his arms. "Daddy, I'm so glad to be home. Wait until you see what Mama and I spent your money on. Hank can't see it yet, but I'm going to model it for you specially as soon as I can get rid of him."

There was a throat clearing sound from the doorway of the bus, the bus driver was standing there. We were so close to the door he couldn't step down. I moved away to let him out and Eva turned, seeing him, said to the Captain and myself, "You remember Bill, don't you?" We all spoke to him. "Mother and I sat up front all the way from Kingston. We've talked his ears off. But he's no slacker either." Eva finished. The driver then proceeded to the cargo compartment, opened it and started to take their things out. The very first item was an overlarge dress bag, I could see the white of a dress through a small window in the bag. It was Eva's wedding dress. Bill had made sure it was securely placed atop the other luggage so it wouldn't get crushed. He handed the dress bag to the Captain, saying, "I understand you've just bought a dress, you might as well carry it. I'm sure it's a beautiful dress, but if it isn't, it'll turn beautiful when she wears it. How'd you ever raise such a daughter?" He finished, addressing Captain Stinsin.

"Mr. Bill, all I ever do with 'er is what I always do with 'er mother. I stay out of their way usually, come when they call, do what they want. Her mother taught me that, worked with 'er mother, works with Eva."

With that the driver started handing me the rest of the bags and I stacked them on the cart. There were six or seven. Eva had brought all of her things home because she was going to be reassigned to another dorm, one for seniors, when she went back in the fall. Shortly, I had them all packed. The Captain carefully laid out the dress bag on top of the other bags.

Bill closed the cargo compartment, turned, said, "Miss Eva, you have a good summer, you hear." Eva stepped to him, took his hand and shook it, stepped up and kissed him on his chin. "Thanks for looking after me. You take care of yourself this summer. Don't want anyone else to be driving me back to school next fall. And watch out for all those cute coeds, you hear." Bill was about sixty-five years old, but all of sudden he was a very pink man. She had him blushing. I knew how it felt and couldn't help myself. I began laughing. It was just funny. "Stop it!" she said to me. I just turned away. Turned back, said to Bill, "She does it to me, too. I'm not laughin' at you, I'm laughin' with you."

"She's something," he said, "missy, you're something, you are. See you come September."

He climbed back on the bus, put it in gear and soon it was disappearing up the road on the turnabout that would take it back out to the main road out of Point Judith.

"What is it they say," Eva spoke, "let's get this show on the road. I want to steer her home." Soon we were aboard the *Eva*, the bags stacked up behind the wheelhouse cabin where they'd be in the lee. The wind was light anyway and would be directly off the bow for most of the trip to the island. I loosed the lines, brought them aboard as the engine kicked over and the *Eva* started moving out of the slip. We had turned to port when I looked in the windshield of the wheelhouse and realized Eva had taken her out of the slip and was conning her toward the opening in the breakwater. Her father was standing to the rear on one side, her mother on the other. Eva saw me looking at her, smiled, mouthed the words "I love you" and puckered her lips in a kiss, a kiss only I could see. I sat down on one of the kegs up in the bow where I could look at her. We were probably half way across, maybe a little more, an hour or so anyway into the trip, when I saw her saying something to her father. My eyes had hardly left her face since we'd left Point Judith. I'd just been sitting there looking at her, wondering how I had gotten so lucky to be loved by her.

Her father opened the wheelhouse door, stuck his head out, said, "Eva says it's time for some music, wants you over 'ere." Soon I was standing in the wheel house doorway and we were singing sailor's ditties again, following as always Eva's lead. She'd sing a verse, we'd join her when she sang it the second time.

We stopped singing when we rounded Clay Head and had Old Harbor in sight. Another twenty minutes and we were mooring in the harbor and soon were sitting in the front seat of the pickup, all four of us with Eva in my lap, as we drove up to the Stinsins. I helped unload the bags, taking Eva's upstairs to her room as the Captain took Mrs. Stinsin's and the wedding dress to their bedroom. As I turned to go downstairs, Eva whispered to me, "Meet me at our place in an hour."

As I started to leave, Mrs. Stinsin said, "Hank, we expect you for dinner at six o'clock. I told Captain Stinsin to get us a baking sized bass for dinner. He did it, and I'll have it ready by then."

"Yes ma'am. I'll be here, prompt."

Eva met me at the door, stood on her toes, kissed me as I left and gave me a smile as I walked out of the yard. I looked again as I got out on the street and she was standing on the porch still looking at me. She waved, still smiling as I walked on down the road. I didn't turn to go to the Hill Top, instead, went the other way, walked on down to the harbor and out on the breakwater two hundred yards or so north of our place on the beach below the Ocean View bluff. Thought I'd sit there for a while as I waited. I seemed like only a minute, but I know it was an hour or more, when I saw Eva in the distance as she started up the road to the Ocean View. I walked back down the breakwater, climbed down the south side and walked toward where the path down the bluff met the beach. We arrived there at the same time. She first took my hand, then pulled me to her. Kissed me. There were other people around, two surf-fisherman not fifty yards away. Didn't bother her. She wanted to be kissed. She was kissed. It was simple.

She'd brought a blanket with her. I'm sure she'd probably said, "I'm going down to the beach to be with Hank, I'm taking a blanket." She would never lie to them, or sneak around them (Christmas Eve excepted perhaps) and they trusted her to do the right thing for all of us. They knew she was in control.

We walked down the beach to our place, spread the blanket and just sat side by side, touching, with our legs bent and our arms on our knees looking out over the water.

"I loved your letters," she said, "I knew you were a romantic inside, I knew it because you were so shy last summer. Your letters proved me right. But then, I know these things. Honestly, I seem to know things that others don't. It even makes me wonder sometimes. Worries me, scares me sometimes when I see things I don't want to see. Sometimes knowing things doesn't make me happy. Depends on what it is I see ahead. Everything I know, though, everything I sense about you, makes me happy. Is there anything about you I won't like? Tell me now. It won't bother me, I'll just change you."

"You know too much, already," I said carefully, "I don't think I've kept anythin' from you, at least on purpose. I'd be 'fraid to," She interrupted me then. "It's afraid, not 'fraid, and you need to say your gs, too. That's why they have them. If you're going to college you need to start working on saying things correctly." "Yes'um, Miss Eva. "I responded. She laughed a little. I then kept on, trying to speak a little slower and more precisely, "You'd know if I kept anything from you. I've never known a woman who knows so much about me. Sometimes it's frightening, the fact that you seem to know all of it, that you know the bad and the good. I understand you knowing the good, you gave it to me, it's been your present. But you've made me tell you things I really wish you didn't need to know."

"Like what?"

"Like all that stuff you got out of me about how I was down south, the raising hell, fighting, the stuff about running with the wrong kind of women. Even, I guess, some of it about how I grew up, my dad being lost at sea, my mother dying, having to go out on my own too soon. Sometimes I think of that life as memories that make me vulnerable. Normally, I've always kept how I feel to myself. Maybe I felt embarrassed by it before. But not with you. You know everything important about me. I don't know, really, how you got me to open up the way I did."

"Are you glad you did?"

"Yes. But that doesn't mean I understand it."

"That part's simple. I wanted to know it. You loved me before you even knew it, so you told me."

"You don't tell me everything about you," I responded. "There's all that mystery in you, how you know so much, why everyone loves you, even the island girls your age and that's not normal. I'm still waiting to hear everything because you love me, too."

"I've told you women need to know and men need to wonder. It's just part of love. Believe me."

"Somethin' is really weird here," I said then, "I'm older, I've fished all over the east coast, in the islands, fishin' on rich people's boats, Key Largo, Cat Cay, caroused for two or three years all over the coast. One girl, one woman after another, one party after another. And I come to this island and it all abruptly stops. Your daddy opens the door, you walk into the parlor and take my hand and look into my eyes and I don't even know who I am. A little bitty girl. A beautiful girl that defines the term, looks into my eyes and I can't talk, can't breath, my heart stops. I'm glad that I was never in love before, I couldn't have done this twice."

"You weren't going to fall in love before you met me," she responded, "fall in sex maybe, but not in love. I wasn't either. Some banker's big mouth son gets his head broken and you get run out of town. You end up on an island in a different direction than you've ever gone before. Here I am, waiting for a man that makes my heart stop, makes it hard to breath, sleeps a little too soundly sometimes - just jabbing you. I was feeling just like you. The only difference was I was waiting for my man to come to me. You didn't know what you were waiting for. All I had

173

to do was teach you. I never had any doubts about my ability in that respect."

"That's for sure. You've made a prisoner of me. I think the word really is, I looked it up in the dictionary anyway, that I'm enthralled. I've been spell bound from my first day on your island."

"I like the way you say it's my island. It is. Every island has to have a pretty girl, every pretty girl needs an island. I figured that out when I was twelve and just becoming a woman. Pretty girls are prettier on islands, and every island's finer if it has pretty girls."

"This is the finest island, then, in the world. I think I remember reading one winter, that there was a time when a Greek island had sirens that lured sailors to them. Women that were so seductive that men sailed to their deaths to be with them. Is that what you are? The siren of Block Island?"

"Well I wouldn't mind being considered partially a siren, I wouldn't mind being seductive. I think I am if your reaction to me is any measure. But I wouldn't want men to sail to their deaths. All I wanted was for the right one to sail into Old Harbor and end up on my porch. Now that's accomplished, I can quit being a siren. It's hard work."

She laughed then, turned into me as I turned to her. She said then, "It's time I got a another kiss, a real kiss, don't you think. It's no fun being a siren if you have to go ten minutes without being kissed."

We embraced, kissed, sitting there on the sand, hugged. I was getting used to the jolt, the electric shock, the numbness in my elbows so I didn't flinch. By now it was shocks of pleasure, a tingling numbness, a warmth even, and more, too, as my body responded to her. I said then,

"Christmas is a long time away."

She looked at me, seeing my physical state, said "I can see it is." She kept on, "Think of the wait as a test. Are you worthy of loving Eva. Of loving me the way I love you. If you are, I want you to know for the rest of your life that on your wedding night you bedded a virgin. One that was waiting for you before she even knew your name. We're young, our families, ourselves, we aren't rich. We can't give each other material things. But, I can give you that; it's the greatest treasure I have to let you be the first man to know me; to let you be the man that awakens

174

me. Now come on," she finished as she stood, "we better head up to the house, get ready for dinner."

"Maybe, we'd better wait just a minute or so," I replied. She realized why I needed to wait and burst out laughing, loudly laughing.

"You can carry the blanket," she said, still laughing. "Carry it in front of you."

We walked north along the beach, a little gingerly at first for me, then normally. Walked hand in hand, step in step after she skipped as she always did so we could be in step. As we walked through the old town section we saw two of the couples that had been with us on Christmas Eve, stopped for several minutes, told them when the wedding was going to be, asked them to put it on their calenders.

We arrived back at the house just in time for dinner. After dinner they sent me on my way. Eva was going to try on the wedding gown for her father, Then they were going to talk about arrangements for the wedding. They didn't need me for any of the discussion, at least not yet.

I left, walked on up to the Hill Top, stopped by the bar for a beer. Leatherby was already there. I hadn't seen him in probably two months or so. I hadn't been stopping by very much, no reason to. It was more fun to go to bed and dream.

I pulled up a stool next to him, asked the bartender for a beer, told him to give Leatherby a drink.

"Thank's for the booze at Christmas," he said, "hit was the best present I got. Hell, it was mostly the only present I got. Ifin it hadn't been for it I'd been lonely. A bottle ain't much of a friend 'til it's the onlyest thing you got."

"I wasn't around hardly any over Christmas," I replied, "I was up to the Stinsin's house almost the whole time. Sorry I didn't get up with you, but I knew the bar keep would get the booze to you."

"I heard some on it," he said, "that you done got yourself 'gaged to Captain Stinsin's daughter. Fine family, fine girl. Best you could ever do. Hell, best anybody could ever do. One time when Captain Stinsin was shorthanded, must been most of five years ago, he signed me on part time. First trip I went with him he brung 'er 'long. Thought at first it were just somebody to get in the way. She weren't bigger 'an anything. Captain sent 'er up the mast and she saw so many fish it liked to worked the Captain and me to death runnin' from one fish to 'nother. When we got comin' in, she hopped right back with me and helped dress 'em, clean 'em. We had a half dozen. She treated me fine, too. Talked to me like I was an adult, and she was a young 'un showing respect to elders. That ain't happened much since I got on the bottle bad. She was pretty then too, even me, as far dissipated as I already was, could see that. Sees a lot too, 'specially for a kid. Even knew how I felt. Just afore we got in the harbor, she even asked what made me go on the bottle. When I didn't answer she asked me if it were a woman. I told her then it was a private thing and it hurt to talk on it. She said she was sorry. But she knew what done it and she a little girl. You a gettin' a real one there. Ain't none better."

We sat at the bar another half-hour or so and then I went on to my room, leaving him with his head on the bar. The bar tender always made sure he made it to his room so I wasn't afraid to leave him.

Chapter Twenty-Eight

JUNE

Our relationship intensified as June arrived. I was working to get the boat ready, or finishing up some of the smaller painting jobs Captain Stinsin had; usually this late in the spring they were jobs on private cottages. Not real money makers, but worthwhile, they kept me in spending money. When I wasn't working or sleeping I was with her. We were mostly exploring ourselves now, our likes and dislikes. Remembering funny things to share. Like the time she was trying to understand a foreign guest at the Ocean View and thought he wanted an enema when all he was talking about, or thought he was talking about, was that his dog had escaped its container and he didn't know how to find it. In trying to describe his state of mind in not being able to understand how it had escaped, he saw the meaning of the word enigma in his German/English dictionary. So he had used it in his conversation. Eva sent a nurse with an enema bag to his room. Five minutes later an embarrassed nurse had stormed back through the lobby.

I told her about the time I'd been perched on the flying bridge ladder on a sport fisherman off Hatteras, fishing a bunch of pilgrims from South Dakota, fishing for blue marlin, when a large blue crashed a long bait we were pulling from a middle rigger. To get in the cockpit faster, I'd jumped from the bridge to the transom, but it was wet and I'd caromed overboard. I came up just as the long bait, a mackerel, went skipping by with the blue all lit up, fin out, and its bill slashing at the bait. They went by just four or five feet from me. I waved to the boat to keep on and it did, left me in the water thirty miles out. The captain called another boat and they'd come over and fished me out. When I was transferred back to my boat one of the pilgrims said, meaning it, "That's a hell of a way to get them to bite, make them mad. Aren't you afraid they'll stick you with the bill?" I'd answered him, "Na, hell, we do it all the time out here, ain't none of 'em ever sticked us yet. If you're too big to swallow, they don't try you. Little guys, it might me different. That's why you don't see no little fellers out here.

We're all full grown, pretty good size." When we got back to the dock there were several of his buddies waiting, he told them all. We still laugh about the South Dakota pilgrims back home. "He's from South Dakota." became the phrase we used to describe a person who'd believe anything.

Mostly though, we talked about the life we were going to live once she got me educated. About the children we wanted to have. I wanted a girl just like her, somebody to treat me like she treated the Captain. She wanted a boy just like me, who would be smart enough to get a girl like his mother.

We talked about her job and her future at the Ocean View, her promised promotion. Her personality and the way she was able to exude happiness to others had quickly made her a prime asset, the person to greet new time customers, the person old time customers always asked for. Eva took her magic with her wherever she went.

One day we talked about the fishing season coming up. She told me then that she was a little worried about her father. He was getting older, but didn't seem to realize it. She had noticed last season on the two trips she took with us that he was slowing some and didn't react as well. She was afraid for him out on the pulpit. Told me to take care of him. I told her, she didn't have to worry, that after her the Captain and her mother were the people I loved the most. I'd look after him the best I could. That was enough for her.

In the first half of the month, before the Captain and I really got to fishing, Eva and I would go to parties. Parties hosted by the couples from the Christmas Eve sleigh ride and bonfire. They were sort of a clique, the couples and Eva. And now me.

By mid-June that started tapering off. Everyone had jobs in the hotels and inns on the island and they were getting busier. Then it was time for the first swordfishing trips. We took our first trip on the fifteenth of the month. Didn't see a fish. We went every day until the twentieth, still hadn't seen a fish. The water was too cold, they weren't coming in to the short trip spots. When we came in that day the Captain said, "We'll ice up now, double load of ice. Fill 'er fuel tanks, top 'em off good. We have to be goin' way out, find some warmer water. We'll be stayin' overnight, makin' a two day trip out of her, get closer to George's Bank. We'll be leavin' 'bout two o'clock, you'll need to get your sleep soon's you can, I'll be tellin' Eva for you. She'll be understandin'. We've had this early season problem afore when warm water stays out. I'll have Rebecca fix 'nough food for the both of us. You'll need to be 'ere in the mornin', 'two sharp. We'll run 'till two hours after daybreak, then start lookin'. Fish 'em all day, hove to overnight, fish 'em 'til the sun starts fallin' fast the next day, then head for home. Get back here 'bout midnight, maybe earlier. Sell what fish we got the next day, lie over in the harbor that night and the next day, and if the fish be out there, we do 'er again. Keep a doin' it like that long's the fish stay off-shore.

"Get your rest now, get to bed. This is goin' to be hard fishin'. Ain't only the runnin' and the fishin' but one of us has to be awake all the time, so you ain't gonna get much sleep out there."

He was right about the sleeping; he'd also guessed right about the fish. That's where the fish were. There was an eddy of water there in the high sixty range, a large piece that had probably spun off the gulf stream as it started its northeast and east curve to England. We fished hard the first day until around three in the afternoon. We stopped spotting the fish then, they'd slowly returned to the depths to feed again. We'd gotten six, three in the two to three hundred range before we dressed them. Two considerably bigger, and one pup. They came pretty spread out and we just threw the keg over, let it play the fish, then brought it aboard, slowly pulled the fish in, lanced them, tail-roped them and except for the two big fish, hauled them in over the gunwale. We used the mast, boom, block and tackle to swing the larger ones into the cockpit. We hadn't had to use the dory.

The Captain had said when he stuck the small fish, "There's Rebecca's." He'd taken the fish for his wife, she'd have friends over, give some to relatives, ice some down. She preferred the younger fish. The small one was about a hundred and a quarter - just the right size for her. It would be the last one he'd take that small. He generally wouldn't 'stick' the pups, considered it wrong. But he humored Rebecca. If she wanted one, it had to be right.

After the fish went down that day, the Captain motored farther south, getting a little farther east as well. He'd figured that the eddy was slipping south and east some and he wanted to be able to stay in it the next day.

179

Toward six o'clock he cut the engine off. We hadn't eaten since we'd consumed the egg and bacon sandwiches Mrs. Stinsin had made for us to eat on the way out. That had been around six in the morning. We'd been too busy once we started fishing, just had time to drink from a water jug on occasion. Now we started preparing dinner. The Captain brought a small sterno stove out of a compartment in the wheel house, sat it on the midship deck, lit off a can of sterno. When it got going good, he went in the fishbox, got out a pot that Mrs. Stinsin had sent and put it atop the burner on the stove. In ten minutes it was hot and we were eating the fish chowder Mrs. Stinsin had sent for our dinner. We also had sandwiches. When we were through, the Captain capped the sterno can, extinguishing it.

Then we set about cleaning the fish, dressing he called it, and put them in the fish box and iced them down. We finished just as it began to get dark. At first there was a clear moon but then fog moved in and soon our world was limited to the thirty yards around the boat. The Captain turned the running lights on. The bow light, masthead light and there was another low wattage light looking to the stern on the back of the wheel house.

"Now, Hank," he said then, "we got a special way of things out here when we overnight. Ain't like inshore. We ain't far from the steamer lanes into New York harbor, we're just inshore of the New York to Boston route, and smack dab in the steamer lanes into Providence. 'Sides them, there might be a passel of them big draggers out of Point Judith, some of 'em out of Falmouth, working out here or runnin' to somewheres or back from somewheres. We have to keep a sharp eye out. We're so small ifin they run over us they might not even know it.

"You done learnt how to run the boat last season, heck, you knew how to run one of 'em afore you got up here. Nighttime ain't no different so far as runnin' 'er is concerned. But you got to keep a sharp lookout to keep from gettin' run down. 'Specially in fog like this 'ere. We'll do three hour watches. But ifin on your watch you can't stay awake you need to be callin' on me to get on up. Four eyes sleepin' on a four eyed boat gets you kilt out here. You understand?"

"Ain't no problem, Captain, expected it when you said we'd be layin' hove to out 'ere. Ain't really no other way to do 'er."

"We's mostly lie quiet, engine down so's we can hear good." He continued. "With this fog we ain't gonna see much, dang sure ain't gonna see the one that runs over us if we only 'pend on our eyes. Best thing out 'ere in the fog is your ears. Ain't no trouble in hearin' the fog horns on 'em ships. Hear 'em a mile, two miles, more even. But that don't solve it all. Hearin' the horns. In the fog the direction is changed all 'round. You know there's a steamer near you, but 'cause of the fog you can't figure whichaway she be.

"What you need to be doin' is gettin' ready to start the engine as fast as you can when you first hear the fog horn, but don't start 'er then. You got to get set, but don't start 'er yet. Need to keep 'er quiet for 'other piece. Keep 'em wheelhouse doors open and listen for the noise the bow wake makes as the steamer cuts through the water. Listen for the props too. Them big props, 'specially ifin she ain't loaded much, makes a big splash noise ever time one of 'em blades hits back into the water. It be a swooch, swooch, swooch, swooch, type of sound, each time one of them big propeller blades hits the water on the down go she makes a swooch. Once you get 'perience, you can tell how fast she's a goin' by how fast the swooches is. Way she works is that when you first hear the bow wake and prop wash you won't be able to figure where she's goin' in relation to us. But ifin you keep listenin' to the bow wake and the prop swooches, you'll find yourself gradually turnin' your head in one direction 'til you don't feel the urge to keep turnin'. That's where the steamer be comin' from. You keep lookin' there you'll see 'er. Ifin she's comin' head on when you first see 'er, get them engines on, hit full throttle and get somewheres else, fast. Ifin she ain't comin' head on, goin' to pass you by, still got to turn the engine on, get the boat faced up to the bow wave or 'pendin how the *Eva's* layin', stern to it. Don't want no bow wave on the sides of 'er. Throw 'er 'round too much, ifin the steamers real close, could swamp us, maybe put us under without even hittin' us. Ifin I'm sleepin', I'll be awake soon as I hear that engine turn over, but it'll be too late for me to do much by then 'cept hold on.

"Ain't be meaning to scare you none. But's important that you know what to do out 'ere when we got this fog on us. Didn't have fog could see a steamer's lights a mile, two mile away. Ain't much danger then. With this fog it's different. Ever five years or so a boat just don't come home. No distress calls, no nothin'. Ain't even been rough. Just ain't come home. Mostly, we think it's the steamers. They's so big they won't even know they hit a boat this small at night. 'Sides, they mostly lookin' for each other, lookin' to 'void something big 'nough to hurt 'em, ain't worried 'bout us none."

"Captain," I said, "I've had occasion to worry on this before; ain't first time I hove to in the fog. First time up 'ere. Down home all the southerin' steamers stay inside the Gulf Stream, catching the Labrador current runnin' south. Sometimes they's within thirty miles of the beach and we're fishin' out near that far pretty regularly. Sometimes she be foggy there, too. Even in the daytime you got to treat it the same when you got this much fog. Course ever'body's awake then, you got more ears a listenin'. The drill's the same though, same way you just 'plained it. 'Sides I promised Eva I'd take care of you, ain't gonna be lettin' you get run over."

All that got was a grunting sound, then he said, "'Bout ever two hours, want to run the engine for ten minutes to throw some charge back into 'er batteries. When they's running you got to be specially alert. Harder to hear with our engine runnin'.'"

We made it through that night with the same size boat we started with, None of it had been cut off by a ship coming out of the fog. We had hard boiled eggs, cold ham, and a pot of coffee for breakfast. Went back to fishin'. Took four fish, all good sized, headed in around three in the afternoon, me cleaning the fish and icing them down. Got in Old Harbor at eleven.

I slept until ten the next morning, met the Captain at the boat at eleven and we ran over to Point Judith, sold the fish, took on a new load of ice, fueled up, headed back to the island. Ate. Went to bed, Got up at one, were past the breakwater by two, back on the off-shore fishing grounds by eight or nine o'clock. The warm water was where the Captain had figured it would be. The fish started rising an hour later. We took five that day, lay overnight, thank God no fog, and took another five the second day. Back to the island, sleep until ten, over to Point Judith, sell the fish, take on ice, take on fuel, back to the island, sleep, up, out as long as the weather held.

Thankfully, it didn't hold. We needed a rest. I needed time with Eva.

On the thirtieth a northeaster came down the coast. A dry northeaster, a lot of wind, no rain, and some sun. But it was blowing too hard to get far out to where the fish were staying. It blew us out for three days. We caught up on maintenance the first day. Then we just took off, waiting for the weather to break.

Chapter Twenty-Nine

INTERLUDES

DANCING

The next days were the happiest of my life. Eva was finishing up a week of working days, in four days she'd start on the night shift. The shifts rotated throughout the summer. So for the next few days she was free in the evenings; the northeaster had put me 'on the beach'.

The evening of the first day, I picked her up at the house at nine. There was a dance at the Ocean View she had wanted me to take her to. I had told her that I didn't know much about dancing.

She said to me then, "You'll be surprised what you can do when you're with me."

We walked the island's little roads, hand in hand, sometimes arm in arm, or arm and shoulder, arm and waist, whatever it was from time to time, strolled really, I guess it was, to the Ocean View. Wisps of lilacs floating around us always, the smell of her. She had told me she used a perfume with the scent of her favorite flower.

I had on the new suit, the summer suit, that Eva had shamed me into buying. I was glad I did. Most of the people at the dance would be off-islanders, tourists, guests at the Grand View and the other hotels and inns on the island. They'd be dressed to the Ts.

I was still a little uncomfortable. I'd never been to a fancy dance at a nice place with the prettiest girl in any town on my arm. I'd been to things in the islands down south, in the keys, where rich boat people congregated. But they weren't dressy. Wear shorts, clean shirt, take your knife off your belt, go get drunk with the best of them type of parties. Make a fool out of yourself parties. Hit on the owner's wife, on the beach next day, parties. But this was a real dance with a real orchestra, real instruments even, not just three guys standing around hitting the top of steel drums, saying Mon this and Mon that. This orchestra even had a vocalist, a chanteuse I guess they call it when it's a woman, at least that's what the dictionary said.

Since Eva had returned I'd been working on my vocabulary, especially when I was going to be with her. When she had told me that we were going to the dance if the boat was in, I'd taken the dictionary on the boat, read it under the masthead light when I was on watch, in the mornings before the fish rose. I'd found the word. Others as well.

I was beginning what I figured would be for me a long process. But it was what I wanted. It was an uneasy feeling to be with her when we were around other people, educated people. I always had to be careful what I said. Usually, I didn't say much. I guess they thought I was the silent type. I just didn't want to embarrass her. When we talked of it, she told me that I couldn't embarrass her that way. She loved me too much. If anybody looked down on me, she'd look down on them. That would take care of the snotty noses, that's what she called some of them, privately.

We arrived at the dance at nine thirty. The orchestra was in the middle of a tune so at first Eva and I walked together around the fringes of the ball room. Frequently, a hotel guest or an islander would come over to speak. She'd introduce me. Often the guests would bring over their children to see her, exclaim over how good she looked in her dress, how beautiful she was. I generally just stood at her side. Every time Eva would introduce me she'd reach for me, put her arm around my waist, tell the person that I was the man she loved and that she was going to marry me. Often, they would ask to see the ring and Eva would thrust her hand to them as if she was wearing the Hope diamond.

After we had made a circuit of half the room, the orchestra switched to a slower dance and Eva put her arm around my waist and led me to the dance floor. Not on the edge of it either, right dab in the middle where I couldn't hide. Would have been hard for me to hide anyway, I was too big and the woman in my arms was the prettiest thing there. No-one could keep their eyes off her, couldn't help but see me when they looked at her. We were the center of attention.

When I took my first step onto the floor, I didn't have a clue as to what I was supposed to do. Then Eva turned me to her, placed her arm around my shoulder, put my arm around her waist, took my left hand, said, softly "Follow me."

We glided around that dance floor for what seemed like hours. The music would change, Eva would whisper, "Waltz," "Polka," "Jitterbug,"

"Charleston," whatever. And we'd do it. She'd teach me. She turned my two hundred twenty pounds into ounces, I felt almost so light that I thought I might fly off the floor every time we swirled together.

We danced until the music stopped. At two o'clock we were sitting on the veranda with our shoes off. She said then, "It's time to head for home."

Porches, Blankets and Things

We walked, holding hands, in the grass down the Ocean View lawn, our shoes in our off hands. Walked down the street to Old Town Road barefooted, swinging our arms some, took a left and soon were at the Stinsin's house. "Let's lie down in the chaise lounge for a while, it's too early yet; I'm not through with you," she said. I took my jacket and tie off, laid my shoes down and soon we were lying beneath a light blanket, facing each other, then in each other's arms. We weren't talking much at first. Just kissing, hugging. Soon our hands were exploring as much as she wanted them to. When I was beginning to get out of control, when I started to rise over her, she asked, "Do you love me?" "Yes," I answered. "Then please stop." She said.

I hovered over her for another five seconds, then sank back down in the cushions of the lounge. I knew that if I'd gone on we might have consummated our physical beings, she might have let it go that far because she had wanted it, also. Her hands had been on me through my clothes. She knew about me. But she'd asked me to stop. She had depended on my love for her to save us from doing the thing that would destroy what was so important for her to be able to give me on our wedding night. She wanted to come to me a virgin when she was Mrs. Gaskins.

I realized then as I came down off where I had been moments before, that she had my head in her arms, was stroking my face, kissing my face, saying "Thank you, My Man. When I'm with you, you have to save me. I love you." We lie there in each other's arms. Fell asleep.

The next thing I knew a big hand was shaking me. It was Captain Stinsin. All he said was, "She needs to be gettin' to bed. You best be gettin' your clothes changed, can't go to work lookin' like a high falutin' tourist." He walked on off the porch, heading in the general direction of the country store. I realized that the sun had come up, it was getting lighter by the minute. I looked over at Eva, she was awake, hair mussed,

186

still beautiful. She put her right hand on my cheek, looked deep into my eyes, said. "Thanks, My Man. I had a lovely time, all of it. It's time to go in, I have to get ready to go to work." With that we got up from the chaise lounge, I went to the table got my jacket and tie and as I turned I felt her hands on my waist and she pulled me to her, we kissed, she whispered in my ear, "Around nine at our place on the beach. You bring the blanket." She smiled, turned, went to the door and went in. I stood there for a minute, walked off the porch and headed up to my place at the Hill Top, shoes in hand, to change my clothes.

There wasn't much else left to repair and get ready on the boat. The Captain and I performed regular maintenance all the time and kept the boat up regular. The second day we had changed the oil, sharpened the darts, checked the lines for frays. Checked the guy wires. Today we stopped around two, the Captain saying, "Best get caught up on as much rest as we can, goin' to be 'nother round of long days lessen this northeast wind finds a pocket of warm water and drives it in 'ere. Ain't likely on a northeast wind, ain't like a steady brisk southeast wind. Get much sleep as you can case the wind backs off to the westward tomorrow and we can get out."

We walked up the breakwater and through the streets together, him breaking off to go to his house. I kept on up the road to where the Hill Top road intersected, turned up it, went to my room, set the clock for seven, undressed, got in bed and went to sleep.

At seven thirty I was walking downtown carrying a blanket, going by the Stinsins as I did. I could see Eva in the parlor, laughing and talking with her parents. I went on toward Old Harbor, stopped at a concession bought myself a lobster roll sandwich and sat outside eating it, washing it down with iced tea. Other than the occasional beer at the Hill Top I still hadn't had any booze, hard liquor, except the hot toddies over the holidays, since I'd come to the island. Since I'd first seen Eva.

Around eight-thirty I walked over to the breakwater climbed down it to the beach and walked south to our place. Spread the blanket and sat there as the lighted sky from the sun that was setting behind the bluff above me diminished, painting the blue grey in the east of a minute before into the darker grey and then the darkness of the nighttime sky. Right before complete darkness came, I saw her come down the path, turn and head for me. I rose to meet her. Right away her arms were around my neck and we kissed.

"Have you been waiting long?" she asked, as she pulled back from our embrace.

"It seems like forever when I'm waiting, but once you get here I can't even remember waiting."

"Writing love letters appears to be good training for the man I love. I'm always waiting, My Man, for the next beautiful thing you say to me. Funny, too, you mean it. Don't ever stop saying the words I love to hear from you, even when we're old, wrinkled, dried up, sitting on a porch somewhere, both of us smoking pipes. Anytime you're around I'll just turn my hearing aid up. Won't want to miss the beautiful words."

"How about this, then," I said, being careful to say it right, "I love the air around you, the space you've just walked through, the ground you're on, the place where you are and the world that lets us love each other. I know that's corny. But it is exactly how I feel and I mean every word of it."

"We're learning something else," she responded, "even I'm learning something I hadn't thought of. This loving thing we have is fun. Every day is a carnival, a blessing in a way. Come, let's sit and talk. I want to stay a long time, but I've got to get to bed earlier tonight than I did last night."

We sat there on the blanket for a while in her favorite position, she huddled under my right arm, head on my chest some, my arm around her, her left arm around me. The moon began to peak over the eastern horizon, at first just a thin slice of light like the edge of a bright tiddly-wink, then it rose almost so fast that we could see it move until in five minutes the bottom of the moon left the surface of the sea. In that period of time, in that spell really, it cast its glow on us. Our skins were glowing with moonlight, Eva's lips were almost luminous, her eyes a deep indigo purple, the moonlight reflecting from them as if the moon was shining into a mirror. We sat there as the moon rose, then when it was a hand high off the horizon, she pushed me back on the blanket, moving her arm from my waist but still leaning on me until I was on my back with part of her resting on me.

We lie there another few minutes, then we were kissing, then we were doing other things that lovers do. Chaste things, though.

Absorbing the contours of each other, leaving the whole of us until the right time. But it was the right time for kissing and feeling, until her little hand guided mine away from where it shouldn't have been going. But her hips, her legs, shoulders, breasts even, were areas to be touched, felt, discovered, until she indicated they weren't. My body was also something to be explored as far as she wanted it. I just respected her wishes, let her make the time magical, there in the moonlight in our place beside the sea.

"It's ten-thirty," she said. I'd lost all track of time. Lying on my back, her in my arms, looking at the stars and moon, the gleam of the sea, the sparkle in her eyes, the pucker of her lips, strands of her hair, her golden honey hair, rising and falling as she breathed. "Both of us need to sleep," she said. "It's time for you to walk me home."

The Stinsins were still up, each of them reading, as we got to the house. We walked up on the porch and paused. As I kissed her, she said, "Let's go swimming tomorrow after work; I'll get daddy to let us use his truck and we can go over to Mohegan Bluff, there's a beach there that on this wind should have a decent break. We can body surf, you can ride waves, can't you?"

"What time?"

"Pick me up at the hotel at five. I can change at the beach," she finished, laughing, pecked me on the lips one last time and went into the house.

Swimming in the Sea

We arrived at the beach around six the next afternoon. As usually happens when late afternoon approaches, the wind laid down a little. What wind remained was out of the northeast and wasn't blowing directly onto the beach where we were. There was a headland to our north that stuck out, with a point of rocks extending out that was breaking the slop of the chop, smoothing the water on the lee side where we were. But the ground swell still wrapped around the point of the rocks and bent into the cove, making rideable waves that took a left break far across the little cove. The tide was half high. The beach was empty. It wasn't a regular bathing beach. Too rough for most. We'd have it to ourselves.

We walked down a steep bluff to the beach which was bordered by rocks and bushes at the base of the bluff. As we arrived at the bottom,

Eva said, "You go on, test the water while I change into my suit." I kept on going to the water's edge, took off my jeans, walked in up to my knees, let the spent waves splash up on my legs, to the edge of my bathing suit. I heard her a few moments later, "It's okay now, you can look."

I turned. She was dazzling. Gorgeous. She wore a two piece black bathing suit. Bikinis hadn't made it to Block Island yet, but it was the next thing to one. I had seen her breasts in the moonlight, briefly, there on the chaise lounge just a night ago. If anything they were as beautiful in the skimpy halter top she was wearing. I hadn't realized that she had fairly wide shoulders, hadn't realized it I guess because, except for a fleeting moment, I hadn't seen her carriage as a complete package. She had a great rear, great breasts, beautiful hair, beautiful face, sexy lips, all the right things necessary to beauty. But this was the first time I'd seen so much at one time. I was overwhelmed for a minute, until she spoke, "Like it?"

"Love it." I answered. As I did, she started running, ran past me further out into the surf, I watched her as she ran by and then as she was by. I followed and soon we were swimming for the rocks where the swells first came around the point. She got there first, but I wasn't far behind. The depth of water here was a little over our heads, probably not much, but an inch too much can kill you, unless you know what you're doing. She did. Me too. We noticed then a set of waves building up, coming around the point. She started getting ready first. With no bottom to push off of we had to start swimming a little before the point of catching a particular wave, had to get our bodies horizontal on the surface, moving in the direction of the wave's movement before it arrived.

She let the first two waves go by under her, then started stroking hard for the third wave. I'd already made up my mind I'd try for the wave after hers. I didn't want to catch a wave and leave her out beyond the surf break by herself as I rode a wave to the beach. I shouldn't have worried. She swam like an otter. As the wave began its curl to it's left, she was on it in three strokes and all I saw over the lip of the wave were the soles of her feet for an instant as she cut left down the face of the wave. An instant later I was on the next wave, head out, my hands down to my side, by left dragging some to help me cut left across the wave as it carried me toward the shore. Soon it had broken clear across the cove and I was in the break, in the white water, heading into the beach. Eva was down twenty yards to my left. She'd been able to cut across her wave better then I had mine, and further in. She was still riding the foam when I bottomed out, stood and started to walk to her. As I did I noticed a black halter top floating back out to sea, took a step or two, grabbed it. When I looked over at Eva she saw I had the top.

She didn't react the way I thought most women would react in that situation. There were no hands placed over her nipples. No arms crossed over her breasts. She just walked slowly to me, head high, arms at her sides, her upturned breasts, nipples puckered from the cool water, in full view as she approached. Her only reaction was to smile. I could feel blushing all over me. From my toes to my head. There I stood, not able to take my eyes off her, wondering whether I should, but not even trying to. She kept on smiling as she walked up to me, stood so that her breasts were within a foot of me.

She looked in my eyes, reached for her top, and put it on, turned around slowly, asked, "Will you fasten it for me?" I fastened the back strap. She turned back to me, raised on her toes, put her hand on my face, kissed me, said "That's My Man. Come on, there's plenty of waves," With that she was running into the sea, diving under the combers as she made her way beyond the breakers, swimming back over to the point around which the swells were making. I joined her then on every wave. No need to wait beyond the break so I could protect her, she was better in the water than me. We'd ride in side by side sometimes, seeing which one could make the best cut. When the up wave rider would catch the other we'd tumble sometimes, get caught in the break, under the break in the white water. Once when we were tumbling, wiping out I guess, she lost her top again and one of her breasts was almost in my right eye. She knew it. When we got to shore she asked, "Get a good look?" I answered, "Yes.

She threw the top further up the beach, turned around and joined me in the surf. For another twenty minutes we surfed, both of us bare breasted, but me, in comparison, barely breasted. Finally she said, "Lets catch one more and go in." She missed the next wave and I was waiting, top in hand, on the beach when she waded in from her last ride. I noticed then, a slight glitch in her walk, like she was favoring one side of her body over the other, made one of her hips look higher than the other at a particular point in her stride. I asked her about it.

"When I get really tired," she said, "A little kink develops in my left hip, usually goes away after a minute or so. If you're looking close enough my right hip will look a little higher when I'm compensating for the kink. And one thing you've been doing is looking although I didn't know you were looking that low."

"I've been looking higher so much, almost got tired of it," I replied, smiling.

She reached down then, grabbed a handful of sand and threw it on me, ran back into the surf laughing. I dropped her top, ran after her and soon we were rolling over in the edge of the surf, laughing, playing, me getting excited some. When she noticed that, she pulled me to her, kissed me hard, said "Not yet," laughed, rose and walked out of the sea, picked up her halter top, looked over her shoulder, said "I'd better get dressed."

"You'd better."

While she was getting dressed, I toweled off. Soon she came out dressed, walked over to me, put an arm around me, said, "Here you hold this, you've been holding it all afternoon." She handed me the halter top, laughing, then finished, "I love you My Man. You are so much fun. I would have been fighting any other man off of me. You respected me. You saw the fun in it. You make me feel so good. I love you for every reason there is to love someone and on top of that or included in that, is that you are great fun and I feel so safe with you. I'm saving myself for you, and you're saving me for you, for us. But, we're having fun in the process."

"For me, One High Hip," I said trying a nick-name, speaking carefully because I was with my grammar teacher, "what we've been experiencing is not only a once in a lifetime thing for us, but, the way I look at it, it's a once in a lifetime thing for the world. I don't think this has ever happened to anyone, any two people before. I'm convinced, first you convinced me, then the way we are together reinforced it. I know it's important that we wait."

"Yes, that's the way I feel, way I've always felt since I was a girl and mama first told me things about sex. She told me how beautiful it was, it is, with daddy. Embarrassed me when she told me. Didn't think my parents did anything like that. Then it dawned on me, they had had to. But, she told me of how on her wedding night she had blossomed under daddy's spell. That's what she said then when I was just a girl. Now, I'm not so sure it wasn't just under daddy," she said laughing, then continued "but, as I grew older, the age when some girls start exploring with things like that, I always remembered what mama had said, could see them around me, happier than anyone I knew. I figured their way was the way for me. So I waited for the right man. Here you are and the wait is almost over. For the both of us. Just six months, a little less and I am going to know what I've been waiting for, you're going to know whether it was worth waiting for."

"I intend to tell the whole town," I said.

"What are you talking about, telling the whole town?"

"There will soon be a night in December when there will be the marriage of a big rough fisherman to the prettiest and greatest woman in the world and sometime around midnight, everyone on this island is going to hear a great noise, ringing from the tree tops, well bush tops anyway. They are going to hear a word screamed. The scream is going to be one word. 'YES.' That's going to me announcing to the world that the woman I love is no longer a virgin and that I can stand up straight again."

She started laughing then and we laughed until we reached the truck. She got in the passenger side as I got prepared to take off the wet trunks and get into my jeans.

"You keep your eyes out your window while I slip out of these wet trunks." I said to her.

"Okay." She said.

I turned my back to the truck, slipped out of my trunks, reached for my jeans, when she said, "You've got a skinny rear end," and started laughing hilariously. I just sighed, finished dressing, got in the driver's seat, her still laughing and looked at her. Laughing, she turned, reached for me and pulled me down to kiss, but she couldn't she was laughing so hard.

We headed back toward her house. I noticed that it seemed like the wind was lying down a little more than the normal evening lay.

When we pulled up to the Stinsins, they were sitting on the porch. I drove the pickup in the back and Eva and I walked up to the porch, me carrying my swimming trunks, towel and blanket. This time Eva was carrying her halter top. I spoke to her parents, kissed her and started to leave when Captain Stinsin said, "Looks like the winds beginnin' to lay down, we ain't goin' to be able to get out tomorrow, still be a little too rough, but day after for sure. Going right on back out where we was a gettin' the fish afore we was blowed out. Be a two day trip, get some rest."

Mrs. Stinsin spoke up then, "Come for dinner tomorrow night, I'll have it ready at five-thirty so you can eat early."

By noon of the next day the winds were light and variable, the seas calm. In the afternoon we loaded ice, checked the *Eva* again making ready to sail early the next morning. We had her ready by two o'clock. I told Captain Stinsin that I was going to take a nap, would be at his house in time for dinner.

For dinner that evening Mrs. Stinsin had prepared ham and cabbage, boiled potatoes and macaroni and cheese. A sticking to the sides of your stomach meal. As we sat there, Eva spoke up, "Mama and I are going to prepare the same thing for your dinner tomorrow night on the boat. Put the ham, cabbage and potatoes in the pot so all you'll have to do is put the pot on the Sterno burner and have a hot meal. The macaroni and cheese will be in a pie pan. You can sit the pan on the engine manifold while it's still hot and the macaroni will get warm enough." The woman knew everything.

We finished dinner, with pie for desert. Then we sat around with coffee until seven, when Captain Stinsin said, "Know it ain't even dark yet, but one in the mornin' is racin' to get 'ere, best get to bed and get what sleep we can. We got a rough spell on the water comin' up, probably be able to fish three or four two day trips afore we get blowed out again." He rose, excused himself and went up stairs.

I rose to leave, told Mrs. Stinsin how much I had appreciated the meal. She told me that the Captain would have tomorrow night's dinner in the morning. As I left Eva came out on the porch with me. We walked to the yard where we could see to the west where the sun was setting over the sound and the mainland beyond. We stood there silently for a moment looking at the gold sky tinged with cloud puffs of pink and orange. I said then,

"Gonna miss me, One High Hip, be two days, really three before I'll be seein' you?"

"I miss you the second you're out of my sight."

"I'm goin' to miss you, too. Like your dad a lot, but he's not built like you. His top don't, excuse me, doesn't, slip off like yours. Wouldn't be anything there to attract my attention even if it did. I'm goin' to miss seein' things, I've never seen any such things floatin' out there in pairs,"

"You'd better be careful how you tease me. I might decide to starve your eyes if you keep talking like that. Starve them until Christmas anyway. You're going to be feasting then, me too. You going to serve me a feast?"

"Whatever you want, now, then, forever."

"What you want, what I want, I'm saving for you, for my husband, for me, for us." She said in response, then continued, "You'd better be heading to the Hill Top, you've got a full day, probably several days. I start working a week of nights tomorrow. I'll make sure I get up with you on your lay days, but I won't be around at night."

We turned to each other, kissed, then she walked me to the road, squeezed my hand, said to me, "I'm going to love you forever," as I turned and started up to the Hill Top road. I looked back several times, each time she was standing there; she'd see me look then wave to me. As I turned to walk up the Hill Top road I glanced back one last time. She blew me a kiss, turned and started back to the house. I was in bed in ten minutes, dreaming of her in fifteen.

BOOK TWO

Chapter Thirty
JULY 4ᵀᴴ, 1952
OFFSHORE

By daybreak the next morning we were well out to sea on our way to the in-shore side of George's Bank, close to where the fish had been the last days we'd fished. We were five or six miles inside that point; the Captain had accounted for three days of wind, but it was really the temperature of the water that mattered and he'd found the warm eddy. It was still out here. The wind had picked up a little since the previous afternoon but it was still fishable, not too uncomfortable.

About the time we started looking for fish we began to notice one sailboat after another passing by inshore heading in the general direction of Block Island Sound. After a while, I asked, "There's a passel of wind sailors out here, today; ain't 'ever seen this many, this year or last. Something special goin' on?"

"We ain't fished the fourth last year," the Captain answered, "hits a race 'tween a bunch from down your way and a bunch of rich 'ens up 'ere. Its the Annapolis/Newport race. One year they run 'er south, next 'north. Party heavy when they get where they's goin'. She'll be over today, bunch of 'em 'ill head on over to the island, be a bunch of rich drunks ever'where tonight, pissin' on the streets, puckin' in the flower beds. Rich bastards, most of 'em anyway, think they get a pass on doin' wrong. We'll see the same batch goin' south tomorrow, half of 'em or better come outta Annapolis and 'ill want to be gettin' on home."

We fished the rest of the day, the fish rose later than usual, Captain said that it wasn't unusual for a late rise after a spell of wind. We took four fish, a large one, three in the two hundred, three hundred pound range. Saw two others, got up on them but the Captain called that they were 'pups', so he didn't 'stick' them. Just drifted up on them and scared them into the deep. That night we warmed up the ham, cabbage and potatoes in the pot, put the pan on the manifold and warmed up the macaroni and cheese and ate like we were at the Stinsins. We put the running lights on around nine, and started shifts at ten. Fog had enveloped us by eleven, a thick fog.

Eva's shift at the Ocean View was over at twelve. She stayed behind for another half hour to summon a doctor to help an elderly guest who was having an asthma attack. She remained until she was sure the doctor had everything under control and that the grave shift manager was fully aware of the situation. She left at twelve twenty-five, began her walk home. Five minutes later she was walking up Old Town Road when a car almost hit her. It stopped. A man got out and walked towards her.

Chapter Thirty-One

THE CALL

It was three-thirty in the morning. I was in the middle of my shift sitting inside the wheelhouse with the door open listening for fog horns. It was still foggy - pea soup foggy. The Captain was lying in the cockpit wrapped in a blanket. I was listening to some of the boat chatter on the radio, trying to stay awake. Suddenly, I heard on the radio,

"Captain, Captain, she's not come home. Captain." I recognized the voice right away. It was Mrs. Stinsin. Hysterical. I picked up the microphone, put it to my mouth, said,

"Mrs. Stinsin, he's sleeping. What's wrong?"

"Hank, she hasn't come home. I just woke up and she's not in her bed. I called the hotel, they said she left around twelve-thirty."

"Captain," I yelled loudly, wakening him up, "you'd better come talk to Mrs. Stinsin, something's happened to Eva. She hasn't gotten home yet."

He was at the radio in an instant. I could hear both of them, Mrs. Stinsin so frightened that she was almost hysterical. He told her, "We'll leave now Rebecca, run her full out but we're still three, three and a half hours out. Call the Chief, get him to looking. Tell him we're comin' fast as we can." I'd already started the engine, began turning the boat on a northwest course. The Captain told her then, "We're coming already. I'll keep the radio on, tell the Chief he can call me, you can call me."

He took the wheel then, I'd been steering generally toward the island; he knew the direct course. Made an adjustment, five points on the compass, headed right toward Old Harbor. Throttles cracked wide open, not worrying about the fog. The hell with the fog. It would already be well after daybreak when we got to the harbor. If we got run over, we'd just be run over.

We had run her for two hours full out when we emerged from the fog bank. The east sky was just beginning to lighten. We could see way off in the distance to the west some, almost beyond seeing, the Southeast Light when it swung it's beam around. We were so far offshore yet that it was just a blink. But it marked home. From where we were coming the light was just about a point off the course we were making. The Captain received another call from Mrs. Stinsin,

"Will, the police are looking for her everywhere, but nobody's seen her; I've called everybody, her friends, our friends, I've called them all and none of them has seen her. Nobody's seen her since she left work last night. They're organizing a search for her, to get search parties ready to go when the sun gets up good. Will, I'm scared. Something is bad wrong. Eva would never do this, even if she was staying at someone's house she would have called. I'm afraid."

"I'm coming, Rebecca, fast as this old boat 'ill go, we were almost to Georges when you called first time. Figure we'll be there in an hour, hour and a half at most, we can see the Southeast Light some already."

In a half an hour it was light enough to see fairly clearly, we could actually see the lighthouse itself, make out Mohegan Bluffs. Lights were flashing atop the bluff to the west of the lighthouse. Tiny pinpoints from this far out. I hadn't noticed them before.

Way down to the south, down toward Montauk Point I could barely make out a sailboat, a single sailboat going south, getting set up to round the point.

Chapter Thirty-Two
THE SEA

The first blow was the one that put her into unconsciousness. It was also the one that would kill her. It had knocked her head into the headboard of the bunk, knocked her brain violently into the inside of the back of her skull. It caused a coup contre coup injury to the back of her brain, a bruising, bursting of blood vessels. If not treated by ice, by cooling initially to slow down the swelling and ultimately by having a hole bored through her skull to let the blood and brain liquids drain, it would build up over time, the pressure gradually increase on her brain throughout her skull until the pressure from the swelling and bleeding began to kill her brain part by part until it could no longer operate the body functions of life, breathing, heart beating, thinking.

The rest of the blows had broken her nose, her sinus cavity, had cut her head in the front and on top, made her bleed profusely. She didn't feel them. But they were what the men saw, convinced them she was dead. She was dying, almost not breathing, the coup contra coup injury's impact on her brain already beginning to slow down her body organs. The men didn't see her slight breathing, never bothered to check her pulse, it was so light they probably couldn't have felt her pulse anyway. They rolled her over the side, hardly making a splash. She went under right away, disappeared from sight almost immediately. O'Brien threw over her dress.

She felt the chill of the water. Felt the coolness. Slowly felt that she was under the water. Her feet, her legs, arms, instinctively began to move in swimming motions before she was conscious of what she was doing. Then she realized that she was under water, looked around saw a faint lightness and began to slowly stroke for it. In a minute her head broke through the surface. She instinctively took a breath.

She wasn't really conscious, not fully conscious. She was just swimming. Her body was. The shock of the water had partly roused her brain from the deeper sleep the brain injury was causing. She saw a light flash, automatically started to make feeble swimming motions in it's direction. The current was helping her. She didn't know it though.

Four knots an hour, a strong current taking her in the direction of the light.

A half hour later she was still swimming. She wasn't conscious of the time, her brain was beyond the point of counting time, it was beginning to die now, killing part of her with each brain cell that died. Her motions were getting weaker, but still her body swam. After a while there were dim periods, groups of seconds when she could barely see, or if she saw, that part of the brain where those messages went was now unable to relay the message further, was dying.

An hour after they put her over the sun was rising in the east. She was within the sound of the surf breaking ahead of her, a light surf. She barely heard it, even when she swam into it; that part of her brain was dying now. The swelling at the rear of her skull kept growing, compressing her brain into itself. Killing it and her.

Her hands touched a rock then and the next feeble stroke touched sand. She stopped swimming. The centers of her brain that controlled her limbs had just died. A wave washed her toward the rocky beach, then its backwash took her part way out again. She was powerless to stop it. She felt something then, the injury hadn't killed the touch center yet. She felt something under her arm.

Leatherby had been fishing all night, trying to get a summer striper. Had come down to Mohegan Bluffs to fish and to drink. Finish the bottle of rum he'd gotten that afternoon for sketching a summertime girl's face on her boyfriend's chest. He'd gotten pretty drunk, fell asleep around three o'clock. The sun rose over the horizon. Shined directly into the slits of his partly closed eyes. He awakened slowly. Looking around. He checked his surf pole in its sand-spike. The line was limp, the tide had moved his terminal tackle close into the beach. He stood up, went to take the rod out of the sand spike when he noticed something awash in the surf. Rolling over with the waves. He looked closer. Looked like a body.

He forgot his surf pole, walked toward the thing in the surf. It was a body. He went closer. Noticed it take a breath, blood bubbles coming from it's nose. Five seconds later it took another breath. He rushed to it then, noticing as he got closer that it was almost nude, only underwear. Woman's underwear. It was a woman. He grabbed her underneath the armpits and pulled her out of the water, up on the beach, far up on the beach above the high tide mark. He laid her down partially on her back, partly on her side. Then her lips moved. He thought she was saying something. He got on his knees beside her, leaned over until his ear was almost touching her lips.

"Crossed oars." the woman whispered. Twice more he heard her whisper the same words. He was sure of it. Then she whispered, "Mama. Daddy. Hank." Then she said no more. Lay there, taking a breath only at long intervals. He thought for a minute that it might be the Stinsin girl. He knew she'd been dating Hank.

He noticed then that she had been beaten. She was disfigured, her face askew. So he couldn't tell for sure who it was. Knew, too, that she had head injuries, serious head injuries. Now that he had her out of the water he could see blood draining from her nose, coming from her ears. He opened her eyelids. Her eyes were full of blood, it flowed down her cheeks. She was hurt bad. Needed help. He ran for the path up the bluff.

The cool water had slowed the swelling just long enough for her to reach the shore. Had Leatherby not been there, not seen her, not pulled her on the beach, she would have rolled over in the water until she drowned.

The swelling continued, the pressure on her brain increased, it began more rapidly to die. By the time Leatherby got to the top of the bluff, the pressure had killed the part of her brain that controlled her speech. He had heard the last words she would ever say. She went into a coma as Leatherby ran down the Mohegan Trail for a house a half-mile away where an outside light shined.

He banged loudly on the door until someone woke up, frightened by the noise he was making. A man came to the door with a shotgun, wanted to know what he wanted. Then the man recognized him, put the gun down and opened the door. In a minute he had gotten hold of the Chief, told him a woman had washed up on the beach just west of Southeast Light. That he had pulled her out of the water; she was at the base of the bluff. He told the Chief that she was still breathing, but looked like she was hurt bad. Told the Chief he'd meet him on the road at the top of the bluff.

As he ran back to the place where the path from the beach met the road, he began to hear sirens. That would be the Chief coming he thought. The louder one would be at the firehouse calling the ambulance crew together. By the time the Chief met him at the path, he could hear the sirens of the ambulance and other police cars coming down the road.

He took the Chief down the bluff to where the woman was. He noticed her breath again, even weaker now, blood still bubbling from her nose. The chief reached down, shook her, but got no response except a shallow breath,

"Christ, it's the Stinsin girl, its Eva," the Chief said. "Somebody's beaten her bad, beat the heck out of her. Leatherby run back up to my car, get the blanket out of the back seat, rush it back here so we can cover her." Leatherby was back in a minute.

The Chief started to cover her when he noticed her hands were clenched into fists; something was gleaming between the fingers of one hand. He opened the hand and there was a chain with a crucifix cross, and with something else, something like a charm. It looked at closer. It was crossed oars, fused together at their middle points. Leatherby saw it.

"Chief, that's what she said, something about crossed oars, then just Mama, Daddy and Hank. That was the only thing she said, then she stopped."

By then two other officers had gotten to the bottom of the bluff, an ambulance crew was half-way down the path. The Chief spoke to one of his officers,

"Go back up, go to the Stinsin house. Tell Mrs. Stinsin we've found Eva. Tell her she's hurt bad; that we'll meet her at Doctor Vann's office, probably be fifteen, twenty minutes. Then see if there's any airplanes at the airport that can carry her to Providence. If she makes it to Dr. Vann's, he's gonna want to send her on the Providence hospital. She's got bad head injuries for sure."

The officer ran off the beach, passing the ambulance crew on the way down. Pretty soon the ambulance crew was administering to the girl, to Eva. As they went to put her on the stretcher, she gave a sigh.

Then one of them noticed that she wasn't breathing any more, even slightly. They checked her heart. It was still.

Chapter Thirty-Three
SWEET SORROW

She could see again. She was looking down at a body, a familiar body lying on a stretcher on a beach. The same beach where she and Hank had body surfed just days ago, where she had shocked herself, shocked him more. Where she had proudly shown her body, her breasts particularly. Teased him. But he'd proven he loved her as he always did. Proved he respected her.

She looked back up the island, could see her house now, it was miles away she knew, but she could see it like she was standing in the driveway; neighbors had gathered in the yard with her mother, crying. She was saddened for her mother, but there would come a time when she would make everything right. Make it right for all those she loved. It's what she always did.

She looked out to sea, could see the *Eva* off in the distance, running hard for Old Harbor. Her father at the wheel, Hank beside him.

Then she was standing in the wheelhouse door. Next to her father. Wished she was there to sing ditties. Those times, though, were in the other life. Where the road started, not where it had ended.

She talked to her father then, knew he couldn't hear her but she needed to tell him. "I love you Daddy. I'll miss you. Look after Mama until I send for you." She saw then that his eyes were tear filled, wanted to wipe them for him. Saw his fear, too. Wanted to charm his fears away. But charm was gone. With the rest of it.

She looked at Hank and it was like she was in his arms again, fronts touching, his features were so close. He couldn't see her. She knew that. And she couldn't kiss him now. But she wanted desperately to kiss him, to hold him one more time, lots of times. It couldn't be, wouldn't be until a time even she didn't know. Thought, then, for just a moment what it would have been like had they not been waiting for Christmas. Would he survive what had happened to her better for the waiting, or better had they not waited. She wished she knew. Then thought again, was glad she didn't know. Supposed his memories of what might have been would be even stronger. Remind him of her forever.

Then she thought, questioned really, how long is forever? It hadn't been as long as she'd thought.

She felt herself being drawn away from Hank, from the *Eva*, the sea on which it was and the earth upon which all else was. Being drawn up, moving faster, into the sky. One last time she looked at Hank as he receded from her view, first gradually, then faster. She hurried to whisper to him, "I love you," one more time, then blew him a kiss and she was rising from everything she had ever been. A tear ran down her cheek. She sent it to him with her kiss.

We had run her hard, hard as she'd go. Racing for Old Harbor. For Mrs. Stinsin. To find Eva. As we closed the island from the southeast, we could see the lights on the bluff, the blinking lights. Could tell they were police cars or ambulances. We could even see people down at the bottom of the bluff; from the distance they looked like scurrying insects. We looked at each other, the Captain and me. Not saying anything, not wanting to say anything. Afraid to say it, to think it even.

For a moment, a fleeting moment, I felt a kiss on my cheek. Knew it was her. Knew somehow that she was trying to say goodby. Then it was gone, the fleeting moment. Had to have been my imagination; she wasn't there. I hadn't seen her. Couldn't have been dreaming. I was wide awake.

I felt something else on my cheek, something moving. I reached up with my finger and felt a tear. I hadn't known I was crying. But a tear was on my cheek. Something made me capture it, cup it in my hand, bring it to my face, then the scent of lilacs was with me one more time. I knew for sure then. She was leaving. I turned to the sky, said aloud, "I love you, too."

The Captain looked at me. Understood. Started sobbing.

Chapter Thirty-Four

TEARS

She had died at the moment of her sigh, the moment I felt her kiss upon my cheek. She had made the Captain and I know it, though we couldn't know it. It was Eva. Even in death the rules didn't apply.

I would never again be on a boat and look up, look over at land in the distance, without thinking of that last moment with her, how she had managed to transport herself through the differing dimensions of death and life for one final instant, to console us, her father and me. I would dream of it in countless rooms, in countless places. It would be with me forever.

By the time we arrived in Old Harbor, other fishermen were waiting to hop aboard, care for the boat, so that the Captain and I could rush ashore. Soon we were pulling up in the Stinsin yard. It was full of neighbors, friends, all standing, some weeping. One of them said, "They're at Dr. Vann's."

The Captain drove us over several roads until we arrived at a house with a doctor's office attached. There were two police cars, an ambulance, other cars in the parking lot, the yard and on the street. The police cars and ambulance still had their emergency lights blinking. There was also a crowd in the yard, milling some, mostly just standing there. They were talking as we drove up. Grew silent as we got out. Just looked at us. Pitying looks.

They made a path for us as we went to the door. We opened it and entered, could see an open door down the hallway, hear sobs. We walked down the hallway to the door. Eva was lying on a gurney, covered except for her face and the hand that Mrs. Stinsin was holding as she lay her head on Eva's chest, stroking her face with the other hand.

Eva's face was misshapen, bruised, cut. Blood was clotted in the golden honey hair. They had closed her eyes.

I noticed then that the Captain was swaying, then he collapsed at my feet. The ambulance attendants and the doctor carried him to a chair, administered to him. I went over then to Mrs. Stinsin, laid

209

my hand on her shoulder. Then bent over and took her in my arms, hugged her. Said nothing. There was not one single thing in the world I was capable of saying, bending over with Eva's body lying there like it was on a table. I could see the beauty that had been her, could see it only because I had seen it when it was her. It wasn't her, though. I kissed it anyway. It was cold to my lips. She was gone somewhere. My love, our love was with her. It was gone from the emptiness that she had filled, the emptiness that now was me. Again. We were both gone, Eva and I. We weren't what we were and would never be in this place, on this earth.

The Captain had come to, was rising from the chair with the help of the attendants. They helped him over to the gurney. He stood there for a moment looking at Eva's body, her beaten face. Took his hand, ran it through her bloody hair. Bent over and kissed her face. Straightened, turned to Mrs. Stinsin, said "Come Mama, there's nothing we can do here." He took one arm, me the other, made our way out the door, down the hallway, out to the truck. We put her in the truck. As we did the preacher motioned to me. I understood, said to the Captain, "I'm goin' to stay a bit, can't leave yet." He nodded, started the truck, left.

I walked over to the preacher, tears still running, streaking my cheeks. A "hunk" she'd told me I was and I was sobbing like a baby. Couldn't help it. It just came. The preacher stood with his arms around me, just standing there. Eva had loved him, too. Differently, but she'd loved him, respected him. Because she did, I had respected him. Respected him still. In a moment, he spoke,

"I'll make the arrangements. I have taken care of all the Stinsins since so long I can't remember. I'll take the burden off them. Off you. It'll be a while though, they have to send her over to the Medical Examiner in Providence for an autopsy. It's required. They need to establish what happened as close as they can. It'll take two or three days. I'll plan the services for five days from now. They'll be in the church. She'll be interred in the family plot in Island Cemetery at the intersection of West Side and Center Roads."

"Do what you think the Captain and Mrs. Stinsin want. Eva would want it to be done that way." I replied.

"Will you tell them or do you want me to tell them?" He said, "I'll be dropping by the house as soon as I leave here."

"If you can wait a minute," I said, "we can go to the house together. I want to check with the Chief before I leave, find out what I can."

"I'll wait out here for you."

I went inside. They were wheeling her out, her face covered now, taking her to the ambulance for the trip to New Harbor where they'd put her on a Coast Guard boat for the trip to Point Judith. There a hearse would be waiting to take her to the Medical Examiner's office in Providence.

I stepped aside so they could get by, tried not to look down at the gurney. Did, though. She was just a shape beneath a sheet. "God," I screamed inside, screamed silently, "It ain't fair that you took 'er." I then said to myself, "She was your special angel." They went on by, the Chief stayed behind standing in the doorway of the room they had come from. Said to him, then

"I need to talk."

"Thought you might."

"What do you know?"

"Lots of it you could see. She was badly beaten. Doc Vann is pretty sure it was pressure buildin' up in her brain from bleedin' that actually killed 'er."

"But how'd she get in the water? Get on the beach?"

"It's too early to tell for sure; looks like she jumped over or was put over from a boat after she'd been beaten. Somehow got ashore, swimming, currents. We don't really know. When she was first seen she was awash in the surf."

"Who found her?"

"Leatherby was night fishing for stripers. Drinking some, there was an empty rum bottle with a fresh smell to it that we found. He fell asleep sometime in the night, woke up when the sun rose and glared in his eyes. Went to check on his rod in its holder, saw something in the surf, went to it, found her and pulled her out. She was rollin' over as the waves came in."

"He see anything else?"

"Hank, she was alive when he pulled her out. Died maybe twenty minutes later."

I stood there for a second, I hadn't heard that; all the Captain and I knew was that she was dead. I remembered then the feeling I'd had, the kiss as we were making for Old Harbor. The lilacs in the tear. That had been shortly after sunrise. Right when she had died.

"Leatherby said she was limp when he pulled her out, not moving at all that he could notice. He did hear her speak, she talked before she died. Not much. But talked some."

"What did she say?"

"According to Leatherby she kept repeating two words several times. 'Crossed oars.' Said it three or four times."

"Crossed oars? What's that mean?" I asked.

"Don't know for sure yet. It's a clue somehow, related to something else we have, but other than that we don't know what it means. She didn't explain what she meant. Leatherby said it was mumbles, he could hardly hear it, had to get down on his knees, get his ear close to her mouth just to hear it. Then we have this," he continued, reaching in his breast pocket, "when I got there her hands were clinched in fists. Tight. Doc said it was probably because of her head injury, that when that part of her brain stopped working the muscles clinched up. I saw something between the fingers of one hand, managed to open it, found her clenching this."

He finished pulling what looked like jewelry from his pocket. I saw that it was a gold chain and after he opened his hand fully I could see a gold cross, with a crucifix figure embossed on it and hanging separately from the chain a set of crossed oars fused together like a charm.

"This is a key to what happened?" I asked.

"Yes. I'd appreciate it if you didn't say anything about it for a while; right now it's the only clue we have other than her body. I want to ask around see if anybody's seen anything like it. Word gets out, whoever lost it might take off, maybe get a duplicate. Do whatever he can to explain losing it. Keep it quiet for while; won't be long. It's bound to get out soon; fact is if I don't get a reaction to it early on, I'll be putting it in the paper."

"What else do you know?"

"She said something else according to Leatherby, just three words. Said them in order. Think you ought to know, said 'Mama, Daddy, Hank.' Those were the last words she said.

"Other than what I've told you we know nothing yet about how it happened, the particulars. We know she left the hotel around twelve-

212

thirty. Left to walk home. The next time anybody saw her anywhere was when Leatherby pulled her out of the surf. We haven't had any time to ask around; there hasn't been enough time for most people on the island to even learn of it. It's real early in the investigation, but, to be honest, I don't think we'll get much volunteered information. There weren't any reports of screaming or anything like that last night. You know how islanders are; if they'd heard anything the phone at the police station would have been ringing off the hook. Not a call after midnight.

"I'm thinking that somehow or 'nother whoever did it got her on a boat, beat her there. There were signs she fought whoever it was. When we got her in the Doc's, he noticed right off that four or five of her fingernails were broken. She had bruises all over her upper body, separate bruises, lots of 'em. Usually means that the victim has kept on fighting. Once they stop fighting the beating usually stops. If she was doing that much fighting she was probably screaming. If she'd been getting that much of a beating here on the island, people would have been able to hear her screams and the phones would have been ringing. I could be wrong, but I think it happened on a boat. When he, or they, got finished, they tried to kill her, thought she was dead and threw her over."

"What do you mean, 'when they got finished?'"

"Hank, Doc thinks she was raped. There were signs. Doc thought there must have been more than one of them."

I shuddered. Could see her on a boat; see men on her. Felt sick. Overwhelmingly sick. Threw up right there in the doctor's office. Over me, the floor. The chief rushed me to a chair, got the trash can. I sat, was sick again.

I slowly steeled myself. Blocked out of my mind the scene of it. Then I felt a white heat, something rising up the back of my neck. Felt hate seeping into my brain, my heart, into my soul. In all the places she'd filled with love not long ago, love that was still there. But it had a new companion. Hate for those that had done it. Until now I hadn't thought of hate. Anyway one's own hate isn't something that's thought of, it just comes. Then I said, not realizing I was speaking aloud,

"I will kill 'em, I will kill 'em."

"Hank," the Chief said, "you let us take care of it. It's our job."

"Chief, I find 'em, I kill 'em. You find 'em, I'll come for 'em and take 'em, kill 'em. Don't be gettin' in the way. I like you, but that happens, they get found, they'll not see the inside of a courtroom if I'm alive. They get found I'll be a dangerous man; you'd best take care if it happens, they get found. Don't get in my way."

"Hank, we'll talk later. For now there's things you need to help the Stinsins with. Arrangements. Just being with them. We probably won't know much more until we get the autopsy reports back, maybe nothing even then. Keep in mind, you do something the law don't allow, you could get locked up, maybe worse."

"You think there's anything worse than this?" I asked, as I rose and made my way outside. He followed me out. Said, "Let me give you a ride to the Stinsins."

"Take me to where she came ashore. I need to go there."

"Get in."

I walked over to the preacher, told him that I was going with the Chief, that I'd see him shortly at the Stinsins.

I got in the Chief's car and he drove me the mile or so up on the bluff.

"You go on back," I said, "I'm goin' to be awhile. I'll need to walk after. I'll get on back later."

As I got out of the police car I noticed that there was another police car, with an officer sitting in it at the top of bluff. I paused, turned back to the Chief, said "I'd like to be alone."

"Ok, but there's an area marked off down there, don't disturb it."

As I started down the path both cars moved off. When I got to the bottom, I could see the area marked off, scuff marks led from the area to the path I'd just come down. The tide was lower now and I could see two drag marks leading from the edge of the sea to the marked area on the beach. It was where Leatherby had dragged her when he pulled her from the water, her feet dragging. I walked down to the edge of the sea, sat next to the drag marks. Where her feet, her body had been when she was still alive. Nothing happened. I couldn't think of her. Mind just blank. But I was weeping anyhow. Alone. I rose, started to leave, but something made me pause; I wasn't satisfied.

I bent over, took off my shoes, undressed, left all my clothes in a pile, there next to where she'd been just hours ago. Walked naked into the water, first knee high, then higher, and soon I was swimming to the point where we had surfed just days ago. There wasn't any need to go on with this life. There wasn't anything worth having left. Just a blank world, Except for the hate. It made no sense to stick it out. For what? She was gone.

I tread water, waiting, there off the point. Waiting to get tired. Too tired to swim back. Waiting for it to be over.

I glanced back to the shore, saw the waves breaking. Saw something. Saw her feet, the soles of her feet as she caught a wave, saw it just as it was, had been. Then she was back out, treading water again, not saying anything. Just being there with me. Loving me. Then she smiled, turned to catch another wave, I went with her. To the beach, riding the foam. I looked up and she was walking to me, smiling.

I shook my head. I was alone still, treading water off the point. I began to realize though, that I wasn't really alone. I had memories still, wondered, would they be enough? Could I live on memories. Memories and hate. I knew then that neither of them would ever leave me until it was all over. Something came over me, a feeling I couldn't describe. A feeling that I still had a purpose, purposes different than before. Before she died. To keep her alive by keeping her memories of her in my mind. To find those that had killed her. To bring them to justice. Our justice, Eva's and mine.

I found myself back on the beach putting my clothes on. Being scratched by the sand stuck to them, hadn't needed to be neat considering why I had swum out. As I got to the top of the bluff, the Chief met me. Had come back to make sure that I didn't do anything foolish. He had draped his Sam Brown gear over the window of his car, his shoes and socks were on the front seat. Said when I got to the top of the bluff, "Thought you might need a ride anyway."

I looked at him standing there, shirt unbuttoned, barefooted, said "Thanks."

He knew what I was thanking him for.

Chapter Thirty-Five

NUMBNESS

I didn't feel like going to the Stinsins. There would be lots of things I didn't feel like in the months to come, in the years to come. But I went anyway. I could cry with them; I could cry without them. And I did until I left the island.

When the Chief drove me back to the Stinsin house there was still a crowd of people in the yard. Friends and neighbors. I recognized most, either from the neighborhood or from church. They parted as I walked to the porch, crossed it and opened the door, went inside.

The Captain was sitting at the dinning room table, the preacher next to him. The Captain's head was on his arms, which were resting on the table. I pulled up a chair, sat down and put my arm over his shoulders. I didn't say anything. Just cried with him. After a while I asked, "Where's Mrs. Stinsin?"

The preacher answered, "She's in bed. Several ladies are sitting with her."

I went back to crying. Didn't know what else there was. Only the hate and this wasn't the place for it. At least I thought it wasn't. The Captain got himself under control some, almost stopped crying, turned some and put his arm around me.

"Thanks." He said.

"Why thanks?"

"Because of you she was in love. She didn't die without ever havin' found someone to love. She had you. Thank you for lovin' 'er."

"No, I owe you thanks, you and Mrs. Stinsin, for havin' 'er, for letting me be a part of 'er, for letting me love 'er, for approvin' of me."

"She made you different," the Captain said then, "you changed from one day to the next. She did it to you. Wanted to do it to you. She always got what she wanted but she never wanted what she shouldn't.

"It don't figure. I'm a religious man. But it don't figure. Why was it 'er. The preacher's been talkin', he's a smart man, come the right time I might be listenin' to God talk. Not now. But he'll be makin' the arrangements. What Eva would have wanted. But afore I get my religion back, if I ever get it back, I want you to promise me something."

"Anything."

"If I ain't around when they find them as did it to 'er, I want you to kill 'em. Hurt 'em bad as you can afore you finish it."

"I swear it." I answered.

The preacher tried to interrupt then, but the Captain said, "Be quiet preacher, we goes back a long time, our kin been 'ere forever and I respect you. But you best be quiet, I ain't got much tolerance for the Lord right now, or His messengers. There might be a time to talk with me on this, now ain't it. Appreciate you makin' the burial arrangements. We'll want 'er with the Stinsins. Get the bills sent to me. Need to be alone with Hank 'ere."

The preacher left the dinning room then, pausing on his way out to squeeze the Captain's shoulder, then mine. I heard him going up the stairs.

The Captain looked at me then, tears running down his face, said "What're we gonna do, can't take much of this feelin'?"

"Captain, I don't know what to do. Everything hurts. It hurts walkin' through 'at door, sittin' 'ere. This was where she sat. We ain't ever gonna get any of it out of our minds. Good things, bad things, gonna be in our heads forever. We got to live with it cause we ain't never gonna be shed of any of it."

I stayed at the Stinsin house until after the funeral. A constant stream of 'casserole' ladies kept food in the house. Mostly they ate it. The Captain and I just sat around drinking coffee. Never went to bed. We'd fall asleep in chairs when our eyes finally closed. Get up, clean up and begin sitting around again. I'd go in and see Mrs. Stinsin every day, sit with her for a while. We'd try not to talk of Eva, but always did; always cried. Mrs. Stinsin came down from their bedroom the day Eva returned to the island.

She stood along side the road as the hearse went by taking Eva to the church. I'd gone out just to be with her. She waved at it. Stood there waving softly at it until it was around the corner. I helped her back in the house, sat her on the couch. There were two ladies there, they'd been upstairs. One of them said, "We'll take care of her." I walked over to the Captain, sitting again at the dinning room table.

Told him I was going for a walk, be back in an hour. He waved his hand in acknowledgment.

I walked up to the police station. Went in to see the Chief. An officer showed me to his office. Knocked on the door, "Chief, Hank Gaskins is here."

"Send him in."

I went in, the Chief was behind a desk, motioned me to take a chair at one corner of it. "Guess you want to know some things?" he said. I nodded.

"You want it soft, you want it hard.?"

"I want it all, don't care how I get it."

"There might have been more than one that raped her. It was a brutal rape. She fought 'em hard, at least as long as she could. Even with her being in the water, there was still skin under the nails that weren't broken. I told you her hands was clinched tight when I got there. Probably helped preserve the stuff under her nails. There were hairs in her bra, mens hairs, one a blonde and one dark haired. May of been more of 'em. They tore up her female parts, tore her up inside. Examiner said she'd been a virgin."

"I know," I said. "There was nothin' about 'er that weren't perfect, whole."

"Her dress washed up about a mile down the beach from where she was found. It had been ripped down the front. Medical examiner said from the way it was ripped, it had been torn from her by somebody. Hadn't been ripped by rocks or nothing. Said he thinks they took off her underwear before they raped her. Weren't any tears on her panties and the bra wasn't broken, stretched some but not broken like it would have been if they'd tore it while they was raping her. There weren't any marks on her body that the bra straps would have made had it been on when they beat her.

"Medical examiner says they must have knocked her unconscious first somewhere else, took her to the boat, then undressed her, took her underwear off, then raped her and tried to kill her, thought they'd killed her outright. That means that before they put her in the water one of them put her panties and bra back on. Probably threw the dress over. Medical examiner thinks they were probably trying to make it look like some kind of accident if she was found; he thinks she may

218

have been kept in the boat for a while after they raped and beat her. He thinks they sailed in close at Southeast light before they put her over, figuring if she floated up near there people might think that the rocks had somehow killed her, falling down the bluff, maybe getting caught in a rouge wave on the beach.

"Leatherby doesn't remember hearing any engine runnin' offshore of the light, but admits he was drunk and had fallen asleep. So it could have been a motor boat of some kind, but the best bet is that it was a sailboat, just slipped in close and let her over."

"How'd she get to the beach alive?"

"Examiner says the injury that caused her death takes a while to do it. Gets slowed down some if it gets cooled, the body temperature gets down some. He figures that she was unconscious when they threw her over, the water revived her some and she started swimming. He figures the boat was pretty far in when she hit the water. The water slowed down the swelling in her brain, didn't stop it, just slowed it down some. Said the longer she went on the weaker she was getting. He's surprised she ever made it to the beach. Swelling of the brain kills one function after another until the person dies.

"I know it doesn't help any, but it was already too late to save her when Leatherby pulled her out. The process had gone too far by then."

"You find out anything about the chain, the cross and the oars?"

"I've been to every house on the island since it happened. No-one recognized it. All the stores. Nobody remembers seein' 'it. I'm thinkin' that it was an off-islander. Summertime, boats in and out of the harbors every minute. Especially last weekend with the finish of the big race over at Newport. New harbor was full of the race boats, crews ashore letting off steam. Bars full, fights everywhere. The people over at Newport have sent over the order of finish and we'll be checking it out as we go along.

Then there's the ferries letting off hundreds of visitors every day, some day visitors, some overnighters. Since it happened probably been five thousand people through 'ere, five hundred boats and most of 'em don't bother registering with the harbor master on race weekend. I don't know for sure but my feeling is that whoever done it is long gone. Ain't any islanders come up gone that shouldn't be gone."

"Can I have a picture of the chain and the things with it?"

He paused, then yelled out in the front office for the officer that had taken me back to the chief's office, told him to made me a Polaroid of the items. When he brought the photo back, I stood, put out my hand to the Chief, shook his, said, "Thanks. I'll stop by every now and then to see what's going on."

"Hank," he said, "I ain't givin' up, none of us is. She belonged to the island, one of ouren. I'll keep after it long's I can."

I said thanks and left.

I sat with the Captain and Mrs. Stinsin at the funeral the next day. She'd been beaten so badly they kept the casket closed except when they opened it for the Stinsins and me. They had done as good a job as they could I guess. But it wasn't Eva, wasn't the girl that loved me. I looked for the ring, wanted it to be wherever her body was going. It was on her. I didn't kiss her, didn't kiss the dead person lying there. I'd had my last kiss from her on the *Eva* as we came up on Southeast Light days before.

At the funeral the preacher said whatever it is that preachers say. Didn't hear him say anything about God's will, 'better places' and such. Don't think the Captain would have tolerated it, knew I wouldn't. The preacher just talked about how wonderful she was, had been. He talked of her, while I thought of her, went into the memories.

After a while the pallbearers were carrying her out to the hearse for the ride to Island Cemetery. The hole in the ground was at the side of the Stinsin lot, near several lilac bushes that almost made a little cove amongst the graves. I was surprised for I had expected it to be in the middle so that when the Captain and Mrs. Stinsin passed she could be between them. The preacher said some more words. I wasn't listening to them. I just stood there watching my life being lowered into the ground. As they removed the straps with which they had lowered the casket, people started coming over to the Stinsins and me, saying words that meant nothing, really, well meant words, though. I just went through the pantomime, letting my hand be grasped, lowering my head, pretending I was listening, nodding an acknowledgment of words I hadn't heard. Except when Bill the bus-driver grabbed my hand, said, "She was something, she was. I'm so sorry." I hugged him, responded, "I know it especially pleases her that you came."

We walked to the Stinsin home; was a considerable walk for us in our condition. South on Center Road, then east on Old Town to their house. The 'casserole' ladies were on the porch. We could see them as we approached. I stopped the Stinsins as we approached the driveway, told them that they needed to be alone without me; that I needed to be alone. Told the Captain, "I'll come by a week from today. See what we're goin' to do now. Can't talk on it now, know you can't. I love the both of you." I turned, went back up Old Town to the Hill Top Road. Passed Bill walking to the ferry dock, nodded, continued on. Went to my bed, laid down and began to cry again.

We went back to sea a week later, wasn't anything else to do. Went out 'sticking' swordfish. We found out the first day that all we could talk on was the fish. Anything else we said led back to her. One of us would say, "Remember when she . . .," and one or the other of us would cry, then the other. By the third day we had tacitly agreed to talk only on the fish. Again, we caught our share the rest of the summer, more really.

Both of us were crazy, taking chances, going out when it was too rough. Beating the hell out of the sea, the fish and ourselves. Then it came to a head.

It was a mid-September day; we had stuck a big fish, almost had her to the boat with me pulling her as gently as I could with one hand, a lance in the other, when a large mako came up under, hit her tail, and disappeared. The strike pulled the dart out and she was lying there on the surface, maybe fifteen feet away, twitching, when, about fifteen or so seconds later the mako returned, came from under the boat heading towards her. A big male, claspers showing.

Didn't think on it. The white heat was on me, up my back, in my head. I jumped off the *Eva* with the lance in front of me, stabbing the free swimming shark right before I smacked into it. All hell broke loose. The mako literally exploded, wrenched the lance from my hand, took off across the surface tearing up fifty yards of water. I didn't give a damn. Just swam the rest of the ten yards to the swordfish, grabbed what was left of the tail, pulled it on over to the boat, not worrying about the shark. Could still see it thrashing, a hundred yards off now. I bumped into the *Eva,* looked up and the Captain was standing there, shaking his head from side to side, had the thirty-thirty in his hands.

221

He glanced out to where the shark was thrashing, put the rifle down, bent over, threw me a line, said, "While you're bein' dumb as a corncob, why don't you just put this 'ere line up under her gills so we can haul 'er in."

I snugged it under one pectoral fin, then under her gills and tightened it. The Captain bent over the gunwale, lowered his hand, I took it and he helped me back aboard. We hauled the fish in. The Captain looked astern, said, "Looks like the mako is done for, just lying there twitchin' erself. Might's well go get 'er long's you've decided we're out here shark fishin'." Soon we had the mako aboard, dressed and in the box with the swordfish.

That night, both of us were outside sitting side by side on the gunwale, drinking coffee. Just sitting, not talking. It was a cloudless night, no fog, a million stars. He said to me, "That all you done today don't do no good, son. Being crazy won't get it. She wouldn't 'ave wanted you to do it. She'd been aboard she'd be right smart mad on it." I didn't respond; he didn't say anything else. I didn't go overboard the rest of the season.

The season wound down and soon was over. I hadn't gone to school. Been admitted but couldn't go. The Stinsins understood and never said a word about me not going. The Captain and I started the painting some but it wasn't the same. It was only painting. I woke up every morning with nothing to look forward to. The year before Eva had been going to come home for Thanksgiving, for Christmas, when school was over. She wasn't coming this year, wasn't writing letters.

I'd started drinking some, at the Hill Top mostly. Some nights when the memories hurt the most I'd get drunk and sometimes get mean. I'd never been mean on this island. But I'd had all I could take. Somebody would say the wrong thing, especially about a woman, about all women. Usually I didn't say anything first, mostly they weren't even talking to me. I'd just hit them anyway. Generally, I won the fights I started, but not always. When I lost I liked it better, it hurt then, hid the other hurt, the one I really couldn't stand. Got me a reputation, the fighting did. One like I'd had back home before the meanness had left me. Before this island and her.

The bartender started cutting me off early on a regular basis when he saw I was getting drunk. That was okay with me, I liked him, knew he was doing what he had to do. I'd just go to my room, grab a bottle from under the bed, lie down and drink myself to sleep. Up early the next morning. Drunk again at night. Sunday evenings I'd go to the Stinsins for dinner. None of us went to church anymore.

Often Leatherby was at the Hill Top painting. The first time after the funeral when I saw him there, he came over, told me he was sorry. I thanked him for what he had done; told him that we appreciated that he'd tried to save her and that she'd been with an islander when she died. That he had been able to tell us that she was thinking of us when reason, then life, left her. I'd drink with him until it was time to stagger home.

It went on day by damned day. Me feeling like a husk with nothing inside me. I was just a covering that covered nothing. I began to realize that I couldn't stay much longer on the island. I had to get off, go somewhere. I couldn't live in the constant memories. I couldn't rest my mind when every bush, every grain of sand, the waves rolling in, reminded me of her.

Christmas Eve the Stinsins had me for dinner. A quiet dinner. All of us separately remembering the last Christmas. We didn't make it to desert. All of us were crying. After awhile, I told them I had to leave, that I couldn't stand staying any longer. I'd be leaving tomorrow. Hoped I could come back, but didn't know when, didn't know for sure if ever. Said I'd write to let them know where I was. They were the only family I had. I was like their son. But it pained all of us to be together, each of us reminding the others of her.

They understood. When I rose to leave, Mrs. Stinsin came to me took me in her arms, said "Time is what we all need. You come back to us. We love you." I told her that I would, that they were the only people in the world that I had left to love, but I was going crazy. She hugged me tighter, then let me go. While we had been hugging and saying goodby, the Captain had gone over to a drawer in a buffet, opened it and took out some blue-backed papers, came to me, grabbed my shoulders and hugged me, said, "I ain't sayin' goodby, just you have a good trip. You'll be back 'ere. These here are some legal papers for you. Keep 'em, use 'em when your time comes."

"What they about?" I asked.

"They're the papers to the lot in the cemetery, the one right next to the Stinsin lot. We had her buried on the side of ouren, stead of the middle, so's you can be side by side when the time comes. Wanted you in the family for ourselves."

I just stood there.

"Don't need no thanks. Know how you feel, that's 'nough," he said, as he put his arm around me and walked me to the door. As we walked out on the porch it had started to snow, already a dusting. He walked me out to the road, reached up and kissed me on the cheek, turned and started walking back to the house, said as he did,

"Stay clear of 'em bad boys, you hear."

I went on up to the Hill Top, told the bartender that I'd be leaving early the next day, Christmas day. Told him how much I owed for the room, left it with him to give to the manager. Leatherby, who was at the bar, had heard the conversation. He turned to me, said "I figured you'd have to leave for a while anyway, didn't know it'd be tomorrow. I been afixin' something for you, almost done. Stay here while I get it." I had planned to stay there until I was stone drunk or the bartender cut me off.

Leatherby was back in fifteen minutes, carrying a package wrapped in brown butcher paper. It was about three by four feet. He handed it to me, said, "Open it. It's yours, made it special for you."

It was a painting of a swordfish boat. I remembered, then, that I had asked him to paint me one. I said to him, "It's great, how much do I owe you?" I was looking at the picture closer as I asked him. He didn't answer me. I realized then that it was a painting of the *Eva* out on the swordfishing grounds. The two men on her were big men, oversized, like the Captain and me. Leatherby had painted a picture of the boat with us on it. Only thing missing was the dory being towed. There was a line there but it just trailed in the water. He hadn't had time to paint the dory in; it looked ok, natural even, the way it was. One of the men was up on the pulpit getting ready to "stick" a swordfish you could see finned out in the water beneath him, The other man was standing midship with a keg in his hand. I noticed then that there was another crew member up on the platform, the crow's nest. A woman with her long honey colored hair streaming behind her. He'd painted Eva in the picture. Looking just like she'd looked when she had sailed with the Captain and me. I started weeping, the meanest man, the toughest man on the island sitting in the roughest bar on Christmas Eve, sobbing.

Leatherby put his hand on my shoulder, hugged me, said, "Know you loved 'er. Wanted you to have this painting. I'm goin' home now, you have a good trip," he finished.

"Thanks, Leatherby," I said still crying, "I'll treasure it." He left then. I just sat there looking at the picture, thinking of her, getting drunker. The bartender closed the bar early, around eleven.

I walked to the Stinsin house, left Leatherby's painting on the porch, wasn't room to take it with me the way I was going. I'd write them, tell them I'd send for it as soon as I was somewhere permanent.

I caught the first ferry in the morning.

Chapter Thirty-Six

FLORIDA WINTER

I had the bus driver let me off at Uncle Dick's. It's where some of the guides and mates hung out on the south end of the purple isle, Matecumbe. Islamorada, Florida to the tourists. Uncle Dick operated a mail drop where a lot of the itinerant mates and guides would get their mail. It was the headquarters for fishermen. I dropped my duffle outside the door; no need to worry that someone would steal it. Stealing wasn't a healthy occupation in this part of the keys. Get you killed.

Went to drinking, waiting for the charter and back-country boats to come in across the way at the marina. I was in the sport fishing center of the keys. When the mates and guides got there, I might know some of them. They'd know which boat needed a mate, know where the jobs were.

By three o'clock some of the guide boats started coming in, they'd been fishing for bonefish mostly; there had been a high blue sky, little wind, several days of warm weather, with tide moving up on the flats for the better part of the day. Perfect conditions for bonefishing. Some of them had probably actually gone to the edge of the 'glades', running over to Shark River channel, to Flamingo, fishing for redfish and trout, hoping to find a place where snook were laying.

Later the charter boats came in loaded with dolphin, yellow colored by now, they'd been out of the water for a while. But I could see them in my mind fresh caught, with the brilliant blues and greens. They were beautiful fish, big blunt headed bulls, more graceful cows. Jumping jacks the both of them. There were several sailfish put on the dock. Weren't many releases back then. Most fish were brought in, billfish even. They'd be dressed, eaten. What wasn't eaten fresh was smoked and ended up in little packages of smoked fish sold in all the bars up and down the keys.

By the time the charter boats had started showing up across the street, I had made arrangements for a place to stay. Don, one of the guides, had made a deal with the owner of a Constellation, big yacht that had caught on fire and burned some before they got it out. It was docked in a secluded canal surrounded by mangroves on the ocean side about a mile up the island where several commercial stone crab and crawfish potters moored their boats; there was a tailboat moored alongside, as well. The owner of the Constellation was letting the guide live aboard and in return the guide was repairing the burn damage, fiber-glassing the burnt areas on days he wasn't booked. The guide offered me the same deal. He figured one more body was less fiber-glassing work for him. Took him up on the deal. Knew I'd be itching some, fiber-glassing is an itchy business. But, what the hell, it wasn't the worst thing.

He told me of a boat, the *Pardon Me*, that had lost it's mate. He had married a pilgrim; turned him into a pilgrim. He'd just up and left; been taken to Atlanta where she was from, where her money was. The boat had been in its slip when I got off the bus. A big Mathews sport fisherman; yardarm forward and all. Hadn't sailed that day.

Around five I saw a heavy set man walk down a dock across the street, step on the transom of the *Pardon Me*, then down into the cockpit. I paid my check, told the bartender I was leaving my bag at the door, would be back for it. I crossed the highway to the marina and walked down the dock to the boat where the captain was working on the radio in the cabin. I hailed him,

"Captain, hear you might be needin' a mate?"

He turned, looked at me, yelled back, "You one of 'em?"

"Yep."

"Where you from?"

"Ocean City, Maryland by way of Block Island."

"Get aboard, ain't no reason to conduct business so everybody on the dock can hear it."

I climbed into the cockpit as he wiped his hand on a rag, held it out, said, "I'm Captain Boinis, Demeatris Boinis. Most people call me Meach. '

"Hank Gaskins. Hank 'ill do for me."

We spent a half-hour learning about each other, checking out the experience of the other. He said he needed a mate; when he heard me say I was from Ocean City he figured I might know a little bit about fishing. When he found out I'd fished the keys, south Florida, the islands some, he realized I knew more than a little bit. He knew one of the captains I had worked for at Hillsboro Inlet two years before and knew him to be a good fisherman. He questioned me about live baiting, kite fishing, even fishing electric gear for groupers and big red snappers, tile fish in the deep way out in the stream. I'd done it all one time or the other, one boat or the other. I learned that he had done it all, too, would fish any way a charter party wanted, preferred bill-fishing though, fishing for sails close in, marlin fishing further out, both of them over in the islands, giant tuna, too. He had a two week trip to West End coming up the end of January, trip to Bimini in mid-February. Have to take the boat up to Lauderdale to refuel, provision some, before he cut over to the Bahamas. The mate bunked on the boat when they were on trips. Had too really, wasn't any other place when they were in the islands.

Otherwise it was full-day or half-day fishing, day by day offshore here in the keys. Fishing had been good, so far the sails had showed up riding the stream north, then when fronts came through they'd been riding the northwest wind back south, tailing fish they'd be then, easier to see - harder to bait. He told me what I already knew, the fish would ride the northerly white caps south in the stream, using the waves to help head the northerly current. Their tails would be out of the water most of the time but more often than not they weren't feeding. Sometimes, you might get them to take a live bait. But normally not. He used a lot of live bait, went out evenings in a skiff where the channel from the marina and the cut under the bridge went across the reef on the way to the deep. Used tiny jigs to catch blue runners, goggle-eyes sometimes, chain rigs to catch pilchards when they were around. Usually had a live well full when he went out. Sounded good to me.

He'd pay me twenty-five dollars a half day trip, forty dollars an all day trip. We'd split any mount money fifty-fifty, also split the fish money down the middle. I kept my tips; he kept his. Days we weren't sailing we'd service the boat in the morning, do maintenance, whatever needed to be done, make sure she was fueled, catch live bait, whatever, have it done by noon in case a make-up party got together for an afternoon trip. If none showed up, we'd take off at two, come back next morning. Seven days.

He asked me where I was staying. I told him. He knew the guide I would be living with, knew the boat also. Told me that the setup would probably work ok, figured I could walk a mile to the dock. Last thing he asked was whether I drank much, caroused and such. Told him I did, but I'd never missed a sailing. Was never drunk on the boat when it was time to fish. Admitted I got in fights and such if I was pushed to it, sometimes when I wasn't. But it never bothered me showing up the next day for work. Asked me then,

"Figure you ain't married?"

"Ain't never been married."

"Me neither, things ain't never worked out that way."

"Yeah."

We shook hands then. I would start the next day. A full day trip for sailfish.

I spent most of the rest of the winter fishing the *Pardon Me* with Captain Boinis, He had a good reputation for catching fish already, but it got better when I started working. We began to throw a lot of fish on the dock, lots of sailfish; caught two white marlin in the week before we left for the islands the first time. It wasn't unusual to put a load of dolphin on the dock, twenty, thirty, couple of times when we found schools hanging around large pieces of floating debris we boated fifty or more.

One day when we were out early we found a whole palm tree floating north in the stream. We put a line on the tree so no other boat could fish it. The party caught over 400 before they got too tired to catch any more. Took me three days to filet and sell them all, but it put a nice piece of change in the bank. For the next two days we could hear the charter boat captains further north talking about the palm tree. They were probably still catching dolphin from under it at Hatteras.

Chapter Thirty-Seven
DAY IN - DAY OUT

The first trip to the islands was successful as far as the fishing was concerned. The charter party was a mobster from Chicago and his young wife. He wasn't doing his job with her and she tried to hook up with me. There had been a time when it would have happened, damn the consequences. Now, I just wasn't interested. Had somebody else in my mind, thinking of Eva.

Sometimes in the islands when I was staying aboard the *Pardon Me*, I'd wake up in the middle of the night, go out in the cockpit and lie back on the transom or fish-box and just look up at the sky. She was there somewhere, mingled amongst the stars and moon. I'd try to see her, identify her star. I'd imagine one was hers and I'd talk to it, tell my star how much I loved her. Tell her how my life was so empty without her. Tell her I would find them someday. Those that killed her.

I would wait for her to hear me, to talk to me, but the time wasn't to be, yet. When I would start crying, I would head for the bottle. I'd get drunk and imagine she was talking to me. But then the sun would start to rise, the stars would fade and soon I couldn't see her, even if I was drunk. I'd start the coffee then, cook breakfast in the galley for the Captain and me.

Around ten o'clock the mobster and his friendly wife would mosey on down to the boat and off we'd go to help him show off his manhood; show her even fat men could catch fish. And he did. We might have to back all over the ocean to help him, I might have to secretly handline hundreds of yards of line, staying below the gunwale of the boat, when a big fish went deep. We did it all the time, Captains and mates, caught the fish for the party without them knowing. We'd let them be the big man on the dock standing next to a marlin, sailfish or some other large sea creature. Generating the tips, mount money and usually fish money as well. Sometimes we'd sell the fish on the dock, sometimes take them to the commercial packing house in Marathon when we were home.

The first trip to the islands was a success. We sent the mobster back to Chicago and sent his wife back as deprived as she was when she came down. Back at Islamorada we were quickly back to our routine, full-day, half-day trips, weathered in some days. Fiber-glassing when I wasn't fishing. Itching for days after.

In midweek before the Monday we were to leave for the islands in February, Captain Boinis left for two days to go to a funeral in Panama City where he home-ported in the summer. One of his former mates had been killed in a fishing accident. When I got back to the Constellation, Don was there. When I told him I had a couple of days off, he said,

"Why don't we go up to *Sal's*?" Sal's was an upscale bar up in Key Largo where most of the money people went. Where the money was the girls were. Where the rich people mingled with the conchs, with fishermen like us; where they slummed.

"How we goin' to get all the way to Key Largo? Ain't either one of us has a car?"

"I got the next best thing."

"What?" I asked, thinking he must have a motorcycle stashed somewhere.

"I got the keys to the tailboat."

A tail boat is a powerful work boat with oversized props and an oversized diesel engine. It was used in Florida in those days, and elsewhere I suppose, in the towing of barges in narrow quarters, in the inter-coastal waterway, in local rivers, in any tight piece of water. A regular tugboat would have a barge in tow maybe thirty to fifty yards astern, the tail boat would have a line on the stern of the barge and follow the tow down a waterway. When the tugboat started around a left bend the tail boat would pull the stern of the barge to the right so that it could get around the bend. It would do the opposite on a right bend. A little bit like a hook and ladder operation I guess. Anyway, tailboats were powerful little boats with big engines turning oversized props.

"How come you've got the key? Don't want to be messin' around with something ain't legal."

"Owner knows me, knows I live next to it. He's up in Dania, got anothern there, only uses this one when he gets tows down 'ere, which ain't often. Gave me a set of keys, asked me to look after 'er, check 'er out after storms, wants me to run 'er ever now and then, make sure she stays loose, make sure she stays pumped out. Told me to run her outside some, keep a check on the steering cables and such."

Pretty soon we had thrown the lines aboard the tailboat, hawsers really, lines big enough to swing the stern of a barge around. We headed out of the gut to a channel across the reef into the ocean. Once we were clear of the reef we turned her north and headed up the coast for Key Largo.

After an hour's run we passed Tavernier and in short order we came to the light marking the entrance to the channel into Key Largo. We slowed her as much as possible to keep the wake down, barely making steerageway. Just inside of the key, *Sal's* was the first place on the waterway. It was waterside, built on pilings with a small deck running down the side of the bar with tie piles attached to the outside part of the dock. We tied up, bow and stern. I looped the large bow hawser over a pile and Don looped the stern hawser on another pile. Tailboats don't just have regular cleats, they also have large stanchions on the deck, bow and stern, in order to take the strain of tows. We fastened the hawsers to the stanchions. Walked through the tables and people on the deck and went into the bar.

Three hours later we were drunk. The next thing I knew Don was pouring a drink, some kind of cream drink down the front of a woman's dress, saying "Just puttin' some back." Her husband hit him. When two others jumped Don, I joined in, settled things, picked Don up, said, "I think they want us to leave."

"Fuck 'em."

With him under my arm, hollering obscenities at some of the richest people in the country, I took him out, walked him through the people on the deck, reached out over the tailboat and dropped him in. Then jumped aboard.

"You okay to run this thing?" I asked.

"Can run 'er drunk or sober."

"Best get 'er turned over, won't be long afore that bunch 'ill have the cops on us. I'll get the bow line you look to the stern." I said as he got the engine running. I went up to the bow, jumped up on the dock grabbed the hawser and threw it on the boat. Almost as soon as I was back on the boat, Don was warping it around to head out the channel, using the stern hawser on the pile as a fulcrum. I moved to the stern, waited for Don to give me enough slack to sling the hawser off the deck piling. He had another idea. As soon as he had her pointing east down the channel, he cracked the throttle. The line was so taut I couldn't swing it loose, then I thought it'd break and come back aboard and put us in danger so I ran back to the bow, yelling at him as I did to "Take it off 'er, it's gonna snap." Then the deck of the bar started shaking from the strain.

By now the people on the deck were falling out of their chairs, plates falling off the tables. The inside bar backed up to the window that separated the deck from inside. I could see glasses and bottles falling off the shelves. As Don kicked it to her, the whole place started shaking with people falling off bar stools and chairs. It got noisier, with everyone screaming, the tailboat's big diesel roaring. Then the piling we were attached to began to tilt our way, bringing a part of the deck with it. People started falling into the channel, dressed up ladies, dressed up men, people that had never seen anything like it before. Hell, I hadn't seen anything like it before. Then the whole damn thing came into the channel. The deck, the pilings, the wall of the main building, the whole thing. It went on for another ten seconds. Then I felt the boat throttled back some, then put in neutral.

Don stuck his head around the wheelhouse door, said "Think you got some slack now. Best not try to get the hawser off the piling, just take it off the stanchion and throw it in the mess."

I did, still in shock.

He throttled her back up and out the channel we headed. I said to him then, "Probably be best not to turn the runnin' lights on, case some of 'em get unconfused enough to want to figure out where we come from."

He was laughing, then I started. We laughed all the way back. After maneuvering the tailboat back in the mangroves, we hid her as best we could. We weren't worried about the other fishermen, they were conchs, like Don. The people in Key Largo were snow-birds, yankees mostly, rich bastards.

The next morning the Miami newspapers had a big story about the boat they called Tillie the Tug. They gave her the name. The natives, the locals thought it was a pretty good story.

We decided not to give any more of our patronage to *Sal's*.

Chapter Thirty-Eight
RUNNING BEAR

Considering that I didn't think that Sal was a happy man, I considered myself lucky to have spent the next week in the islands; this time in Bimini, my kind of place. Great fishing, lots of partying, lots of drinking, lots of bumping fuzzes for those that were up for it. I wasn't. Every time I felt myself begin to respond to a girl I'd think of Eva and that would be the end of it.

We came back from the island trip to Bimini into a mini-crisis. Captain Boinis had been dating a rich girl who spent the winters with her parents on a private island near Vaca Key. For whatever reason she was known as Running Bear. Sometimes they would have trysts on the boat; sometimes she'd get them a room at one of the hotels. Sometimes they just went to the beach. She couldn't stay away from him.

Her parents had been strongly opposed to her being with Captain Boinis. He wasn't good enough for her, and they had made it so difficult for the Captain that he had finally told the girl that he wouldn't see her anymore.

As we pulled into the dock at Islamorada at the end of our Bimini trip, the dock-master ran out onto the dock, yelled,

"Don't tie her up. You got to get back out."

"What the hell you mean?" Captain Boinis said, "Just got back, it'll take the rest of the afternoon to get her ready to fish tomorrow. I ain't goin' back out." Captain Boinis said.

"You got to, your girlfriend's parents just called. They had an argument and she's done walked out in the ocean. They thought she was just joking 'till she got across the flats and the shallow reef. They got scared when she kept right on goin'. Say she's way out now."

"What 'bout the Coast Guard?"

"The Marathon boat is down for service, take too long for one from Key West to get there."

The Captain looked down to me, said "Might as well get goin'." With that he took her back out of the slip, down the channel and turned her south when we got abreast of Alligator Light. In twenty minutes we were passing the south end of Long Key, heading for Vaca. Captain Boinis began to turn her a little west, getting closer to shore.

I happened to look seaward, saw something splashing about a quarter mile offshore of us and we were a mile off the beach ourselves. Yelled at the Captain, "There's something to port, up the port bow 'bout a quarter mile out." He turned the boat offshore, soon saw the splashing and headed for it. We were about a hundred yards away when we could see it was a girl swimming in her nightgown. When we came up on her we could see it was Running Bear still swimming strong in a butterfly stroke. I couldn't swim fifty yards butterfly, here she was a mile and a half from land. We throttled back, settled about ten yards from her. She glanced at us and kept right on swimming offshore. Captain yelled at her then,

"Wendy! Come 'ere and get in this boat. What the hell you doin' way out here?"

She never said a word, just kept swimming. The Captain yelled at her two or three times more to get in the boat. She ignored him. Finally he yelled at her,

"If you don't get over 'ere I'm coming in to get you, I'll drag you in 'ere."

I said to him then, "You better not do that, you ain't that good. She's done swam 'most a mile and a half, she's liable to drown you ifin you get in there with 'er. Let me see if I can snag 'er clothes with the boathook, ifin I get 'er close, grab aholt of somethin', we'll bring 'er on in."

I hooked the back of her nightgown pulled her to the boat and the Captain reached over and grabbed one of her hands. I dropped the boathook, grabbed her other hand and over the side she came. We put her in the fighting chair. Every time the Captain tried to talk to her, she just smiled at him, sitting there in a wet sheer nightgown.

I told the Captain then, "I'll run her back." He stayed in the cockpit with her while I got the boat heading north for the marina. I got on the radio and called the dock-master, told him we had her, to call her parents and tell them we'd be at the dock in about a half-hour.

In the third week in March she and the Captain were married. I was the best man. Her father gave her away, gave the Captain the deed to the private island. Gave him a job in his air conditioning business back in Washington. Captain Boinis became a vice-president. I became unemployed. Time to head north anyway.

Chapter Thirty-Nine
THE RETURN

I sobered up the morning after the Boinis' reception, had no idea how I had gotten back to the boat where I lived. It made no difference. I was heading to Hatteras for the marlin fishing. Figured I could sign on a boat at *Oden's* when I got there. I got my things together, had my duffle bag packed by noon, left it while I walked down to Uncle Dick's to see if I had any mail.

I had a letter from Mrs. Stinsin.

MARCH 20TH 1953

"Dear Hank,

I need your help with the Captain.

He hasn't done anything since Christmas, but to sit in a chair in the parlor and drink coffee. He gave up his painting contracts right after you left. He hasn't worked since. The only time he leaves the house is when I send him for something. I'm afraid for him because he still can't handle what happened. I've talked with him and argued with him. All he does is start crying if I mention Eva. I'm afraid he'll hurt himself. I know he loves me, but now it's not enough.

He won't talk to the preacher; won't even let him in the house. He hasn't been to church since it happened. The only person he's talked much with is the Chief, trying to find out what's going on with the investigation. And there's nothing there for him, either. The investigation is apparently stalled.

He hasn't started getting the *Eva* ready for the season. I don't think he's planning to go swordfishing. If he doesn't, there's nothing much left for him. If I can't get to him, he won't even have the fishing. That's what makes me so fearful for him.

If you're coming north this year, could I impose upon you? Will you come see us? Help me with the Captain? Maybe, if you can get him going to sea again, he'll find something to live for that will help him through this bad time. He was different before you left and kept himself together better. Maybe if he sees you, has you around him, has another man that loved her with him, he can draw strength from it.

If you have other plans and you can't return to the island yet I'll understand. I feel bad that I need to call on you, you who have suffered so much with this family already.

We love you,

Rebecca

I didn't write her a reply. I sent myself.

Chapter Forty

THE CAPTAIN'S JOURNEY

I hitched a ride from Homestead, just outside of Miami, on a refrigerated tractor-trailer heading to Boston with a load of produce. It took the better part of two days to get to Providence, the truck driver let me off there around midnight Friday. I caught the early local bus from Providence down to Point Judith and arrived at five Saturday morning.

Right as I walked out on the Point Judith docks, a lobster boat was about to leave. It had just dropped off a load at the packing house, picked up fish scraps for bait and was heading back out to pull more pots and re-bait. I recognized her as a Block Island boat, hailed her, asked if she could drop me by the island, either harbor, on the way to fishing their pots. They recognized me. Knew my story.

I was lucky they were on their way to run the strings of pots they'd set offshore of the island. Taking me along wasn't much out of the way. In an hour or so I was walking into the center of the island from New Harbor, heading up to Old Town Road and the Stinsin's.

When I got to the house the lights were on downstairs, I could see the Captain sitting in a chair in the parlor, saw Mrs. Stinsin walking through the kitchen door carrying a cup of morning coffee. I walked up on the porch, dropped my duffle bag, not concerned with the noise, opened the door and walked in.

Mrs. Stinsin dropped the coffee, put her hands to her face, squealed, rushed to me and threw her arms around my neck, exclaimed

"You came back! You came back!"

The Captain was rushing me now, soon the three of us were in a three way embrace. We stayed that way until I pushed them back from me, said

"I need some coffee, need to get warmed up before we catch the ferry."

"What'd you mean you need to catch the ferry?" Captain Stinsin said, "You just got here."

"I didn't come up here just to look at you," I said, "I came up here to make some money swordfishin'. Saw the *Eva* over at the Point Judith yard on my way here, don't look like much been done to 'er to get 'er ready. We might's well start on it now I'm 'ere, now you got some muscle, somebody to do the work for you.

"Mrs. Stinsin," I said, "hope you got something you can get up for breakfast, some leftovers or something you can fix for our lunch and dinner today, some food for tomorrow, too, we'll be stayin' on the *Eva* tonight, be back on the ferry tomorrow in time for evenin' services. If you don't mind, my suit's in the duffle on the porch, if you could press it I won't look quite so bad in church."

We put in a full day on the *Eva* on Saturday, scraping and painting, patching. Burnt some worm holes. Made arrangements for painting the next week, to put new zincs on her. The Captain and I slept the night in the wheelhouse, mostly not talking. Didn't have to. We were thinking the same things. Thinking of her. I suppose each of us cried at times, but it wasn't the incapacitating type of weeping. Crying at the sweetness of her. The memory of how captivating she had been. It was for what was missing; it was crying for what had been not for what was gone. We caught the early ferry back on Sunday.

When we walked in church that evening, the murmuring that always is present before services start, abruptly stopped. By the time we were halfway down the aisle, people were stepping out of the pews, shaking the Captain's hand, then mine, the ladies hugging Mrs. Stinsin. No-one saying anything. They didn't have to.

We walked on down to the pew where they had always sat before; it was empty and we sat down. Soon the preacher walked out of the back room, walked up on the pulpit looked out on the congregation. When his eyes found the Stinsins, he paused, smiled, said to them, "Welcome home." I don't remember what the sermon was, makes no difference. They were back in church where they belonged. It had been a part of their life, now, again it was a part.

Mrs. Stinsin had insisted that I stay at their place. I was apprehensive. Didn't know what memories I would have, could I live with whatever memories came. She wanted me to take Eva's old room, but I couldn't do that. Told her, "Please, I'll be better off in the back bedroom." She understood.

I stayed the summer there, every night dreaming of the nude spirit of that other time retreating through the door in the moonlight. Even when there wasn't moonlight I'd dream it, just put moon light in the dream. I talked to her, dreamt she talked to me, telling me things I wanted to hear. I had thought it would hurt, and it did at first, the dreaming, the talking, but then it came to comfort me. It was if she had left it, the dream, or the memory, behind to help me find my way.

By the first of June we had the *Eva* ready, wasn't as pretty as she'd been the year before; we hadn't winterized her right the previous fall. Hadn't the heart then to do anything but haul her. But she'd do, make it through the summer. We took her out to the east the first time on the eighteenth, took two swordfish, took three the next day. We had a long spell of good weather, sailed every day up into late July. The fish were inshore, in good numbers. We were exclusively 'short tripping'.

At sea we had begun to talk of her some. Ashore, too. Talk about how she had looked, how good she was at sea, not just for a woman, but just how good period.

One evening in mid-July we were sitting in the parlor drinking coffee, when Mrs. Stinsin said,

"Hank, the Captain is going to stop fishing this year on the first of September. He's getting too old to do much longer of a season."

"I can take care of it," I answered, knowing she knew that I was saying I could take care of him.

"There's 'nother thing, Hank," Captain Stinsin said, "its 'bout you, 'bout your future. Me and the missus has talked on it 'siderable. We ain't aimin' for you to be 'ere in September."

"What are you talkin' 'bout. Sure I'm goin' to be 'ere."

"Hank," Mrs. Stinsin said then, "when it happened to Eva, a week after the services some ladies helped me go through her things. There were some papers she had put together about your college. Her letter was there, too."

"Mrs. Stinsin, that's all over now. I didn't go. Couldn't. That's history now."

"Not really," she said, "when I read everything I took a liberty. I wrote the people at the University of Maryland, told them what happened and that you wouldn't be showing up for school last fall.

There were several letters back and forth and the final word is, you're accepted there this fall - they just postponed it a year."

"I can't go. Haven't even thought on it since afore the other happened. We got the fishin' to finish up. Me and the Captain's got things agoin' again."

"Hank," the Captain said then, "the fishin' don't matter none anymore, not much anyway; I'm gettin' to old to keep it up much longer, the *Eva's* getting a real parcel of years on 'er hull, engine, too. I keep at it, gonna take a passel of money to fix 'er up the way she needs. And the fish, they's beginning to lean out - ain't like it used ter be. I need to be gettin' out of it pretty soon. But that ain't the best reason for us to be stoppin' it. It's what she wanted. She put 'siderable work in it, gettin' you admitted. She were 'ere she'd make you go, you know it, we all know it. It's what we want, too.

"Sides you stay here or come back next summer for the fishin', you'll be doin' it for me. Ifin I do it, I'll be doin' it for you. It don't make no sense. Best thing for ever'one is to quit the fishin'."

Mrs. Stinsin said, "He's right. Eva would want it, so it needs to be done. And the Captain's right, each of you is fishing for the other one. It doesn't make any sense. I've got the papers upstairs, all you need to do is sign them and send in your first semester's tuition. We'll lend you the money if you don't have enough."

"I've got plenty of money. I've still got all the swordfish money from last season. Left it in the bank up 'ere. Never spent a dime. Was saving it."

Before the evening was over I had agreed with them. Signed the papers and wrote a check. Mrs. Stinsin would mail them off in the morning.

I was asleep that evening when I felt a body sit on the side of the bed, a hand on my forehead. I opened my eyes and Mrs. Stinsin was sitting on the bed in her robe.

"Hank, we were talking in bed just now, the Captain and me, and we discussed how you are like a son, and we decided that we needed to tell you now that we love you like our son. We want you to consider this your home. When you're here, she is. When we know you're coming, we know she is. You've saved the Captain for me. I've got him back.

He's almost his old self now, he'll never be all the way there, but he's regained himself to the point where there's plenty of him to love.

"You'll never know how much you've done for us, coming back and making us whole again. I know it was hard. I thank you for it."

"Mrs. Stinsin, she would have wanted it; when you wrote, it was like she did. I really didn't have any choice. None of us ever has where she's involved. Even now."

She gave a little laugh then, leaned over and kissed me on the forehead. As she did I noticed that something had blocked out the dim light from the doorway. It was the Captain standing there in a pair of pajamas. He came on in, stood beside the bed, took Mrs. Stinsin's hand, said to me, "Thanks for comin' home. Don't know what would have happened, but weren't gonna be good none. You've got it so I think I can get on by it. We all lost 'er, but somehow she gave us each other. There's a salvation in that. Thank you son," and he leaned over and put his hand on my forehead, as if in touching me he was touching her. They turned to leave then, saying goodnight as they left the room hand in hand.

Three weeks later we were down near Montauk Point, we'd put three fish in the boat, I was back up on the platform when I saw another fish inshore of us, yelled down to the Captain, waited for him to ask me "whereaway she be." I didn't hear any response, yelled again. Nothing happened. I climbed down the mast to find out what was going on. When I went around the wheelhouse door I noticed him slumped over the wheel, wedged in it somehow.

When I got to him he was unconscious, pale. I cut the engine off, grabbed him and dragged him on the deck where I could lay him out. I tried to revive him, couldn't. Checked his breathing. Didn't see any. Didn't feel any. Couldn't find any pulse. I tore his shirt off, put my ear to his chest listened for his heart. There was no beat to it. It was still. He was dead.

I cut the engine back on, turned and ran for home at top speed. I radioed into Block Island, got the Chief, told him what had happened, asked him to have the Doctor at Old Harbor, an ambulance, too. Told him that I thought it was too late, but it would be better if they were there when we got in. I also asked him to let the preacher know, have the preacher go to Mrs. Stinsin and be with her at Old Harbor when I got there.

It took almost two hours to get home. As I came around the south breakwater and headed for the harbor's entrance, I could see the ambulance, a police car, their lights flashing, could see a group of people on the north breakwater where the *Eva* would be moored.

As I got close another fisherman jumped aboard from a dingy to help with the mooring. As he was up on the bow hooking the buoy, another dingy bumped into the side of the boat. It had Mrs. Stinsin, the Chief, and the doctor aboard. I helped them over the gunwale while the youngster that had rowed them out took the *Eva's* stern line back up on the breakwater. Mrs. Stinsin rushed to the Captain's body, knelt there beside him, took his big old hand in hers. I knelt beside her. We stayed there while the doctor worked on him, examining him. In a couple of minutes the doctor looked at us, shook his head from side to side.

"Looks like his heart just gave out," he said "I'm going to put down that I was attending, put the time down as right now. Okay with you Chief?"

"Best way." The Chief responded.

"Mrs. Stinsin?"

She nodded her head up and down. She was still kneeling, holding his hand. She reached up to push his hair off his face, wiped a smear of fish blood from his face. I was holding her elbow now, supporting her. She wasn't crying hard, not sobbing, just letting the tears flow.

She was seeing him in all the ways he'd been. She was running through the memories as she knelt there holding his lifeless hand, his ring hand, thanking him for those memories with her tears.

I firmed up my grip on her elbow, started to raise her, when she pulled away from me, said "Let me stay here longer. This is my memory of his dying, not in some fancy box in a funeral home. Here on the boat we named for her. This is the way he would have preferred it, on her boat, her man with him. This is the way she would have wanted it, too. At sea."

She stayed there for another while, on her knees still, just looking at the Captain. I had closed his eyes as the *Eva* neared the breakwater. He was lying there as if he was asleep. In peace, really. I supposed that if he had felt it happening, his only regret was leaving Mrs. Stinsin. For the rest of it, his passing, he was probably glad because he would be seeing Eva. His morose days and nights would never return now. He'd be with her saving a place for Mrs. Stinsin.

A dory banged alongside the boat, the ambulance crew was coming aboard, four of them. They'd be the ones to carry him ashore, then to the funeral home. As they clambered over the gunwale they just stood there behind us. Being respectful. They were islanders, all. Volunteers, the sons and brothers of fishermen, some probably fishermen themselves. They'd take care of one of their men of the sea. It's what they had always done, taken care of each other, out there or here in the harbor.

The next time I raised up on Mrs. Stinsin's elbow, she rose turned to all the men there, the Chief, the Doctor, the ambulance men, said "Thanks. Take care of him for me. Hank, take me home."

I helped her into the *Eva's* dory, rowed it to the breakwater, helped her out and tied it to the mooring line. Then we climbed up the breakwater, my hand under her arm to help her. We reached the top and started walking to the Captain's pickup for the ride home. As we walked I noticed the men on the *Eva* were waiting until we were gone to take the Captain off.

As we approached the pickup, I realized that I didn't have the key, it would be in the Captain's pocket. I'd get it later at the funeral home. I asked one of the policemen if he could give us a ride to the Stinsin house. Soon we were at the house.

The next days were a blur. Not as bad for me as the period of Eva's dying and funeral, but bad. I was all Mrs. Stinsin had, except for cousins, other relatives not close enough to mean as much as me. Eva had brought us all together, God was tearing us apart.

We buried the Captain next to Eva's grave, to her right looking up. Mrs. Stinsin would take the place to his right when her time came. It was appropriate, she'd been his right hand for forty years. I now owned the lot next to Eva. To her left. With her in the lilac cove. Supposed when my time came I'd be here with all of them. My body would, the essence of my being, my soul, I knew would be wherever Eva was. She would arrange it.

After the interment, the usual happened, 'casserole ladies" and all. Friends, relatives visiting. I just stayed in the parlor, speaking when it was necessary, mostly staying quiet, helping Mrs. Stinsin. She stayed downstairs, didn't go to her room this time. Did what she knew the Captain would want and he wouldn't want her to take to her bed and hide from her anguish. She stuck it out until the last one of them left. I helped her to her room, went back downstairs and sat in a chair. All night. Thinking.

He'd been as close to a dad as I could remember having, certainly the closest friend I'd had. When he had told me as I was leaving to go south, "Stay clear of 'em 'bad boys', you hear.", it had been his way of telling me that he loved me like a son. I thought of him, the fishing, what I'd learned, thought of it until dawn.

I spent the next three weeks looking after things for Mrs. Stinsin. She didn't want to sell the boat; didn't want anyone to have it. It was the Captain's and Eva's, mine too, now. Asked me to sink it so no-one could ever have it again. Asked me take it out where the Captain had died. Put it under there. I made the arrangements, quietly; didn't know one way or the other whether it was legal to intentionally sink a boat.

Another boat went out with me and when we were where I figured we had been when the Captain had his heart attack, I turned the engine off, opened the seacocks in the engine room and the forward hold. Got in the dory and rowed off about thirty yards, the other boat hovering nearby. It took her almost forty minutes to sink. The last thing to go under was the mast with the platform. As it went under I thought of Leatherby's picture, the one with Eva on the platform. The one the Stinsins had been holding for me. I was really saying goodby now. I rowed the dory over to the other boat, took the *Eva's* hatchet, chopped several holes in the bottom of the dory. When she was about half full, almost swamped, I climbed across the gunwale of the other boat and watched the dory sink. Threw the hatchet after it. All of it was gone now. She'd fish no more; she was resting where she couldn't be run down by a steamer in the fog. Fitting, really. The grave of a dead boat should be on the bottom, not rotting in some marsh somewhere.

In my last week there I fixed up everything I could find in the house that needed fixing, changed the oil in the pickup, checked the antifreeze. Made arrangements for others to check on Mrs. Stinsin after I had left the island. The night before I left, Mrs. Stinsin and I made arrangements to keep in touch. I had already been given my address at school in some materials sent to me. Mrs. Stinsin was going to wait a week and send some of my stuff, the stuff I couldn't carry. She'd send my picture of the *Eva*, Leatherby's painting, as well.

The next morning she walked me down to the ferry dock to start my journey to the rest of my life. I threw my bags on the ferry, stayed on the dock with her as long as I could. "Take care of yourself," she said as the ferry began to move, "I love you. Write!" I bent over, kissed her, said "I love you, too. Thanks for everything." turned and leaped for the ferry, barely making it, but grabbing a rail and leaping over it. I turned to wave. She blew me a kiss, yelled "Good Luck." I blew her a kiss back, yelled "I'll be back."

BOOK THREE

Chapter Forty-One
THE NEXT LIFE

SCHOOL

We were making introductions around the room in my first class, an English class in the late afternoon on a Monday. We were supposed to stand, give our name, our age, what we had been doing since we had graduated from high school. When it came my turn I gave my name, told her, Mrs. Rogers the teacher, that I had been a fishermen. That wasn't enough for her, she asked me then, "I want more than that, that's not enough, what have you been really doing since you graduated. You've been out more than four years. Surely you've done more than fish." She hadn't asked any of the kids, the recent high school graduates, what they'd been doing other than their jobs. Her attitude made me believe that for some reason she didn't like me, or didn't like older students. I stayed silent for a moment or two, trying not to get too hot. Then she said, "Don't be embarrassed. You're a big man. No need to be shy. You speak like a farmer not a fisherman, anyway."

She had done it, she wanted it, I'd give it to her. "Up until the last couple of years" I said, "I fished, partied, got in fights and fornicated all I could. That satisfy you?"

She came right back, "That's nice to know, but what about the last two years? What have you done? What do you want out of life?" My dandruff was scorched I was so hot. I didn't hold back any,

"Well Mrs. Rogers" I said, "In the last two years I fell in love with a wonderful woman, she agreed to marry me. Then a pack of animals grabbed 'er off the street, raped 'er, murdered 'er and threw 'er off a boat up at Block Island. Then I buried 'er. That was summer 'fore last. A month ago I buried 'er father. His heart gave out from the strain. Then I took his boat out in the deep and sank it 'cause his widow asked me to. As far as what do I want most out of life, I want to find them that killed 'er; when I do I'm gonna kill 'em. Won't make any difference what the law says."

253

You could hear a fly going by. I sat down. After the teacher recovered, she went on with the rest of the kid's introductions, muted now though. We got our first assignments, had some preliminary instruction and the bell rang. As the class got up and started to leave, Mrs. Rogers said to me, "Mr. Gaskins, can you wait for a moment?" I stood to the side of the door as the other students left. She said then, "Please have a seat." I sat in front of her teaching dias.

"I'm sorry, Mr. Gaskins. If I had known it was going there, I would never have asked the questions. I can't even lie and say it was accidental, I meant to embarrass you. I've found it pays to get the older student's attention. But, I am really sorry. It won't happen again."

"Don't pay it no never mind, Mrs. Rogers," I responded, "you couldn't have known. And I have a problem, I get a little too hot sometimes, don't rein things in fast enough. My fiancee is the one that got me into college, actually filled out the application 'fore it happened. She wanted me to get my way of talkin' right first, told me that English would be the most important subject for me. So I want you to keep right on pushin' me."

We both stood then, I reached over and shook her hand.

Every Monday afternoon the rest of the school year Mrs. Rogers tutored me after class, in English, especially in the way to speak it. From then on I was her special project. It only took me three years to finish my undergraduate studies, even with having to do regular work to support myself. But the whole time I was at College Park she groomed me, civilized me.

I had written to Mrs. Stinsin about Mrs. Rogers right after the initial confrontation, then wrote her when the relationship changed. Soon Mrs. Stinsin and Mrs. Rogers were writing. They were the same age. Educated. Widows. They hit it off. The next summer, Mrs. Stinsin invited Mrs. Rogers to spend a couple of weeks on the island. I stayed back in College Park to work at a bar, getting money for the next semester. Going to summer school, making up for lost time with my education..

They must have hit it off, because they became close friends. Of course they had a lot in common. Me, I guess. Spent their other summers, conspiring, I think, on the ways they could make me better. They were both grooming me.

With Mrs. Rogers's help I graduated, took the entrance exams for law school, did well, was accepted at my first choice. Made Law Review, graduated in 1959, first in my class; got a job with a prestigious law firm in the nation's capital.

After two years I felt like I was being held back; taking a back seat to the relatives of the partners, young kids really being given as gifts what I'd had to work for. I'd made a little bit of a reputation, saved some money, resigned on amicable terms and started my own law practice.

It was 1961. She had been gone for nine years. I was thirty years old.

Chapter Forty-Two
THE LAWYER

I had made many friends during my time at the big firm, had made a reputation as an up and comer, a good lawyer, possibly going to be a great lawyer. I'd had no other distractions, no family, no other interests, no lovers, none of the things that take time. I'd worked sixteen, seventeen hours a day, seven day weeks. Focused.

Shortly after I started my own practice, consisting initially of a secretary, a researcher (they call them para-legals now)and myself, I noticed that some of the clients of the old firm were showing up. I kept on doing things the way I had done them-preparation, preparation, preparation. Kept on winning. Winning begat more clients, and more winning begat more and so on. In two years I had six other lawyers working for me, salaried; I wasn't ready yet to share control of anything; didn't want any 'partners' to argue with, hadn't found any I'd want to argue with.

I had begun to notice, though, as soon as I opened my own practice, that there were several tough female litigators in the trial courts that could more than hold their own with the best male litigators. Had the tendency to go for the balls of any litigator that thought just having a couple was enough. This was before females in court were a common sight. Before they had arrived at the position where they could get money clients, bill top dollar. I'd been impressed; two of the six lawyers I had hired were women.

I had especially noticed a plaintiff's lawyer that I thought was the best of the bunch, good as any man, better than most. Her name was Joanne Parsons. I found out through asking, that she'd worked her way through college and law school as a lifeguard in the summers in Ocean City, waiting tables at night. She'd been there the year before I'd left for Block Island, the summers since until she got her law degree. She'd begun her private practice cold turkey. Tough even in those days, tougher for a woman. She'd made it, was now very successful, had a boutique practice concentrating on representing plaintiffs who had been involved in accidents with tractor-trailer trucks. She was one of the first lawyers to discover that most major trucking firms belonged to a consortium that self-insured a substantial percentage of the coverage of their own trucks. She'd won two or three large cases in her first two years, from then on it had been mostly settlement workouts, with just a trial here and there to keep the trucking industry honest.

She was the first woman I had felt any interest in since Eva left. It wasn't the same interest, not the love interest part. It was the respect side of it. Not that she wasn't good looking, because she was. It was that I admired her work in the courtroom. I wanted to get to know her, be around her, learn what made her tick. What had made her good. Was curious.

It took me six months, sometime early in 1964, before I had the opportunity to introduce myself. It was at an embassy party that one of my clients had gotten me invited to, the Italian Embassy up in Northwest. I didn't know many people. I was mainly standing around with a drink in my hand, trying to figure how to parley my presence into more business when I noticed her. She wasn't standing alone like me. She was the only woman in a group of young men. She was in a low cut short cocktail dress, lots of cleavage and great legs, a lot different than her working clothes.

I remained where I was, observing her when I could without being conspicuous. It didn't take me long to figure out that she wasn't with any particular man. She was a bright light, attracting men like moths. It appeared that she was getting bored with all the attention. If I went over, the worse that could happen was that she'd have another moth, but not for long. I wasn't the fluttering kind.

I made my way into the center of the group, started to introduce myself, when she said,

"I know who you are. You're the man that's willing to hire female lawyers."

"And I know who you are. You're the tractor-trailer nemeses." I responded.

"Well, I guess that makes us kindred spirits of a kind. Why don't you take me to the bar; I could use another glass of champagne."

Like that she had taken us out of a crowd, put us together as a pair. We spent most of the rest of the evening together, danced, talked about the law a lot, used words to feel around each other, to figure out if either of us was worth the other's efforts. We came to the same conclusion when I suggested that we leave, go to a jazz joint in Georgetown. Charlie Byrd was playing and tickets had been impossible to get, but they knew me there, they'd work us in.

We caught a cab, twenty minutes later we were approaching the doorman who was surrounded by a crowd waiting to get in. I was just about to brush through the crowd to approach the doorman so he could let us in, when he looked in our direction, yelled

"Joanne, come on up we've got your reserved table ready."

She looked at me, gave me a smile as we walked up that seemed to say, "Hey guy, I know people, too." I smiled back, just shook my head and we were packed in and seated in just a few minutes. I said to her above the noise,

"Looks like I'm not the only one that knows their way around town."

"Looks like it. Surprise you?"

"No, I've seen you operate in the court room."

"I've watched you, too," she said, "we're a lot alike, sort of snaky really. Crawl around, crawl around, crawl, then strike. That's what makes cross-examination so much fun. Set them up, knock them down."

I laughed, she was absolutely correct. We got paid to have fun. Paid good money to have fun at someone else's expense. Sharks I guess we were, 'em 'bad boys' as the Captain used to say.

After the last show we left, caught a cab to her place. I told the cab to wait when we got to her apartment house in Bethesda, walked her to the foyer door. I asked for her number, told her I had a good time; that I'd call her. Left her there, got back in the cab, waved as we pulled away.

I called her the next morning, asked her to go to dinner that night. She agreed, then said, asked really, "You didn't try to come in last night?"

"It's not right yet." I responded.

"I hope you'll let me know when it's right,"she said.

"I hope so, too. See you at eight."

I had been, was, unsure. I hadn't been with a woman, had sex since the spring of 1951, before I left to go to Block Island. Ten, eleven years before. I hadn't felt the urges, even, since the tragedy. Felt like I had been castrated; had learned to live with it. Part of living with it for a man was being the only one to know of it.

We went out for several weeks almost every night, except for the nights when one of us was in court the next day. We began to learn about each other, our backgrounds, her's particularly. There was a lot of mine I couldn't talk about. Mostly steered the talk about me to the practice, court, law school. But I primarily listened to her. She'd been raised in moderate circumstances, had to put herself through school, had developed her confidence as a life guard, swimming out in rips with a torpedo buoy and hauling drowning swimmers back to shore. Hundreds of times a summer. Coping with the worst in people waiting tables in a bar at night, learned to take care of herself in every way. By the time she got to law school she had no doubts that she was going to be a top lawyer; hadn't even been afraid when she'd opened her practice. She hadn't had a secretary her first three months, hadn't been able to borrow enough to do more than pay the rent. Still wasn't scared even then.

She'd taken court assignments in criminal cases two days after she began to practice. Within a week she was handing the equally inexperienced prosecutors their shorts. In the next week she was picking up paid defendants, made them pay up front and a lot. And she had won a lot. Soon she'd hired another lawyer, a female, to help her with the overload. It was at the end of the first year that she'd come across a reference to the mostly unknown consortium fund. She'd been doing research on another negligence case and saw a short reference to it in an Idaho case. Saw the opportunities it might offer. One day that opportunity had been wheeled in her door and she beat the trucking company and the consortium over the head with it, pulled down a half-million jury verdict. That had been the start, three or four more opportunities showed up and she raised lumps on their heads again. Hired a second lawyer, a man this time. She was so good, felt so confident that hiring a man just because he was the best young lawyer available to her wasn't intimidating. She didn't feel that she had to hire women for some kind of movement. She'd been her own movement. Far as she was concerned every woman was on her own. She'd been.

259

But, she saw that I was doing the same, hiring the best, women, men, it made no difference to either of us.

For some reason even she didn't understand, she was dynamite so long as she could wheel the client in the courtroom. By her third year, as soon as the companies and the consortium heard she had a new one, they were beating on her door to settle. Soon nine out of ten were settling. Usually for a lot less than a half-million, but still substantial sums. She took her one-fourth when they settled, one-third when she had to drag them into court. Now she was established. Spent more time managing, less time out-of-court lawyering; still took the ones that had to be tried, took them because they made her brain fluids flow. She had made it and she was proud of it. I knew how she felt. I had all the business I could handle. I told her that I was at a point where I had to rein in my practice or expand it. Where it was, it was a pain in the ass.

We'd gotten closer as the weeks passed, grew to like each other more. I knew that with her it was more than liking, at least hoping for more than liking. I was confused, though, I knew what it was like to really be in love. I wasn't at that point, didn't think I'd get there ever again. I'd had my time with love. A person's not supposed to be there twice. I didn't think so anyway. I liked Joanne, respected her as a professional, a person, as a woman. But when we would embrace, kiss at her door there wasn't the feeling I'd had before. Had I not known what real love was, what Joanne and I were in might have been what I thought love was. It followed, albeit by ten years, the full real thing. The love I couldn't get out of my mind, didn't want to.

I had just about talked myself into stopping the relationship because it wasn't fair to her when, one evening, we were standing at her townhouse door and as I started to leave, she grabbed my arm, said, "I don't know whether you love me, but dammit you like me enough. I'm horny and you're coming up, I need some. I'm not a nun."

We were in an embrace as soon as we were in the door to her apartment, kissing, then she took me by the hand and led me upstairs, taking off her clothes as she did until at the top she was in panties and a bra.

"Get with it Gaskins," she said as she began to unbutton my suit coat, undo my tie.

Soon we were in her bed, turned side by side facing each other. I felt her hands on me, all over. Her mouth. I felt myself getting excited. Then, I smelled the faint scent of lilacs. All I could think of was Eva. I closed my eyes and saw her. All the while Joanne was trying to get things going. Get it up, keep it up, I guess is the way to put it. Nothing was happening. This was the first time I'd let myself get in this position. I'd been afraid of humiliation. Wanted to be a man, a real man, but my mind wouldn't stay where my body was. I was in love with a dead woman, but she wasn't dead in my mind. She didn't want it so; it wasn't so. She was my life, still. I realized it there in the bed of a woman I liked and respected. A beautiful woman. A woman that had to be wondering by now what was going on with me. I gently pushed her away, just a little, still stayed in contact with her, moved my arms around her, said

"I can't."

She was quiet for a few minutes, just lay there as her breathing slowed, as she cooled. Then she asked,

"What's the matter? Is it something about me? I know I'm attractive, hell I'm beautiful, most of the men in this town would sell their souls to jump my bones. So what's the problem?"

"I haven't been with a woman in over ten years."

"You go the other way?"

"I haven't been with anybody."

"You wounded or something?"

"I'm in love with somebody else."

"I've been watching you around this town for years. I've never even seen you with another woman."

"She was here tonight. Just a moment ago."

"What do you mean she was here?"

"In my mind. She took over my mind. I wanted her to."

"If you are going to think of her when you're in someone else's bed, you ought to damn well go to her." She responded, curtly, becoming angry.

"I can't."

"She's married?"

"She's dead."

Silence. I looked over at her, she was looking at me, quizzically, questioningly, then she rolled over on her side, raised her torso, breasts prominently displayed, only incidentally now, supported her head on her hand and forearm. And I began to talk. I started with the fight in Crab Junction. Told her everything I remembered and I had a good memory in those days.

We ended up at the table in the kitchen having breakfast. Drinking coffee. We were dressed. I was; she was in a robe.

"Well Gaskins here we are."

"Yeah, the question is though, where are we?"

"I can't compete with a dead woman, can't compete with a dream." She said.

"I know," I answered, "and I can't change it. Truthfully, I don't really want to. When I dream of her, when I see her it's like she's really here. She's just a foot away, I can't touch her but I feel her love surround me, descend on me. I feel her looking after me. Telling me things. Keeping me safe."

"She was one hell of a woman."

"She was. She is."

"Well, where do we go from here? All I wanted from you was a little sex. If that's not going to happen, where are we?" She continued.

"I hope we're still friends."

"We'll be that, no reason not to be. But I'm a girl that needs certain things. Sex, but more than that. I need a man that is in love with me, not that just loves me. My father loved me. I want to get married and have kids. Time is flying by Gaskins. I don't have time for a man who's in love with a woman I can't compete with. I've got to get rid of you."

"I know that," I said, "but I still like you, respect you as a woman and a lawyer. Want to be your friend, confidant even, not that I think you'd ever need one. Sometime when I'm hurting, when I'm thinking and it hurts, I'd like to be able to think you're my friend, that you'd help if I need it. We're trial lawyers, we don't make many friends. Usually not even with each other."

"Why don't we leave it at that, Gaskins. We'll be friends."

Chapter Forty-Three
THE NEXT LEVEL

We kept on seeing each other on occasion, but as friends. Meet for lunch, sometimes even for breakfast. Either of us have a legal problem we'd call the other, bounce it off, get some advice.

Sometimes I'd see her out with other guys, some I knew. I hoped that she'd find a guy, but in a couple of weeks it'd be somebody else.

Over the next three months the pressure at the office got worse; we had two much business for a small firm before we had enough business for a big firm. I had pondered for the last week whether to make a big hire, start the getting big process my making a dozen hires immediately, then add a half dozen a year. Take the risk that it'd pay off. There comes a point in the progress towards bigness when it takes off, if it's going to, and then profitability takes care of itself. It's right before that point when the seed firm is at the greatest risk. If it exceeds it's grasp, the pay obligations come in faster than clients and the seed firm can fail.

One day I saw Joanne come in the outer office. We hadn't had lunch or breakfast for a week. Figured she had a problem I could help her with, came for advice. I waved her on in.

As she walked in she said to me, "Sit down, Gaskins." I smiled, it was the way she was. Direct. Apparently she had something to say and I was always interested when she was in the talking mood. I sat down, and she 'cut to the chase'.

"Gaskins, we've got it all squared away that neither one of us is going to be screwing the other, I mean literally screwing."

I laughed, as she continued.

"And that gives us a big advantage, we don't have to worry about getting involved in the office. We've got the perfect opportunity. I'm not talking about having sex, I'm talking about not having it. It gives us opportunities neither of us would take advantage of if we were screwing."

It was beginning to dawn on me. She was talking business.

"Look," she said, "we've both been talking about the bind we were getting into, too big for a limited practice, too small for a big practice. We're in the same place, have the same problem. What I'm getting at, is we're the answer to each other's problems. It's been right in front of us."

I sat there looking at her. She was smiling, a hand in the cookie jar smile. She was really excited; I was getting excited. Two small firms with top notch lawyers would bring all their clients to the new firm. Right away we'd have a nucleus to build on, to start hiring other top graduates while the combined billings of the two firms would support the new hires until they began to bring in their nut. We'd avoid some of the built in expansion traps that had buried other firms trying to go big.

"Whose name goes first, G comes before P." I said, smiling.

"I thought you were a gentlemen. Let the ladies go first." She answered.

"I thought we were snakes," I said, "woman I know said good lawyers like us were snakes."

"Yeah, but I'm a female snake."

"Make you a deal. One gets their name on the door first, the other gets the bigger office."

"Deal."

"Lets flip on whose name goes first. You got a coin?" I asked.

"Call it in the air."

I called it heads, it came up tails and Parsons & Gaskins, Attorneys at Law was born. At the end of the first year we had twenty attorneys in the firm, two years later forty.

That was the year we hit it big. The year we got the first really big verdict.

Chapter Forty-Four
ASBESTOS

Two months after we combined our practices a diminutive elderly lady walked into the office. She was helping a man twice her size carrying a personal oxygen tank. She asked to see a lawyer and was shown to one of the intake lawyers, the first lawyers who normally saw new clients, walk off the street clients. Two hours later the intake lawyer was asking to see the two of us, Joanne and myself. His name was Mack Chimes. We met in the library/conference room.

"Ms. Parsons, Mr. Gaskins," he started off, "I think maybe this couple has a compensable injury. He's suffering from some kind of lung disease that's going to kill him and it's work related. He got it from something at work."

I interrupted him, "Sounds like a workman's compensation matter, Lynn Vasaloo takes care of our comp. claims, she's got it organized on an in/out basis, really processes them efficiently."

"Mr. Gaskins this one is a little different. Almost everybody that has worked in this shipyard in the past forty years is sick. This disease, the doctors have just told him, comes from people working with asbestos."

"Where are you going," Joanne said, "wouldn't that still come under occupational disease categories?"

"I suppose that's what the company thinks and they may be right for them. But what about the manufacturers, the distributors? The asbestos industry itself?

"Mr. and Mrs. Moore have brought in some copies of scientific literature and other stuff they say was given to them when the left the treatment clinic last week. Some stranger came up to them, asked them if either of them were being treated for an asbestos problem. When they said Mr. Moore was, he handed them the material.

"I've just browsed it real quick, but it looks pretty damming. If it's true, the industry knew that this stuff was dangerous, was slowly killing people and still they fiercely competed to sell the stuff, advertized new uses of it. There's even one document, a copy of a letter from the president of one company to the president of another company that they were going to keep right on selling and pushing it for use in schools even after they knew it could kill people. That's where they figured the big money was, in public building construction; the industry's bottom line needed it. They'd worry about the risks when they had to."

Joanne and I looked at each other, then nodded, asked

"Where are the Moores?"

"In my office."

"Escort them in here. You stay, too. We may want you to take a lead here."

Mack walked them into the library, the man with the oxygen bottle just shuffled. Walked real slow.

"Mr. and Mrs. Moore, Janet and Bob," Mack said as he made the introductions, "this is Ms. Parsons and Mr. Gaskins; they're the partners in the firm."

"It's a pleasure to meet you, although all of us wish it weren't necessary," I said as I extended my hand toward them. Mrs. Moore took my hand first, gave it a pretty vigorous shaking given that she couldn't have weighed a hundred pounds. Mr. Moore grabbed a hold firmly as well. He might be sick, but he was a shipyard worker, had done man's work, heavy work. In his world what you did, you did like a man until you couldn't. He could still shake hands right.

"Mrs. Moore, Mr. Moore," Joanne said, "thank you for joining us. We've very interested in the case and the story you've brought us."

They sat down, got as comfortable as possible and began to talk.

He'd started at the shipyard right after he came home from the Korean war. It was the best job available, hard work but he was strong, a big man. The yard was building tankers then, building them for Greek shipowners before the Greeks figured out it would be cheaper to start their own shipyards and build their own tankers. He had started working with asbestos at the very beginning. Because of the heat generated in the power plants, the tankers' engines, asbestos was used extensively as insulation. It was one of the best heat resistant substances then known. In the early days they had wrapped pipes and such with sheets, lined the companion ways with it. Later, the yard and the manufacturer had devised a method of spraying the substance on exposed surfaces. No masks were used in the earlier days. Workers just went in the tight quarters of the ships, sprayed an asbestos substance virtually everywhere. It was cheaper that way, just cover everything with it.

Workers had started getting sick in the last couple of years, really sick. Then six months ago he had started having trouble breathing, was really short of breath. Ex-rays had indicated that he had some kind of thickening in the interstices of his lungs. When he had gone back a week later his doctor had found literature on the subject of a newly understood disease that was caused by exposure to asbestos. Several problems, several diseases really. His was asbestosis, a form of pneumoconiosis, a particularly rapid progressive form. He wasn't expected to survive it; wasn't expected to last long.

He'd started going to clinics specially set up by the worker's compensation insurance carriers to treat conditions like his. He couldn't afford to pay for treatment privately so he'd been forced into the clinics. There he'd seen many of the men he'd worked with over the years. Almost whole neighborhoods of men. He'd learned that the clinic was funded in part by a consortium of asbestos manufacturers. It was cheaper for the industry and the employers and their carriers to set up clinics then to farm the patients out. Easier to control the problem also. Keep the publicity down. Keep right on doing business as usual.

He'd just left the clinic one day when the man approached them, asked if he was being treated for a sickness coming from asbestos. When he answered yes, the man had handed Mrs. Moore the packet of material and walked off.

I told the Moores that I'd like to keep copies of the material, do a rush investigation, and talk with them again in about a week when we'd be better able to advise them of what courses of action, if any, they might have. Told them that we'd talk about our compensation next week if we thought it was worth their while to go further with it. That the day's consultations were free of charge. Mrs. Moore spoke up then.

"Mr. Gaskins, we don't have much money. I doubt we can pay you anything. It's all we can do to scrape up cab money for the ride to the clinic. When the company found out about John's illness they laid him off right away; that way they didn't have to pay him full retirement.

That was two years ago, before the problem got so bad he couldn't work, before his retirement had fully vested."

"Mrs.Moore, don't worry yet about paying us. Unless we feel you have a case that is net compensable, by that I mean a case that has a decent possibility of producing enough money above our legal fees and costs that there will be a substantial amount that ends up in your hands, we won't advise you to go forward. If we don't take the case there won't be any fees to worry about."

Mrs. Moore smiled, turned to her husband, said "Told you we could get some help, at least have somebody look into it, wouldn't take all our money, wouldn't have to mortgage the house."

She started to help him up when I thought of something.

"Mr. Moore, you said you were in the Korean War?"

"Yes sir, I was."

"What service, what was your outfit?"

"First Marines."

"You were at Chosen then if you were in the First Marines."

"Yeah."

"You're one of the 'Chosen Few', one of the men that fought your way out of the reservoir."

Mrs. Moore spoke up, "He's got the medals to prove it, too. Fought for his country, came home. All he wanted to do was work. Make a living for his family. Now we find out that the work has killed him, going to kill him."

I asked, "What medals did you get?"

"It ain't part of this. That's only something that's important to those that were there." Mr. Moore said.

Mrs. Moore spoke up again, "He's got the Distinguished Service Medal and the Silver Star. He was wounded twice during the retreat."

"Weren't no retreat," he interrupted her, "we was surrounded. Just picked a way to go and fought our way out. Never went backwards once we started forward. That ain't no retreat. We was marines. We don't retreat." He finished, now out of breath to the extent he had to slow up the process of raising up from the chair.

I asked Mrs. Moore if she would bring the citations for his medals with them for our meeting the next week. She said she would and they left, Mack walking with them to the outer door. We waited for him to return.

When he did we sat around for an hour. Looked at the copies of the documents they had left with us. Dynamite if they could be established as true and with copies of them we would be able to ask for specific documents in the discovery process. Once we started asking for specific documents the industry would run scared. If we knew about the documents specifically they wouldn't be able to hide them. If they produced them we'd be able to use their own people to authenticate them. Probably be able to get them in evidence. More importantly they wouldn't know how much we did have. We could probably make a big part of our case on their records. Our primary job would be to establish the nature of Mr. Moore's work and the medical and other expert testimony necessary to establish the link between the injury and the exposures to the products. We'd have to front expert witness money for the Moores.

We talked some more about their case specifically, but talked even more about the general ramifications that might result from taking on this type of case. First and foremost somebody needed to begin the process. We could afford it. That wasn't a problem. We realized that before their case was over we might be fighting several major manufacturers because it was likely that over the years Mr. Moore had been exposed to products from more than one manufacturer and whichever one we thought was responsible and sued, would defend itself by saying it was another manufacturer. When Mack pointed out that possible defense, I said

"We'll sue all of them, during the process they'll start defending themselves, attacking each other in the process. They'll be conducting discovery against each other as well as fighting ours. They'll weed each other out and in the end, if we do our discovery right, we'll end up with the companies responsible. They might all be responsible if we can tie that letter into the elements of a civil conspiracy."

We beat it around for another couple of hours. Then Joanne said, simply, "Let's do the sign." It was an inside code, our way of saying go ahead. She had a sign in her office that said, "Sue the bastards."

"I think that is exactly what we'll do, and we'll sue all of them until we sift it down to the ones responsible." I said. "Mack, I think, at least for now you should head it up. Start the investigative part; we'll get you another associate to help. Joanne, you're more up on this stuff than I am. Can you think of anything we're forgetting?"

"Well, only one thing. We need to be a little careful. There's only so much money in this case. They're both old. Actuarially, their claim is going to be limited because they are so old. There's only so much money in it and it's going to take a lot of money for the firm to get to verdict."

"We may not make really big fees on this one case, though we might," I responded, "knew that from the beginning. But when the Moores go home after our meeting next weekend they'll be telling all those other people out there, the ones they know, the ones they see in the clinic, that they have lawyers that are going to sue for them, going to try and see them receive what they should because of their injuries. Guarantee you, within days other people who have been poisoned by asbestos are going to be walking in that door. Most of the prep work for the first case will support the other cases as well. We might not make a dime on the first case. But at the end of it the companies won't be able to take the heat, they'll settle out and for big bucks. More than we can imagine right now. Only question is can the rest of the firm sustain itself while we start investing firm assets in the asbestos cases?"

Joanne answered, "We've got two of the tractor-trailer cases that'll settle in the next two weeks, there's four or five more that should settle out in the next six months or so, and there's one I'm going to be trying at the same time. Don't want to settle it, the client's only twenty, a paraplegic. Truck ran a light, driver fell asleep. Ran right over our client's Honda Civic. Broke our guy's neck. They offered five hundred thousand, case is worth three big ones.

"Then we've got all your stuff, the business end, the business litigation. In your world it's mainly about moving the big guys' money around in court, making your big hours as the money flows by. We'll be able to fund this case and grow the firm at the same time. We're going to have to designate one of the senior associates as a firm manager anyway, now we'll just have to speed it up so she or he can take care of the business end while we concentrate on the litigation."

It worked out just about the way we expected. Within a week after we had agreed to take the Moore's case, other asbestos cases began to walk in the door. At first there were three and four a month. We had worked up a litigation package for the Moore case, interrogatories, requests for admissions, other discovery. Everything we did in the Moore case became a template for those to come. Even the manufacturer defendants were ususally the same. We sued all of them in every case and let discovery sort them out. Three fourths of every case was the same. In time all we had to do was fill in the blanks.

In the meantime Joanne kept up her tractor-trailer cases; I kept the business case practice going. We made enough to carry the asbestos cases and to make new hires to assist Mack's original complement of lawyers. By the time the Moore case got to court two years later we had sixty-three asbestos cases pending, had a seven member special group of lawyers working only on asbestos issues. Had expanded our office space by a hundred percent.

After a two week trial the jury returned a verdict for the Moores. It was six and a half million dollars. Surprised us even. Especially in that it was enough of a verdict for us to take our third. Mr. Moore died within days of the end of the trial but he had held on for three years with a disease that killed most men in two. Held on long enough to see the manufacturers pay for killing one of the 'Chosen Few', long enough to know that Mrs. Moore would be able to live in comfort until she joined him.

By the end of the month following the Moore verdict, we had over three hundred asbestos cases and they were growing at the rate of seventy a week. We took the Moore case fee, over two million dollars, and used it to process the other cases and grew the firm by another twenty lawyers. Then another ten. All the while the other parts of the practice were also in high gear. Joanne was winning her cases; I was winning the business litigation cases. We took on additional office space; soon had taken over the whole building. Three months after the Moore verdict a jury brought in a four million dollar verdict in the second asbestos case. With our contingent fee of a third of the verdicts the firm was now in the big time money firm basis. And there were eight more asbestos cases within sixty days of trial.

A week after the second verdict, I received a call from one of the senior partners from my old firm. He asked me if Joanne and I could meet with several of the partners and senior associates the following Monday. I responded, "Depends on what it's about."

"It involves asbestos cases, we have a representation situation and want to start out talking." He answered.

"If it's about asbestos cases we'll want to bring one of our senior associates along."

"That's fine. How about if we get an early start, around nine o'clock?"

"We'll be there," I answered.

When I hung up I called Joanne on the intercom, asked her to meet with me in the conference room. Called Mack and asked him to meet us there with his top two asbestos lawyers.

Once everybody was there I told them of the phone call and the meeting, said,

"I don't think it's any attempt to beat on me because I used to be in their firm and still have a good relationship with them. If it was that they'd want me to meet with them by myself. Their firm is one of the old time firms. They wouldn't be handling a local distributor. If they're in it and they say they are, their client or clients have to be the manufacturers. If they want to talk and I'm right about who they represent, they're going to be feeling us out on some type of settlement that gets them out of these one by one trials. They can do the math, have to know there's five, six hundred cases, more maybe, out here. Multiply that by what we've gotten in these first two cases and the industry is looking at being wiped out. I think this is the first step in negotiations for settling cases. Mack you're more up on this than Joanne and I, do you have any ideas?"

"I think you're right. These manufacturers are facing a double whammy. Their legal fees are going to be enormous; on top of that there are going to be a series of huge verdicts, one after the other. The publicity from each case will generate more cases and they'll be in court for ten, fifteen years, until all the people who are already infected become symptomatic. There is literature out there that pretty well establishes a twenty year or more lead time for some of the related illnesses."

"Joanne?" I asked.

"I think you're both right. They want to start the process of getting out of this mess. Mack, how do we stand now with asbestos cases, what's the number?"

Mack turned to one of the young lawyers, said "Alice is the overall manager for us, supervises the initial intakes, then supervises the calendering of the cases, motions and all that, is also in charge of our basic research into asbestos diseases. Alice?"

"Four hundred and seventy-eight as of yesterday," she answered, "and there's probably another case or two walking in while we're meeting."

Jimmy the other associate spoke up then, "Mr. Gaskins, I think we're going to end up with around fifteen hundred cases. The demographics of the workforce in the steel mills and ship yards in Baltimore and Norfolk during World War II and the Korean War indicates that the onset of cases is just beginning. The incubation period for these fibers to cause disease is lengthy. Most of the victims are just now wondering what's wrong with them. And the word is getting out. The unions, public health people are spreading the word and it's only been recently that our cases have begun to generate publicity."

Mack said, "Jimmy's right. I figure we'll end up with a thousand or more cases."

"Yes," Alice spoke up then, "business wise that's the upside. The downside is that most of these people are men, once they realize there's something wrong with them, they don't last long. The studies show that there's a long incubation period, but once they begin to show symptoms their prognosis is that they may last a year, two at most. Mr. Moore was the exception. We all know that the value of the cases drops drastically once the victim dies. If he dies you're going to be limited in significant ways in respect to damages. There's no claim for future damages if the client is dead. Besides, once he's dead you don't have him for the jury to see, he's not there in his wheel chair with his oxygen bottle, wasting away. I think having the victim where the jury can see him is part of the reason for the large verdicts - when they die that's gone."

"Even more importantly," I said, "we want the victim to see that somebody is paying for what they did to him; it's important to try and get these cases processed so that the victim is still here to know that his widow, sometimes his children, are going to be in decent financial shape when he's gone. He's our client. For a lot of reasons, it's important to try to resolve each of these cases expeditiously. Settlement is the only way for our clients to see money before they die. A major part of our duty to them is to have them win, whether at trial or settlement, while they're still here.

"Of course, the industry is going to know everything we know about the progress of the disease. They were the ones who commissioned some of the important studies and then ignored them. They know me, Joanne, Mack, know the firm, know that we'll be putting pressure on ourselves to settle so that the cases don't outlive the clients.

"Let me ask all of you something. It's harder than hell to settle a thousand cases, especially when we don't even have half of them yet. What status do we put ourselves and our clients in, especially the ones that haven't walked in the door yet, when we start talking settlement on a large scale, multiples of settlements. Let me hear your ideas; if we want to lean that way what are our options?"

Joanne spoke up, "I've heard of two ways. We all know of class action lawsuits, but they can get pretty costly, administratively. Take forever to finish if the other side opposes them. Don't know whether the expenses would stay high if the effort was part of a settlement. Usually the clients don't end up with much in a class action - just the lawyers. If we start talking that route with the manufacturers, we're talking a so-called friendly lawsuit and they ought to be friendly enough to pay the expenses. But, class action lawsuits, friendly or otherwise, still take a lot of time because of the notice requirements and other procedural mandates and don't usually produce large enough sums for the clients.

"There may be another way though, it's something three cosmetics firms got involved in out in California when they all used a specific ingredient in their various skin treatments and the treatments started causing birthmarks on several thousand women about a month after the products went on the market. The manufacturers pulled their products off the market fairly early on, but realized that there was a possibility that two or three thousand more women might become disfigured before they got word of the problem.

"The attorneys representing about three hundred of the women came up with the idea of what they called a global settlement. The manufacturers and the attorneys for a number of the women agreed as to what the manufacturers would put into a general compensation fund and the manufacturers agreed to separately pay to run an advertisement campaign throughout California notifying potential plaintiffs of the details of the settlement. Way it worked was that the central fund was established as a trust with a committee of the various lawyers administering it. The advertisement told the affected women that there was a substantial compensation fund as part of a global settlement, that they could become a part of it and get a proportionate share of the fund depending upon how many women signed on, that there was a specific time period for joining the settlement, another specific and limited period of time, very short, after which they would receive their share of the settlement. Their receipt of their share would be automatic, albeit on a periodic basis as the fund was supplemented, once the time period for joining was up and the trustees had qualified them.

They were also told that if they didn't join the settlement they would have to proceed with individual suits and the fund would not be available to compensate them; that they'd have to hope the companies still had assets to attach at the end of the process. The advertisement also informed them that they would be required to give up their right to file individual suits if they joined the global settlement. The amount of the fund was set very high and publicized. Over ninety-five percent of the qualified women joined the settlement and the companies were able to deal with the remainder without going bankrupt."

"That appears to be a particularly attractive process for our clients," I said, "given that they are all going to die in the near future, many of them before we can get their cases to verdict. That way they'd be able to see the money in this life. Joanne, why don't you try and contact the attorneys in California and see what you can learn about the process; they may not want to tell you, but, I imagine you'll get most of it out of them. Mack, you, Alice, whoever you can spare from case processing, get right on it - we'll need as much information as possible before the meeting."

It took six months of negotiations before we had our global settlement. By then we had filed an additional three hundred and eighty cases with more clients walking in the door every day. Also by that time virtually every manufacturer, distributor and some large end users of asbestos products who perceived possible liability in respect to their clients had signed on to the settlement. The initial pledge funding of the trust created in the settlement was three billion, eight hundred million dollars. Our fee was one-fourth of the amount to be paid out over three years, with an additional one-fifth of any amount that might be required to be submitted by the defendants in the future to further fund the trust. Professional trustees were hired by the trust to oversee the disbursement process.

Joanne and I started an investment firm, hired professionals to run it and soon it was making money with our money. We each bought ourselves new homes, mine an eight bedroom four story townhouse in Georgetown overlooking the Potomac. It was 1968. I was 37 years old.

We now employed well over a hundred fifty lawyers. Joanne had kept up her regular tort practice throughout the asbestos cases settlement process and it had grown far beyond its former scope that had limited it to tractor-trailer cases. There were now thirty-five lawyers devoted to motor tort cases and the firm had developed almost a boiler plate procedure for processing, settling, or trying the cases. They were never left to stagnate. Every case was always moving forward. Started with intake, gathering information by investigation and in the limited pre-trial discovery permitted, then discovery demands upon the defendants coupled with direct settlement negotiations with their lawyers. If there was no meaningful progress in sixty days, suits were virtually automatically filed. A thirty day grace period to permit the opposing party to think about suit followed, then one more effort to settle. If that didn't work, settlement negotiations were broken off and the case vigorously tried. Often when the other side realized that trial was inevitable there would be last minute attempts to settle. We let it be known that if we had to take the case to within a month of the trial date without a settlement, the only settlement we would thereafter recommend to our clients was one that exceeded our last demand. Because we didn't lose many we took all the way to trial, ninety percent of the cases were settled.

At the same time I had kept up with the business end of our practice. This was more hands on intensive, took more lawyers and the results were not often as spectacular, but the fee remittances were constant; didn't have to wait for ten months or three or four years to see money coming into the firm for work already done. We gave prompt service; expected prompt payment. Both happened. With the public announcement of our settlement arrangement in the asbestos cases the business practice almost doubled overnight. Nothing helps a firm attract all kinds of business law clients like winning a big case against business entities. Rich people like to do business with rich people. Besides, if they were our clients, we couldn't represent other clients against them.

Pat and I had sunk most of the money we had made prior to the asbestos settlement back into growing the firm. Now it was growing so fast and we had made so many good hires, it began to grow by itself.

"Ms. Parsons, Mr. Gaskins," Tim Rayne, the counselor we had hired right out of business school, said one day, "I'm here because I want to bring something to your attention about a certain type of investment I think you should make, but I've got to tell you up front that there's a lot of risk attached to it. Most counselors aren't recommending it, in fact none of them are."

"You mean they think it's a loss generator," Joanne said, "not a viable investment?"

"Yes'm, you're right.

"Well," I interrupted, "why are you here if it's a big risk?"

"Because they're wrong," he answered, "for all their so-called smarts they're not seeing the right things. They're like ostriches, they've got great eyes but they're not seeing because they've got their heads in the ground. If it isn't traditional, if it isn't something they already know about, they don't recommend the investment. They just see the moment, the piece of the world right in front of their noses. They're not seeing what's on the horizon. But things are starting, things are beginning that are going to revolutionize business, revolutionize everything. They don't see it because they're afraid of the unknown and to them unknown means anything other than the way they've always done business."

"What kind of investments?" I asked. "Specifically, what kind?"

"Companies that are beginning to produce software for computer markets, other companies that are getting involved in making chips to be used in computers, companies that make a specific one of a kind item, an item that will become essential for the high speed computer generated flow of information. Items, Mr. Gaskins, that are going to drive the future furnishing of information."

"How confident of it, are you?" I asked.

"Mr. Gaskins, I've sunk every thing I've got, every dime you pay me, into these technical companies, these research companies and I fully expect to get rich doing it. That's another reason I'm coming to you with it. I didn't want you and Ms. Parsons to wake up some morning and read in the paper that I have become rich because of my investments and have you wonder why I didn't put you in the tech market."

"Give us a minute, please, we'll be right back." I said, "no more than fifteen minutes." It only took Joanne and I five minutes. We'd taken large risks all of our professional careers; it had worked for us, there wasn't any reason to stop now. We went back in the conference room.

"Tim," I said, "we're in. We'll go big time. Take twenty-five million out of what we've got invested in the market; take it out so it doesn't hurt, over time I guess, that's your department. Put it into these new companies. But, we want you to try and use the investments to produce business for the law firm. If you make a big start up investment for us, try and direct that firm's legal business to us. That way we'll get two advantages: first we'll get some of our investment back in fees and we'll know that the companies will have competent legal representation; second, we'll be able to keep an eye on what's happening in the companies that are using our money. In other words we can watch our money."

Joanne spoke up, "Hank, it will be easy for the business side to set up a group to handle the high tech stuff Tim's getting us into."

"And once other investors find out we've set up an investment business group in the law firm, we should start to get their business," I said, "especially if we try to limit it to this high-tech stuff. Tim you've got a go on it, do the twenty-five mil as soon as you can reasonably do it; do it in separate names, half for Joanne, half for me. Until we tell you differently, either of us can speak for the other on this issue, speak for the both of us. As soon as we start to see it moving, see some of these companies take off, we'll put more money in the investment pot, lots of it."

That was the day I started the journey to the billionaire class.

Chapter Forty-Five
THE LIQUOR INDUSTRY

I read a newspaper article one morning about an accident between a tractor-trailer belonging to a local firm and a station wagon. Of the occupants of the station wagon, only the father survived. His picture was in the article. His wife and three children were killed. The article noted that among the charges placed against the driver of the truck was the charge of driving while intoxicated.

I guess it was maybe two or three months later when I was in the reception area of our offices when an extensively bandaged man about my age was wheeled through the door. It appeared that he had lost his arms as well as having been extensively burned. I observed the receptionist's intake procedure and soon one of the lawyers from Joanne 's tort practice group, the lawyers that did the negligence work, was escorting the man down to what we called in the firm - the sue the bastards wing.

Every Friday morning the leaders of the various practice groups would meet with Joanne, me, and most of the time Mack as well. We'd go over the cases that were becoming overly difficult and the reasons; think of solutions for case problems and personnel problems. There would be a brief discussion of the numbers of new cases and, when one case stood out, a discussion of that case might occur. The meetings were in essence the firm brainstorming with itself.

The Friday after I had seen the armless man, Joanne 's assistant, a woman who had asked to be called Charlie, directed our attention to a case above the normal run of automobile accident cases.

"Ms. Parsons, Mr. Gaskins," she said, "we need to take a close look at this case involving a man named Clayton, Bill Clayton and his family. He's horribly injured and he lost his wife and his three children. His car was struck by a tractor-trailer. No question of liability; the truck ran a traffic light and there was a police officer on the opposite corner who saw the whole thing. On top of that the driver of the truck was drunk; had just left a bar at a truck stop. The info is all contained in the police report.

"The problem is that there is only minimal insurance coverage for the truck and the owners don't belong to the consortium. The company is probably going to declare bankruptcy just about the time we file suit. The client has very serious injuries. In addition to having severe burns over his whole body, the burning injured his arms so badly they had to be amputated. He also received a severe back injury and the doctors still don't know if he'll ever be able to walk again. He's got a lifetime of major expenses just for his medicals, let alone his loss of income and the other damages to his life caused by the loss of his wife and kids. I don't know whether to recommend settlement at a figure far below what I think the case is really worth because the responsible party isn't solvent, will probably make itself judgment proof by going out of business, via bankruptcy or otherwise. The amount I can settle this case for really isn't going to compensate our client, won't even come close to it."

I had been thinking about the drunk driving aspect as she had been talking. Something was spinning around in the back of my mind. I asked, "What do you know about how the truck driver got drunk, or why he was when he was on duty?"

"Mr. Gaskins, I've reviewed the police report. It said he had stopped by a truck-stop just inside the district line to watch part of an early baseball game on television. Stayed there an hour and a half. Was drunk when he left. I've been out to the truck-stop, typical bar, televisions, several of them, tuned to sports programming."

"What did the inside of the bar look like?"

"Typical as far as I could tell."

"What about the advertisements; what kind of advertisements did you see?"

"Looked typical to me."

"Were they home made advertisements or generic ads that are normally supplied by breweries or distilleries?"

"Come to think of it, Mr. Gaskins, they were mass produced type signs, product signs. I imagine they were produced by the manufacturers or the distributors."

"After we get through with today's meeting," I said, "you and I will take a little ride out to the truck-stop."

That afternoon Charlie and I drove out to the truck-stop which was on a main north-south highway that led from New York City all the way down to Miami. We drove on by it for ten miles, turned around and came back. What I had suspected was correct. Five miles before the truck-stop an alcoholic beverage manufacturer had a billboard directing persons to the availability of their product at the truck-stop. In the next mile there was a billboard advertising a beer product's availability. At the truck-stop itself, there were numerous industry-supplied signs advertising the availability of various alcoholic beverages.

When we got back to the office Charlie and I met with Joanne and Mack. I started off by saying

"Charlie and I drove out to the truck-stop, approached it from the same direction as the truck driver was coming. In ten miles there were at least two billboards advertizing the availability of brand specific alcoholic beverages at the truck-stop. I'm sure if we do a survey from the other direction we'll find the same situation. I have a feeling that the various breweries and distilleries are specifically targeting these truck-stops, that they're actively marketing to truck drivers."

"But," asked Mack, "how does that help us with Charlie's case, we still can't get money for the client from a company that doesn't have any?"

Joanne was seeing further; she looked at me, smiled, waited for my response.

"Oh," I answered, "the companies I'm thinking about have money, lots of it. I think that this case may be another asbestos case. We target the manufacturers of the products; distributors as well. That's the way to get money for the client, probably the only way." I paused, looked around the table, slowly Mack and Charlie began to smile, realizing where I was going. I continued, "Joanne, you've had it figured out since I opened my mouth. What do you think?"

"We go with it. It's the only way our client will ever be adequately compensated for his injuries. It'll take a lot of advance work, lot of discovery, be a long, drawn out process before we reach the end of the first trial. The client, even though he has serious injuries is not likely to die early, so we can afford the time to do it right. The firm can handle anything that comes up, financially."

"Here's my thoughts on the first step." I said. "Charlie, we're going to want you to get up teams of lawyers, two in each team. Get them cameras, send a team north, one south. Have them travel this north-south route taking pictures each way of every industry sponsored sign from Key West to Canada. We're also going to need a team to pick out an east-west route from the West Coast back here and do the same. We need to get this going now."

Joanne interrupted then, "While they're out on the roads, I'll get people here in the office to access all the records we can get on the number of alcohol related accidents involving truck drivers on the two routes we survey. We'll be able to extrapolate from those figures the number of such accidents nation-wide. Additionally, we should be able to readily access the names of the various industry entities, relative standing in the industry and things like that. We'll be able to access annual reports, minutes of stockholders' meetings and things like that. We probably have lawyers here in the firms that are stockholders in many of them. I am, and at least until we get the information I will be."

"That's the way to start this thing out." I responded, "get all the information we can before we show our cards. By the time we file the suit papers with all of our demands for discovery we'll have a lot of the information we're requesting. When they respond, they'll lie, and we'll be able to catch them on it. Joanne, you should also have your pleading people start preparing the pleadings alleging civil conspiracy, all the other charges we'll need to bring, have them start getting the general discovery papers ready. There have to be industry publications out there identifying the manufacturers. Use it to identify the defendants, we'll have the photos of the billboards, every sponsor of one is a potential defendant, remember, too, we've got to include the driver, the truck company and the owners of the truck-stop as well. When the time comes, we'll file against them all just as we did in the Moore case."

We gathered reams of evidence, thousands of photographs of billboards, tens if not hundreds of thousands of pages of evidence, caught the companies in hundreds of lies. It took two years for Mr. Clayton's case to arrive at the verdict time. In the interim, due to the publicity our case had engendered we had over two hundred separate cases pending against the industry. In the week after the jury in Mr.

Clayton's case returned a verdict of eighteen million dollars in damages for him, sixty- three other cases walked in the door.

In the aftermath of the Clayton case we ended up with almost a thousand clients, including six states who retained us to represent them in cases claiming that the industry's actions had caused the states to make extra health care expenditures, both to treat the victims of drunk drivers who couldn't afford to treat themselves and to treat alcoholics who had been partially enticed into using the product because of over aggressive advertizing campaigns.

Eventually, we went the global settlement route. The total settlement was a truly impressive sum. Thirty billion dollars over time. We were in it for an average fee of twenty percent, a fifth-six billion dollars. By the end of 1970 Joanne and I were among the fifty richest people in the world.

I was thirty-nine years old.

From that point on Joanne and I mostly turned the firm over to the relative youngsters coming up, turned it into a professional corporation, started making equity partners, making opportunities for the best of the youngsters. We'd come in once or twice a month, attend the firm's conferences, mostly as observers, giving advice only when asked or when it was necessary to keep the firm out of trouble, letting the guys and gals that had started out as junior associates take over the firm. It kept our names, kept our support, but it really became theirs to run.

Chapter Forty-Six
POLITICS

It was then that I began to be involved in political life, behind the scenes.

I also intensified my efforts to find the men that had killed Eva. The contacts my money made for me in Washington led me to those who traveled on the fringes of the nether world of crime. Some were for hire, hell all of them were for hire, but some of them even tried to earn what they were paid. Occasionally, over the years to come one might report to me that he had found them. I would pay then for more than the finding of them. I would pay for someone to set me up to kill them. I had never forgotten my promise to the Captain. But it never panned out.

I double checked, sometimes found out that I was being conned. Life then became unpleasant for those that tried to con me. It was an advantage of money. Of having it. Eventually, though, I stopped hiring people; I didn't really give up, just recognized that I didn't have it figured right; that I really didn't know how to get the job done, how to find them. Something told me that she'd find the way; that it would spring up somehow when the time was right.

Even before 1970, I had become involved in civic things, pro bono work, sponsoring clinics, meeting with public service lawyers, offering advice, sometimes funding.

I had also become involved in politics; found I liked the game. The excitement of it. Even the underlying vacuousness of the process, the hypocrisy of it all, the 'balls' of it. Bombast and bluster emanating from nothings, from empty suits, usually. I just played with it. Sometimes supported the most outrageous ones, the real buffoons, just to see how easily such people are accepted as real. But that part of my life changed at the end of the first year of my involvement on the fringes of politics.

When I had first come to Washington, first socially and then more than socially, I became a personal friend and a confidant, later an advisor to a young Senator from Florida, a man who was different, who really cared, who really meant what he said and had something to say. And who would become a candidate for President. We were both forty years old when he ran for President in 1970. I helped behind the scenes in his campaign. I would write his speeches. The delivery was his own. Later I funneled money, got Joanne to funnel money when it was critical to the campaign. He won. Barely.

We had become closer friends, very close during the campaign. When he became President I returned to my more or less titular role in the law firm, to my office in the investment firm, but was on call for the President. I was called often to be used as a sounding board for his ideas during times of crisis. Other times, too. Socialized with him often, sometimes with him and his special 'friends', the ones his socialite wife didn't know about. Usually at my townhouse. I'd have intimate dinners prepared before he arrived and then sent the staff home. The Secret Service contingent mixed with my bodyguard in the back and the front foyers, not outside where they could be seen.

Most of the time there would be one woman, sometimes two. She, or they, would just show up at my office in the investment firm near the time I usually went home, ask me if they could go home with me that night. That was the signal. I'd set it up, take them home with me. The neighbors would think I was at it again. I really wasn't at anything. But, because of the President, I ended up with what should have been his reputation as a real 'ladies' man'. I didn't mind. The President would arrive late, come in the back door from the alley. They'd have dinner. I'd join them sometimes, sometimes not. Then I'd go on up on the fourth floor and go to bed. In the morning they'd be gone. I'd always receive a message two days later on Presidential stationery. Two words - "Thanks again."

But there were many meetings for other things. Governmental things. He needed a sounding board, he needed the counter to the advice he was getting, he needed someone to play the devil's advocate. I would often be seen going in the White House; sometimes be seen conferring with him as we walked in the Rose Garden. I wasn't seeking publicity, didn't want it really, but it came anyway.

When my relationship with him became known, it increased the already considerable stature of the law firm as a power broker on the national scene. Raised the stature of the investment firm as well. It was good for business. That was fine with me, good for the firms. But my relationship with the law firm was mostly a pride thing for me by this time. Joanne and I had created it, it had our names on the doors, on the buildings in some cases. The firm now had lawyers in five cities; had taken over whole buildings in some of them. Joanne and I put a significant amount of the money we received from the law firm into legal services for the poor all over the country. But, my relationship with the President was still one of the big pluses for the law firm, brought clients walking in the doors all over the country.

Then the President was assassinated by a crazy man. That's what they said. Wasn't true. More to it than a crazy man.

Chapter Forty-Seven
COMMISSION AND JUSTICE

The new President, the former Vice-President, called me within an hour of his swearing in and asked me to meet with him between events that evening. He and the former President had been great friends as well as political associates. He'd come to the townhouse a time or two with the President; always when there were two ladies for dinner. We had become friends, also, during the campaign and after. We respected each other, I thought we did anyway, know I respected him, and thought, too, that we shared the hollow feeling that grief left in us at the killing of his predecessor.

I slipped in the side door on the Executive Office Building side of the White House about eleven that night. Was ushered in by two Secret Service agents. We met in the Oval Office. After we greeted each other and spoke briefly of the tragedy, he got down to the business of the moment.

"Hank," he said. "I want to continue with you the way the President did; to feel I can call on you when there is no one else I can bounce things off."

"Mr. President," I replied, "you know that I will do anything my country asks of me; anything you ask."

"Well, I know that a lot of things the President asked you to do took you away from your practice, that your firm has had to do without you at times. Will they care if you continue as you have? Being available to the Office of the President-pro bono."

"Frankly, Mr. President. In the overall scheme of the way things work around this town, my relationship with the President, a relationship with you, works as a big plus for the firm. It brings clients in. Big clients. The kind that pay their bills. Even the big fees we charge. There will be no problems with the firm.

"Where is Joanne now?" the President asked, "I haven't seen her in years."

"Mr. President, she bought herself an island in Tahiti, built a palace there, got herself married to a good guy, they're raising bambinos right and left. The practice really doesn't need either one of us."

"That's what I wanted to hear," he responded. "Because I have a big job for you. The most important job you've ever had."

"What's that, Mr. President?"

"We're forming a commission to investigate the assassination. As you know there have been hundreds of questions raised. How could it happen? Who was behind it? Things like that."

"I've heard them. Some of them are worse, even."

"I know," the President responded, "and we've got to give the people the answers to those questions. But careful answers. The right answers. By right answers I mean the best answers. And the best answers may not be the truth. We need answers that won't destroy the world. That won't destroy the country. That's why I want you on that commission."

"What do you mean?"

"You know what I mean. You've been around this town. The firebrands have to be headed off. The congressman from Massachusetts and his friends in Congress."

A junior congressman from Massachusetts had been throwing the blame for the assassination everywhere he could, on every cause he disapproved of, on every enemy and he had many of them. He was throwing the conspiracy word around, trying to attach it to anyone, any philosophy he disliked. Anyone that wasn't like him. On anyone that wasn't an Ivy League elitist. The new President was from Arizona, a graduate of that state's public university system. The last two presidents were from public school and public college systems, neither was from the Ivy League. It had driven the congressman crazy, at least that's what I thought. He'd never been much, a big fat glob of bluster, the biggest promisor of all time. At times he had almost advocated anarchy when the recent president had championed a cause contrary to the liberal causes the congressman advocated. And he was at it again.

"What are you suggesting, Mr. President?"

"Simply that the country has to come first. That's why I want you on the commission. You'll do what it takes to protect the country. Even if it needs protecting from the truth."

"Mr. President, I appreciate your confidence in me, but there is no way the country will accept me as the chairman of that type of a commission. I've always been behind the scenes. Nobody outside of the Washington scene knows me."

"I didn't mean as chairman. I'm going to name a retired Justice of the Supreme Court to be the chairman. He'll be the figurehead the people of the country need; maybe what the Congress needs. I want you to be on the commission because you are what the country, itself, needs right now. Somebody willing to let the mist fall over the things that can destroy us. Someone who doesn't mind working in the fog."

"I think I know what you're saying." I said, "and I don't disagree with you. Right now, with the way things are in the world, you, we, have to be careful. I'm not sure how it will work, though."

"Hank," he responded, "the Chairman is not as sharp as he used to be. He is mainly name now. He'll be looking for someone on the commission to rely on. If you're on it he will naturally turn to you to operate the staff. He'll recognize that he can't do it. You'll be the choice. No-one else on the commission will have the combination you have - ability and a desire for privacy, personal obscurity, the resources of a major law firm, other private resources. He can let you do all the work. Then he and the other big names that are put on the commission can get all the publicity. You are really the key to it for me. You can't say no."

Of course, I said yes. And the key turnings of the investigation were controlled by me. The investigation was ultimately designed to produce inconclusiveness because I could find no specific cause or suggestion that would not, in turn, damage the country more than it damaged those that were responsible. But later, the real information, the truth, the real names were furnished in complete confidentiality to those who would do the right thing, with the accidents strung out across such a period of time that no connection would be made. The American way, I guess. Justice? I thought so.

My money made it possible.

The Commission was the first time, really, that my name became known to the public in a public capacity, despite my attempts to stay in the background. I resisted all of the requests for interviews, referring them to the Chairman or one of the other members. Avoiding publicity to the extent that I could. But I became known, anyway. And the firm prospered more. So did I.

Over the years the new president continued to need me, as would his successor, and others, also.

Chapter Forty-Eight
RETURN TO BLOCK ISLAND

Mrs. Stinsin and I had been writing periodically over the years. I had made arrangements for a substantial sum to be wired to her bank account each month. She had resisted it, said she didn't want it, didn't need it. I sent it anyway. I needed to send it even if she didn't need to receive it. Mrs. Rogers had retired and moved to Block Island and was living with Mrs. Stinsin and I would get letters from her as well. I'd reply to both of them. I decided to take the summer of 1972 off, spend it on the island; see if I could return there, stay there. I wrote and told them I was coming.

I walked off the last ferry of the day at Old Harbor, stepped on the island for the first time in sixteen years. I hadn't told the ladies when I was going to arrive, just that I'd be there soon. I put my luggage to the side of the ferry dock while I arranged to rent an old pickup at the car rental shack. Drove back to the dock, threw my two bags in the back and headed for the Stinsin house. When I got there I drove it on in the back just as the Captain and I had done years before. By the time I walked back to the front porch the ladies were there, standing almost demurely, but flushed with excitement. I climbed the porch steps into two sets of arms.

We spent the next several hours just sitting in the parlor, talking, catching up on all the news, primarily the news about me, about the firm, they wanted to know all about Joanne. I could see they were wishing for me, hoping maybe, that after all this time I had found someone, that Joanne might be that one. I told them she wasn't; told them there was no-one; didn't expect there to be anyone.

I managed to convey to them the extent of my financial standing in the world, not bragging, just wanted them to know that I wanted them to call on me when they needed anything. That I wanted them to spend the money I had been sending. I had checked and knew they had been putting it aside. They told me they knew I was rich, but that they didn't need the money. I wanted them to know that anything they could possibly need in a year would probably represent no more than an hour's earnings of the working of my money. That the money worked twenty-four hours a day. Joanne and I had added another hundred million dollars to our investment portfolio in the tech and computer research companies. The investments were starting to grow already, we had doubled our investment; in the two decades ahead we'd see our investment grow twenty fold, then more even.

Once you have a certain amount of money, I told the ladies, it just grows. You don't have to do a thing, it just keeps getting larger no matter what you do. Told them that's where I was in the money department. That's why they should use the money I was sending. It was almost like it wasn't really mine, I told them. There was this big boatload of money out there somewhere, growing bigger all the time. We could take what we needed, what we wanted and it would be as if nothing was gone. They smiled as I tried to describe being rich, really rich; then they agreed they'd let me help if it was what I wanted. If I wanted to keep putting money in Mrs. Stinsin's account they wouldn't complain, might not spend it, in fact wouldn't spend it unless they needed to. What did they need? They had everything they needed. They said. If it made me feel better I could keep sending it, but only if Mrs. Stinsin put my name on the account so if anything happened to her the account would be mine.

We had dinner in the dining room where I had eaten that first night the Captain brought me to the island. Where I had first seen her. Been overwhelmed by Eva. As we ate they came. Memories on top of memories, memories of the Captain, of a Christmas past, of Leatherby, of being out at South Channel in a crows nest, memories of 'sticking' the great fish, memories even of the 'bad boys', but mostly memories of her, her standing on the deck of the *Eva* with a hatchet in her hand, fish blood on her face, smiling at me, at my reaction to her. Memories of swirling with her on the dance floor at the Ocean View, body surfing down below Southeast Light. Memories of being "My Man." I seemed to awaken then, from the reverie of my memories, where I'd been but moments before. Mrs. Stinsin and Mrs. Rogers were looking at me, smiling, and I realized that I hadn't been talking, responding to them, that conversation had stopped while I was living in the past. They had known where I was. Had respected it, knew I needed it, needed times of memories. I smiled back at them, said, "Just traveling." Mrs. Stinsin responded, "We knew."

After dinner we sat in the parlor drinking coffee, talking, me catching up on what they had been doing. They knew all about me. They'd followed things in the papers. Had two scrapbooks full of what I had been up to. After a while I got up, said, "I'd better be leaving, I've rented a house on the bluff at Clayhead for the summer."

"It's too late to get settled in a new place tonight, you can do that in the morning. Tonight you're staying here, staying with me." Mrs. Stinsin responded,

"That's too much trouble."

"Nonsense, no more trouble than the first night you showed up in my parlor. Put you in the back room then, do it now. I'll be troubled if you don't stay the night."

I went outside to the pick-up, lifted my bags out of the truck bed, brought them in, took them upstairs, on into the back bedroom. Mrs. Stinsin hadn't changed a thing. It was as it had been then. I undressed, got in the bed, went to sleep.

Chapter Forty-Nine
LILACS

In the middle of the night I dreamt of the scent of lilacs.

She was there.

I was aware of her just as I had been aware of the woman in my dream, or had it been a dream, those many years ago. Was it a dream now? I didn't care. That she was here, somehow was enough. A woman's body, naked body was on mine, sliding, moving, breasts pressed into my chest, lips on mine, lips then whispering in my ear "My Man, My Man. My Husband." I felt myself responding, realized that I was complete, ready. And then we were love-coupled. There in the ethereal world of the dream she made for me, we consummated the love that we had denied ourselves in the other time, the time of this earth, the time of our youth. It was as I had known back then, had always known since, it would be. Loving her physically was dying, without death. Being with her fully was the suspension of breathing, the suspension of my heart, my circulation, all of it subsumed into the intense pleasure that only she would ever bring to me, a pleasure only she could bring. The spirit of she that loved me, was loved by me. She had made us wait in that other time. Now the waiting was over. I was experiencing what no other man had ever known. A love so strong that it reached beyond the grave. She had joined me and then joined us. In the darkness of the night, in the silence of the night, she had returned to me.

This time she did not leave to preserve what was to come, this time she had brought it all to me, stayed, was giving it to me, to us. This time there was no reservation. There was no premature ending. It was from the beginning to the end of it. Until she looked down at me, smiled. Until I was spent.

This time as she slid her body from mine, she turned me to lie on my side facing her and I saw her face clearly, the beautiful face aglow on a moonless night, luminous as if she was the moonlight. The golden hair shimmering in a light that was not of this world. I didn't really know where we were, where I was. This world? A dream world?

295

She pushed her bottom arm under me, her top arm over me, stretched up and kissed me again. Then lay there in my arms.

I wanted to talk, but couldn't in the place that we were. It was her time, her place, to talk if she wanted. That was okay. Just to be looking at her, to feel her lying on me, next to me, in my arms, talking, was more than I thought I would, see, hear or feel ever again.

"You have been good ." She said then, "When they made it that I could not be with you on this earth, it was important that a man who had lost so much as am I, should reap other rewards, other great things. You have done so. I am proud of you.

"Now is the time to go on to other things. To use your wealth to influence what happens in the world, to save it from those such as the men that took me from you.

"I shall come to you, not often, only when it is necessary, until the time I come to take you away with me to where I live, where it is that I am, anyway. They call it something else here. It is not living that we call it. Nor death either. You will see.

"I will bring you messages. I will bring you love when you need it. It will not be often, but I will come. I will come to you in the darkness to bring to you my light, to comfort you, to embrace you, to take you into the body that was saved for you when we were so young. I will love you always."

I realized then that I could talk, she was letting me talk, "When will you come again?"

"When I should."

"When am I to expect to see you? To hold you again?"

"It cannot be known when one should come until the time one should. I will be with you when it is needed by you or it is needed for me to be with you - or when I want it so."

"What is your message? Do you have a message for me?"

"There is never a single message, one begets another. There are messages. I want it that you should help your President end this terrible war. That you should make those pay that assassinated your friend. I want it that you should find those that sent me to this place where you are not. As for them, when it is the time, the right time, I want you to ask them if they remember me, what happened to me. Then give them to the 'bad boys'. "

"I haven't been able to find them? How can I find them, the ones that sent you from me? "

"I am not permitted to name them, though we know everything here. It is that we are not permitted to make the things that happen there, happen or not. Only earthly beings can do the things there. I have been permitted only to visit you, visit you in this way; most of us do not get to go home, ever. Even in dreams. But I am Eva. Even in a dream, if a dream is what it is. I will come again because it is what I will want."

"If I find them," I asked, "how am I to know where the 'bad boys' are. You know they are never in a place, a particular place. They go where they will. It is their nature. When I find them, the men that killed you, how will I know where to give them to the 'bad boys'?"

"When you find the men, and you will, I will send the 'bad boys' to take them from you. You can be sure of it. You serve the men on the table, I will send the revelers to the festival, to the feast."

I said then, "Tell me what happened, how did it happen, how did they kill you?"

She told me.

I was sorry I had asked. She drew me into her memory of that night. I fought them for her, screamed in my anger. And she was gone, merging into the blue of the sea of another world.

I felt a hand on my shoulder, shaking me. I opened my eyes. Mrs. Stinsin was shaking me, Mrs. Rogers standing behind here. "Hank, what's the matter? You were screaming and when we came in you were fighting something." Mrs. Stinsin asked.

I lay there for a moment, then said, "I'm okay now."

"What was it Hank?" Mrs. Stinsin asked again.

I lie there silently for several seconds, then said, simply at first, "She was here."

They both looked at me then, knew what I was saying. Then Mrs. Rogers said, "Hank you were dreaming, or having a nightmare. You want her here so bad that your mind made it happen. It was in your mind."

"Mrs. Stinsin, I asked her about the night they killed her. She took me there. Then I saw them killing her, I was fighting them and I began to see her drift away, drift away from me into the sea. Beyond my reach. Then you were shaking me. I opened my eyes and the two of you were here."

"Hank, you were dreaming, a nightmare. Come, get up, we'll go downstairs, I'll fix a pot of coffee."

I slowly threw back the covers, got up in my pajamas, walked to my bag to get my robe and turned and left the room.

Eva had transcended time to come to me, even if it was in a dream. I knew it; could see in the ladies eyes that they knew it, also. I said then, "We never need to be afraid of this. Afraid of her. We knew she was special when she was here. God's special angel. She's no less that now. She will come when she wants, in a dream or not, however she wants it, when she thinks she should. There is nothing to fear in it."

We talked no more of it. Ever.

And it was then that I began to write this journal. To tell our story.

I spent the rest of the summer on the island, walking the bluffs, the dunes and the thickets, walking along the ponds, walking mostly along the beaches. Every time I walked through our place beside the rock where the Ocean View had been I could feel her presence; when I walked the beach where Leatherby had found her, I always cried. Tears just came in that place, a place of tears for me, from where a tear had been sent to me in that other time, a place where tears come from and where they go. I would promise then, promise Eva as I had promised the Captain that I would find them. Kill them.

Often I would hire a restaurant, usually the great restaurant at the Hotel Manisses, the Indian name for Island of the Little God, to set a table for me at the special place below the Ocean View bluff, to have a waiter serve dinner to me there, usually a wonderful thing they did with stripped bass, the rock fish of my first island, served with baby patty squash they grew in the Hotel Manisses garden, and champagne, the best they had. And they had good champagne. Two crystal flutes. They would set it up early for me, in the afternoon around four, four-thirty, perhaps a little later. I would eat, with people walking up and down the beach in the late afternoon sun, looking at the crazy man sitting at a table next to a rock, dressed for dinner, eating dinner, being served by a waiter.

When the shadow of the bluff behind me began to fall over the table, I would ask the waiter to serve the champagne and he would open it, pour the glasses and I would take one, toast the other seat at the table and drink the champagne. Sometimes, if the memory of her was particularly upon me, I would drink the whole bottle. Then the waiter would call me a cab; I'd leave the pickup in the Hotel Mainisses' parking lot and walk to retrieve it the next morning. When I'd leave sober, or relatively so, I'd write in this journal. Taking solace in the writing.

Some days I'd have one of the restaurants fix a picnic lunch, enough for two really, and I'd drive to Southwest Point, North Light, or the beach beneath Clayhead Bluff, and sit there and think of the old days, think of her, the Captain, the swordfish out in the deep, think even of the 'bad boys'. Fondly even, they did their thing, the 'bad boys', what they'd been put on this earth for. I held no grudge. Admired them really.

One afternoon when I had walked to the beach where Eva had come ashore the last time, I sat down at the edge of the wave wash, sat there for a while, my eyes full of tears, then undressed and walked into the surf, swam out to the point, caught several waves to shore. Could see her in my mind, walking to me in the shallows. But it wasn't the same; never would be like it was, not here, not in this place, this time, this life.

When I had first arrived at the island at the beginning of summer, I had noticed from the ferry that the Ocean View Hotel was gone. When I inquired, I found that it had burned down the year before. It was for sale, a developer was about to purchase it. Going to build condominiums on the parcel.

I made inquiries. Found the identity of the owners; they lived in Philadelphia. A brother and a sister - the Patterson siblings, heirs I guess would be the correct term. I called Mack, asked him to send our best acquisition's person to the owners. To tell them that an anonymous buyer was interested in the property. Mack called early in the morning two days later.

"Hank." He called me Hank now, "There's a problem, the owners have a buyer and have already agreed to sell."

"Have they signed a contract yet?"

"Haven't signed yet. But, the brother says their word is their bond."

"How much have they been offered, did they tell you? "

"Said half a million."

"Mack, call them up, see if they'll see me at two o'clock tomorrow. My name ought to be worth a meeting. Just tell them I need to see them on business. If they agree, I want you to charter a plane, have it here on the island first thing in the morning. Get a two engine job. Tell the pilot it will be a round trip, there'll be some waiting in the middle of it, and that we'll be arriving back at Block Island after dark."

I went to the best lawyer on the island, paid him to draw up a deed for the Ocean View property, to prepare an indemnity agreement, paid him to arrange to have the title searched immediately, to prepare settlement papers and to be ready to come with me the next day. Paid him three times the going rate. In advance.

The next afternoon my Block Island lawyer and I walked into the Pattersons' office. Both of them where there. After introductions were made all around, we sat, and I spoke.

"Mr. Patterson, Ms. Patterson, I understand that you are the owners of the old Ocean View property on Block Island?"

"Yes, we own it." Mr. Patterson said.

"I want to buy it."

"We can't do that, can't sell it to you."

"Why not? Everything is for sale for the right price."

"We've already agreed to sell it." The sister said.

Her brother said, "Once we agree we honor it." His sister nodded her head affirmatively.

"Here's a certified check," I said, "a deed and an indemnification agreement. You have to make up your minds now or we walk out, wait until your proposed buyer settles and then deal with him. That might even be cheaper. But that's up to you." I slid the documents over in front of the two of them. Then I placed the million dollar certified check on top. Thirty minutes later we were walking out of the office and within the next hour we were in the air on the way back to Block Island with the signed documents in our possession. The lawyer would take care of the recording and such the first thing in the morning. I paid the pilot to stand by to carry the attorney anywhere he needed to go to finish the deal.

The Ocean View property was mine, ours really, Eva's and mine. Before I left at the end of the summer, I had signed the contract for the rebuilding of the hotel. Upgrades to four star status from what had been before. But in the same basic elongated design, with a cupola in the middle, that had stood on the bluff for almost a hundred years. The way it was when I first stepped upon the island. I also had the architect recreate the ballroom exactly as it had been the night we danced, the night she taught me to dance. There was only one other difference. It was to be the *Hotel Eva.*

At the very end of the summer I went to a yacht broker in Newport, told him to find a boat builder, commission him to build a replica of the *Eva* by the next summer. But to up-grade it, twin engines instead of one, a larger wheelhouse, cabin space below, electronics, especially radar, but to keep its outer appearance as close to the original as was possible.

I returned to Washington in September.

Chapter Fifty
THE WAR

We thought we could do what the French could not. We always had done so, surpassed the French. We were wrong.

The President had called me one day said he wanted to talk to me about Viet Nam; asked if I could come over that evening. I went as I always did when a President called, through the side entrance to the Oval Office. I knew, of course, about the war in Viet Nam. About the twenty thousand advisers there. Everyone knew. It was no secret. He spoke almost as soon as I entered.

"Hank, you know we're involved in Viet Nam with advisors, equipment, munitions and things."

"Yes sir, Mr. President. I know."

"Well," he said, "I'm thinking of sending additional troops there, lots of troops. Thinking about taking over control of the war. Crush everything until we win the thing. What do you think."

"Why? Why do more?"I asked.

"Why! Its there." he answered. "There's a war there."

"But why would you want to get in a bigger war with an enemy that has destroyed the military apparatus and will of France. Why fight an enemy that will never give up?"

"The Chief of Staff says we can win it in six months."

"I think he's a fool if he's saying that, if that's the advice he's giving. They'll never stop fighting over there."

"We have the mightiest air power in history. They can't match it. Russia can't. The Chinese can't." He responded.

"What will you do with it?"

He answered: "With what?"

"With the air power? With the damn war?"

"We'll bomb the hell out of them. We'll stop communism in its tracks. Do it over there, so we don't have to do it closer to home."

"Mr. President, with all due respect, you haven't answered my question. Why do it? I doesn't make sense to me. It will destroy you, your presidency. All bombing will do is kill people. Level buildings. It can't win a ground war in Asia."

"We have to stop them somewhere."

"They'll turn on each other over there, Russia, China, Viet Nam, if they get a chance and we give them the time. Growing this war is a damn mistake, a folly that will destroy you. Why, Mr. President? "

He was never ever to tell me why. The war expanded to a national tragedy for us. It destroyed him.

Chapter Fifty-One
BUFFINGTON

The Viet Nam war grew into a monster until it turned on him, killed him. One night a month before the party primary convention where he was expected to easily win his party's nomination, almost two years after I had described his thinking as wrong, two years after I had described his decision to drastically increase the country's efforts in Viet Nam as folly, he dropped dead in his tracks. His heart simply stopped beating. The Speaker of the House who he had named as his Vice-President, and who was next in line of succession succeeded him into the presidency.

During the two years of his failing presidency, I had decided that I wanted to spend more time out of Washington, didn't want to be called on as frequently as before. And I had begun to remember the time of my youth when I had fished out of Ocean City, out at the Jackspot, further even, when I had spent more time on the sea than on land, at least it seemed so looking back. I didn't want to spend all of my time, my summer time in Block Island, wanted a place closer. Decided to buy a place in Ocean City, or near it.

When I was growing up there was a place where we took the girls when we could get them to go. Took them to party, to drink, dance to the sounds of the radio from a car parked outside. Sometimes do other things. It was an un-lived in house on a large estate south of town on the mainland. For as long as we could remember the house had been called the haunted house. Haunted by a woman who had lived there only one summer. A woman who had not even died there, or so the story went.

It had a name the estate did, Buffington. The owners had not visited it in over fifty years and it had declined until it was an old gray house with Victorian towers on the corners, tower rooms and all. The windows had long since been broken, or stolen, the doors broken in. Shingles blown off in storms. A haven for vandals, for kids looking to scare girls.

The property was directly on the mainland side of the bay opposite the north end of Assateague Island. High wooded land, surrounded by marsh, extended almost to land's end. It was there on a point that the house had been built, surrounded on the north and the south by pine trees that bordered the marsh. There was a gut leading into the point about twenty yards from the house. The owners had dredged it out, built a boat house there giving the property fairly deep-water access directly to the bay. The main house and the boat house had been built just prior to the entry of the United States into World War I and it was the war that gave the house a special story passed on to us when we'd been young.

The Buffingtons, Chad and Eleanor, had been married in June of 1916. He was the son of a wealthy Pennsylvania railroad company family. She the daughter of a banking family in Philadelphia. 'Mainliners', high society. He had bought the Ocean City property when they had gotten engaged at Christmas time in 1915. Had sent a double crew of craftsmen, carpenters and the like to build Eleanor a mansion at the shore, the Maryland shore, a great house on the mainland protected by the barrier island to the east. The ocean visible from the second and third floors over the low sand dunes across the bay. It was to be self-contained. With servants cottages and the like. Everything they would need for when the honeymoon was over. Everything they would need in the summers they planned to spend there. The summers of the rest of their lives.

They had married, spent a month in England. Their liner, a British vessel, had a torpedo shot at it on the way home. It had been a dud, made a clunk. Was exciting, though, being shot at. The liner changed course, sped up and the U-Boat had been to slow to close again for another shot. They had arrived safely home, taken a series of trains southward from New York, picked up their servants in Philadelphia and proceeded down through Delaware, then the Eastern Shore of Maryland to the spur line to Ocean City. They'd been met by locals they had hired to meet them with trucks and by their drivers who had driven two automobiles ahead of them.. They had been driven to their great house, her bay-side cottage she called it. Arriving on the 15th of July 1916. They had spent the rest of the summer there and most of the autumn, a magnificent time. They had been young and in love.

They returned to Philadelphia by Thanksgiving of that first year, to be there for the society season. And the war came into their lives.

The war had really started in 1914 with the assassination of Archduke Franz Ferdinand at Sarajevo, but the United States had managed to avoid involvement until Germany forced our hand by announcing an unrestricted sinking policy in respect to any vessels approaching England and the European continent. In April of 1917 the United States entered the war on the side of the allies.

Chad was a patriot, besides war was the maker of men, great men's resumes included military service in time of war. Over Eleanor's protests he had volunteered for the Army. His connections and his money had gotten him a commission as a captain. Eleanor had followed him to his first training camp in Kansas in the dust of the eastern edge of the plains. The camp had been rudimentary, was seventy-five miles from the nearest fair sized town. The nearby village only had a minimum number of rental units. She had rented the largest she could find. The entire apartment would have fit in one of the bathrooms of their house in Philadelphia. Then she found that there were no servants to be hired. No chauffeurs and she didn't drive. No laundresses. She spent two months washing her own clothes, washing Chad's on the rare evenings he was permitted to join her. She cooked, had to. It was the first time for her. Had to walk to nearby truck farms, vegetable patches really. Buy vegetables, eggs, chickens that were walking around in farm yards, pay extra for the farm wives to kill them for her. Ring their necks. The headless chickens would sometimes run around the farm yard until they fell from loss of blood. Then she'd carry them to the apartment, pluck them, and cook them as best she could. Cook vegetables, try to bake potatoes in the wood-stove.

When Chad's time in Kansas was over he got orders to go to a camp in Texas for artillery qualification. He had expected that she would accompany him to his new station. They were in love, weren't they?

She refused to go. Said she was going home to Philadelphia where it was civilized. She couldn't take any more of army life. She paid a local truck company to take her to the nearest train station. Chad reported to Texas and then was sent overseas.

He spent the rest of the war in France, then in a hospital in England after he was gassed and shot twice, both times in the leg, the same leg. He would walk with a limp the rest of his life.

One day while he was in the hospital he received a letter from Eleanor. She had met someone else; was going to file for divorce. She hoped he would sign the papers that she had enclosed with the letter. But, if he didn't she would divorce him anyway; it would just take longer. He had waited two days before responding. Thought it out. She had already destroyed their life together. He would love her forever, but he could never trust her. He signed the papers and mailed them to her without comment. Just signed them.

Their lawyers split the property up for them. She hadn't wanted the Maryland property. Didn't need the memories of her first honeymoon while she was on her second. She got their home in Philadelphia.

They discharged him from the hospital three months later and he returned home. He left again as soon as the war was over. Returned to Paris, was accepted by Sylvia Beach and Adrienne Monnier, stayed at their place above the Shakespeare Book Store, then paid their rent for them, there met all the writers of the left bank, the ones that would become famous, Ernest, Joyce, the rest of them, even Jean Prevost; became a writer himself, an unsuccessful writer. Couldn't write what others wanted to read. He returned to the United States five years later; took a job with his father's company. Never married again. Never again visited his estate in Maryland. Stopped the maintenance. Just let it deteriorate. He had never put it on the market. It was the only time he had been happy, the time they had spent at Buffington. He wouldn't sell it, just let it go the way of his marriage.

Now I wanted it. Not the house itself; it was too far gone. I wanted the property. It took me four months of negotiating with an eighty-five year old man who hardly knew who he was; didn't remember now why he hadn't wanted to sell. Eventually, he realized that it was now just another piece of real estate. I bought it.

Within a week construction started on my showplace, the place where I would do most of my entertaining, business socializing. Block Island was my personal place, my private place. It was saved just for me. Buffington would be my other place where I'd bring the people that were now in my life, Joanne and her family when they were in the country, Mack, others from the law firm, Tim, his people from the investment company, politicians, industry captains. Even friends, sometimes. It would be where I'd hold fund-raisers, formal dinners, yet, also where I'd hang out with hunting and fishing cronies. My place. A big place, ten bedrooms. Twenty thousand square feet of living space, huge kitchen, huge dining room that seated thirty, indoor/outdoor swimming pool, one that ran into the house, tennis court, bars and entertainment centers. The whole works, the entire property surrounded by a fence.

My real home remained on Block Island, where my heart had gone so many years ago. Where I was building my hotel and where I would spent most of the time in the summers until the marlin came. Buffington was different, a toy for a rich man. The place to go to see boyhood friends, most of the rowdy gone from all of them by now; the place to go for the marlin, tuna, too.

The Ocean City Airport's grounds abutted Buffington on its southern side. It was one of the reasons I had been interested in the particular property in the first instance. I planned to buy a plane.

I flew into the airport on a chartered plane two weeks after I settled on the Buffington property to check on the start of construction. After we landed, as I was walking to the limousine that I had hired for the weekend, I noticed a flying school sign, 'Crash Quillin's Flying School - Single Engine - Multiple Engine," there was a smaller line beneath the main message "Get your instrument ratings here." I told my body guard to wait for me.

I went inside and there was D. R. Quillin, a man my age. In fact we'd gone to school together. When we'd been young we'd called him "Dehue." Another wild kid. I walked up to the counter, said

"Hey Crash, what you doing?"

"Do I know you?" He answered.

"I'm Hank Gaskins. We went to school together."

"I remember now," he said "you got run out of town a long time ago. Made it good since, I hear. Top lawyer up there in Oz. What you doing down here?"

"I just bought the old Buffington place. Building a house there. They just started construction. Came down to check on things."

"I heard that some rich guy had bought it. That's you?"

"Yep."

"Congratulations," he replied, "welcome home. If there's anything I can do, just let me know. I'll take care of your plane, help your pilot find his way around. Be glad to do it."

"I've got something else on my mind right now. I've got a place up in Block Island, Rhode Island. It's no more than two or three miles from the general aviation airport up there. They're about like here; mid-sized operation, runway just under four thousand feet. I travel up there a lot; intend to travel here a lot, especially in the summer at both places. In the fall I'll be bringing friends down for the hunting, in the summer for the fishing.

I've got a custom Bertram being built in Florida. We're cleaning out the old gut on the Buffington place, using a clam shell to dredge it some. We'll dock her there. So I'll be bringing people down frequently. I saw your sign, stopped by for some advice.

"I want to buy a plane big enough to carry six or seven people, or more even, not counting the pilot. Has to be able to land easily here or on Block Island. Has to have enough range to get to Florida non-stop. Want twin engines, all top of the line electronics, everything I'll need for instrument flying. Not interested in jets. Has to be a prop plane. Doesn't have to be the fastest thing in the sky, most of the flying will be pretty short trips to here, little longer ones to Block Island. After I get the plane I'm going to want to get a license to fly the thing. I don't have any license now. I'll be starting from scratch.

"Off the top of your head what kind of a plane am I looking for? Money is no object, whatever I get I'll be modifying the cabin, 'gussing' it up. So as long as she'll carry six or seven passengers, I'm not concerned about the amenities in the cabin."

He was silent for a minute, then said, "You want an Areo-Commander outfitted with long range fuel tanks. Probably a 690 B model. She's high winged, easy to get in and out of small airports. Can handle four thousand foot runways. Usually no problem. She's twin engined. Can fly on one almost as good as two. Can take off with one engine, land on one engine. With the extra tanks she can take you to Florida, anywhere about that distance. Cabin access is good on them. I know you don't care but the top of the line has a great cabin setup already. You can buy them completely instrumented, usually carry a pilot and a co-pilot."

"What about lessons, can you work with me, get me multi-engine rated so I can be one of the pilots on my own plane if I want to?"

"Certainly, but if you've never had a license, never piloted a plane before, it'll take a lot of time."

"I've got time. Can you start next weekend, keep at it on weekends until I have all my hours, until I get licensed?"

"Yeah, I guess so, would if we had an Areo-Commander here, or a twin engined plane to give you lessons with. Don't have one available right now. The one we have is in the shop getting its motors overhauled."

"You'll have an Areo-Commander, 690 B model, here next weekend. Can we start lessons at eight a.m.?"

"If we have a plane I can start anytime. You want to know how much I charge?"

"It doesn't make any difference how much you charge. I won't cheat you and you won't cheat me. Agreed?"

"Yeah, agreed. You're on. Next Saturday."

"Do you have any brochures, anything like that, about these Areo-Commanders?"

He got me one. I turned to leave,

"We'll be landing at seven-thirty next Saturday. See you then." I said, then asked "Why do they call you 'Crash Quillin'? Doesn't appear to be a very reassuring name for someone in your business."

"They call me 'Crash' because I survive my mistakes. I've learned to glance everything in. Skip them in. I'm good at crashing. I crash them and walk away, well sometimes I get carried away. I fly antique planes a lot and they're always crashing. Never crashed a contemporary plane. Just the old ones."

"See you next Saturday." I said, as I left the office and walked to the limousine.

I called the manufacturer of the Areo-Commander, told them who I was. Told them I wanted a fully equipped Areo-Commander, long range tanks and the works, custom cabin, the best they had. They told me the price, I ordered the plane. Told them I wanted it by the following Friday, would pay a premium for it. They argued for a while,

I raised the premium. They got on the phone, told some other client there had been a delay with his order, would take an unexpected six months to finish his plane. I hired a pilot, sent him to the factory and my plane flew out Friday morning, overnighted in Washington at National and it arrived at the Ocean City Airport the next morning at seven-twenty with me aboard.

By the following June I was instrument rated, multi-engine rated. I kept the pilot on the payroll of the investment company. Usually used him. Sometimes, though, usually when the weather was good, I'd fly back and forth without a co-pilot. It was my plane wasn't it? Funny thing, when I was flying solo with passengers aboard the passenger cabin would be quiet from wheels up until I cut the engines off.

In the years that followed the Areo Commander was a frequent sight flying south along the beach of Ocean City on its approach to the airport. Circling Block Island to get in the right approach pattern.

I home based her at Ocean City, left it under "Crash's" supervision. He did most of the checking on her, fueling and so forth, especially when I didn't have a co-pilot, which became increasingly more frequent as my confidence grew.

I named the Bertram *Eva Still*. She arrived the late spring of my first year at Buffington. She was complete in every detail. Bridge, bridge controls, Bimini top, outriggers, center rigger, starboard side gin pole with block and tackle, bait rigging station, live well, built in fish box, all the electronics, fully equipped galley and bar, saloon, big sleeping area up forward, two smaller ones on the sides, shower. She was a fully found vessel.

I hired Jimbo to be the stand-by Captain of her; he was available anytime I needed a captain. If we were fishing a tournament I'd pick up a local mate, an Ocean City boy, no need to settle for less than the best. Otherwise it would just be Jimbo, me, and whomever I had invited to Buffington to go fishing. Often I'd take her out by myself, fish my guests without the benefit of captain and mate. I hadn't forgotten the old days, the old ways.

Often times I'd take her out myself. Just me. No-one else aboard. Head out past the Jackspot. Sometimes I'd fish; sometimes not. Sometimes I just wanted to be on the ocean. To be surrounded by the sky and the sea. When the moon was full, visibility clear I'd hove to overnight, out there by myself. Out beyond the effects of the lights of Ocean City. Out beyond the glow in the west. Radio in and tell the help I was staying out overnight. Then turn the running lights off, drift with the current. Put the back rest of the fighting chair in the horizontal position and lie back and look at the stars, for hours. Thinking of Eva usually. Sometimes I'd fall asleep, and dream. It was a way to be with her. The *Eva Still,* herself an island drifting in the tide and the breeze. Sometimes in the morning I'd be down off Chincoteague, having drifted down there in the night and have to run for a couple of hours to make the Ocean City inlet.

I had also leased a hunting marsh on Assateague and was hosting guests whenever it suited me for hunting and fishing. Meetings as well. In short order, Buffington became a famous place, the place others liked to talk about. Locals too. That was okay. They were my people, mostly. The locals. They protected me from outsiders. Many a guest would drive down, get lost trying to find Buffington. Usually, the locals would play dumb when the temporary 'come heres' asked for directions.

Over time my fishing and hunting invitations became some of the most sought after invitations in Washington. It wasn't just the hunting and the fishing. Partying accompanied most of the sport stuff. Partying at night. Usually without me. Sometimes all night after I had gone to bed.

Chapter Fifty-Two
END OF WAR

One evening while I was spending the night in Washington, I got a call from the new President, the former Speaker. He asked if I could come to the White House for a confidential meeting. When I arrived there were two other men there, the Secretary of State and one of the President's senior advisors. The President spoke.

"Mr. Gaskins," the President began, "I need to speak with you in complete confidence. Nothing that is said here can go outside this room. Agreed?"

"Certainly, Mr. President. But everybody calls me Hank. I'm very comfortable with people using my first name."

"Hank it is then. I might as well get right to why I called you over. I'm going to China in three months. So far no one knows except the Secretary of State, a half dozen others here in the White House and in the State Department. We're going to wait to make an announcement until we have everything we need lined up, so that the trip will bring results. We're going to try and get out of this Viet Nam mess. "

"Mr. President, the trip is long overdue. You're to be complimented for being willing to take the political risks involved. To open up to a third of the world. Negotiate with them."

"Hank, that's why I've asked you here. I want to reduce the risks as much as possible. You know Jonathan Waters don't you." He said, pointing to the third man present, the senior advisor.

"Yes sir. We've met around Washington, several times. Jonathan, it's good to see you again."

"Hank," the President continued, "I'm sending an advance team to China under the guise of a trip to Pakistan. The team will include the Secretary of State, Jonathan, and we'd like you to be a part of it. We need somebody that can move around without being seen to be doing so. Somebody that no one will be paying much attention to."

"Mr. President, of course I'll help any way I can. I just don't know what I can do in Pakistan, or China for that matter."

"The most important thing, Hank, for what I have in mind is the ability for the person to appear to be nobody in a general sense; while those who have been prepped will know he speaks for me."

"I understand, Mr. President. But surely the Chinese will know that the Secretary of State shares your confidences."

"I know that. It's not the Chinese I'm talking about. The Secretary is already up to speed on that. I need someone to sneak into North Viet Nam. He has to get there in a way that no one sees him or knows he's there. Other than the ones expecting him. We need to create the framework for stopping this damn war. The Chinese will help, but the Vietnamese want a direct contact with a representative of mine that they can trust. In contacts through the Swiss Embassy your name was brought up. We don't know why or how your name was known to them. It may have been your work on the assassination commission, what happened afterward. But, in any event, the Swiss told us that the North Vietnamese suggested you.

"We're afraid of publicity if the meetings don't pan out and the word gets out that we held the meetings at all. With your reputation we don't have to worry about that. You've always shunned the spotlight. We need you."

I flew into Pakistan with the Secretary of State's party. During the layover it was easy to slip away. Tim Rayne had called people, asked them to meet me, give me what I needed. I was ready when they appeared at the hotel, told them to take me to the far end of the airport. Had them just leave me off there. A jeep showed up, I got in and was shuttled to the military side of the airport. I flew into Hanoi in a Pakistani military transport plane that was sneaking military supplies to North Viet Nam.

I would meet with the associates of the leadership of North Viet Nam. We arrived at tentative positions on the cessation of hostilities that each of our countries could adopt. Both proclaim, both talk, about victory. I took the proposed agreement back to the President and his people. After his people went over it, the intelligence people, the military people, and the politicos, they made minor adjustments and I flew back, this time direct by Air America. Met again with the Vietnamese. Hammered out the last details, especially concerning P.O.W. issues.

A month later the China trip was consummated between the two countries, China and the United States announced their joint plan for concluding the war. It was accepted by the antagonists in Viet Nam.

My part in the agreement stopping the war would not be known until twenty years later when they unsealed the tapes of the Oval Office conversations and a researcher listened to the original tape. I still refused to tell of it, of the trip, the role I played. At last the folly was over. But it would affect the country for the rest of the century and even beyond.

Chapter Fifty-Three
MRS. STINSIN'S JOURNEY

Over the years I became an enigma to the Washington hostesses. It was known that I had influence beyond the effect of the money. Over the years in Washington, at dinners in a hundred mansions, I sat next to some of the most beautiful women in the world. At almost every dinner party, I would find myself sitting next to some famous beauty, infamous beauties sometimes.

After Eva, after loving her, all the rest to me were caricatures. I could not forget her; didn't want to. My memories of her sustained me and they were enough.

Eventually, I found they were sitting me next to gay men. They were desperate to solve the riddle. They were just further from the truth of me, then. Later I was described as "self sufficient", then "self contained."

They didn't know that I was in love with a woman who had been killed twenty, then forty years before. They would have thought it was just a memory I was loving. It was that, a memory, the memories. That was only a part of it. She was as real to me as life itself was real. Since the night when she had brought to me her innocence, she was real again. I would go to bed, in the later years as an old man, and wake up in my dreams as a young man, loving Eva. Being with her even. In my mind in the darkness of the night. When she wanted me to dream.

I was spending the summers and the fall mostly in Block Island and at Buffington. I had a special suite at the new Hotel Eva, on the south end of the hotel looking east out towards South Channel. When I was there I'd spend most of my days on the new *Eva*, the boat I'd had built at Point Judith. Would go out mostly by myself, but sometimes Mrs. Stinsin, even Mrs. Rogers would go with me. Sometimes, rarely though, we'd see a swordfish basking on the top. When we did, we'd just hang around it as long as it stayed on the surface. Mostly though, we'd just ride. Talk about Eva, the Captain, talk about how it had been. Sometimes when I was alone I'd just cut the engines off, drift, and think. Sometimes I'd fall asleep, dream of what might have been.

Dream sometimes of what was. Dream of life as it was, not as I wished it were. There were times when I'd be on the lawn at the hotel, see fog rolling in offshore, take the *Eva* out, put her in the fog bank and just sit there waiting for the foghorns, with the feelings, the thoughts of yesteryears. Waiting for steamers to come swooshing by.

I repeated my ritual dinners with champagne at our place on the beach. Usually have the hotel set it up. Sometimes the Hotel Manissess from down the street a ways. Sometimes a local would come by, sometimes they'd speak, sometimes just pass by with a wave. They knew of my love for her, of the unsolved murder, of the girl that had swam to her island to die. They knew of the man that never stopped loving her. It was an island special story, the rich man growing old with his memories of a great love, the love of one of them. The lady of the island she became in the stories they began to tell of us. It was okay. Had she lived they would have still told stories of her, different stories perhaps. She would have been still, though, even in life, the lady of the island. I returned to the island for my memories because my memories were my life. Most of what I did now was a search for my memories of that other time. Before they killed her.

I would always go to Buffington, to Ocean City, when I received word that the marlin were there in numbers, or the tuna even. I'd get the call, head for the Aero-Commander, head south over Long Island, then over the open ocean on a straight shot, be landing at the Ocean City Airport in under three hours. Turn the plane over to "Crash," he'd see to her servicing, have her ready whenever I needed her. Everything would be ready at Buffington, ready with the *Eva Still,* and we'd be offshore at dawn letting the baits out as the sun left the horizon. Spend the day dancing with the gentlemen of the long noses. Sometimes when it was the fat guys, the tuna, we were after, we'd anchor using a buoy ball, chum until we had the tuna up behind the boat. Boat what we wanted, let the rest go. If we hooked up with a big one we'd release the boat from the buoy and chase the tuna down, come back to the buoy when we had the fish or we'd lost it.

When the fishing was hot, or in the fall when the hunting was, I'd have guests from all over at Buffington. Rich people, not rich people, politicians, public figures, sports people, fishermen from the past, just people I thought I'd enjoy being with, people who could carry on intelligent conversations. Lots of times Ocean City locals. They were the best really. Talked common sense, something I didn't get much of any more in Washington.

Several times I flew Mrs. Stinsin and Mrs. Rogers down from Block Island in the summer. Took them marlin fishing, showed them where I'd grown up.

But Block Island was different. It was my personal place.

In January of 1983 I received a call from Mrs. Rogers. It was seven o'clock in the morning.

"Hank," she said, as I heard her sobbing, "she's dead. Rebecca's dead. I just got up, went to her room and she won't wake up. She's not breathing."

I sat there for a moment. I knew it was coming. Mrs. Stinsin was old, the age for dying, the dying you do when you've spent your time. But it was still a surprise. Death usually is.

"Mrs. Rogers," I asked, "have you called anybody?"

"I called you."

"Mrs. Rogers, I want you to go in the kitchen and start a pot of coffee going. Sit down and try to relax. People will be there shortly. I'll take care of everything. In a few minutes the Chief will be there with you, the preacher, too. I'll call them. They'll start the process of what needs doing. I'll be there by noon."

"Okay." she said.

I called the doctor, the chief and the preacher, had them go to Mrs. Rogers. I called out to the general aviation terminal at Washington National had them get the plane ready. Couldn't get up with the pilot. Made no difference. Most of the time now I was doing the flying anyway. Often by myself.

I landed at the Block Island airport at eleven-thirty in a snow storm, slipped and slided to the end of the runway, barely got her stopped. Taxied to the small terminal where I kept a truck, took the truck, was at the cottage in ten minutes.

We buried her four days later next to the Captain. The Stinsins, all of them, had left me.

A couple of days later the local lawyer told me that I had inherited the cottage. I met then with Mrs. Rogers, told her that she could live in the cottage for the rest of her life, treat it as her own. I'd pay for all the upkeep, utilities and send her whatever amount of money she needed.

She told me that she wasn't going to stay on the island. Thanked me for the offer, but she wanted to go to her home, where she'd been born. She still had relatives there. I called the law firm, had them make the legal arrangements necessary for her to be taken care of as long as she lived.

I met with the Chief. Told him of my plan for the cottage, wanted it moved to the southeast edge of the old Ocean View property next to the *Hotel Eva*, wanted it fixed up, and shielded from view by shrubbery, trees and such. Would need a caretaker for it; someone to make sure it was ready every time I visited the island. I asked him if he had any suggestions. He referred me to a house-mover, and a contractor. Then told me that his grandson might be the right person to hire on as a caretaker.

I met with the grandson, told him what I would be wanting. Before I returned to Washington I had made all the arrangements with the Chief's help. His grandson Julian would be put on the payroll of the *Hotel Eva*. When he wasn't taking care of the cottage or me when I came, they would use him there. I left then, returned to Washington.

Chapter Fifty-Four
THE COTTAGE

The cottage was ready the next summer. I'd shipped mature trees and shrubs over from the mainland. A small barge load. Julian had hired a landscaper and between them they had managed to conceal the cottage from the hotel. It was situate at the edge of the bluff at the far southeast corner of the property, just above the place on the beach, our place on the beach. I had kept the cottage furnished as the Stinsins had left it. It faced out to sea now, that was different. Now Eva's bedroom almost touched the rising sun when it left the horizon.

That's when I went to it the first time. Went to the cottage after Mrs. Stinsin died. At dawn on my first day back on the island in the summer of 1984. I had flown in during the night. Julian had met me at the airport, taken me to the cottage. Took my bags in, put them in Eva's room. It was the first door on the right, upstairs. The best room, really. Julian left me there in her room, left the old pickup in the driveway behind the cottage, locked the gate as he left.

I went to the bed, sat where I had sat thirty-four years ago when I was the first man to ever sit on her bed. Realized as I sat there that I had been the only man to ever sit there. I remembered again the kiss that had stunned me. I could hear her laughter again, just as it had been that other time. I began to wonder, too, wondering if I was crazy. I knew I imagined, that I dreamed, day dreamed and night dreamed, in ways others didn't. I had known it for years; lived with it for years; under the circumstances wouldn't have wanted it any other way. I knew I was actually living in ways noone else did. I had parallel lives. The real one with all its money, privilege, power over others, the dream one with all its power over me. And I lived them at the same time. In the instances of the same time.

I'd be riding in a limousine going to a business meeting, going over in my mind the details of what was coming up and at the same time I'd be on the old *Eva* with her. I'd be going over figures, talking to her all at the same time. I'd be standing at a party talking to people, while I was talking, I'd sense her standing beside me. It was like my mind was divided in halves, both operating at the same time, one in this world, one in her world.

I felt that way sitting there on her bed. My mind was in the present, my body as well, but I knew her spirit was there, sensed it there, knew she was smiling. Knew she was glad that I was there in her room again.

I decided to take a short nap, something I had started doing years before. I took my suit off. Opened the closet door. There hanging by itself was a wedding dress. I had never seen it. It had been there all the years.

I had a thought then I didn't want to have. The thought of her dying just down the beach a ways from where I was in the present, her swim and her dying in the dawn of that other day just as the sun was rising then, as it was rising in the present time. Her struggle and her dying as the Captain and I were rushing to find her, to save her.

I felt again the kiss upon my cheek. I reached up and there was a tear again. A tear upon my cheek. I brought it to my mouth and breathed it in, took inside of me the scent of it.

I woke up at five in the afternoon. Lying on Eva's bed with my arms around a wedding dress, my clothes on the floor. At peace with myself. Rested, truly relaxed, for the first time in over thirty years.

I had been awakened by Julian coming in the cottage. I got up, hung the dress back up, got dressed, went downstairs and met him in the parlor.

"Mr. Gaskins," he said, "I am setting up dinner on the beach for seven-thirty. That should cover the sun going behind the bluff at the time you are finished. We've stocked your favorite year of Mums' champagne, enough for the summer. I'll make sure the waiter always has some chilled, unless you tell him otherwise. The table will be set for two as you asked. Tonight the chef is preparing chateau briand. Just tell the waiter what you want for tomorrow. We've made arrangements for your breakfast at the hotel every morning at seven, the southeast corner of the dinning room overlooking the sea. Lunch will be brought to you here. Just tell them what you want for lunch when you come for breakfast.

"Maids from the hotel will come over every day at one, make up the rooms, pick up your clothes, make sure they get washed and ironed. Return them the next day. We've installed phones throughout the cottage. You have two lines. One goes directly outside, the other through the hotel switchboard. Hotel security will also cover the cottage, they've put extra security on for when you're here; the Chief supervised setting it up. You have any trouble just ring the switchboard. You don't have to worry about anything. Someone will be looking after the cottage around the clock when you're in residence. The gun you wanted is in the box on the floor in the bedroom closet. I've also put a schedule of hotel events on the counter in the kitchen."

"Thank you Julian," I said. "It looks like everything so far is perfect. I appreciate you looking after me. How's your family, your grandfather, how's the old Chief doing?"

"They're all doing fine, sir. The Chief is getting a little long in the tooth. He's getting some years on him. I don't thing he'll be able to keep the pace up for much longer."

"He's a tough old bird, son. I expect he'll bury me before it's over. Thanks again for putting all this together. You've done fine."

He smiled, said, "I'll leave you now sir. You need anything you just call."

I turned the water on for a bath. Got in the tub, stayed in it until I was wrinkled like a prune, pink like a peach. Later I dressed in one of the tuxedos in the closet, walked down the pathway to the beach, our place, where a waiter was waiting at a table set for two. I had dinner there, ate the steak, drank the wine. I'd had the table set for two because of her. If she came, if she ever came. If she could see me from where she was I wanted her to know that I thought of her, always, especially when I was on her island, the island of the little god.

I wondered if she was its little god; she was my goddess, my deity, a personification of the force of my life, what gave me life still, thirty some years after she had left the rest of it, had left this world. I lived mostly in my thoughts of her, my dreams of her.

Just as the shadows cast by the bluff behind me began to encroach on our spot, I motioned to the waiter and he took the champagne from its bucket, opened it and filled the glasses. He left. Julian had trained him well. I toasted the empty seat across from me, whispering to her, "I love you," and drank. Then I drank her's. Sat there, drinking champagne until the shadow moved out into the sea, began to cast darkness on the beach. I rose, walked back up the bluff to the cottage. Sat on the porch. I sat there and thought of my life, thought of the way it had been changed by coming to this special place, this special island, its special people, truly an island of some god, little or otherwise. It had been a magical place, tragic yes, sorrowing at times, but a magical place. It had happened here. Magic. Was still happening here. To me it was.

I went up later to her room, laid down, made sure I could see the ocean to the east out there in the semi-darkness.

The sea is never totally dark. It has its own light, even on the darkest night. Almost as if its surface is the mirror of the sky, of the stars, of the greyness of the fog even. And before the last light of night is totally gone, the new light of morning begins to emerge from the east.

Then, I thought again of her being dropped over the side of a boat, out there perhaps in sight of where I was sitting, thought of her sinking, waking up in the darkness of the deep, then fighting her way to the surface, trying to swim, making it only to die on her island. I could feel the coolness of the water, the fear she must have felt when she saw the flash of Southeast Light in the distance, knew she was far out. Imagined her knowing that she was dying as she felt life leaving even as she was swimming to shore.

Then I got sick. Threw up for hours, mostly dry heaving. It was the first I'd been physically sick since that time. When I could leave the bathroom I went down to the kitchen, went into the cabinets. Eventually, in the back of one of the floor cabinets, behind the big pots, the pot I'd made 'slick' dumplings in on our Thanksgiving, I found Mrs. Stinsin's toddy bottle, an old bottle of rum, a third gone, coated with years of dust. It probably hadn't been used since before the Captain died.

I put it on the kitchen table, drank from the bottle, drank myself drunk. Staggered to bed. I woke up with the sun in my eyes, the place beside me on the bed depressed as if it had been slept on, it was warm, too, the sheets on that side of the bed. And I smelled lilacs. I laid in bed for an hour, waiting, but she didn't come. I took it as a message. It was the last time I was drunk.

That first summer of eighty-four in the cottage was the most peaceful time of the part of my life that started when she died. It was as if I was with her, though I wasn't. I spent it hiking throughout the island, walking where her feet had been, in her footsteps. I explored the edges of all the ponds and there were lots of ponds, explored the beaches that circled the island. Walked every foot of them. Went one night to Clayhead Bluff, drove up in the pickup. Julian had put some firewood in the back. I carried it to the place where we'd had our campfire on our Christmas Eve. Made a fire, laid back on the beach, could almost hear the strains of "Danny Boy," heard again the poem that she had recited on that evening.

> "My true-love hath my heart, and I have his,
> By just exchange one for another given:
> I hold his dear, and mine he cannot miss,
> There never was a better bargain driven:
> > My true-love hath my heart, and I have his
>
> "His heart in me keeps him and me in one,
> My heart in him his thoughts and senses guides:
> He loves my heart, for once it was his own,
> I cherish his because in me it bides:
> > My true love hath my heart, and I have his."

I knew now, if I hadn't fully realized it then, how true it was. Her heart in me had guided my life since that time, she had cherished me, still cherished me, came to me when I truly needed her. We had each other's hearts. I wondered if that's why she comes, can come, why I wait? Our hearts are in the other. We are really the one person, even death can't sever us.

I fell asleep that night, there on the beach in the warm July breezes. Woke up just as the last embers of the fire began to pop, sending sparks into the darkness. Saw someone on the edge of a dune looking my way. Startled me for a moment. I noticed then, as he disappeared behind the dune that it was Julian. He was looking after me. They were looking after me. Julian, perhaps the Chief, the security staff at the *Hotel Eva*. Realized then that the feelings I'd had of being followed as I ambled about the island had been Julian and his friends making sure I was safe.

Later, in the summers after, Julian would tell me that I'd become an icon. My story, Eva's story had become a tale of the island. An old man having dinner, going on beach parties, hiking, with a ghost created from a great love. A love changed by tragedy, but never terminated by it. I was a man, they said, not beset by a spirit, but blessed by one.

One night during that first summer in the cottage, I heard a band playing love songs, the music was coming from the hotel. I checked the schedule that Julian had left. There was a dance at the Hotel Eva, billed as a dance from the fifties. I couldn't resist. Went to the closet, got out a tux, the trimmings, dressed.

I left the cottage property, walked to the hotel. They wouldn't take my admission fee, just smiled, said "Mr. Gaskins, it's all yours." I walked on in the ballroom. It was exactly as it had been that other time. The bandstand in the same place, the floor the same, even the decorations looked the same. I took a table for two in the corner, asked for champagne, stayed there for hours, occasionally taking a sip, mostly just watching the dancers, imagining her. Thinking of the time we danced. Then I became conscious that I was crying, some of the people were looking at me. One of the ladies with the hotel started to me, but I put up my hand to her, mouthed "I'm okay. Thanks.," and she drew back.

I got the outward manifestations of my grief under control, stayed there, grieving inside, but at the same time grateful that she had made me dance in that special time of ours, grateful that I had a memory so strong that it made me cry. Thought, too, of those that had no such memories. How empty their lives must be. I had lost her, true, but I'd had her, and she me. Our searches had been over. We had found the one person in the world for each of us. That was no small thing. It was a large thing, too large, really, for luck. Thought why had it been that I had gone north in the time of my trouble. I'd never gone north before. It was something, I thought, the thing, the being in the place we know not, that knows us, arranges it, but only when it can be great. Something had brought me Eva, brought me my greatest happiness and my terrible sorrow.

I sat there listening to the music, watching the dancers, thinking, until I noticed that the dancers were gone, the music stopped, the dance over. I got up then, the last one to leave, walked by the desk at the foyer, two ladies were standing there saying goodnight to the guests. I walked over, took the young lady's hand that had started towards me when I was crying, said, "Thanks for looking after me. It was lovely. Brought back so many memories, but I guess you could tell that."

"Yes, Mr. Gaskins," she said, "we know of her. The two of you. Everyone knows. We were crying, also, a little. Both of us. Your story has become everyone's memory. She was a very lucky lady to have had you, even for a little while."

"I suppose that's right," I responded, "we were both lucky. Thank you for reminding me again that both of us were lucky. Goodnight."

"Goodnight" they both replied, almost in unison.

I left, returned to the cottage, went to her bed and wept.

Chapter Fifty-Five
SUMMERTIMES

The times of summer that I spent on Block Island, passed one after the other. The patterns never changed. My love story became the lore of the island, articles were written about it. The locals respected my privacy as much as they could. I was a private man, but when you dine on the beach with someone who isn't there to other people, waited on by white coated waiters, walk the island incessantly, go boating in a boat named for a murdered woman you had loved, cry at dances, your life can never be completely private. And it didn't bother me. Noone ever bothered me. People would wave sometimes when I was dining on the beach or walking here and there, I'd wave back. They'd speak at the dances, smile, I'd smile back when I noticed. But I was never bothered. Something about the island. Everyone, even the guests minded their own business, other than common courtesies, never interfered.

The second year of the cottage, the girl at the dance, the one that had started to help me, had cried with me, told me she was getting married at Christmas, to a lobsterman, wanted me to come to the wedding if I could.

I had my pilot fly me to Block Island for the Christmas holidays and went to her wedding in the church where Eva and I would have wed had they not killed her. Saw what it would have been like. It was a beautiful wedding. As the bride and groom came back up the aisle she noticed that my eyes were watering. She paused, her arm in her husband's, reached up with her other hand and wiped the tears from my cheek. Said,

"Thanks for coming. For everything."

"Thanks for inviting me."

She stood on her toes, kissed me on the cheek and continued on up the aisle.

I went to their reception in the church hall, thinking of never having seen the Captain and Mrs. Stinsin at a reception, a wedding reception. Wondered if they were seeing this one from where they were.

327

I had contacted her husband, privately, as soon as she had told me they were engaged. He was a local boy, man really, related to one of the couples that had been on the sleigh ride with Eva and I on that other Christmas. I asked him to let me ride along when he fished his pots, he agreed. While we were at sea, working the pots; he operating the hauler, me emptying the pots, re-baiting, and culling, I told him of his wife's treatment of me, what it had meant to me. Told him what it meant to me the way everyone on this wonderful island was treating me. Told him that I'd like to give him and his bride a honeymoon. He said then,

"Mr. Gaskins, I got it covered. We're goin' up to Boston for Christmas week. I can handle that. Appreciate your offer though."

"Son," I said, "I was thinking Paris, London, Tahiti, wherever in the world you want to take her. It'll stay just between you and me. No-one else would know. I owe so much to the people of this island, and it means so much to me to be able to give something back. Think about it if you have to, but I hope you'll consider it. Hope you'll do it for me. I need to do it. "

"Mr. Gaskins, I'll have to clear it with her, ain't starting out without tellin' her."

"Thought you would."

They both came to the cottage three days later. Told me they'd accept my offer, were grateful for it. The money they'd been saving could be used for more lobster pots. I asked them where they'd like to go. They suggested a weekend in Paris, I changed their minds to a month.

I then went to the preacher, set it up with him to let me know when any of the island natives were getting married. Told him I was going in the honeymoon business. For years after, I sponsored hundreds of honeymoons, set up a special company in Providence, a travel company, to accommodate my honeymoon venture. Before I knew it, that company had so much outside business it became profitable.

Chapter Fifty-Six
BIDING TIME

For the next twenty years I waited, mostly. In the mid-nineties, I told Tim to start taking me out of some of the tech stocks, diversify my holdings. I'd become concerned about all the companies whose stocks were running up when there was no profit in them. Thought the market was becoming a dangerous playground. Set up a real estate division. Began to buy up property, all kinds of property. In the process of diversifying, I added several more billions to my wealth.

Most of my time in the summers was spent on Block Island, the rest at Buffington. By now I had homes in Aspen and Palm Beach. I'd visit them in the winter. Have Jimbo take the *Eva Still* down to Palm Beach, fly the plane down, it was getting older now but I was comfortable with it. Kept it maintained, refurbished, engines replaced and the like.

We'd work on the sailfish out of Palm Beach, do the tournaments. Go over to the islands some. I'd bought a cottage at Cat Cay, we'd spend some time there, fishing the Cat Cay tuna tournament, the Bimini marlin tournament. But, no matter where I was I thought of her. How it would be if she was with me.

I was dreaming, most of the time. Waiting to die, I guess. Went on living, using my wealth to do anything except what I really wanted to do. To be with her, really with her, not just in dreams, if they were only dreams.

One time she came, I think she actually came, maybe, anyway, walked out of nowhere into a dream, as I sat in my study at Buffington looking out over the bay and Assateague beyond, out to the ocean where the moon was rising, with the barrel of a pistol in my mouth. She took the gun from me. Left as the sun was rising, I could see her leave but I couldn't see her leave. She just faded away. After she was gone, if she'd been there, just after whatever she was faded, she spoke back over her shoulder, but I couldn't see her shoulder or her, but I knew she was looking back, speaking to me, just a word.

"No."

The second time she came, almost actually came at least in my mind, was in the middle of the night in the Boston hospital. In the summer of my heart attack. It was 1998. I was sixty-nine years old. Was lying in the bed as happy as I had been since she had died. My time had come; I'd waited for forty years or more to find her where she was, to go to her; to spend all time with her. I had been lying there for two days, dying, smiling. I had the nurses talking about the happy dying man, not something they were accustomed to. But I was happy, even when it hurt bad I was happy. The pain would come. I'd embrace it. Loved it. Another step closer.

Then one night, when the lights in my suite were turned down and I was lying there looking at the ceiling, I thought I felt a warmth enter the room and she was standing there, naked, beside the bed pulling back the sheet. In my mind. She left when the rising sun's rays began to enter the room. Before she did, she sat for a moment on the side of the bed, turned to me, said simply,

"Not now. Soon."

And whatever she was left.

I was released at the end of the week, went to the island to recuperate. Was back in full harness in a month. It was at the end of the next month, August, when I got a call from Washington. I was staying at Buffington for the marlin fishing. It was the President's Chief of Staff.

BOOK FOUR

Chapter Fifty-Seven

Promises Remembered

THE SENATOR

Over the years since the Viet Nam era Presidents had come and gone. Some had used my services when they needed someone with money to handle a discreet matter. To raise a ship; to sink a ship. To find people to do things people don't do. To help when things are ticklish. Sometimes, rarely though, I'd be called on just to lobby for legislation, when it was felt I might have some special influence, or my money might. Some presidents hadn't called on me at all. That was okay with me. Either way. So long as what I was asked to do was, in my own mind, a benefit for my country, I'd do it. When I'd be asked to do what wasn't good for my country, it didn't get done by me.

But my money and the relationships I had with some of the presidents, with members of Congress kept me in play. I didn't necessary want it; it was just the way it was. Politicians are sucked to money like Japanese Beatles to a trap. The nature of the beast.

I was ushered into the President's inner office. After he had begun to sip Wild Turkey, he began

"Hank," he said, familiarly. I'd never met the man before. Knew his Chief of Staff, not him. "we need your help to do a little lobbying for us."

"Mr. President," I interrupted, "I don't usually get involved in that sort of stuff. It's not up my alley. I've done it a time or two, but not much. I'm a little too plain spoken to be effective as a lobbyist. You don't want me." All the while I'm cursing under my breath. I didn't appreciate being brought up to Washington for something relatively unimportant, non-critical, like lobbying a bill in Congress. Hell, I paid lots of money to people to do it for me. Didn't like doing it myself.

"I thought that it might be a little different this time." He said.

"What do you mean Mr. President?"

"It's an issue I think you might be interested in. Involves fishing issues. Stuff you used to do. At least that's what I've been told."

"Mr. President, what exactly are we talking about," I responded. Interested now. "I don't know whether you've heard about our big environmental issue this year," he continued, "we're directing our attention at the oceans. The coastal seas. We've got all kinds of measures in the legislation to begin the process of reinvigorating the near oceans. Pollution measures, discharge issues, the works. An important part of it involves the fishery. That's where we're having the most trouble."

"What do you mean, sir," I asked, "specifically?"

"A big part of our program is to ban all commercial fishing for open ocean sport fish, giant tuna, the billfishes, all of them, but especially the swordfish. They're almost wiped out. We're going to ban all long-lining within 200 miles of the coast; become assertive in using navy ships to run over long line gear throughout that zone along both coasts, run over the float balls, break them, cut off the buoy flags, board the vessels whatever it takes. The legislation we're proposing authorizes severe limitations on commercially taking these fish, several other sports species as well."

"Sir, offhand, I think it's a good idea. I don't know what I can do. I'll do what I can, but -"

He interrupted me then. "Hank, every one of them over there on Capital Hill has their eye on the prize. Money, campaign money. Money talks. You've got it. Your various business entities are major contributors to members of both parties."

"Mr. President," I replied, "we just grease them. Most of the contribution decisions are made by the heads of the various companies. Most of the time I don't even know who we're giving too. Contributions are just a side show I don't pay much attention to."

"That may be so, but they don't know it. Every single one of them over on the hill thinks you know where every political dollar goes. I'm not asking for an extended effort. Just two or three key senators. Where the log jam is. The ones that are holding it up. If you could take a couple of days, work on them, I might be able to get the job done. And it's a job that needs doing."

I agreed to help. Hell he was the President. I agreed with the purpose of the legislation. He actually wanted me to work on five or six senators. The next morning I called around to three or four of my key people, found out that we had been contributing to every senator on the President's list. He had known it, I'm sure.

I then set up a series of dinners at my Washington townhouse with the senators, except one who couldn't work it in to his schedule, but did agree to meet with me in his Capital Hill offices. The dinners went according to plan and purpose. I enlisted their support; told the President. Told him, that I was meeting with the remaining Senator, the former congressmen who had been screaming conspiracy back in the days of the assassination, now the senior senator from his state. My appointment with him was at eleven on a Tuesday morning. I was on time, was ushered in promptly. We spent a half-hour just talking; found out we both were boat people, he had sail boats, always had them. I told him I was into power-boating, sportfishing really. Had an old Bertram, fully equipped. Used it out of Ocean City, mostly. Palm Beach some, marlin fishing, tuna. Before long it was arranged that he and his two aides would go on a tuna chunking trip with me on the *Eva Still* the weekend after the upcoming one. The second weekend in September. I'd fly them down on that Friday afternoon from National. They'd be weekend guests at Buffington.

We then got down to the legislation. His state harbored a large number of long-liners, though most of them were gradually going out of business due to depleted stocks, especially the depletion of the swordfish. It was going to be hard for him to support the bill; his State's commercial fishing industry supported him, had contributed to his last campaign.

"Senator," I asked, I was getting tired of the subject "how much did they contribute last cycle?"

"They were up around fifteen thousand dollars. I know it's not much money in your league, but that's a lot of money for those guys." He answered.

"Senator, my various companies will contribute fifty thousand dollars to your next campaign. It will be in bits and pieces over the next two years. But it will get there."

He looked at me, never said another word on the subject, but nodded his head affirmatively, nodded almost imperceptibly, but I saw it; he knew I saw it. We then began to talk of other things, Washington things, the upcoming fishing weekend. We finished, I excused myself, left his inner office and went into his reception room. His receptionist was momentarily out of the office so I waited for her to return so that I could give her the information, the details about the fishing trip. While I waited I walked around the office looking at the Senator's trophy wall, his wall of pictures, plaques and certificates showing his accomplishments.

One caught my attention. It was the picture of the senator, not as he was now, but of him as a young man. Maybe twenty-five, thirty years old. He was sitting in the cabin of a boat. The cabin appeared to be the cabin of a fairly large sail-boat of some kind. But that wasn't what attracted my attention at first. It was that on the wall of the cabin behind him were crossed oars, the type that are used in rowing, sculling races. The crossed oars represented some kind of an award. I stood closer, tried to make out what kind of award it was.

I noticed something about him in the picture. His shirt was opened down the front. He was wearing a golden necklace. There was something hanging from it. I got closer, concentrated, squinted. I was stunned! It wasn't the first time I had seen the necklace. The Chief had handed it to me forty-five years before. I had a photograph of it in the cottage on Block Island. A Polaroid. It was the same necklace the Chief had taken from Eva's hand on the beach near Southeast Light the morning she died. There was the same cross, with a crucified Christ on it, and the crossed oars, almost copies of the oars on the large plaque on the cabin wall.

The receptionist returned. I stared at the photograph for another minute, burning the imagine into my mind. Fighting the white heat rising up my neck. Getting control. I turned, walked calmly over to the receptionist's desk, gave her the information and left.

Chapter Fifty-Eight
THE END GAME

I went to my office. Made two calls. Within the hour I was meeting with two men who operated a discrete business. I'd used them before when things needed doing, discretely. They found out things; arranged things. Things no one but they and their client of the moment ever knew about. One of them had retired from wet operations at the CIA a decade before, had used his international contacts to create perhaps the most effective private espionage, and other 'things', firm in the world. The other had joined the company in the second year, concentrated on domestic investigations, the high line type. The stuff people like me needed to know and needed done for whatever reason. He had been a police detective in New York City in the early seventies, investigating the mob, successfully. Within the hour they left, promised a report for me by the beginning of the next week.

The following Monday they presented me with an extensive written report. Gave me a verbal summary. I wrote them a check for the forty thousand dollars that had been agreed upon. When they left the older one paused as he was about to open the door to leave, said

"Mr. Gaskins. He's the one, his chief of staff was on the boat, and there's another aide in his office that was on the boat. The one-eyed one. When they got back from the sailing trip he had a severe eye injury and a doctor that was with them arranged to have his eye removed. He has a glass eye, wears the eye patch because he thinks it makes him tough. The three in the Senator's office have stayed together ever since it happened. The doctor's over at State General, head of the surgery department. Once they got back to Annapolis, right after he arranged the operation for the other one, it looks like he split from the rest of them."

I called him back in, said, "I want the doctor to be questioned on this, I want to know what he says. Record it if you can. Then I want him disappeared. I'll take care of the rest of them my way." He set the price. I wrote the check. Money buys anything. Enough money.

I read the report. The Senator's boat, the *Party Time*, had been entered in the Annapolis to Newport race, hadn't reported in at the finish. That's why she'd never come up in the Chief's investigation. My people had discovered that she'd almost been dismasted and had been taken directly to a repair yard for repairs. They'd also discovered an old timer, sort of a drunk, but still somewhat lucid who loved to talk about the old days.

He had known the senator, known who he was anyway, knew the family. Course he wasn't a senator back then. Just a wild mean kid, a blowhard with money. The old timer hadn't been a drunk back then, but a drinker, a fisherman who hung out in bars some when he was ashore. He'd been in the bar in Newport when the Senator and his buddies had been thrown out.

My people had checked the old records at the repair yard in Newport. The *Party Time* had left the yard about noon on the day before Eva was found on the beach by Leatherby. It had been sailed to Block Island. The harbor master's office had no records of her checking in. They hadn't kept records from that far back. However, the investigators had spent two days on the island, checking the bars. Had talked to the owner of one of them. The bar owner had been a bouncer at a bar called Maggie's the night Eva disappeared. He remembered about her, the whole island knew of her murder.

When he was asked about the summer of Eva's murder, he said,

"It could have been about that time that summer when a bunch came in Maggie's. Caused a disturbance. I can't remember exactly when it was, but I had to put two of 'em down, then threw 'em out. Don't 'member for sure of the specific day, but it was 'bout that time of summer. But you know I put a lot of drunks out in those days. It's been a long time. Back then I went south every September after the high season was over. I left pretty soon after that. Didn't think much more on it."

The investigators had slipped into the Senator's office dressed as telephone repairmen checking on phone lines. While one of them kept the secretaries busy the other had taken a picture of the photograph on the wall. They had taken it to an expert on sail boats; he had identified the make and model of the boat. When they checked the records in Annapolis they found that the *Party Time* was the same make and model of sail boat that had been repaired in the Newport boat yard back in the summer of 1953.

They had checked the Annapolis newspaper records for the time of the race that summer and came across an interesting item. The *Party Time* had struck a submerged object as she approached the Virginia capes on her return trip from Newport, had sunk. Her crew, however, had been pulled from a life raft within a half-hour by a passing trawler. One of the *Party Time's* crew had received an eye injury in the sinking.

There was a lot of other information about the four of them, the Senator, his aides, the surgeon. I read the whole report.

Three mornings later I read where the Chief of Surgery at State General had been killed in an automobile accident. His Mercedes had been found wrapped around a tree on Rock Creek Parkway. He'd been working late, stopped by a bar for a few drinks. Met a couple of guys, they left together. His car had been found down a slope in the park by a hiker around ten the next morning.

That afternoon one of my people delivered a tape to me. It was the doctor. He confessed to his participation in what had happened, implicated the others. The tape was left with me. I made copies of it.

Then I began to plan. The thoughts, the ways, virtually flew into my mind. I didn't even have to think about it.

Chapter Fifty-Nine

THE FISHING TRIP

I flew down to Ocean City on the Thursday morning before the fishing trip, flew alone. I had given the pilot the week off as soon as the investigators had left my office. When I got to Buffington I called Jimbo, told him I'd be taking the *Eva Still* out by myself on the weekend, he'd have an opportunity to spend it with his family.

Early that afternoon I went to a chicken processing plant, obtained four plastic buckets of chicken blood and offal. Told them I wanted it for chumming. That was the truth. Went down to the docks, to the fishing company packing houses. Bought two dozen bluefish, and three boxes, flats they called them, of butter fish. Bought three buckets of prepared chum. Bought ice. Returned to Buffington, went aboard the *Eva Still*, put the buckets and the fish in the fish box, iced them down. Put the harness I'd rigged on a bunk in the forward cabin.

I went below to the compartment in the cabin where I kept a gun. Every sports fisherman I had ever been on had a gun aboard. Never knew when you'd have to shoot something. Mine was a military issue .45 cal. Colt. Checked the gun, it was clean and operable. Checked the magazine, saw that the gun was loaded. Made sure I had spare fully loaded magazines. Wrapped it back in the oil rag. Put the handcuffs that the investigators had gotten for me with the gun.

I stopped up at the house, told the staff to prepare for three guests, staying with us Friday and Saturday nights. I was back in Washington by dark. I spent the evening leaving instructions.

The next afternoon the Senator showed up with his chief of staff and one-eyed aide, only fifteen minutes late. Soon we were airborne, clearing the various restricted air spaces around Washington, heading east. Before long we were over the Chesapeake Bay heading on a direct line for Ocean City. After about an hour we flew over the north end of Ocean City, turned south and I began the descent as we proceeded parallel to the beach. I could feel the plane shift as the three of them moved to the starboard side of the plane to look at the island as we got lower, nearing the airport. I took her on past the inlet, then banked to starboard, flew down the north side of the airport so they could see Buffington, then circled to port around the airport, back over Assateague Island and out to sea a little, banked to port again, lined her up on my approach path, passed back over Assateague, scaring ponies I was so low, flew just a few feet up crossing the bay and put the plane on the very end of the runway. Taxied to "Crash's."

We were met by two members of my staff. Everybody got in the Suburban and we were driven the short distance to Buffington House. The other staff member would follow in the Jeep with the bags.

They entertained themselves, swam in the pool, drank, watched a baseball game on television, played pool. Later we had dinner. Went to bed around ten. Five-thirty comes early in the morning.

I called Julian from my bedroom. Told him what I wanted for Sunday morning. Told him I'd be getting on the island around one or two in the A.M. Would need to be picked up at the airport.

Chapter Sixty

LILAC FRAGRANCES

We cleared the inlet the next morning just as the sun was full up, out of the sea. Blinding almost, as I conned the *Eva Still* out and put her near the Jackspot line, the course to the shoal. I intended to take her north of the shoal and east a little, in deeper water, still shallow enough to set up a reasonable chum line. It would take a while to get there. I'd changed the engines three times over the years, but never stepped up the power. I liked to keep her the way she was. A good decent boat. I could have had the best boats. But, didn't need them. Liked the older boats. My Bertram was comfortable for me. She was the way it was when I was a relatively young man. We'd grown old together. She'd been kept up though. I'd taken care of her, she'd taken care of me. The way it is with good boats if you treat them right.

We were where I wanted to be by nine-thirty. Took me another half hour to get the anchor set so the slick would go out to the southeast, offshore a little and to get the buoy rig hooked up right with a spring line, a bridle, on the offshore side to keep the stern to the east. Went back in the cockpit. The Senator and his aides were eating the breakfast the Buffington staff had prepared. I'd told the staff that we'd be in late and would be going to a restaurant in Ocean City for dinner. Said they could have Saturday night off, I wouldn't need them again until Sunday noon.

I waited until the Senator and his people had finished eating before I set up the chum slick. Tied one of the chum buckets overboard so it'd swish back and forth in the little sea that was running, letting chum wash out through the holes in the buckets. I set one of the blood and chicken offal buckets midway on the transom, punched a small hole in the side near the bottom, positioned the bucket so that a small but steady stream of blood would go overboard.

I went below, up forward where we kept the rods. Got three out, went to the bait rigging station, rigged up two of them with bluefish, the other with a butter fish. Left the leaders and rigged baits in the box on ice. Leaned the rods against the gunwale. After twenty minutes or so, I started cutting up butterfish, chunking pieces out into the chum line. In another half-hour I saw the first swirl back about seventy-five yards. Took the rods, got the Senator and his aides ready. The *Eva Still* was equipped with a single fighting chair in the middle of the cockpit with an extended foot rest, adjustable back rest. One angler would use it, the others would use belt rod holders and fish standing up. Of course the Senator got the fighting chair, the aides the belts. That's the way I planned it, wanted it, anyway. By then there were several tuna working the chum line. A small school.

We put the lines out and hooked up with two fish right away. School tuna, in the forty to fifty pound class. Took them about twenty minutes to land. I gaffed them, threw them in the fish box. We had five tuna in the boat by lunch time. It wasn't enough yet. I wanted to make sure I had enough aboard. We stopped putting out bait during lunch, kept the chum lines going, were into the second bucket of chum, the second bucket of blood.

By three o'clock we had eight more school tuna aboard. We were in violation of catch limits. But it didn't matter. Then we had a triple header on. They were all hooked up at the same time. The two aides were standing at the stern, one to the Senator's right, one to his left, their legs bracing them against the transom cushion. The Senator was in the middle, back from the transom a little, in the fighting chair. I had him strapped to it. He was huffing and puffing in the chair. Fighting a good sized tuna. I was standing behind the three of them. It was time.

While they were busy I went below, got the gun and returned to the cockpit. The two aides were looking aft, straining on the rods, their legs against the transom. I walked with the gun at my side, behind the one on my right, the one on the port side of the boat, the Senator's Chief of Staff, raised the gun, put it to the back of his head and blew his brains out. He toppled overboard, rod and all. I turned to my left. The aide with the eye patch and the Senator were frozen, eyes wide, eye wide in the aide's case, looking at me. The aide backed into the starboard gunwale, keeping his eye on me; his fish yanked the rod from his hands and it went overboard. I shot him then, in the forehead, saw the little hole in the front as the pink mess blew out the back of his head. The force of the bullet blew him back, blew him overboard.

345

"Jesus Christ!" The Senator yelled. I shot him then. Twice. Once in each knee. He dropped the rod. The tuna popped the line on it.

The Senator was grabbing his knees screaming. Pleasing me. I went below, got the tape recorders, the hand cuffs. When I came back into the cockpit he had managed to get out of the chair, was lying in a scupper with a gaff, trying to crawl to the cabin door. Planned to gaff me. I shot him again, in the back of one of his upper thighs. He dropped the gaff. I dragged him to the center of the cockpit.

"What the hell's going on. You crazy?" He yelled, as he lie there moaning. I pulled his arms behind his back and cuffed him and put tourniquets around both legs to slow up the bleeding. I didn't want him to die before my time. Before we had our talk. I rolled him over, leaned him up against the cabin bulkhead, on a little elevated deck where he could see out over the stern. He sat there moaning. Cussing some. I got the empty buckets, the wash bucket, the empty chum bucket and blood bucket. Reached into the fish box, pulled all the tuna out laid them on the deck. Probably four hundred fifty, five hundred pounds all told. They had bled profusely in the fish box, beating themselves to death against the sides. I reached in, partially unscrewed the plug so that some of the tuna blood would drip overboard through the scuppers.

I got more chum and blood buckets, set them up overboard, tying them off on the side cleats. Then I began to cut up the tuna, first slitting their throats and bleeding them into a wash bucket. The Senator sat still, his back against the cabin bulkhead, moaning, watching what I was doing. Soon I had a bucket of pure tuna blood, had to get the spare wash bucket. Filled it, too. By now the cockpit was a mess, blood everywhere, all over me too. The fish blood on the deck mixing with the Senator's blood that was dripping into the cockpit. All of it draining overboard through the scuppers. I then cut up the tuna until I had all the buckets full of large pieces of tuna and a pile of it about three feet high on the deck of the cockpit. It had all taken about an hour.

"What the hell's going on?" He screamed at me again, "you son of a bitch, cocksucker, what the hell you doing. You killed them. What the fuck's happening here."

"Want to talk, that's all." I answered.

"Talk!" He screamed. "You call this talk?"

"Just getting ready for it." I answered.

346

"You kill two people, shoot me, because you're getting ready to talk?"

"No, not because I'm getting ready to talk, you're getting ready."

"What the hell are you talking about?"

I didn't answer him. He'd ask again before everything was ready, or when it was. I had noticed during our brief conversation that there were more swirls back in the slick, different swirls, not tuna swirls. Creatures that stayed on top. Or just under the surface. Then I could see them, two of them at first. They finned out. The sharks had come.

I said to him, when I saw the fins, knew he could see them if he looked, "We're doing different fishing now, we're chumming for sharks, seeing how many we can get up behind the boat. You're a politician, good company for them."

He looked out at the slick, could see the fins as I began to throw over pieces of tuna, poured one of the buckets of blood into the fish box, loosened the plug more to speed up the blood flow out of the fish box and onto the deck and then out the scuppers into the slick.

In ten minutes the water was swarming with sharks. Blue sharks from offshore, brown sharks, a couple I recognized as lemons. One big old hammerhead, so far. I kept the blood flowing, turned the fighting chair around, sat in it, said to him,

"Most people don't know that a long time ago I was in love. Was engaged to be married. Most people think that's something I'm not capable of. Love and marriage. I imagine you were one of those people that thought that way about me, even when you were sitting behind your fancy desk, taking my money."

"This can't be about the money," he said, "nobody kills two people for that kind of money. You can have it."

"You're right it's not about the money. It's about love."

"This is about love? "He asked. "You're blowing brains all over the ocean and it's love? You're crazy."

"Well that's true, I guess," I said.

"You're crazy as a bed bug." He responded.

"Senator, I don't imagine you know much about how crazy a bed bug can be. You didn't exactly grow up with them in your fancy houses in Boston, out on the Cape. In your fancy school, Harvard wasn't it? You don't know about crazy, mean you know about, common is down your alley, but crazy, you don't really know much about crazy. Not yet. I think you'll meet crazy in a little while if you don't tell me what I want to hear. You're going to get one chance to talk to me and live. Otherwise I'm going to have you killed. You're a Senator, you know about dealing. This time it's not the welfare of others, the money of others, it's a deal for your life."

It was beginning to get dark. I got up, went in the cabin turned the flood light on, stepped back in the cockpit, adjusted the light to shine down the slick, walked to the stern, just two or three feet away, sloshed some more tuna blood in the fish box to make sure the stream of blood wasn't interrupted. Looked out, down the slick, there were eight or nine sharks finning behind us now. I could see another one coming up the slick, barely saw him in the dimming light, even with the floodlight. It was fighting the current a hundred fifty yards back, dorsal fin out, tail beating, throwing water up. Looked like a big old broad headed tiger, wasn't sure though. Threw several other pieces of tuna in the slick, a half dozen butter fish. Took the rest of the tray of butterfish with me when I got back in the chair, put them in my lap. Started talking to him again.

"Remember your old boat the *Party Time?*" I asked, sitting there in the fighting chair, throwing butterfish over my shoulder into the slick behind the boat, smiling.

"The *Party Time*, what the hell's she got to do with this?"

"Remember when she sank?"

"Hell yes, I remember. But what's that got to do with me?"

"Your aide hurt his eye, right?"

"Yeah, but where are you going?" he said, "You can't do this to me. I'm going to have your ass for this."

"I don't think so, if we don't make a deal, you don't tell me what I want to hear, you're a dead man. Remember," I continued, "the doctor that was on that trip that helped take care of your aide's eye injury?"

"I remember him, he was a friend of mine. But, he's dead, had a car accident just in the last week."

"I know he's dead. It wasn't an accident. I had him killed," I said as I threw several butterfish over my shoulder back in the slick.

There was a period of silence, he was thinking, trying to think through his pain.

"Who the hell are you?" He said.

"I'm just a man with ten billion dollars and a thirst for justice."

"What the fuck justice are you talking about? This isn't justice, going around shooting people."

"Well," I said then, "I guess that depends on each man's sense of justice. The man that's administering it has a right to his opinion. Right now that's me. If you don't tell me what I want to hear my justice will be the last justice you ever know."

"I don't even know you, for God's sake. I just knew you were out there in the world. Knew you were rich. I don't know you."

"You know me now. You're meeting me now. All you have to do is tell me about something."

"For God's sake, I'm bleeding here, bad, what do you want me to say."

"Just listen first; you'll get the idea." I said throwing more butterfish in the slick.

I put the audio tape of the doctor's confession in one of the recorders, turned it on so he could hear it. As it played, I went back to the stern threw more tuna chunks in the wake, checked that the blood was still flowing overboard. Started cutting up the bluefish, sending them back in the slick, creating a smorgasbord for the toothy ones. They were real excited now, staying on top, fighting for the chunks of fish, the scraps from the chum bucket, smelling the blood. By now the sea behind the boat was covered with a blood slick, for a quarter mile back.

I heard the tape stop. He'd listened to the doctor's confession. He knew now why he was here, but not why I had him where he was, the predicament I had him in. By now it was dark. He started talking as soon as I turned to him.

"I'll give you money, keep quiet about all this, do anything you want."

"What would I do with your money? I give more to beggars on the street."

"What do you want me to say?"

"You heard the doctor's confession. Is it true?"

"He's lying, doesn't know what he's talking about."

"Didn't."

"Fuck you."

349

"Senator, fucking isn't going to cause you any more problems."

"He was just trying to blame somebody else. Somebody bigger than him. God-dammit, what the hell do doctors know?"

"Not much, maybe. That's why you're here."

"He was only trying to stay alive himself. It's all bullshit. This whole goddamn thing is bullshit, you're bullshit. I'm not telling you anything."

I got the two other tape recorders, sat them near him where they would pick up his voice. Put tapes in them. Turned them on, told him

"This is a half-hour tape, the one side. That's how much time you have before you begin to die. You start talking, you live. We fight it out when we get ashore. Otherwise, I'll have you killed."

I left then, went below, got the harness I'd rigged, got the extra line, went back out in the cockpit. He was quiet. The recorders were running, recording silence. I hit the rewind button on the recorders. Waited until they were rewound. I sat the other gear in the chair, turned and checked the chum bucket, it was almost gone. But I had another bucket of tuna blood and a big bucket of chicken blood and offal. Sat it on the transom, punctured it and let the blood out in a steady stream now. Poured some more tuna blood in the fish box. Threw some more pieces of tuna over, cut up some bluefish threw them over. The action behind the boat was hot now, sharks fighting sharks, tearing up the ocean, in a feeding frenzy. I stood there looking down the slick, looking for something. Not yet.

I went to him, rolled him over on his stomach, tied his upper arms as tight as I could get them. Put him in the harness, the webbing under his arms, around his buttocks, his chest and back. Rolled him over on his back; he tried to kick me then but it hurt him so bad he screamed, the bones were broken, probably in both legs. I loosened both tourniquets. His blood began to flow more freely. Flow out on the deck. He said then

"What are you doing? What's all this stuff you're putting on me. If you're going to kill me, do it."

"I'm not going to kill you." I said.

"What's going on?" He asked, as I stepped over to the gyn pole, unfastened the hook from the block and tackle, released it and pulled the hook on the end of it over to him. I spoke,

"I'm not going to kill you. They are," I said pointing at the sharks behind the boat, now flashing in the luminous water created by the floodlight, "they're going to eat you. If you don't start talking I'm lifting you in there with them."

"I don't believe you."

I had the hook from the block and tackle fastened to the upper part of the harness. I walked over to the gin pole, hooked the block and tackle back on it, started pulling on the line rigged to the block and he started sliding over the deck to the gunwale beneath the gin pole.

"You're not going to do it. You can kiss my ass. You're not going to do it."

I paused on the pulling, said to him. "The woman you raped that night, the one you killed, threw overboard off Block Island, was my fiancee. We were in love. You think I won't do it. You'd better start thinking better."

A look of understanding came on his face, understanding and fear. For the first time he understood that I was going to do it.

I began to pull on the line again and he slowly raised. He was trying to kick me but with the broken bones all he could do was twitch. Swivel his hips. Soon I had him elevated above the gunwale. I started to lower him into the sea. He couldn't grab anything with his hands, they were cuffed behind him. He tried to hook the gunwale with his chin, tried to hold himself out of the water. I grabbed his head, pushed it backwards, lowered him until he was in the water. I let out more line, letting the current take him back off the stern in the slick. He was yelling when he had his head up, screaming. I snubbed the gin pole line to a cleat, walked to the transom, looked at him porpoising in and out of the water as he struggled in the current. He wasn't ten feet from me.

"Please," he pleaded, "please get me out of here."

"Will you talk?"

"Go to hell." He screamed just before he went under.

When he surfaced, I was ladling tuna blood on him, throwing it over his head, throwing tuna chunks in the water near him. By now several sharks were circling him, jerkingly, making passes. Darting in, turning away at the last minute.

"Stop it, get me out of here." He yelled.

I threw more blood on him. Then a blue shark, six maybe seven feet long hit him, hit him in the thigh, tore a small chunk from him. He screamed.

"I'll talk," he yelled, "anything, just get me out."

I threw several chunks of tuna away from him, over to the side, went to the gin pole and began to reel him in as fast as I could. As I pulled him from the water another shark hit him in the foot. I couldn't see what kind it was. I noticed as I pulled him over the gunwale, dripping blood on the teak covering board, that he was missing a part of his right foot, three toes were gone, just his big toe and the one next to it remained. He was really bleeding now. I lowered him to the deck. Laid him on his side at first. The next thing I did as he lie on the deck moaning, almost ashen he was so scared, was to put the tourniquets back on to slow the bleeding. I didn't want him to die before he'd told me everything. I left him all hooked up, didn't free him from the harness. He didn't notice he was so terrified.

I propped him up, his back against the cabin bulkhead, got the three tape recorders, set them up in front of him, turned them on, said "Talk."

He confessed to everything, gave every little detail. Twice I almost shot him right there, almost killed him. I was white hot all over, didn't want him to have the privilege of another breath, but I held back. Wanted him to finish. It was part of the plan. In maybe twenty minutes he was finished.

The blood had kept on dripping behind the boat as he talked. The sharks had stayed with us, some of them eating each other, eating the smaller ones. In a frenzy really.

I went to the stern ladled more blood over, threw the rest of the bluefish and butter fish over, most of the tuna. I noticed there were a couple of huge sharks at the edge of the light. Couldn't see what they were, they were circling so far out.

I went back to the Senator, undid the tourniquets, slapped his legs to get the blood flowing, went to the gyn pole and started pulling on the line from the block and tackle. The line tightened, pulled the Senator over on his back.

"What are you doing? I told you everything."

"Everything?" I asked, as I kept on pulling.

"There's nothing else." He screamed at me.

"What about the ending?"

"I told you about it. After I killed her, we put her over in the water." He said just as I was lifting him over the gunwale.

"Not that ending. This ending. You haven't told me about this ending."

I pushed him out over the gunwale, began to lower him. He screamed.

"You promised!"

"I lied."

I lowered him the rest of the way into the water, let the line out so that he was behind the stern in the light where I could see him. Got in the fishing chair to watch. Before long two sharks, a blue and an oceanic white tip were on him. Eating him. He was screaming when he wasn't gagging on the water he was taking in.

I felt a breeze then, felt a slight breeze waft across my face and with it came the scent of lilacs. Lilac fragrances.

Suddenly, he was in the air, five feet out of the water in the jaws of a huge mako. The 'Bad Boys' were here. She had said she'd send them to the festival, to the feast. And she had. The big mako splashed back into the water, swam off a bit, the Senator's foot sticking out the side of its jaws. Then another one hit him, another mako took a large piece of his ass. That one wasn't particular I guess. I let it go on until he stopped screaming. He was dead, then. They'd mostly been hitting him below the waist, most of the upper torso hadn't been hit yet. but there wasn't much left for them to eat but his upper body. Everything below his hips was gone.

I needed the rest of it for the statement I wanted to make, so pulled what was left of him from the water. He came aboard much lighter than when he'd gone overboard. I let the mess hang there from the gyn pole. Wrapped a line around it, wasn't much blood left in him now. Snugged him up to the gyn pole. I threw all the chum buckets, the blood buckets overboard, threw the rest of the fish to the sharks.

353

I turned the engines on, turned the salt water wash down pump on and washed the decks as best I could, getting most of the mess overboard. Then I took my clothes off, threw them overboard. Washed myself down. Stood there for a minute naked. Drying in the summer breeze, the last of the summer breeze. Then I climbed up on the port gunwale, a naked old man I was, seventy-three years old, feeling younger though - just for a minute. In any event I made my way around the outrigger carefully. I didn't want to go in the water with the 'Bad Boys', the other sharks either. Made my way up to the bow, unhooked the boat from the buoy, left the anchor and the buoy there. I wasn't going to be needing them anymore. Went back to the cabin, got out a change of clothes, white shirt, white duck trousers, new white topsiders. Put on my Greek captain's hat. Was fashionable. Nautical wise. Made my way back to the flying bridge, climbing the ladder alongside the gin pole, being careful not to brush against the Senator. He wasn't saying much now. Wasn't doing much in the living department either. I smiled at him anyway, then patted him on the head and climbed on up on the bridge, put the engines in gear, headed for home. The legless, gutless, remains of the Senator were hanging from the gin pole, swaying as the *Eva Still* rolled in the seas. It was around ten o'clock.

I got in the slip at Buffington shortly after mid-night. Tied the boat up, left the Senator hanging where he was. Wanted him, the top half of him anyway, to be found. An important message. I put one of the tape cassettes on the fighting chair, the dark of the cassette contrasting with the white of the chair. It couldn't be missed there. I took another tape of the Senator's confession and a copy of the tape of the doctor's confession and a photograph, put them in a multi-stamped envelope I had prepared, addressed to the Washington Dispatch. I put another tape and a copy of the report in another envelope addressed to the Chief in Block Island. I drove over to the airport.

Chapter Sixty-One
JULY 2003

At the airport I deposited the envelopes in the mail box at the terminal. Drove out to the plane. Did a quick pre-flight. Crash had topped off the tanks, checked the oil, left me a note saying everything was A okay. I started her up, taxied to the west end of the runway, there was just a little easterly wind. Twenty minutes after I had moored the *Eva Still,* I was out over the Atlantic, heading north by northeast for Block Island. An hour and a half later I was approaching the east end of Long Island, then crossing it, Montauk Light blinking to my right. In another ten minutes I could pick out South East Light on Block Island.

As I closed the island I turned my landing lights on and off twice, then left them on. I'd told Julian that was what I would do when I was five miles out. The runway lights came on, I circled to the west, approached over Block Island Sound. Touched down at four a.m. Julian drove me directly to the cottage, said as I got out of the pickup,

"I did as you asked. The table's there, two bottles of Mums. Glasses. The flowers."

"Thank you Julian," I said, "it's a pleasure having you look after me. You're fine people."

I had made arrangements for Julian, for everyone. Julian left, walking back up the driveway in the waning moonlight, closing the gate as he did.

I went inside, undressed, ran a bath, took a cool bath. Just a short one. I didn't need hot water to relax me now. I was completely relaxed. I laid back in the tub, remembering her, remembering them all. I had kept my bond with the Captain, with her. I fell asleep, and she sent me a dream.

She was there in my arms in the tub, snuggled between my legs with her back to my front, reaching back over her shoulder and caressing my face. And I was kissing the back of her head, her neck, her shoulders. I said,

"I love you."

"And I, you." she responded, as she turned to face me. Her bared breasts floating on the water.

And we made love there in the tub, soft, slow, sweet love, not even enough movement to splash water. Languid loving. Stretched out loving. Dreamtime loving?

She said when we were finished,

"You have kept your promises."

Then I noticed that I was awake, alone in the tub. No sign of her. No sign she'd been there.

I dressed in the best clothes I had in the cottage, a tux, studs, pleated shirt, black bow tie, cummerbund, the works right down to the pointy toed black patent leather shoes. The ones that hurt my feet. I didn't care. They were my best shoes. Took my journal, my diary, a pen. Took the last cassette tape, put it in my jacket pocket. Put the gun in my other pocket. Went down to the beach in the darkness. Thinking as I did that I was again walking on the grains of sand she had walked upon a half-century before.

By five o'clock I was sitting at the table, the two glasses of Mums gleaming as the sun's rays began to lighten the eastern sky. I thought, dreamt; didn't know really where it was that I was thinking. This world, that world, was I in my mind? Was there a separate place there? Where was I? Was I crazy? Why worry now? Then I didn't care.

"Is it not enough that you are loving me?" She said to me where-ever I was, said it standing in front of me, holding out her hand.

I saw myself taking her hand. She pulled me up out of the chair, ran her hand over my face, my body. I was looking at myself. I was standing five feet distant from the young man standing there, tanned, wide shoulders. Seeing the way I had been in the years of my youth. I was seeing me at the beginning of it all.

She reached for me again. Pulled me down where we had lain so many years before. I laid there with her on me. And I felt her just as clearly as I had felt her then. She caressed me there, then took me to the center of her, whispering,

"This is the way it will be. Trust me."

And I am awake, back in the chair as if I had never left it, a glass of champagne halfway to my mouth. Not really where I was a moment before. The sun is peaking above the sea's horizon. The journal, everything, almost completed. One bottle of champagne finished. The love songs playing. The gun heavy in my pocket.

I begin to read what I have written, the last things that I have just written, reading my words sitting here on the beach of my remembrances.

"I was kept here, a prisoner in a life I did not want, waiting for the time when I could spend my days, all of my days, in her arms. Loving her always; loving Eva.

"Everything I have done, everything I have become, has risen from the times in the evenings of my dreams of being in her arms. She created me when we were both alive, making me more man than I ever would have been had I not loved and been loved by her. It was the memory of her that sustained me until this time. And her visits, if they were visits. To me they were real.

I read then, "It has been a short time - only one life time. But, forever to live it." Then I write the last words in my journal.

"Love just is."

I feel the gun in my pocket as the sad love songs play. Wherever it is that I am, whatever it is that my mind has become, looks at you as I rise. You caress my hand as I take the unopened champagne and the two glasses in my other hand and then we are walking up the beach to the path, hand in hand, as in the earlier time. Up the bluff. We pause at the top, turn to the east as the rising sun leaves the horizon, its last kiss of the eastern sea finished for another day. You turn to me then, the sun gleaming through your hair, each strand a filament of gold. Rise on your toes, kiss my cheek. Then we are walking across the grass. Up to the center of the island and the paths of yesteryear. Seeing nothing but ourselves, not conscious of the pick-up when it passes, just walking to the gateway. Walking to our place. You skipping a little like you used to do.

As we walk, I watch you in wonderment.

Chapter Sixty-Two

DENOUEMENT

Special to the Washington Dispatch, Monday, July 26th, 2003
GRUESOME DISCOVERY

The world was shocked to learn of the discovery yesterday of Senator Cliff O'Brien's mutilated body aboard a boat in Ocean City, Maryland. The senior senator from Massachusetts was considered the often controversial dean of the Senate. The boat, with its gruesome cargo was discovered on an estate known as "Buffington." The property and the boat are owned by the reclusive billionaire, Hank Gaskins, one of the pre-eminent lawyers of the last half of the last century and a confidant to Presidents over the years. He was belatedly credited with playing a prominent role in bringing the Viet Nam war to a close. He made a fortune capitalizing on advancements in the law, later formed an investment company that is now one of the ten biggest in the world. He later made billions in investments in computer related companies.

He was not on the scene when the body was found about mid-afternoon by an employee. Gaskin's whereabouts has not been ascertained.

The Senator's office staff informed the Dispatch that the Senator, his chief of staff, and an aide left Friday afternoon on Mr. Gaskins private plane to spend a weekend with him tuna fishing in the waters off Ocean City. As of this writing police have not been able to locate the chief of staff or the other aide of the Senator.

The employee who found the body told this reporter that he had seen a cassette tape on the fishing chair on the boat when he had gone aboard to see what was hanging from a pulley on the side. When he saw it was part of a body he rushed from the boat to call the police. Inquiries of the police as to what was on the tape have gone unanswered.

The police have announced an all points bulletin for assistance in locating Mr. Gaskins or the Senator's staff members. We shall have more on this story as it unfolds.

By staff reporter, Jennifer Parker

Special to the Washington Dispatch. Tuesday, July 27th, 2003
A STORY OF LOVE, MURDER AND REVENGE

The story of the death of Senator O'Brien has developed into one of the strangest murders of recent history. Yesterday this paper received in the mail copies of two audio tapes and a copy of a photograph showing Senator O'Brien as a young man. They were apparently mailed to this paper by Mr.Gaskins. The voice on one of the tapes appears to be that of Senator O'Brien. The paper has not yet been able to identify the voice on the other tape as of this time. Both tapes appear to be detailed confessions by the relators of their participation in the kidnaping, rape and murder of a young woman by the name of Eva Stinsin on Block Island, Rhode Island in 1952. The persons talking on the two tapes appeared to have been under great stress, both are heard sobbing throughout the recordings. Senator O'Brien appeared at times to be pleading for his life with someone, but no other voices can be heard on the tape.

The confessions contained on both tapes appear to also incriminate Senator O'Brien's chief of staff and one of his aides in the murder of Ms. Stinsin.

Upon inquiry, the police, after learning of our possession of the tapes, have admitted having obtained a copy of the Senator O'Brien tape. This paper has furnished copies of the other tape to the police.

Additionally, at a press conference held last evening, the Ocean City Police Department has stated that the manner of death of Senator O'Brien appears to have been due to attacks by sharks while bound. Several shark teeth have been recovered from the body; one large tooth has been identified by local experts in the Ocean City area as belonging to a large mako shark. When the Senator's remains were discovered his arms were bound to his sides and he was hanging from an apparatus used to land large fish on sport fishing craft. No other cause of death has been identified.

The police announced that they are still attempting to locate the two aides of the Senator and have issued warrants for the arrest of Mr. Gaskins. Inquiries by this paper of Mr. Gaskins' various business entities have met with little success.

359

We have learned from sources on Block Island that Mr. Gaskins, at the time of the 1952 murder of Ms. Stinsin, was engaged to be married to her. Although a resident of Ocean City, Maryland, he had gone to Block Island to work in the swordfishing industry. He had been at sea when she was discovered to be missing. Mr. Gaskins never married. His single status over the years had been the subject of much conjecture in Washington gossip columns.

According to Block Island police files made available to the press late yesterday, Ms. Stinsin had disappeared while walking home from work. She had apparently been raped and beaten while aboard a boat and then been thrown overboard, but had managed to swim ashore before she died. She was found by a local resident just after dawn on an island beach, but had died before help could be summoned. The Block Island police also released photographs of a necklace and two charms that had been tightly clenched in Ms. Stinsin's fist when she was found. They appear to match the jewelry seen in the photograph received by the Dispatch in the package the paper received. One of our reporters visited the Senator's Capital Hill office and has confirmed that a copy of the photograph hangs on the wall.

The Dispatch has also learned that a cemetery on Block Island was cordoned off by local and Rhode Island State Police yesterday afternoon and remains cordoned off as of this writing. Due to the presence of trees and shrubbery in the area it is not possible to see the area within the cemetery where the police appear to be congregated.

By staff reporter, Jennifer Parker.

Special to the Dispatch - Wednesday, July 29th 2003

GASKINS FOUND

Mystery Deepens

The Block Island police department has announced that the body of Hank Gaskins, the billionaire sought in the murder of Senator O'Brien, was found Monday afternoon in a cemetery on Block Island. A statement by the Chief was furnished the press. It states in its entirety:

"Yesterday morning a resident visiting the Island Cemetery reported to the police that a man was lying on a grave, and appeared to be unconscious. I was on duty at the time and responded to the scene. There, in a cove in the lilac bushes, I discovered the body of

360

Mr. Gaskins lying on his back next to the grave of Ms Eva Stinsin. He was dressed in formal evening wear. A half empty bottle of champagne was found beside him and to each side there was a champagne glass partially filled with champagne. A breeze had caused lilac blossoms to drift on him and on the grave of Ms Stinsin. Although a handgun was found on his person there were no signs of violence at the scene. In fact Mr. Gaskins appeared to be smiling. Initial indications by the state medical examiner note that Mr. Gaskin's heart just stopped. Several years ago he had a heart attack.

"On Tuesday the Block Island Police Department received an envelope that included documentation and other evidence about the murder in 1953 of Ms Stinsin. The envelope was from Mr. Gaskins and among the evidence contained in that envelope was a report, a photograph, and a tape recording. The contents of that envelope indicated that Senator O'Brien, his chief of staff, another of his aides and a doctor who died in an automobile accident last week, kidnaped, raped and beat Ms. Stinsin on a sailboat and dumped her overboard thinking she was dead. She managed to swim ashore but died here on the beach from head injuries.

"Mr Gaskins was engaged to marry Miss Stinsin at the time of the murder and vowed in person to me at that time, fifty years or so ago, that he would find the murderers and kill them.

"It appears that Mr. Gaskins had spent the time just before dawn on Sunday on the beach below his cottage on the *Hotel Eva* property. A local resident found a journal, or a diary of some kind on the beach and turned it into the police department. We have not had time to go over it, it is very extensive, but it appears to be a chronicle of Mr. Gaskin's life. The last sentence in the dairy, dated Sunday past is 'Love just is.'

"There was a witness interviewed, a lobsterman, who saw Mr. Gaskins walking on the road to the cemetery just after dawn Sunday morning. His remarks speak for themselves,

'I was driving to Old Harbor to my boat. I was going to fish my pots. As I came around the last curve before the cemetery, I saw Mr. Gaskins. He was dressed in a tuxedo and had a bottle of champagne and two glasses in his left hand. He was being pulled along by a young woman who had his right hand and who was almost skipping beside him. It looked like she was hurrying him. She was very beautiful. I waved at them, but they didn't notice me. They both were smiling at each other.

'The woman was carrying an armful of lilacs.' "

The chief concluded his statement by stating:

"Fingerprints were recovered from the champagne bottle and from the glasses. The ones on the bottle and on one glass matched Mr. Gaskins'. The fingerprints on the other glass match the fingerprints of Ms. Stinsin we have on file from the time of her murder."

The chief then declined to take any questions.

By staff reporter, Jennifer Parker

THE END

Printed in the United States
33758LVS00005B/40-279